Brooke poked Quill's firm bicep. "Hey, what's your problem? I'm havin' some fun for once in my boring life. Don't you be mean to Ash—she's my bestest friend. Just because you're super sexy and all…"

"Let's go, Brooke." His posture stiff, Quill stood, radiating tension. His large hand gently closed around her arm. "I'm taking you home. I think you need to sleep this off."

"I'm not tired. I'm having fun." Pulling free of his grasp, she dug her heels in, crossing her arms over her chest with a huff. "You're such a tyrant. I'm staying right here with my friends."

"Honey, don't make me carry you out of here. You've had too much to drink. It's up to you which way you leave. You decide, but we *are* leaving." Quill's clipped tone incited her temper.

"You're not the boss of me!" Brooke glared at him, sticking her tongue out in his direction. The others turned away snickering behind hidden hands.

"Oh, baby, you are so going to regret that." Quill scooped her up, and the world turned upside down. He headed toward the exit, and she bounced along hanging like a rag doll over his shoulder.

"Put me down this minute, you Neanderthal!" She punched and kicked the Protector to no avail. The jolt of a sharp spank to her backside shocked her. "You did not just hit me? I'm—I'm telling your mother."

"Baby, that was a love tap."

Praise for M. Goldsmith and A. Malin

"This paranormal romance has a very unique premise and characters who display intriguing abilities. I quickly found myself rooting for them to overcome their obstacles. The ending was very satisfying, and some of the secondary characters were so interesting I am hoping for more of their stories set in this world."

~*Roni Denholtz, award-winning author*

~*~

"This book kept me so interested to keep reading to see what would happen next. Love the names of the characters. Would definitely want another book continuing with series."

~*IBooks reader*

~*~

"Fabulous book!!! From the first chapter, the authors placed me in a new magical world where I can see and be part of the exciting story of Ash. Loved the characters, their edge-of-your-seat adventures, but more importantly the beautiful love stories the authors wove through the book. I could not put the book down and look so forward to reading the next series."

~*Barnes and Noble Reader*

~*~

"Could not put it down. Cannot wait for the next book."

~*Barnes and Noble Reader*

The House of Water

by

M. Goldsmith
& A. Malin

Guardians of the Elements, Book 2

The House of Water

The Wild Rose Press, Inc.
PO Box 708
Adams Basin, NY 14410-0708
Visit us at www.thewildrosepress.com

Publishing History
First Fantasy Rose Edition, 2019
Print ISBN 978-1-5092-2911-6
Digital ISBN 978-1-5092-2912-3

Guardians of the Elements, Book 2
Published in the United States of America

Dedication

M.G.:
For my daughter, Kyra.
Your help and support mean everything to me.
I love you.
And for Lila and Henry, my biggest fans,
I'll miss you always.

~

A.M.:
To my husband and kids.
Thank you for putting up with the last minute dinners,
late nights, and general craziness.
I couldn't have done it without your support.
I love you guys.

Chapter One
Brooke

Brooke Barrington always dreamed of having a different life. She stared off into the reflective surface of Aether's Grand Lake. Dispersed along the water's edge, large and small rocks of every shade of gray and blue dotted the vast shoreline. Climbing onto one of the sun-heated slabs of stone, Brooke closed her eyes and absorbed its warmth on the clear spring morning. The blemish, which lay hidden beneath the compression glove she always wore, tingled. Invisible sparks sent fiery heat to the center of her hand. She gouged her fingers through the dense fibers and into her irritated flesh.

The landscape around her grew fuzzy, and the world spun. Brooke dropped her head to her knees and took a few slow measured breaths. "This is crazy, and I don't do crazy," she mumbled. Crazy was not a word in her vocabulary; terms such as order and responsibility dominated there.

Peeling the glove from her sweat-covered hand, she examined the scar which marked her left palm for as long as she could remember. Tracing its outline, a chill ran down her spine, and she yanked the glove back into place. Quill's words rang in her ears ricocheting around her head like a pinball in a machine. "Do you know what this symbol means? You, Brooke

Barrington, are the Guardian of The House of Water." According to Quill, no typical human had ever been born with a mark before or displayed control over the Elements. She shook her head. Could a biochemist really be a Guardian and find her home in magical Aether?

Power saturated the air enveloping Brooke in a wave of energy. This hidden world, tucked away among the trees and mountains where no outsiders could enter, drew her in like an undertow in the sea. The people of Aether answered to the four Elements: Fire, Water, Air, and Earth. Images of this wondrous place implanted themselves inside her, sprouting, and taking root. Brooke lifted her head, riveted in the magnificence surrounding the Grand Lake. The visions and sensations emitted from this mystifying place held a familiar aura. No matter what happened or where she went from here, the people, the beauty, and the power had etched a permanent imprint in her heart.

The water called to Brooke luring her to its crystal-clear depths. Kicking off her shoes, she rolled her jeans to her knees, and submerged her legs, inch by inch, into the sparkling lake. Brooke leaned back on her hands. "If Quill's right and I am the Guardian, shouldn't I be able to influence Water somehow?"

Swishing her feet in circles, the water lapped up onto the edge of the giant boulder she occupied. A sudden splash of chilled water leapt up and rolled over the rock drenching her pants. She yanked her legs back from the turbulent lake and jumped to her feet. White water rose, and waves crested over the surface, foamy and choppy like the ocean. Goosebumps spread across her icy flesh. Covering her mouth with her gloved hand, she gasped. "Oh my God! Am I doing that? This isn't logical. H2O is a chemical formula. One oxygen and two hydrogen atoms connected by covalent bonds. It's only plain water, isn't it?"

Abruptly, the swells settled. The water calmed, and its smooth surface reflected the landscape once more. The feel of her soaked jeans sticking to her, like an uncomfortable second skin, drew her gaze downward. Brooke pulled at the saturated fabric, and whispered in a shaky voice. "What is happening to me?"

"I told you already. You're the Guardian of The House of Water. You just need to believe me."

Quill. Heart pounding, Brooke spun around and honed in on his deep, sexy voice. She glared at him. "You nearly gave me a coronary. What did I tell you about sneaking up on me?"

"Sorry, I thought you heard me coming. Guess you were too busy practicing your Guardian tricks." He laughed, a cocky smirk plastered on his face.

"You don't understand, Quill, I can't be the Guardian. It's impossible. I'm ordinary, plain old Brooke Barrington, scientist, nerd—"

"Honey, there is nothing plain or ordinary about you. You're special. The first time I saw your picture, I knew it." Placing his hands on her shoulders, he gazed into her eyes. "I recognized you somehow. I understood, in that moment, you were destined to change my life and I yours. Why won't you believe me?"

She slapped her thigh. "That only happens in movies. Get real. People don't fall in love with a picture. You're nuts."

A flirtatious gleam twinkled in his emerald eyes.

"You're definitely wrong about that, just like you were wrong about being a terrible kisser." Quill shot her a wink.

She ran a fingertip over her lips basking in the memory of their first and only kiss. Nothing but a gentleman since, the alluring, sexy Protector tempted her at every turn. Quill hopped up onto the rock beside her. His shirt lifted exposing toned, muscular abs, and Brooke swallowed audibly. Recalling dreams of her body pressed against Quill's, heat surged through her veins settling between her legs. Brooke squeezed her thighs together and shuddered repressing the enticing image. She forced herself to let go of the fantasy. Now was not the time for romantic complications.

The timber of Quill's husky tone penetrated her thoughts and pulled her attention back to the charming Protector. "Where did you go off to, honey? We were talking about kissing; one of my favorite subjects when it comes to you."

"Quill, please, I told you. I can't go there with you. I have to figure out where my father is before he does something even worse. He's been missing since the Protectors destroyed the lab." Brooke leaned over, elbow to knee, massaging her temples. She silently counted to ten, lifted her head, and met his gaze. "Oh, and let's not forget this small issue of you insisting I'm the Guardian of The House of Water. Which, by the way, we both know is not possible. I'm not an Aetherian and neither were my parents."

"I don't know how it happened, but it doesn't make it any less true. You have the mark on your palm to prove it." Quill picked up her hand, pulled off her compression glove, and traced the symbol on her palm with his calloused hand.

The seductive stroke of his touch heated Brooke's entire body fueling the flames of her libido. Fast as rushing water in a stream, she snatched her hand from his grip. "I've told you a thousand times, I was burned as an infant. It's only a coincidence it resembles the mark. I am not the Water Guardian for heaven's sake!" Shooting him her best dirty look, she grabbed her glove and shoved it back into place.

Quill laughed. "Quite a coincidence, don't you think? Creating those waves before"—he pointed a finger in her direction—"that was all you. And let's not ignore your intense attraction to the water. You've been at this lake nonstop. Face it, honey; you're drawn to the water like a moth to a flame. You may not want to admit it, but there is no doubt in my mind. You *are* the Guardian. I think it's time to come clean with our friends. Ash and Hawk love you, and they can help."

Since arriving in the village, Brooke's relationship with Ashlyn, Fire Guardian of Aether, had blossomed into a sisterhood. Her affection for Hawk, Ash's intimidating-looking fiancé, was a surprising bonus. The handsome, brooding lead Protector treated Brooke like a little sister. Who knew someone so big and strong could be so sweet?

She first encountered Ashlyn five weeks ago when mercenaries, sent by her father, Dr. Charles Barrington, kidnapped the Guardian near the village's border. Ashlyn, held captive and tortured for the purpose of extracting her powers, formed an instant bond with Brooke. In spite of all her father had put Ash through, the beautiful Guardian never held Brooke responsible for his actions. Her new friend welcomed her with an open-heart teaching her all about Aether. Although Brooke had helped Quill and Hawk free Ashlyn, guilt still clung to her.

Brooke adjusted her glove. "Maybe we should talk to Ash and Hawk. This way, they can tell you you're wrong. None of this makes sense. Where are the facts? The logic?"

"Some things in life can't be explained. Sometimes, things just are. Like you and I are destined to be together, and you *are* the Guardian of The House of Water. The sooner you face these facts, the better you'll feel." Quill's voice dropped low and sexy. "By the way, I'd be happy to take your mind off things altogether if you'll let me." He stepped further into her space nuzzling her neck. "You know, escape everything for a while. Come on, baby; what do you say?"

Placing her hands on his chest, Brooke shoved the flirtatious Protector. "Knock it off! I told you I can't do this, so stop tempting me." Her fingers met solid muscle. "Agh, you're like a brick wall."

"You should check out the rest me." Quill waggled his brows. "And don't think I didn't notice you said I was tempting. I'll take it. It's a start." Dropping his arm around her, he pulled her close. "Let's go home."

She lifted his hand flinging it off her shoulder. "It's your home, not mine, and maybe I should stay with Ashlyn? I'm sorry; I don't want to lead you on. This"—waving her hand back and forth between them—"is not going to happen. I like you, Quill, I really like you, but I'm wrong for you. I don't belong here. I'm only staying in Aether until we find my father and stop him."

In truth, Quill's place had become more of a home to her than anywhere she'd ever lived. Her mother had radiated love and warmth, but her father's presence had toxified their family's home. The polar opposite of her father, Quill's laid-back, relaxed vibe created an environment which provided a sense of safety. Unlike Charles Barrington, Quill never let her forget she was cherished and desired.

"We'll see. In the meantime, breakfast, *our place*, let's go."

"Fine." She plopped down and slipped her damp feet back into her sneakers.

Quill reached for her hands, pulled her up into his arms, and placed a kiss on the crown of her head. They walked away from the Grand Lake hand in hand, leaving behind the sweet fragrance of water lilies.

"It's so beautiful here. I can feel the power all around me." Since she'd arrived, Brooke dreamed of belonging in Aether. "You really think I fit in? I'm not exactly Guardian material."

Quill stopped in his tracks bringing her to a sudden halt. "I wish you could see yourself through my eyes." He ran the back of his hand down her cheek. The adoration shimmering in his gaze warmed her heart. "You're everything."

Despite Quill's best efforts to make her feel welcome, remorse continued to gnaw at her gut. Most of the Aetherians understood Brooke was not complicit with regard to her father's actions, but she believed there were some who would never trust her. Locating her father would go a long way in proving to everyone, especially herself, she deserved to be an Aetherian.

****

Quill

He froze in his tracks, and his mouth dropped open.

Brooke leaned back sprawled out like a mermaid on one of the large flat stones near the water's edge. Air rushed from his lungs, and Quill rubbed the center of his chest easing the tightness. Her golden hair, pure luminescence, shimmered in the brilliant sunlight splashing across her lovely face. A few stray tendrils flew free in the breeze escaping the confines of her tightly twisted bun giving her the appearance of an angel.

The pull of imaginary forces drew Quill to Brooke's side. Discovering the Guardian mark on her palm had come as a shock to him, but her denial had gone way beyond shock; it had taken on a life of its own. During the past few weeks, he'd done everything in his power to convince Brooke of her fate. Gentleness, bluntness, cajoling, nothing worked to convince her of her destiny. Calling for reinforcements, he invited Hawk and Ash to breakfast. Quill had agreed to keep Brooke's Guardian mark a secret for the time being, but he worried she might never come to terms with her true fate. A push in the right direction seemed like a good idea, but what if she didn't agree?

Walking toward his house, Quill tucked Brooke into his side keeping a firm grip on her hand. Her skin, so soft and warm, called out for his caress making his fingers itch with desire. Yet, no matter how hard he tried, she resisted him at every turn like she resisted the idea of being a Guardian. Quill's passion for her, however, could not be tamed. His heartbeat launched into a rapid rhythm, his body heat rising from the simple touch of her hand. A strange sensation washed over him, so foreign, he feared he'd become unrecognizable. He did not get hung up on women. He did not get attached, ever. Brooke must have cast some kind of spell on him. A swift breeze swirled around them kicking up clouds of dust in their wake, and his body hummed with sexual tension. Hovering near the surface, Quill's powers hijacked him fighting for control.

Hunger for Brooke consumed him. Biting the inside of his cheek, Quill resisted the urge to tear the band from her hair and let it loose to flutter in the wind. He fantasized about gathering the silken strands in his fingers and pulling her close. The God and Goddess had endowed Quill with great strength, but the power Brooke held over him eclipsed even his Elemental gifts. Her beauty surpassed the physical and emanated straight from her soul. A pureness and innocence surrounded this brave woman. Destiny seemed determined to meddle in his life. Now, he only needed Brooke to recognize the inevitability of their Joining.

"I invited Hawk and Ash to join us for breakfast. I know I should have told you earlier, but it's time to confide in them, and I didn't want to give you a chance to back out. They can help us with a plan to find Charles Barrington. They're our friends, Brooke." Quill hesitated and glanced over to gauge her reaction. "I can only imagine how hard this is for you, but you have to trust me. I would never lead you astray."

"I know you mean well, but this whole thing is crazy. If you really want to tell Ashlyn and Hawk—okay—I guess I have nothing to lose. I do trust you, and them, too, but you have to understand how overwhelmed I am right now. My life has been turned upside down. I don't even know who I am anymore. This entire situation feels surreal."

"I get it, and I promise you"—a stray piece of hair escaped her bun, and on impulse, Quill tucked it behind her ear—"I'll help you get through this. You can count on me. I know I joke around a lot, but my feelings for you are serious. I'm more serious than I've ever been in my entire life, and if it makes you feel any better, I don't know who I am anymore either." He grabbed her hand and tugged her in the direction of his house. "Come on, let's get back for breakfast. I'm starving. Ash's mom is sending muffins. Plus, there's lunch to consider. And I'm having dinner with the guys tonight, so I don't want to throw off my timing and be too full or anything."

Brooke rolled her eyes. "Heaven forbid you have to interrupt one of your carefully timed binges, or worse yet, miss a meal. Please, let's go. I don't want you to have to wait for your muffins and mess with the delicate balance of your eating schedule."

Chuckling at her sassy response, Quill playfully nudged her shoulder. They fell into step, moving along in a companionable silence until reaching the front porch of his house. "You ready?" he asked.

"I guess so."

He ushered her ahead of him, but her feet stopped moving the minute she crossed the threshold. Quill bumped straight into her back, and she stumbled forward. Thrusting an arm out, he hooked it around her waist and dragged her against his chest. He peered over Brooke's shoulder to see why she'd stopped. Ashlyn and Hawk didn't budge from their lip lock.

"Oh, for God's sake," Quill grumbled. "Can't you two keep your hands off each other? We haven't even had breakfast yet."

The green-eyed monster poked him with an embarrassing truth. Quill was jealous of his best friend. After the immeasurable suffering they'd endured, no two people had earned a happily-ever-after more than the couple sucking face in front of him. Although their PDA pushed the limits of appropriateness, Quill wanted what they had, and he wanted it with Brooke.

Hawk didn't take the bait. The corners of his mouth simply lifted. His eyes held a spark Quill had never seen in his friend before. True love and happiness looked good on Hawk.

Ash rose to her feet, kissed Quill on the cheek, and then embraced Brooke. "Sorry, guys, we can't help it. Eighty-two years of avoiding each other leaves a lot of pent up—"

"I know what you two have pent up, and if you don't mind, we don't want to see it right now." Brooke laughed aloud at Quill's comment, and he relished the sound. "We need to talk to you guys. Brooke has something to tell you, or should I say, show you? Right, Brooke?" Her light mood shifted in an instant, and her smile faded before his eyes.

Dancing around the room, Brooke hemmed and hawed. "I, um, need to tell you about what Quill and I discovered. Well, he seems to think—I, uh." She planted her feet and drew in a long breath before her words flew out in a rush. "I'm the future Guardian of The House of Water." Their friends burst out laughing, and Brooke's face fell. She flushed a bright pink, bowing her head.

"Really, Brooke? I never imagined you'd get sucked into one of Quill's pranks." Hawk clutched his sides. "You can't expect us to believe—"

Ashlyn raised her hand. "Hold on a second." Her eyes widened. "You're not kidding, are you?"

"No, she's not. Show them, Brooke." Quill nudged her.

Hesitating, Brooke peeled back the compression glove covering her left hand. She flexed her fingers a few times before turning her palm toward their friends. Ashlyn gasped, her hand flying up to cover her mouth. The mark of the Water Guardian sat in the center of Brooke's palm. It was a bold triangle pointing downward toward her wrist with a dot in the center, resembling a brand. The symbol, a deeply embedded impression in the skin, gave the appearance of having blistered and healed in a blush tone.

Ashlyn traced the outline of her own Guardian mark. "I can't believe this. I mean, I knew there was something about you, but never in my wildest dreams did I imagine you were a Guardian." Ash enveloped Brooke in a hug. "We're like sisters. I knew you were special. I just knew it."

Wiggling free of Ashlyn's hold, Brooke protested. "Wait a minute. Wait one minute. This is a mistake, a fluke. I told you, I was burned as an infant. This is a scar. I am not the Guardian."

"Of course, you are. It all makes sense now. Ash being drawn to you. You coming back to Aether. It's destiny," Hawk affirmed.

"I was sure you guys would see the logic and talk Quill out of this lunacy. I'm not the Guardian." Brooke threw her hands up in the air. "My mother told me the story of my accident when I was a child."

Quill's voice softened. "Sweetheart, are you sure your mother wasn't trying to protect you? Maybe hide the truth from your father? I wonder if she was an Aetherian? Think about it, could she do anything extraordinary?"

Brooke stomped her foot. "Of course not, she was a regular person like me."

Ashlyn's amber-colored eyes radiated warmth. Her gentle voice exuded comfort. "You are my dear friend. You saved my life. I would never lie to you. I believe in my heart, with all that I am, Quill is right. You are the Guardian of The House of Water. It's not a coincidence the God and Goddess brought us together. Now that we know who you really are, it's more important than ever we find some answers. We should talk to the Elders; they can help with—"

"No, no way. I don't want to tell anyone, especially them. They scare the crap out of me. It's like they can see inside me. It freaks me out."

Hawk laughed. "They do have a powerful effect on some folks. I'll tell you what, let's come up with a plan, and then we can tell the Elders once we have it all worked out. Sound okay to you?"

Brooke nodded shoving her hands into her pockets. "It sounds reasonable and logical. Actually, I was thinking of going back to my apartment in the city. I grew up there. I'm hoping my father might've left something behind that will help us find him."

Heat crept up Quill's neck filling his entire body with tension. Clenching and unclenching his fists, he took a deep, calming breath. Despite his best efforts, a breeze gushed through the air. A stack of magazines and some loose scraps of paper fluttered at first, but then picked up velocity, flying around the room.

Quill's tone came out more clipped than he

intended. "What the hell are you thinking, Brooke? When were you going to tell me? We're a team. How can I get you to see us as a *we* not an *I*? Something needs to change, or I'm going to go crazy."

Debris whizzed around the room. Hawk's quick reflexes didn't save him from getting beaned in the head by a whirling paperback. "Dude, get your shit together!" Hawk shouted, rubbing his temple. The lead Protector straightened, glaring at him.

Hawk's deep baritone snapped Quill out of his power-fueled display. The various objects soaring around the room froze midair then dropped to the ground like sinking stones. A riot of wild, red curls fell in Ashlyn's face. With a whoosh of breath, she blew the wisps out of her eyes.

Brooke scowled, raised both palms to Quill's chest, and shoved him backward. "You are the most aggravating man I have ever met in my entire life. Keeping up with you is exhausting." To Ash, she said, "Are all the men around here so dominant, so alpha? How do you stand it?"

They all chuckled releasing the tension in the room. "It's an Aetherian male trait"—Ashlyn looked pointedly between Hawk and Quill—"though some have it in spades. Protectors were given an extra helping in the dominance department. Don't worry, you'll get used to it, or at least you'll learn to live with it."

His beautiful, little scientist grinned, and Quill's heart opened even further. He called up his sweetest smile and said, "I'm glad you're finally beginning to understand the way things work around here. You know you like my alpha ways. Plus, there is no way in hell you're going anywhere without me."

"Okay, Quill, you can have it your way, for now. We'll go to the city tomorrow and see what we can find." Turning toward Ashlyn and Hawk, Brooke pointed her finger back and forth between them. "And you two, not a word to anyone until we get back. Agreed?"

Hawk and Ash both nodded, but Ashlyn didn't stay quiet. "Okay, but remember, tonight we're going out with Laurel, Lily, and Marina for our girls' night. I promised Laurel we would be there to help cheer up Lily. It's been so hard for her since River passed on. Plus, it will be good for you, too. I'll come by around seven. I promise I won't breathe a word to anyone, but you are coming."

"All right, enough of this. I'm starving." Quill gestured toward the bag on the coffee table. "I need one of Rowan's muffins."

Ashlyn grabbed the large, brown bag from the table crinkling it loudly. The men followed her into the kitchen like a litter of hungry puppies. For now, they would enjoy the treats, and tomorrow he would worry about protecting Brooke from her psycho father.

Chapter Two
Marina

One year, ten months, and two days ago…

Landon's slow open-mouthed kisses trailed down her neck awakening her senses. "Mmm." The prickle of goosebumps, rising one by one on her skin, sent a shiver down Marina's spine. A muscular arm snaked around her waist pulling her close. Warm and gentle, his other hand found and cupped her breast. Now wide awake, she turned her body to face her Kanti, Landon. "Well good morning to you, my love. Is there something I can help you with?"

"I missed you. You're so sexy when you're sleeping. I couldn't resist touching you." Landon continued his sensual assault running his tongue along the delicate shell of her ear.

She wrapped her arms around his neck. All this time together and it seemed Landon still couldn't get enough of her. He acted as if they were a newly Joined pair, not one which had been together for more than three quarters of a century. Contentment washed over her, bringing forth a sense of rightness.

Landon gazed into her eyes, panting as he spoke, "My-Rina, to the rest of Aether you are the Guardian of Water, but to me you are simply the most beautiful woman in the world." Licking his way down her neck, he hummed. "You taste like the sweetest nectar. How did I get so lucky as to call you mine?"

Clinging tighter to his sculpted body, she kissed him hard on the mouth. Marina beamed at her Kanti and ran her hands down his sides. Stopping on his well-shaped butt, she squeezed the firm globes, and whispered in his ear, "We're both lucky."

"My sanity is slipping. I need you now." Landon took control rolling her beneath his big body. He entered her with one hard thrust filling her in every sense of the word. Her Kanti continued his relentless rhythm hitting every one of her nerve endings, never slowing his pace until she cried out his name. Breathless, she imagined the sounds of her release echoed through the West Tower.

Cocooned in the safety of Landon's embrace, Marina lost all perception of time. Stroking his stubbled cheek, she peppered kisses on his full lips. He looked like the boy next door, wholesome and handsome. Her friend Ashlyn called him Abercrombie because she insisted he looked like one of their models. He laughed it off, but Marina agreed. Landon was a gorgeous man. His wavy, brown hair, now damp with perspiration, fell onto his forehead. Brushing it away, Marina propped herself up on her elbows and looked into his warm, dark eyes. "I love you, Landon."

"And I you, My-Rina." He kissed her, delving deep, his tongue stroking hers. Groaning, he pulled back winded. "I'm sorry, love, as much as I'd rather stay here in bed with you all day, I have to get to headquarters. The trainees are mastering the art of explosives today. It's their final test." As a senior Protector, Landon shared the responsibilities of preparing future candidates to take their places among the Protectors' ranks.

"The art of explosives sounds like one of Quill's terms."

"Yeah, it is, but we all adopted it. He keeps us laughing. That's for sure. I'm going to be late if I don't get in the shower." Landon continued to hold Marina close; his words held no conviction.

"Landon?"

"Yes."

"You need to let go of me first." She laughed, giving him a gentle push. "Come on, get going. River's going to have your head."

Lifting himself off her, he placed a gentle kiss on her lips, and hopped up from the bed. He sauntered toward the bathroom tossing his next words over his shoulder. "Fine, but we're going to pick this up later when I get back."

She followed his movements, her eyes fixated on his incredible backside. As he rounded the corner slipping from her view, Marina nearly toppled off the bed. The sound of water rushing through the pipes filled the bedroom. Tempted to join him in the shower, she fought the impulse knowing he had to get ready. If Landon showed up late one more time, their lead Protector would come down hard on him. River demanded the highest level of discipline and precision from all of his soldiers, including his close friend, Landon. Exacting in his expectations, River ran the military unit in a tightly organized manner.

Marina took a deep breath tapping into her empathic power. Landon's light and happy mood permeated her senses. A current of fluid warmth flowed through her veins. Reading his emotions and invading his privacy weighed heavily on her mind, but sometimes the urge tested her resistance. Worry about Landon's need to prove his love, even after all these years, left Marina no choice but to delve into his feelings. Had her subconscious mind done something to make him feel insecure?

Growing up alongside Landon and his cousin, Coal, the trio had formed an unbreakable bond. As a young woman, Marina had romantic fantasies that included fire and passion with her future Prince Charming. It took a long time before she viewed the boys as anything other than total goofballs. Any thoughts of a romance with either one was laughable, but boys become men, and feelings change.

Landon's pursuit of her hadn't begun until their teenage years. With patience and persistence, his continued wooing finally wore her down. In the early stages of their relationship, Marina used Landon's passion as a conduit, allowing it to travel through her gift. She cherished him with all her heart. Through the years, they built a satisfying and loving physical connection, but the out-of-control electricity she'd longed for as a starry-eyed girl never surfaced. On occasion, she boosted her sexual desires by drawing on Landon's arousal.

Marina closed her eyes, visualizing a dam blocking the stream of emotions spilling from Landon. Her ability to control her gift evolved, strengthening over time. Now, only the strongest emotions possessed the ability to break through her armor. The creak of the bathroom door returned her focus to Landon, who drifted in with a towel wrapped around his waist.

Droplets of water clung to his muscular chest.

His eyes widened. "You're still in bed? Get your lazy, sexy ass up."

She laughed. "Maybe if you hadn't woken me at dawn, I wouldn't be so tired."

Her Kanti stalked toward her with a lascivious grin. "Well, it's your fault for being so gorgeous." Coming within inches of her mouth, the scent of mint lingered on his warm breath. He whispered in a sexy, hushed tone, "Now get up." With a tug, Landon yanked the blanket back, and a cool breeze hit her skin.

Marina grabbed hold of the comforter, pulling against his strong grip. "Hey! Give me that."

Swatting her butt with a playful pat, Landon smirked shaking his head. "No way."

She puckered her lips in a childlike pout. "Yes way. I'm cold."

"Love, when you make that face, I want to take a bite out of you. You look so adorable." Taking hold of her chin, he turned her face up to his gaze. "Are you seriously going to stay in bed all day?"

"Of course not, I have a million things to do. I'm going to the Council Chambers for some Guardian business, and I promised my grandmother I'd stop by. After that, I'm definitely heading straight to the Grand Lake. I need some Water time."

"Sounds good. I'll see you tonight. And remember, we're going to pick up where we left off." He waggled his brows in her direction. Landon stole one more quick kiss before disappearing out the door.

Marina called out to him, "I love you, Landon."

He peeked his head back into the room and used the same response as always. "And I you, My-Rina."

Her Kanti blew her a kiss and continued on his way.

A few hours later, Marina stood by the water's edge of the Grand Lake, staring off into the distance. Images of Landon's handsome face danced around her head. Mist rose floating inches above the glasslike plane. The hazy clouds rolled like billowing smoke from a burning building. Marina basked in the late morning sun on the warm summer day. She eased her way further, wading in the cool, refreshing water, replaying the sensations of her early morning passion. She licked her lips basking in the memory of her Kanti's unique taste. Contentment filled Marina's heart, but she couldn't understand why the God and Goddess hadn't blessed them with a child. If only she could conceive, maybe the strange emptiness which lived deep inside her could be filled.

She skimmed her hands through the water, creating a steady current in the typically calm lake. Absorbing the energy from her Element, Marina channeled its immense power, allowing it to course through her body. All at once, the air of serenity encircling her vanished as if someone had slammed a door. Powerful vibrations and the booming of several consecutive explosions sent a deluge of ripples through the lake. Water splashed onto the edges of her denim cutoffs, and Marina teetered on her feet.

Swept away by her empathic powers, wave upon wave of anger, fear, and sadness enveloped her. A jolt of pain surged through Marina, hitting her square in the gut. Fighting through the agony to remain upright, she braced herself to keep from falling into the water. The emotional onslaught slammed into her with unrelenting force. Marina's heart pounded in her ears, and she lost her balance, sinking to her knees with a loud splash.

"Dear Goddess, what's happening?" Every nerve in her body prickled. Crawling from the lake, she collapsed onto the sand. Gulping in huge breaths, Marina's chest heaved. Soaked to the bone, droplets of water ran down her body. A chill shuddered though her on the hot day. Sand clung to her dampened skin, and the abrasive grains crawled along her flesh.

Marina bolted upright. "I have to get out of here." She brushed off her legs and took off like a shot into the woods. The clouds of dust and smoke penetrated the trees above her and guided Marina toward the deafening sounds in the distance. Her instincts screamed telling her to run faster.

****

The Present

The West Tower's sole inhabitant, Marina Hill, Water Guardian of Aether, slept fitfully. Sweat beaded along her hairline and ran down her neck and between her breasts. The thin gray T-shirt she wore adhered to her drenched flesh. Thrashing about in the large bed, Marina's legs tangled in the sheets imprisoning her just as her memories did. Tortured by dreams of her past, every night her subconscious flooded with nightmares.

Agony ripped through Marina compelling her to run. Her clothing, soaked and caked with sand, restrained her, making it even harder to move. She raced along the uneven terrain, the ground rushing by in a blur. Immune to the pain of the sharp rocks and sticks cutting into her bare feet, she surged ahead.

A mammoth-sized oak animated before her eyes and reached out one of its giant limbs. The creature seized her by the wrist, its roughened bark keeping her in place. Branches and vines hovered, mocking Marina with menacing intimidation. They snaked along the ground, slithering toward her, winding their way around her arms and legs, holding her hostage. Marina's wet hair hung in her face, blinding her. Heat rose to her cheeks, and she squinted her eyes, peering through narrow slits. Shouting, she struggled against the mighty timber.

Marina awoke with a start. Pressing her hands to her chest, she took a few deep, measured breaths calming her racing heart. Each night for nearly two years, she woke in the same state. Shock, anger, and grief plagued her, but she'd kept her nightmares secret, unwilling to burden her family and friends with worry. The mask of secrecy she wore expended all her energy. Her ruse fooled everyone with the exception of Bey, her grandmother, the Elder Water Guardian of Aether. Their shared empathic abilities, coupled with their close bond, made it difficult to keep secrets from one another. With Bey's help, Marina had been fighting daily to maintain some semblance of a normal life, but after all this time, it still wasn't working. Something needed to change and soon, because she couldn't go on like this much longer.

****

Coal

The weight of the heavy bag suspended from the rafters creaked with every strike of his fists. Sweat trickled down his back, but he persisted with his punishing workout. During the predawn hours, Protector Headquarters, or PH as it was more commonly known, sat empty. Alone in the gym, Coal pushed his body to near dropping. Over and over, he brutally assaulted the gym's equipment, pounding it with unrelenting force, and the world around him faded to a blur. Out of nowhere, the bag leapt from his reach, and Coal's fists hit air. He looked up confused. Quill stood behind the bag; his arms wrapped around the circumference.

"What's with the Rocky routine? Ease up, will you?" Quill's voice echoed in the quiet room.

Taking two steps back, Coal bent at the waist, gulping in huge amounts of air. He scooped up his towel from the floor and mopped his brow before straightening up and draping it around his neck. "What are you doing here at three in the morning?"

"I could ask you the same question. You were going at that bag pretty hard. Are you all right?"

Coal shrugged, unsure of what to tell his friend so he turned the tables on Quill. "I'm fine. Why are *you* here? Something new on Barrington?"

"No, the slimy prick is still in the wind, but the wind is my thing." Quill's voice dripped with venom. "I'll catch that rat bastard if it's the last thing I do. I promised Brooke I would protect her and Ashlyn." Quill was red-faced, drenched in sweat, and breathing like he'd run a marathon.

"Come on, man, what's really going on with you?" Coal questioned his friend.

Releasing the bag, Quill stepped back. He stared at his feet and shook his head. "This thing with Brooke is driving me crazy. I can't sleep. I was out running, and then I decided to come here to hit the weights."

Coal furrowed his brow. "I don't get it. I thought she was staying with you. Aren't you two pretty tight?"

"Yeah, she is, and we are, but—shit—I don't know

24

what's wrong with me. I can't think straight when I'm near her. I've tried every trick in the book to convince her we belong together, but she keeps pushing me away."

"Women are complicated on a good day. Plus, I can only imagine what being in Aether is like for a typical human. Remember, the village is very different from the outside world. We were born here, and I'm still amazed by the power sometimes. Give Brooke a chance. I'm sure she'll come around."

Quill shot a pointed look down toward his crotch. "Tell that to my body."

Coal laughed. "That's what cold showers are for, or working out like mad at three in the morning."

"Listen, buddy, I know you've got this whole strong, silent, brooding thing going on, but I hope you know you can count on me or any of the other Protectors. We're brothers, Coal, all of us."

Quill's words, describing him as silent and brooding, fit to a T. Shutting out his brother Protectors had taken a toll on Coal, but they didn't know about the shame and longing which lived inside him. Unsure he could share his secret with anyone, especially with the one person who needed to hear it, guilt festered inside him. Coal's mind raced with memories of the day which had changed so many lives.

****

The sun beat down through the gaps in the trees, heating the wooded area where the Protectors gathered. Baking in the sweltering July heat, Coal and his cousin, Landon, stood beneath the shade of a couple of tall pines. Raised under the same roof, the boys were more like brothers than cousins. Inseparable their entire lives, they'd entered the Protector trials watching each other's backs throughout their journey.

River held up a mass of wires, reviewing the finer points of explosives' set up and detonation to the recruits. He droned on about the differences among C-4, TNT, and ANFO and primary versus secondary explosives as well as high and low explosives. Coal could set a detonator in his sleep, and his mind tuned out. Landon stared off into the woods.

"You looking for someone?" Coal whispered.

"Nah. I'm missing my girl. I keep expecting her to walk through trees for some strange reason."

Coal tilted his head, his brow lifting. "Why the hell would she come here? Isn't she usually at the lake this time of day?" The blonde-haired, blue-eyed beauty had developed a special friendship with the cousins when they were small. Although she and Landon Joined at a young age, they both remained close to Coal.

River's voice rang out. "Yo, Landon, Coal, am I disturbing you two?" Their heads whipped around at the sound of their lead Protector's voice. "Brack is with you. Let him set up the explosives in the cave down this ridge." The Protectors didn't answer; they simply grabbed the equipment and headed toward the cave River directed them to.

With a wave of his hand, Brack retracted the low hanging branches impeding their path. The young trainee's uncommon ability to manipulate anything botanical came in handy. Coal couldn't wait to witness a larger sampling of the kid's powers. Curious and hardworking, Brack absorbed everything presented to him during his training.

Coal stood back, leaning against a wide oak which

towered like an ancient guard protecting the cave's entrance. Brack set up the explosives with efficient movements, setting the detonator exactly as instructed. Landon continued to encourage their protégé. The art of explosives, as Quill dubbed this portion of Protector training, concluded the final phase of the trials. Soon Brack and the other recruits would be inducted into the brotherhood of the Protectors.

Landon and Brack stood shoulder to shoulder in the mouth of the cave. His cousin nodded toward Coal. "Hey, would you mind shouting to River? He should still be over the ridge. Tell him we're ready to roll here."

"Sure. No worries, give me a minute."

Jogging up the steep incline, Coal cleared the hill. Without warning, a strong blast rocked the ground beneath his feet with heavy vibrations. The trees around the landscape swayed in protest showering him with leaves. Panicked, he turned, racing back down the slope. Slipping on the uneven ground, he clawed his way toward the cave where his best friend and the trainee waited. *Dear Goddess, I have to help them.*

Skidding to a halt, Coal froze. He stood fifty feet from the spot he'd left his brother Protectors, but it may as well have been fifty miles. The massive ledge jutting out above the mouth of the cave began to crumble, and his eyes latched on in horror. Huge chunks of rock crashed down shattering on contact with the ground below like large pieces of broken glass. Coal surged forward again, skating another ten feet on the unsteady terrain. Sand, dirt, and rocks slid down in his wake. Fire crackled under his skin, and his vision blurred.

"Get out! Landon, get out of there!" Coal pressed

on gaining ground. Time took on a distorted appearance dragging along until he caught a glimpse of the action unfolding. Brack flew through the air as if shot from a cannon. The young Protector landed hard crumpling on impact, a safe distance from the impending disaster. Coal's gaze settled on Landon's familiar stance, the one he used when he called on his powers from the Earth. His brave and stupid cousin had saved the kid from being crushed without any regard for his own safety. Before Coal could react, the sheer rock wall gave way in a thunderous avalanche, a waterfall of earth and stone, swallowing Landon in an instant.

"No!" Anger and shock surged through Coal. His fists clenched, and heat rose up his neck. Thick clouds of dirt billowed through the air, obscuring everything. Coal coughed in spasms, his lungs filling, the debris choking him.

A second explosion erupted with a deafening roar, and the world around him rushed by. It propelled his body backward, sending him sailing through the air. His flight came to an abrupt and jarring halt, slamming him into the trees. Pain radiated through his body, and blackness closed in. The last memory Coal registered was of his best friend the second before the rockslide consumed him.

Chapter Three
Brooke

A knock sounded at seven o'clock on the dot. Brooke opened the door to greet Ashlyn. Taking in her friend's stunning appearance, she shook her head. "Really? I took an hour to get ready, and you waltz in here looking like a beauty queen in jeans and a top. Do you even have to try? It's not fair." Brooke pouted.

Ashlyn gave her a playful swat, her mane of red curls falling in soft spirals around her delicate features, lighting up her face. "Oh, knock it off. You know you're the gorgeous one."

Brooke rolled her eyes, but enveloped Ash in a giant hug. "I love you. You're such a good friend."

Seeing Ashlyn free, her vibrant spirit restored, filled Brooke with a sense of peace. Since aiding in the rescue of Aether's Fire Guardian and moving to the village, Brooke had become an adopted member of the Woods family. No one looked out for her more than Ashlyn did, other than Quill of course.

Escaping from Brooke's hold, Ash laughed dragging her to the door. "I love you, too. Now let's go. I don't want to be late."

Brooke yelled goodbye to Quill and slammed the door behind them with a loud bang. The two women fell into step, meandering along chatting about everything except the elephant in the room.

Ash grabbed Brooke by the arm, halting her in her tracks. "This is nice, but don't you think we should talk about your Guardian mark. I want to help you learn to connect to your Element. You need to embrace your power and accept your destiny."

Brooke tugged free and crossed her arms over her chest. "Are you done? Can you give me a break with the Guardian talk? I get enough of that from Quill." She narrowed her gaze, shooting her friend a warning. "And if you say one word in front of anyone, so help me—"

"Haha, you know I'd never break your confidence. I totally have your back, but as soon as we convince you of the truth, everyone in Aether will have to know. So, you better start getting used to it."

"Easy for you to say, you're—you're you."

Ashlyn chuckled. "You crack me up. Okay, I'll tell you what, no more Guardian talk. We'll keep tonight all about us girls and just have fun. All right?"

"I'll try. I've never really had a group of girlfriends before. I'm not sure how to act."

Her friend placed her hand on Brooke's arm giving it a gentle squeeze. "Be yourself. Everyone already loves you."

Brooke injected a bit of sarcasm into her tone. "Yeah, sure everyone loves me." She brushed aside the comment with a wave of her hand. "I don't want to talk about myself anymore. I want to be normal and have fun. To be honest, I can't remember the last time I went out and had fun. I think I'm past due."

"Well then, fun you shall have, my friend." Ashlyn threw her arm around Brooke's shoulder, and the two entered the pub.

Finding a large, empty booth in the corner, they

slid across the bench to wait for their friends. The others walked in a few minutes later and made their way across the room. Brooke felt her body stiffen. Marina stood before her, poised, a vision of refined beauty, the true Water Guardian. *Look at her. Now that's a Guardian. They say she can read minds or something. God, I hope she can't read mine.* Her stomach twisted in tight knots. Taking a large sip of wine from her glass, the tart, fruity liquid slid down her throat warming her.

This morning, her friends' persistence had almost persuaded her of the possibility of being the Guardian, but now, in Marina's presence, doubt returned surging through Brooke like a tsunami. The Water Guardian looked like a supermodel, all long legs and sexy curves. Her blonde hair shimmered reflecting the low lighting in the pub. Gorgeous blue eyes added a warmth to her elegant looks. Brooke brought her glass to her lips, downing another long swallow. The other women joined them at the table, and her head swiveled around, admiring the four beauties. *I'm not like them, gifted and perfect. I'm a plain, old, ordinary human.*

Her new friends sipped their wine using exquisite manners while Brooke guzzled down her entire glass, refilling it before anyone noticed. Ash caught her gaze, giving her an encouraging wink. Brooke picked up a piece of fried calamari and popped it into her mouth. The salty, chewy bite danced on her tongue, and she marveled at the flavor. *Yum, even the food in Aether is perfect.*

The animated conversation flowed around her, but Brooke only nibbled on appetizers and sipped her wine, staying quiet. She swirled the ruby-colored liquid around her goblet memorized by the repetitive motion. Nobody brought up the tragic death of River or the unknown whereabouts of Charles Barrington. Relieved there was no mention of her father, Brooke let out a breath.

Laurel's good-natured teasing of Ashlyn entertained the group. "Can't you two keep your hands off each other? It's getting so we can hardly be alone in a room with you guys anymore."

They cracked up laughing, and Lily chimed in. "Can you blame her? Hawk is so handsome."

Ashlyn responded, "Thanks, Lil. I couldn't agree more."

Brooke's mind wandered latching onto an image of a certain green-eyed Protector. *Hawk is hot but not as hot as my Quill. Oh my God, how can I even think that? He's not* my *Quill.*

As if conjured by her thoughts, Quill and his friends entered the pub a few minutes later. Brooke's gaze connected with his, and her lips parted of their own accord. Helpless to resist, a whoosh of air escaped her mouth in a whisper. The stunning men walked through the bar like a parade of Armani models. Kai, tall and blond, had an adorable dimple in his cheek. Hawk followed close behind. The handsome lead Protector carried his dark, Native American looks and herculean build in a brooding fashion.

"Guess the hotties have crashed girls' night," Brooke said, with a laugh. The alcohol slowly crept its way through her system, and she began to feel buzzed.

Ash jumped to their defense. "They're not crashing. Hawk says they only came for a beer."

Laurel needled her friend. "Damn, girl, that

telepathy thing is really creepy."

"Don't be mean. It's not creepy. You know, when it first kicked in, I didn't believe it was real. I thought I was the only Guardian in history without an extra sensory power." Across the bar, Hawk nodded to Ash. A blush spread across her cheeks. "But it sure does come in handy sometimes."

"Yup, like I said, creepy." Laurel ribbed Ash playfully.

Ashlyn snorted. "Says the girl who rekindled her relationship whilst in a coma. Oh, and let's not forget, he was also your doctor. Yeah, that's not creepy." The girls all chuckled at the retort.

Lily's smile didn't reach her eyes, but her voice held warmth and sincerity. "I think the connection is beautiful. I'm happy for you and Hawk, Ash. You guys are great together. And as a matter of fact, Laurel, I think you and Kai are a perfect match, too."

Brooke couldn't help but stare at the incredible-looking men standing around the bar, but it was Quill's incredible butt which drew her attention. "Knock it off," she reprimanded herself.

"Knock what off?" Ash questioned.

"Nothing." Brooke redirected the conversation. "How 'bout another bottle, ladies?"

She signaled the waiter, and a new bottle of wine arrived shortly. One glass flowed into two, and Brooke's usual shyness and restraint melted away. She lowered her defenses joining in the banter, but her gaze kept drifting back to Quill.

"Hey, Ash, use your mind powers, and get the guys over here," Brooke slurred.

"Um, Brooke, are you okay? You seem a little—"

"I'm feeling no pain. In fact—I'm feeling great. Those men are, without question, the most gorgeous men I've ever seen, and what a bunch of total bad asses—I wonder if there is something in the water here in Aether?"

Ashlyn took Brooke's wine and slid it out of her reach. "I think you've had enough for tonight. How about some water?" She pushed a glass in Brooke's direction. "Here, drink this."

"You're so good to me, Ash. Thanks. I'm super glad you're my friend." Brooke marveled at the smooth surface of the cold, wet glass wrapped in her fingers. Her vision clouded a bit, and the slick glass slipped straight through her hand. One second, she'd been holding the water and the next it poured down the front of her blouse. *Great, nice job. Yeah, I'm definitely the Water Guardian. Not. I can't even drink water without spilling it.* She grasped the now sheer, silky material fumbling with the fabric clinging to her chest.

A familiar voice rang in her ears, and she turned seeking the source. Gorgeous green eyes met hers; concern and displeasure apparent on his face. "Brooke, what are you doing, sweetheart?"

"Quill, how the hell are ya? My shirt got wet—see." Brooke thrust her chest out gripping the soaked cloth, and her top button popped open.

Glued to her damp shirt, Quill's gaze widened. The delicate fabric adhered to her breasts. She crossed her arms over her chest, but the way the handsome Protector's gaze sizzled sent tingles through her body. He slid into the booth, scooting closer. The man radiated heat like a furnace. His muscular thigh pressed against her leg, and her entire body awakened with awareness.

Quill grabbed a napkin off the table and handed it to her. "Here you go, use this."

"Maybe you can help me?" Brooke couldn't seem to stop the words from escaping her mouth. *Oh God, I sound like an idiot. I don't know how to flirt.*

"How much did you drink, sweetheart?"

"I just don't know?" She felt her slurring increase with each sentence she uttered.

Quill clenched his teeth. "I thought you girls looked out for each other. Ash, how could you let her get like this?"

Confusion filled Brooke. "Why are you mad?"

"It's not *you* I'm mad at." Quill's eyes narrowed.

Hawk raised his palm. "Wait a minute there, buddy. Brooke is a grown woman. Ash is not responsible for her actions."

Brooke poked Quill's firm bicep. "Hey, what's your problem? I'm havin' some fun for once in my boring life. Don't you be mean to Ash—she's my bestest friend. Just because you're super sexy and all…"

"Let's go, Brooke." His posture stiff, Quill stood, radiating tension. His large hand gently closed around her arm. "I'm taking you home. I think you need to sleep this off."

"I'm not tired. I'm having fun." Pulling free of his grasp, she dug her heels in, crossing her arms over her chest with a huff. "You're such a tyrant. I'm staying right here with my friends."

"Honey, don't make me carry you out of here. You've had too much to drink. It's up to you which way you leave. You decide, but we *are* leaving."

Quill's clipped tone incited her temper.

"You're not the boss of me!" Brooke glared at him, sticking her tongue out in his direction. The others turned away snickering behind hidden hands.

"Oh, baby, you are so going to regret that." Quill scooped her up, and the world turned upside down. He headed toward the exit, and she bounced along hanging like a rag doll over his shoulder.

"Put me down this minute, you Neanderthal!" She punched and kicked the Protector to no avail. The jolt of a sharp spank to her backside shocked her. "You did not just hit me? I'm—I'm telling your mother."

"Baby, that was a love tap. And really, my mother? If you don't knock this shit off and behave, you won't be able to sit for a week." Quill's voice, dark and sexy, held unveiled promise.

Brooke's body hummed with unexpected arousal. *Oh my God, I think I'm actually turned on.* She'd never been aroused by kinky talk, well at least she never had been before. Heat pooled between her legs. Every step Quill took brought more friction to her overly sensitized body. "Please, put me down. I promise I'll be good."

With slow easy movements, he lowered her to the ground. Her feet touched the cobblestone, and she wobbled on the uneven surface. His muscular arm snaked around her waist, steadying her. Hazy from the alcohol, Brooke clung to him, resting her head on his shoulder. "Yum, you smell so good. You know, I think you're the sexiest man I've ever laid eyes on."

"I think you're drunk, sweetheart, but thanks. And by the way, I think you're super sexy, too."

Tucked in tight to Quill's side, Brooke's body knew what it wanted. Arousal crept its way along her nerve endings. He shoved the front door open with his hip, bringing her even closer, sending a wave of heat through her already boiling blood. Guiding her to the couch, he refused to let her go until she settled in the seat. Quill kneeled in front of Brooke running his hands down her bare legs, stopping at her feet. Slipping off her shoes, his warm fingers kneaded the tired soles of her feet, and a tiny moan escaped her lips. Shivering with sensual delight, Brooke's head fell back against the sofa, her eyes closing of their own volition. His voice interrupted her moment of bliss, and her eyes fluttered open.

"Tell me something? What were you thinking drinking so much tonight?" Quill's incredible green gaze locked on hers, his lips tightening into a thin line.

"I don't know. I guess I was nervous." His fingers drifted to the back of her calves, digging in, massaging her flesh. "Mmm, that feels so good." His hands on her skin dislodged any other thought from her brain. *Oh my God, he's sex on a stick.*

Quill stood, reached for her hands, and yanked her to her feet in one swift motion. "Come on, let's get you to bed."

She stumbled forward into a wall of pure muscle. Through her damp blouse, her nipples abraded against his chest. Her tongue swept across her lips, moistening them. She stepped back placing her hands on Quill's shoulders and followed the hard lines of his chest sweeping down over his six-pack. *Finally.*

Quill halted her movement, holding her at arm's length. "Whoa, babe, what are you thinking?"

"Well if you let go, I'll show you." Brooke edged closer and stood on her tiptoes. Stepping out of her comfort zone, she brought her mouth to his, slipping her tongue between his lips. She sensed the exact moment Quill surrendered because he responded with an intensity mirroring her own. Passion ignited, and the world around her faded away.

In an abrupt shift, Quill's body became rigid. He pulled away, his face flushed, his breathing labored. "What the hell am I doing? You're drunk, Brooke. We can't do this."

"Sure we can." Kissing his neck, she wrapped her arms around his waist.

"Brooke, *stop!*" He untangled her arms and stepped back.

The pain of his rejection knocked the wind out of her. Wrapping her arms around her middle, tears filled her eyes. "I get it. You don't really want me. You've only been saying those sweet, sexy things to make me feel better. I'll leave you alone." One lone tear escaped, inching its way down her cheek.

Brooke turned toward the guest room, her gaze fixed on the ground. Quill took hold of her wrist and in one smooth movement stopped her in her tracks. Spinning her around to face him, his smoldering, emerald eyes drew her into their depths. Linking their hands together, he lowered them until her palm encountered hard male flesh. Quill's erection throbbed beneath her touch. Brooke's hand shook.

His raspy tone hit her low in the belly. "I've wanted you from the first second I laid eyes on you. You're smart. And beautiful. And so much stronger than you realize. I want you so much it hurts, but not like this. I want you when you're sober and not feeling off balance. I never want to take advantage of you, ever."

"Wow, you're—um, well big."

Quill laughed. "You are good for my ego, sweetheart."

"Your ego does not need boosting." Brooke's cheeks heated. "I'm sorry, Quill. You've been so good to me, and this is how I treat you. Please, don't be mad at me."

"Of course I'm not mad at you. This *will* happen between us but not until you're one hundred percent sure. I want you to come to me sober and with certainty. Now, let's get you to bed."

As gallant as Prince Charming from the fairytales of her childhood, Quill swept her into his arms carrying her off. She rested her head on his chest, breathing in his glorious masculine scent. The door to her room stood ajar. Connecting to his Element, Quill sliced his hand through the air, and a gust of wind pushed the door open further. Crossing the room, he came to a stop in front of the bed. Quill raised his arm, waving it at the comforter. A strong wind kicked up, blowing the covers back. He lowered her with slow, gentle movements, transferring her to the plush mattress.

"You're so beautiful, Brooke." Yanking her hair free from its tightly wound bun, he ran his fingers through the strands. "Soon we'll be together in every way. Now, go to sleep. We're leaving in the morning for the city."

Placing a gentle kiss on her forehead, Quill turned to leave but paused in the doorway. Too tired to respond, she could feel his gaze on her, but exhaustion sank deep. A light breeze hovered in the air caressing her aroused flesh, but the minute Quill left the room, the warm winds cocooning her faded away. The sudden absence of air currents moving over her body left her feeling bereft, or maybe it was Quill's absence itself which left her empty inside?

Sleep drew near, and Brooke mumbled in a soft whisper, "He really is spectacular. I'm definitely gonna get me some of that."

****

Quill

The instant he pulled the door closed behind him, Quill dropped his forehead with a low thud against the hard wood. Shutting his eyes tight, he took a huge gulp of air and exhaled it in a forceful rush. Earlier this evening, he'd spotted Brooke in the pub, and everything around him had faded from view except for his beautiful, little scientist. The rapid rhythm of his heartbeat sounded in his ears. Quill was doomed. There would never be another woman for him.

"So damn beautiful," he said, prying himself from her door. Hesitating, he turned back, reaching for the doorknob again. The cool metal rested in his heated palm. "No. I can't do this." Releasing the handle, he turned, dragging his feet along the carpet and leaving his sleeping angel behind the closed door.

The memory of Brooke's wet blouse plastered against his chest sent desire raging through his system. It had taken every ounce of willpower he possessed to resist her. Reaching down, he yanked the front of his jeans away from the ache of his constricted arousal. "Whoa, down boy. Damn, nothing's going to help this but a cold shower." He chuckled, heading into the bathroom, peeling his clothing from his traitorous body, and leaving a trail along the way.

Cranking the faucet all the way to *C*, Quill stuck his hand under the stream to check the temperature before stepping under the spray. "Ah, Arctic blast, perfect." Quill fought to clear his mind from the bombardment of visions overtaking his thoughts. Images of Brooke materialized and embedded themselves in his brain. The way her soft, blonde hair skimmed the line of her delicate shoulders made his hands itch with the urge to tug on the silken strands.

Quill bent under the cascading water, allowing the glacial mist to seep into his overheated skin. He hung his head and remained under the icy spray until his need dissipated. Twisting the faucet, he cut the flow of chilly water, and grabbed a towel. Drying off, he tossed the towel onto the counter, and headed back into his bedroom.

Quill climbed on top of the covers, sprawling out nude. He stared up at the ceiling and said a little prayer, "Dear God and Goddess, I may be leading her straight into the lion's den tomorrow. Please, watch over her."

Clearing his mind, he focused on the Air around him, drifting off into a restless slumber. Random snippets of dreams ran through his brain at a frenetic pace. Subconscious visions flashed before him, and he honed in on one particular image. The devil appeared. The mercenary he'd seen in his nightmares many times loomed before Quill, striking a conspicuous pose.

Devlin clutched Brooke to his broad chest, a hunting knife pressed to her throat. Crimson droplets ran along the blade dripping down her neck. The evil man's disfiguring scar twisted his mouth into a permanent sneer. Brooke's screams pierced Quill's ears making his blood run cold. His powers engaged, and strong gusts of wind shook the room. Objects soared through the air, bouncing off every surface and crashing to the ground. Quill found his center, controlling the forceful currents. Riding on the draft he'd created, he jetted to Brooke's side, stealing his woman back from the demon's deadly grasp.

Darkness fell, consuming everything, shifting time and space. Then, like the ascent of a sunrise, light grew in tiny increments until they were no longer entangled with the predatory mercenary. Quill lay prone on a soft mattress with Brooke straddling him. Desperation filled her eyes, and she tore at his clothing. He sat up, reaching between them. Breathless, he plucked at the buttons of her blouse, ripping it open revealing her bare breasts. Cupping the glorious mounds, he brought one pink tip to his mouth, lavishing it with attention before moving onto the other. Her fingers tunneled into his hair tugging his mouth toward hers. Their lips crashed together in the most intense and passionate kiss Quill had ever experienced. Brooke's lips eased back, her image distorting. He clutched her shoulders, despair consuming him. Dissolving into a cloud of smoke, she slipped through his fingers, fading away into nothingness.

On his next breath, Quill emerged alone, deep in Aether's forest. Where was Brooke? A terrible emptiness filled him. Frantic, shoving branches aside, he searched for her. Sweat trickled down his back, and his heart pounded. The desperate need to find her and make her safe consumed him.

Quill thrashed about on the bed, mumbling Brooke's name until his body quieted and his dreams faded away. The urge to protect her was no less pronounced when the blackness of night gave way to the morning sun. Bright light broke through the slats in his blinds. Eyes burning, head pounding, Quill stared up at the ceiling wide awake. Sweet, innocent Brooke, in her drunken state, did her best to seduce him last night using her latent, sexy charms. He might have found the situation amusing if it hadn't taken every ounce of his will to resist the passionate plea in her eyes. His erection refused to cooperate with his firm decision to put Brooke out of his mind. Whenever he focused on the alluring scientist, he had the same reaction.

Dragging his sleep-deprived body from the bed, he made his way to the cold shower once again. Mindless, he washed, trying not to stimulate himself in any way. He wanted the tension in his body, the edge, to keep him alert. Protecting Brooke from both physical and emotional hurt of any kind took priority above all else.

Quill pulled a black duffle from the top shelf of his closet, and a couple of old shoeboxes tumbled down on his head. Kicking them out of the way, he yanked the bag open, inspecting the contents, his focus sharp. It held his favorite Beretta, two forty-fives, and an assortment of knives. Pleased with his collection, he double-checked the safeties and his ammo. Shoving his mini arsenal into the bottom of his bag, he added some clothes and toiletries then zipped the whole thing up. Slinging the substantial load over his shoulder, he walked out of the room.

Depositing his bag by the back door, Quill crept to the kitchen in silence. He set up the coffee maker and flipped the switch. Brooke would need the jolt of caffeine after her little drinking binge last night.

Grabbing a bottle of Tylenol from the cabinet, he shook out a couple of caplets and placed them next to two large mugs. His girl was in for one hell of a headache today. The aroma of the fresh brew percolating wafted up to his nose. Inhaling deeply, he enjoyed the familiar scent. Quill ignored his fierce need for coffee and headed back to the bedroom where Brooke slept. The instinct to care for her took over, shoving aside his bachelor's mindset.

The bedroom door creaked open, and Quill's gaze fixed on Brooke's sleeping figure. The sun's first rays shimmered through the window, bathing her in warm light. Her arms splayed out across the mattress; Brooke's chest rose and fell rhythmically. Adorable pink toenails peeked out from under the blanket tangled around her legs. The black skirt she wore had bunched up around her waist while she slept exposing her flat belly and a pair of lacy, white panties. Several buttons had popped open on her blouse revealing a matching bra, as sheer as her panties.

He inched closer to the bed, a cool breeze following in his wake. Her berry colored nipples responded to the chill, and Quill's eyes widened. The air skimmed over her body, and the gorgeous peaks tightened further making his mouth water. He adjusted his erection for the umpteenth time. *Man, she really hides a rocking body under her conservative camouflage.* He licked his lips. *Not happening right now, dude. Move on.* He needed to wake her so they could get on the road.

He took a seat on the edge of the bed, careful not to jostle her too much. Stretching out his hand, the tips of his fingers grazed a few wisps of the silky blonde hair fanned out across the pillow. Quill's caress grew bolder, and he stroked his hand down the entire length of her hair. If he could gain access to her apartment in the city, he'd go alone to keep her safe. He worried Barrington might be there, or maybe some of his thugs would be watching the place. Dead. They'd be dead if they came anywhere near Brooke.

Quill rubbed a gentle hand down her arm. "Brooke, sweetheart, it's time to get up."

She groaned. Reaching down, she grabbed the covers, pulling them up and over her head. "Go away. I can't even look at you. I'm completely mortified."

"Nothing to be embarrassed about, it happens to the best of us. It's fine. Come on and get up. I'll make you some eggs and toast. Then we need to hit the road." He made light of Brooke's escapades, but he could think of little else other than her inebriated sexual advances. Quill fought his impulses and tamped down his desire. He wanted her to feel secure and didn't think telling her he wanted to tear her clothes from her body with his teeth was such a good idea. So, he chose to take the high road.

From under the covers, her muffled voice whined. "I need aspirin, some coffee, and a shower. Then I'm going back to bed to hide forever."

"No hiding from me now or ever." Quill chuckled. "Go take your shower, and pack a bag in case we need to stay for a night or two. I'm going to get your coffee ready." He tickled her through the blankets until she laughed. "Good, that's more like it. Now, get your lazy ass out of bed." He left her to get ready and headed back to the kitchen.

Twenty minutes later she appeared looking

refreshed. Brooke brushed by him. The fragrance of summer rain followed in her wake, and Quill's nose tingled from the delicate scent. The need to pull her close and hoist her onto the counter overwhelmed him. Fighting the urge to relieve her of her jeans and panties, Quill struggled to keep his expression impassive. He said nothing. He did nothing. He simply passed her a mug of coffee, Tylenol, and a plate piled with eggs and toast.

"Um, thanks, Quill, and not only for breakfast. I don't know what came over me last night. I rarely drink and when I do, I usually have only a single glass of wine. I feel like a total idiot. I hope you can forgive me, for, um, attacking you." Her cheeks pinkened, and she fell silent.

She looked adorable, so he took mercy on her, going against his natural inclination to tease. "Don't worry about it. Let's eat and get out of here before anyone misses us." He mumbled under his breath, "Not that anyone would recognize this pussy-whipped version of me."

Her brow lifted. "What was that last thing you said? I didn't catch it."

"Nothing." Quill shoved a forkful of eggs into his mouth, chewing while he spoke. "I was talking to myself."

They finished eating, cleaned up, and were ready to leave fifteen minutes later. Quill grabbed both bags, tossed them over his shoulder, and took Brooke's hand. Leading her to the back door, he opened it, surveying the area. His hold remained firm, and they made their way through the woods in a companionable silence. The snapping of twigs under their feet was the only sound in the quiet forest.

They emerged from between the trees, and Quill breathed a sigh of relief. "Going the back way really seemed to do the trick."

Brooke grabbed his arm, halting his motion. "Wait a minute, I forgot my phone. We need to go back."

He let out a low chuckle. "We can't go back. I don't want to risk bumping into anyone. I don't feel like dealing with all the questions—" Quill shot her a wink. "—but don't worry, you can play all the *Candy Crush* you want on my phone." The key bobbled in his hand, and Quill steadied it clicking the button, setting off a loud chirp.

Brooke startled, bringing her hand to her chest. "I'm sorry. I don't know what's wrong with me. I'm a little nervous."

"It's going to be all right, honey; you'll see." He caught her gaze and placed his hand on her shoulder. "I'll never let anyone hurt you again."

Popping the trunk on the gray sedan, he tossed their bags in the back. They settled themselves in the car, and Quill started the engine. He shifted into gear and eased the car out of the parking lot. For several miles the vehicle bounced along the rough, dirt road which ran straight through Aether's forest, coming to a stop at the edge of the tree line.

He cleared his throat, breaking the silence. "Did you know there are lots of ways in and out of Aether? Here's a little history lesson for you. The village's borders are massive, and they're protected by strong magic, but there's a secret to getting in—you have to be one of us."

"So how did I get in, Einstein?"

"Hmm? I didn't really think about it. I guess maybe it was because you were with us, or maybe it's because you're a Guardian."

Brooke rolled her eyes. "You're such a jerk."

Quill laughed. "I heard you like jerks."

She turned a cold shoulder to him and returned her gaze out the window. "Let's go, jerk."

Pulling onto the deserted country highway, the car coasted along the smooth pavement. The silence between them grew deafening. Quill couldn't stand it another minute. "Are you ever going to speak to me again? I'm a little confused. Are you mad at me because I keep saying you're the Guardian, or are you upset about getting a little smashed last night?"

"No, I'm not mad at you. I'm kind of a wreck about going home, that's all. I haven't been back since my mom died. And then there's my father. Ugh!"

"I get it, but if you're worried about something, anything, I want you to tell me. I can't help if you don't let me in."

"Thanks, Quill, maybe you're not such a jerk after all."

"Please don't tell anyone. You'll ruin my reputation as a badass. I've worked hard to cultivate it over the years." He flashed a mischievous grin in her direction.

Brooke's answering peals of laughter sent warmth coursing through his body, but the farther they traveled from Aether the more his powers tingled under his skin. A slight breeze kicked up in the car blowing the wispy strands of hair escaping from her tightly coiled bun. Concentrating his focus, his powers responded, retreating back inside his tense body, and the air grew still once again.

Back in Aether he'd been working with Brooke on both martial arts and weapons training. They'd practiced non-stop, and she'd become quite adept with a weapon. Pride filled him, but Quill wasn't ready to let Brooke know how much it thrilled and excited him, not yet anyway. Still, he preferred the idea of her being safe back in Aether rather than facing any potential danger which may lie ahead.

Leaning closer, Brooke draped her hand over his arm. "I can tell you're worried. Don't be. There's a twenty-four-hour doorman in the building, and he'll know if anyone's been there."

Quill covered her delicate hand with his own much larger one, securing it in place. "Okay. I'll tell you what. How about we don't worry about it until we get there? Let's pretend we're on a date, a normal couple heading into the city for a few days away. What do you say?"

"Sounds nice."

"I'll tell you what sounds nice. You and me. Alone. Like a real couple, doing real couple things. In all sorts of places and in all sorts of ways."

Yanking her hand from beneath his, she gave him a little smack on the shoulder. "What am I going to do with you?"

He turned for a quick second, wiggling his eyebrows in response. "I'm pretty sure I can help you out with some ideas to start with."

They laughed together, relieving the lingering tension between them. The remaining hours passed in a comfortable, easy manner. They chatted nonstop the rest of the way. She asked him silly questions about his favorite foods, movies, and everything else under the sun, and soon the cityscape appeared outside the windshield.

Quill craned his neck, gawking at the giant skyscrapers which grew straight up from the concrete. The car drifted a bit, but Quill steadied it before Brooke noticed. His palms tingled, and he clutched the steering wheel with a bit too much force, his knuckles whitening. Danger lurked around every corner in this enormous maze of a world. The closer they got to the city, the more his Protector instincts kicked into high gear.

Before long, they pulled up to a tall, red brick apartment building, and Quill couldn't keep the wonder from his voice. "Wow, this place is huge. Must be thirty stories high."

"Actually, it's thirty-eight floors. There's an underground parking garage on your right. Pull up, and I'll give you the code for the keypad by the entrance."

Quill came to a stop in front of a large, metal door. Brooke called out the numbers, and he punched them into the keypad in rapid succession. The hairs on the back of his neck rose. A mild breeze flowed through the car, picking up in intensity while they waited for the garage door to rise. His head darted from side to side, scanning the busy street, searching for anyone suspicious.

"What the hell is taking this damn door so long? I have a bad feeling. We need to get inside, now." Quill reached behind him and yanked his Beretta out of the waistband of his jeans. He'd tucked it in place as a precaution before they left Aether. Placing the weapon on his lap, he resumed his vigilant surveillance.

After what seemed like an eternity, the immense door rose at a snail's pace. It rattled along its metal track, the loud sound reverberating. Quill didn't wait for it to finish its ascent. Tires squealing, he raced under the gap, screeching the car to a halt. In a flash he re-entered the code lowering the door behind them. Looking back over his shoulder one last time, he caught a glimpse of a broad-shouldered man, dressed in all black, standing in the entryway. The door closed with a shudder. Maybe it was his imagination, or maybe it wasn't.

Chapter Four
Marina

Bringing her knees to her chest, Marina curled into a fetal position. Her damp clothes stuck to her sweat soaked body. The nightmares she suffered from continued to plague her with no relief in sight. Each morning she examined her reflection in the mirror. Dark circles marred the skin beneath her swollen eyes, and soon all the makeup in the world wouldn't help to conceal her sleepless nights.

The tightness in her chest loosened a bit, but a dull ache still lingered inside. Marina took a few deep breaths and uncoiled her frame. Stretching her limbs out in every direction, she groaned from the release of her protective posture. She wished she could somehow block the memory of that day, the one which replayed in her subconscious like a film loop on repeat. Every single night, both the surreal creations of her brain and the harsh reality which had become her life swamped her.

****

Marina wove her way through the uneven terrain of Aether's forest. The rough surface of the ground tore at the flesh beneath her bare feet. Numbness crept its way through her body, a shield to her senses, blocking her own physical pain. However, her power of empathy could not be contained, and agony ripped into her gut, weighing her down. Marina crumpled, holding her stomach, the pain closing in.

Fighting with strength and determination, she straightened to her full height. Her breathing ragged, she scanned the surrounding area catching sight of dark plumes of smoke rising in the air above the dense canopy of leaves. Using the hazy cloud as a guide, Marina forged ahead, weaving between the trees. Her arms scraped against the massive timbers, and crimson droplets dusted the surface of her damaged skin. Resisting the urge to rest, she staggered. A low hanging branch snagged her shirt yanking her backward, knocking her to the ground.

Her arms and legs flailed helplessly. "Let...go...of...me!" Punctuating each word with a kick against the trunk, she growled. "Damn it!"

Grabbing hold of her shirt, Marina ripped it free from the tree's grasp. Ignoring the dirt and debris clinging to her wet clothing, she moved robotically determined to reach the source of emotions bombarding her senses. Shouts reverberated in the distance. The voices gained in volume and intensity as she broke out into the clearing. Her gaze settled on the hills nestled among a series of natural caves dotting the landscape. The sounds of her childhood echoed through her mind. Once a place of innocence, exploration, and happiness, she feared it would now hold only memories of sadness, pain, and loss.

Time paused for a brief moment, sputtering, and restarting again. The scene was utter chaos. She stood frozen, her feet planted, witnessing the horrific frenzy of activity taking place in front of her. A cramp doubled her over, and she wrapped her arms in a protective hold around her middle. Stabbing pains jolted into Marina's brain. Her hands flew to her head, tunneling into her hair, and digging into her scalp. The empathic overload crippled her; its possession impossible to fight.

Clouds of smoke and dust hung in the air. The caustic soot choked her, and her lungs seized. Heaving coughs wracked her body, and gritty, dirt filled tears ran down her face. Protectors hustled, their pace frenetic. River's voice rang out shouting orders amid the pandemonium. His words jumbled in her head, distant and muted. A group of people hovered over a motionless Protector sprawled beneath a tree. Nearby, a young, shell-shocked recruit sat covered from head to toe in a thick layer of dirt. Protectors fanned out over every inch of the terrain, but where was Landon? Marina placed her hand over her racing heart, attempting to regulate her breathing.

A flood of sorrow and anger swirled all around the Guardian. Filtering out the influx of emotions assaulting her, Marina, shaky and panicked, searched her powers for Landon's essence. His name fell from her lips in a hushed whisper. Her gaze darted around, seeking even a mere glimpse of her Kanti. Over and over, she called to him, her volume rising above the commotion until she found herself inexplicably screaming. "Landon! Landon, where are you? Landon!"

Her desperate cries must have drawn River to her side because he was next to her in a heartbeat. "Marina, dear Goddess, what's happened to you? You're hurt. Sit down." Taking her by the shoulders, he eased her to the ground.

Marina's breath whooshed out. "Where is he, River?" She grabbed hold of his shirt. "Where's

Landon?" Dirt caked her shorts, her T-shirt hung in tatters, and blood oozed between her toes. She knew she must've looked and sounded like a lunatic.

"You're going to be okay, honey. Let's get the medical team to look at you, and then we'll talk."

"No! You tell me where my Kanti is right this minute!" she shouted at the top of her lungs. More than a few heads turned in her direction, and a sudden influx of sympathy grabbed hold, churning her belly, infiltrating her senses.

"Marina, please; take it easy."

"No! I will not! *Where…is…Landon?*"

"There was a collapse at the mouth of the cave he was working in, and we believe he is either trapped or—"

"Or what?"

"We think he might've been hit by falling debris, but we aren't one hundred percent sure yet. All we know is Landon pushed Brack free before the overhang gave way. Coal may know something, but he's unconscious. He was blown clear by the explosion and straight into a tree. Listen to me—" River stroked a gentle hand down her cheek. "—we are doing everything we can to get him out of there as fast as possible. All of the Protectors are working on it, and Kai will be here any minute. Meanwhile, I'm going to send someone to look at your injuries. Let me check on our progress, and I'll be right back. Hang in there, honey." River kissed the top of her head before heading off.

Her body sagged. "This can't be happening."

Tears streamed down her cheeks in rivulets, and Marina didn't wipe them away. Even the heat of the summer's day didn't stop a cold chill from seeping in bone deep. Her tongue stuck to the roof of her mouth, and she swallowed around the lump forming in her throat. Marina's gaze zeroed on the dozens of Protectors working around the entrance of the cave excavating dirt and rocks using their powers or pure muscle.

Quill leaned into her space, calling her name. Gently, he shook her shoulder. The smell of antiseptic burned her nose, but the accompanying sting never followed. A firm tug on her legs turned her attention to two people crouched in front of her, tending to her blood-covered feet.

She looked up, her head canting to the side. "Quill, where did you come from?"

"I've been here. I've been calling your name."

Her voice choked with emotion. "What's happening? Did they find him yet?"

"Let us take care of you. You've been injured. I promise I'll tell you the second we know anything, but right now we need to—"

"No! No! No!" Shrieking, hysterical panic laced her voice.

Quill responded in a calm, reassuring tone taking her in his arms. "Hey, it's going to be okay. Stay with me," he ordered. "Take a deep breath." She complied. "Good," he said. "Another and let it out slowly this time."

Her voice, scratchy from screaming, rasped out in a whisper, "I can't leave. Oh, dear Goddess, I can't feel him." Marina's voice rose again, sounding shrill even to her own ears. "There's nothing there."

"Try to stay calm. We're going to get him out. I'll

be right here the whole time."

"Okay." The word slipped out of her mouth, a mechanical response.

Marina found it impossible to measure the passing of time. Had it been minutes, hours, days? The flurry of activity down below kicked into high gear, and desperation battled against hope inside her. River stood at the mouth of the cave, his face a picture of seriousness. Quill held her hand muttering reassurances.

Shaking his hand off, she gave him a small shove. "Don't worry about me. Go. Help them."

He got up, took a few steps, and turned back. "Are you sure?"

Her gaze narrowed, and she pointed down the hill. "Go."

Layers of rock and sediment flew in every direction, and finally Landon's boot poked out from beneath the rubble. The Protectors' efforts increased tenfold, and soon a prone figure emerged. Landon lay motionless. Marina held her breath and waited for any sign of life, but none came. The medical team flipped him over, and Kai jumped into action. He stopped after a few minutes and gave a subtle shake of his head. Using her powers, she dug deep, searching, reaching out, and feeling for any sign of Landon's light. But there was nothing, not even a flicker. An empty space resided where the glow of her Kanti had once lived. Her vision clouded moments before everything went black—

****

Coal
Nearly two years ago
Coal blinked a few times, but the bright light

forced his lids to slam back down. Nausea churned in his gut. *What happened to me?* Confusion battered his brain, and the pounding in his head made it impossible to recall anything. "What the hell is going on?" He croaked out in a scratchy, hoarse voice, "Where am I?"

"You're in the Medical Center." Quill's voice, distant at first, drifted closer. He took a seat on the edge of the bed, the mattress dipping from the Protector's weight. "You're all right, buddy. What's the last thing you remember?"

The rhythmic throbbing in Coal's head matched the pulsating pain in his shoulder. "Wait a minute," he mumbled. Snapshots of his cousin and the trainee ricocheted around his head in a terrifying rush. He bolted upright, the room tilting and swaying with his abrupt action. "Holy shit. Landon! Brack!" Coal took hold of the bedrail, steadying himself with a white-knuckled grip. "Where are they? Are they okay?"

Quill's face fell, and he rubbed the nape of his neck. Coal didn't want to hear the words, but his friend's voice answered all the same. "Brack is going to be okay. Landon pushed him clear. I'm so sorry, Coal, but Landon is gone." Quill hung his head.

Coal fought to get the words out. "W-what the fuck happened?"

"There was an accident with one of the detonators. It went off too early. River is losing his mind. He's overseeing the investigation otherwise he'd be here. We're going to figure out what happened. You have my word."

"I can't believe this." Coal rubbed his temples. "How can he be dead? He's the strongest guy I know."

"I hear you, man. He was a great guy, but I have to

tell you, it's Marina we're all worried about. She was there, Coal. Nobody knows how or where she came from, but she was there minutes after the explosion." Quill stood and began pacing around the small room. "She's a mess and in shock. She had no shoes and abraded most of the skin off the bottom of her feet. Kai says she won't be walking for a bit. We're not sure what she saw before she passed out, and they're still working on her wounds." Quill walked to the side of the bed and dropped a reassuring hand on Coal's shoulder. "Both of your families are on their way, but she needs to be told—"

"I'll tell her. It should come from me. He's my—he was my cousin, and my best friend, and so is she."

"Are you sure you're up to it? Kai says you have a pretty serious concussion. He put ten stitches in the back of your head, and you dislocated your shoulder. Someone else can tell her. It doesn't have to be you."

"Yes, it does. Poor Marina. She and Landon have been together since we were kids. Man, he loves—loved her so much. This is a total shit show." His heart heavy, Coal leaned back against his pillows, closing his eyes.

How was he going to tell Marina her Kanti was gone when he couldn't even wrap his brain around the idea? He scarcely held a childhood memory which didn't include both his best friends. The trio had shared all their hopes and dreams as kids. They had no secrets from one another. Well, except for one huge one Coal had been keeping. If someone really looked, perhaps he could see the secret not quite hidden below the surface, but merely camouflaged. Except nothing mattered anymore but how he was going to get Marina through this. His secrets, his feelings, meant nothing. Would there ever be a good time, the right time, to reveal this particular secret?

****

The present

Quill's incessant nagging to join him and some of the other Protectors had finally worn Coal down. Getting through this evening wouldn't be easy. Guilt and repression had become his new best friends since Landon died. Pushing the door open, he entered the pub. Quill's booming laugh penetrated through the din of music and voices filling the noisy bar. After Coal's conversation with the Protector the other night, he suspected Quill's sudden urge to hang out at the pub had more to do with keeping an eye on Brooke than male bonding. The ladies were having themselves a girls' night tonight. While he could relate to Quill's need to be near Brooke, coming to the pub and acting all chummy didn't exactly appeal to him.

Inching his way across the crowded room to join his friends, Coal dodged the small clusters of people gathered together enjoying their evening. The soles of his boots stuck to the floor distracting him, and his gaze momentarily shifted to his feet. He curled his lip and lifted his feet from the remnants of a beer puddle. A flash in the corner of his eye snagged his attention, and his head whipped around. *Marina.*

Coal's chest tightened, and everything faded from view except for the stunning vision before his eyes. The shimmer of long, blonde hair, swaying in time with the motion of her hips, temporarily blinded him. She wore a blue dress, tied at the neck, leaving her back and arms bare. Coal's fingers itched to touch the delicate-looking skin. He longed to cover it with kisses, leaving nothing but pleasure in his wake. The dress hugged her sexy curves, and the neckline plunged enough to satisfy a little bit more than his curiosity. Coal swallowed the lump in his throat.

So he stood, gawking across the bar at the one person he desperately wanted but couldn't have. No matter how hard he tried, he couldn't stay away. It was like trying not to breathe. Coal was convinced his feelings would never be reciprocated, but he couldn't let go of them all the same. Over the years, he learned to bury his emotions, and they now resided in a dark, private place. The constant struggle drove the Protector to his ultimate limit.

Their gazes connected. Marina smiled from across the room, her pale cheeks flushing an adorable shade of pink. His heart skipped a beat. Constructing emotional barriers helped him keep his feelings buried, but his physical reaction to the beautiful Guardian told a different story. He licked his lips, hungry for her. The urge to lunge at her, grab her, and wrap those gorgeous long legs around him while he pumped into her heat consumed him. Instead, he lowered his lids for a split second and then smiled back in a casual manner. Coal buried his fisted hands into the front pockets of his jeans using all of his inner strength to resist her magnetic pull. *Not here, not now.*

Fire tingled inside him, but he snuffed it out in an instant. Reaching his friends at the bar, Coal glanced over his shoulder, greedy for one last glimpse of the object of his lifelong desire. He knew he couldn't go on like this, stuck at a crossroads. Sliding onto an empty stool, he grabbed the pitcher in front of Hawk, and poured a beer. Before he even said hello, he took a long, slow swig of his brew savoring the bitter hops.

Quill's eyebrows rose. "Nice to see you, too."

Coal lowered the mug to the wooden surface of the bar with a thud. "Uh, sorry. I was thirsty."

His friends laughed but didn't bother to question him. They'd learned by now, any efforts they made to engage Coal would remain an exercise in futility. He'd closed himself off since Landon's death, but his friends stuck by him proving their steadfast loyalty no matter how much he pushed them away. Through the years, he'd come to rely on his fellow Protectors for support. His family dynamic complicated every aspect of his life, and Coal learned where to seek asylum when things got out of hand. The Protectors' bond functioned more as a brotherhood than one of fellow soldiers, but Coal's internal conflict ate away at him keeping him at arm's length. Maybe the time had finally come to man up?

Chapter Five
Brooke

"There's no one out there. You're acting totally paranoid." Brooke reassured Quill for the hundredth time since they'd entered her family's apartment. "You've searched this entire place. Twice. Now will you please sit down and relax. You're making me nervous."

Quill dropped onto the sofa with a sigh. "I'm sorry, but I know what I saw. The reason I'm here is to protect you. That's what Protectors do—and men who are in love."

Meeting Brooke's eyes, he pinned her with his smoldering gaze. Goosebumps broke out over her entire body followed by uncontrolled shivers. Everything about this gorgeous man appealed to her, even if she pretended otherwise. He'd been slowly chipping away at her solidly built defenses ever since she'd arrived in Aether. Last night, with her inhibitions checked out, she let her true feelings surface. Now she would have to deal with her wisecracking hottie and the repercussions of her actions. Blaming intoxication wouldn't fly. He would never let her off the hook so easily.

Quill's uncanny ability to turn teasing and flirting into an Olympic event made her squirm. The sexy Protector had swept into her life on a gust of Air, his lightning speed rescuing her from Devlin's lethal blade.

He moved like a hurricane, claiming everything in his path, including her heart. As much as Quill drove her mad, she secretly loved the challenge he presented.

His shoulders dropped into a more relaxed posture, and Brooke couldn't help but drink in the sight of his incredible body reclining on the couch. His sandy-colored hair curled up at the ends, brushing the top of his collar. The blond waves caught the sunlight streaming in through the French doors, lighting up his handsome face.

The way he undressed her with his sexy, green eyes practically melted her panties. No one had ever looked at her with so much love and passion the way Quill did. Maybe he was right, and destiny *had* brought them together. Brooke rubbed her temples, a headache forming. She'd love nothing more than to give into temptation and explore her feelings for Quill, but she needed to find her father and make things right for the Aetherians.

Quill's voice brought her back to the here and now. "Hey, you still with me? You've got that cute little wrinkle above your nose you get when you're thinking too hard."

"When are you going to learn I always think too hard?" Brooke scowled. "And I don't have wrinkles." She jutted her lip out in a pout. "I don't know where we should start, or what we're looking for."

"Don't worry. We'll go room by room. I'm sure we'll find something." Quill got up and stretched out his long frame, raising his arms above his head. His shirt lifted exposing a hint of his rock-hard abs. Brooke swallowed with an audible gulp. He grinned, and the sound of his husky voice made her a bit unsteady. "See something you like?"

"Yes, um—No." Putting her hands on her hips, she glared at him. "Stop distracting me, Quill. We need to focus here."

Laughing, he responded, "By all means let's focus. I'll focus on you, and you can focus on me."

Brooke crossed her arms over her chest. "Really?"

His hands shot up in surrender. "Sorry. I was only kidding. You're the boss. Where does your gut tell you we should start looking?"

"I'm not sure. Let me think for a minute." Brooke took a deep breath, released it, and then closed her eyes for a moment. When she lifted her lids, she jumped back at the sight of Quill's handsome face inches from her own.

His brow furrowed. "Are you okay? You totally checked out there. I called your name like a hundred times."

The room spun, and Brooke brought her hand to her forehead. "Whoa." She plopped down onto the sofa. "I feel a little lightheaded. That was so weird."

"What the hell happened? You scared the shit out of me." He'd been tense since they'd arrived, but the concern in his eyes reached a whole new level.

"I'm fine. Sometimes I get these odd flashes of pictures in my head. It's kind of hard to describe." She shrugged. "The first time it happened, I was sure I'd flipped out. I was thirteen and finally got invited to go skating on the pond with some kids at boarding school. When we were getting ready to leave, I felt this really weird jolt, and my vision went fuzzy for a second. When it cleared, I saw the frozen pond right in front of me even though we were still inside the lobby of our dorm. All the kids were skating around, laughing, and then I heard a loud noise. The ice under my feet started to crack, branching out like the threads on a spider web. The sound got louder and louder as the ice gave way, and one by one, we all fell through. It was like watching a movie. Then suddenly, it all vanished, and I was back inside. I'll never forget it as long as I live."

"Holy crap. So, what did you do?"

"I told them what I saw, and they thought I was joking. When I refused to go, everyone made fun of me. Six kids fell through the ice that day. One nearly died when she got trapped in the current underneath the frozen water. In case they didn't already think I was a freak, let's say this little incident cemented it. I'm sure you think I'm nuts, too."

"Of course I don't think you're nuts. You know, Guardians are empowered with a special gift, one beyond the ability to control her Element. Some are rarer than others, like Ashlyn's telepathy with Hawk, but I've never heard of the flashing vision thing before."

"Really? A Guardian gift." Brooke let out a sigh. "My mom always called me a dreamer with an overactive imagination. I think she was trying to rationalize it in her mind. I tried to tell her about my visions, but she wouldn't discuss it." She rubbed at her scratchy, tired eyes. "This time it was different, strange. Usually I'm part of the action in my vision, but in this case, I was an observer, standing right there watching my parents fight. My mom raced by me and when she slammed the bedroom door, the vibrations went straight through me. My father's face was bright red. He was yelling and pounding on the door. It was like a Vine

Video, flashing by in six-second increments. I didn't see the whole story, only brief, fragmented pictures. I never have control over it. The whole thing sort of hijacks me. The really weird part is, it was only one of two times I wasn't a part of the action taking place."

"I'm not surprised. Your Guardian powers were dormant without a connection to Aether. You've had no one to mentor you in our ways. Most of the kids in our community start developing their gifts in adolescence. Since you came to be with us, your powers have awakened. You're becoming a true Guardian, Brooke."

"Oh God! Not this stupid Guardian thing again. Give it a rest, will you?"

"Okay, so you want to call this another coincidence? Do us both a favor, and at least be honest with yourself. You're controlling Water, and you have visions. Come on, Brooke, admit it; this can't be a matter of chance. Tell me something, when was the other time you had a vision without being part of it?"

Brooke got to her feet and paced around the coffee table. "I didn't put it together until now, but it was when Ashlyn was being held in the lab. In my vision, I saw a beautiful redheaded woman crying. The next day, I followed a lab tech bringing a tray of food down to the sublevel. The rest, as they say, is history—Listen, I'm done talking about Guardians with you right now, so can we please go check out my mom's room?"

He ran his fingers through his hair and gestured with his hand toward the door. "Fine, lead the way."

She groaned. The same conversation may as well have been recorded for the amount of times they'd gone back and forth. The level of frustration between the two had grown tense. The idea of Quill being angry with her didn't sit well, but he wouldn't let go of the romantic fantasy of Brooke being from an Aetherian bloodline. Was Quill right? Did she have a special Guardian power? Her left palm tingled, the mark she wore reminding her of its presence beneath her protective glove. Her head spun in dizzying circles.

An internal war waged within her; curiosity verses nervousness. Brooke dragged her feet from where she stood, moving toward the door of her mother's room. Her shaky hand fumbled with the doorknob, opening and closing around the brass handle repeatedly. The cold metal against her palm sent a shiver straight to her toes. Quill came up behind her, draping his hand over her whitened knuckles, steadying her.

His warm breath tickled her ear. "I can do this myself if it's too hard for you."

"How do you do it?" She leaned back, resting her head against his broad chest. "It's like you can read my mind."

Quill's muscular arms wrapped around her, cocooning her. The heat generated from his hard body seeped into her flesh, warming her to her core. He had a unique way of making her feel safe and cherished, and Brooke had never been more grateful for his support.

"It's because you're mine. Let me help you. I can't stand to see you so upset."

"You're sweet, but I need to do this." She stood up a little straighter. "But I'm glad you're with me." Brooke placed a kiss on his cheek. "Let's go."

Tightening her grip, she twisted the knob, and entered her mother's bedroom. All at once, the familiar fragrance lingering in the air assaulted her. "Oh my God, my mother's perfume. I can't believe I can still smell her after all this time." Brooke's voice cracked, "Is it real?"

For a fleeting moment she contemplated running, but a magnetic force held her in place. Brooke's knees gave way, and she wobbled; her equilibrium off kilter. Quill's arms banded around her waist, pulling her close, grounding her. Warm words washed over her, providing comfort. Guiding her to the bench at the foot of her mother's king-sized bed, he sat, tugging her onto his lap. He shifted her weight, and Quill's muscled thighs tightened under her butt.

"Let me up. I'm too heavy. I'm okay now."

"You're exactly where I want you to be," he said, keeping a firm grip on her, "and you're absolutely not too heavy. Listen to me, okay?"

"Do I have a choice? You're kind of holding me hostage here."

"Don't get mad, but I think you should try to tap into your gift. It's obvious you're deeply affected by this place, this room. Give it a try. Lean on me, close your eyes, and concentrate. Let's see what happens, no pressure, I've got you."

Brooke responded without words, leaning back against Quill's toned chest. She closed her eyes and inhaled a cleansing breath. He smelled divine, and she had to control the desire to run her hands up and down his fabulous body. If only she could get her mind off the hot Protector beneath her and focus, she might find out if this quirk of hers meant something. Did she really want to know the truth? In this moment, more than ever, she believed Quill might be right about her. If she could let go and tap into this supposed gift, she'd know without a doubt if she were the Guardian of Water.

She opened her mind to the sensations of her last vision. Searching her heart, she dug deeper than ever before. Even with her eyes closed, the room spun until it settled on an image of her mother. Olivia wore a colorful scarf around her head. Brooke recognized it as the one she had given her mother the week before she passed away. Her blue eyes appeared sunken and her cheeks hollow. The flashing image of her mother bending low and tucking something deep between the mattress and box spring of her bed held Brooke spellbound. Quill's strong hands sank into her flesh, gripping her with a hint of bite, and her eyes sprang open.

She looked up at him. "You told me to try to get a vision and then you seem totally freaked out when I do. Do you want to explain that to me?"

"It's like watching you slip away and then disappear. Scares the crap out of me. If anything ever happened to you—" He trailed off, drawing her body into his own, securing her with a firm grip.

"Nothing's going to happen to me," she replied, giving him a squeeze. "Now let me up. I saw something in my vision I need to check out."

Quill loosened his hold, but his hands never left her body. He placed a gentle kiss on the top of her head before settling her in place between his legs. Regaining her balance, Brooke stood. He pulled his hands away but stayed close. Even in the midst of this life-changing moment, his touch seared her. In her head a new mantra rang out, *Focus, Focus, Focus.*

Leaving the shelter of his warm body, she approached the side of the bed. She squatted and wedged her hand between the mattress and box spring.

Brooke struggled against the heavy weight, blindly clawing, wiggling her fingers, and driving her arm deeper into the tight space.

A light breeze lifted the ends of her hair, the heavy mattress rose, and she looked up at Quill. "Thanks."

He gave her a wink, and she returned her attention to the task at hand. A tiny metal object sat in the center of the box spring. Brooke scooped it up, uttering a silent prayer of thanks. Its existence confirmed the veracity of her vision. She flexed her grip, and the small piece of metal stabbed into her palm leaving an imprint. Plopping down onto her butt, she leaned against the bed clutching the prize to her chest.

Quill dropped the mattress, took a seat on the plush carpeted floor beside her, and nudged her with his shoulder. "What is it?"

Brooke inched her hand away from her pounding heart. She opened her fingers one by one to reveal a flash drive in her palm. Her eyes focused, and her brain went into overdrive. "What could be so important about this minuscule piece of technology, and why would she hide it?"

"Only one way to find out. You brought your laptop, so let's go check it out." Quill helped her to her feet. Keeping hold of her hand, he dragged her into the living room where she'd left her computer. Clearly, she wasn't the only one bursting with curiosity.

Quill pulled her down onto the couch next to him and nestled her in close to his side, slinging his arm around her shoulder. The computer rested on the coffee table in front of them, surrounded by the fashion magazines her mother loved. Brooke wiped her palms down the front of her jeans. She raised the lid, and the laptop sprang to life with a flash of light. Hands shaking, she wrestled with the drive but managed to slip it in place. A frozen image of her mother filled the screen, and Brooke's heart leapt at the sight. Olivia Barrington wore the same colorful scarf she'd had on in Brooke's earlier vision. Scraggly wisps escaped from beneath the fashionable silk covering. Her mother's kind blue eyes stared back at her, and her own eyes filled with tears.

Brooke leaned into the comfort of Quill's arms. She buried her face in his chest, her muffled words caught in the fabric of his shirt. "I don't know if I can handle this? I'm totally freaking out."

"You can do this. You're one of the strongest people I know. I'm here, and I'll never let you go." Quill hugged her tighter to his body before giving her a little push toward the computer.

Her hand hovered above the keyboard. The stroke of her finger animated her mother's picture on the small screen. Olivia sat at the desk in Charles' home office staring into the camera with tears pooled in her eyes.

Her mother's voice, soft and weak, elicited goosebumps along Brooke's flesh. "Hello, my gift. I have a lot to tell you and not much time." Olivia halted, casting a glance over her right shoulder. "Charles will be back soon." She stared at the camera and wiped away a few stray tears. "I don't know where to begin, except to say, I'm so sorry. I should've told you the truth earlier, but I was trying to protect you. I am not long for this earth, my darling girl, and what I have to tell you will be difficult to hear. But the time has come for me to be honest with you. Let me start by saying, I do not now, nor have I ever, loved Charles Barrington

III. We began dating"—Olivia made quote marks with her fingers—"if you could call it that, when I was in college and Charles was in medical school. I don't know why he wanted me, but he was relentless in his pursuit. I kept turning down his advances, and then he started buying me gifts. I returned them all. Then one day an envelope came from Charles' father. There were documents inside insinuating my dad was embezzling from his company. He threatened to make the information public if I didn't marry his son." Olivia's gaze dropped to her lap, and she brushed away her tears.

Hitting pause, Brooke interrupted the recording. "This is nuts, my grandfather blackmailed her. I feel like I can't breathe." She dug her fingers into the tight knot forming in the center of her chest.

"You're doing great, baby. Come on, keep going. Let's listen to what she has to say."

Brooke nodded, tapped the key, and resumed the recording. Her mother's voice filled the room once again. "His father promised if I married Charles right after my graduation, he would leave my dad alone. I am ashamed to say, I sold my soul to the Barrington family that day." Olivia rubbed at her tired-looking eyes. She propped her elbows on the desk, dropped her head to her hands, and rested it there for a few seconds. Her mother looked up, this time, fire blazing in her eyes. "At first, Charles was pleasant toward me, but as time passed, he grew cruel and abusive. He slept his way through the entire university, but I stayed with him to preserve my father's reputation."

Swiping her finger across the key, the video froze again. Brooke looked to Quill. "My grandparents died when I was a baby. I never knew them. Why would she have stayed?" He didn't speak. He simply gave her hand a gentle squeeze and pointed toward the laptop. "Fine, okay, I know I'm stalling, but this is crazy. And you know I don't do crazy. My life is spinning out of control." His brows lifted, and he canted his head toward the computer. She rolled her eyes at him. "Stop looking at me like that. I'm doing it." Clicking the keyboard, the story continued to unfold.

"Right before we got married, Charles forced me to join him at a medical conference. I don't know why he made me go, well that's not true, I know why. Charles loved to humiliate me, especially in front of people. Probably because I refused to sleep with him before the wedding.

"One night while we were at the conference, he'd had way too much to drink and went off with another woman. I sat alone at the hotel bar contemplating my life. A man named Kai Sanders, who we knew from school, took a seat on the stool next to me. Charles despised him, but he was so sweet; I never understood why. Kai thought I was upset about Charles cheating on me, but the truth was I didn't care at all. Everything felt hopeless to me." Olivia choked up, but managed to squeak the words out. "I didn't intend on being unfaithful to Charles, but I was all alone, and Kai was so kind, not to mention handsome. Being intimate with Charles was never something I wanted, and the closer the time came to the inevitability of it, the more terrified I became. He was controlling in every way. Kai was his polar opposite." The corners of her mother's mouth lifted, and she had a faraway, dreamy look in her eyes. "Whenever I felt trapped or afraid, I would close my eyes and think of Kai." She leaned closer to the camera, and tears streamed down her face. "Oh God, there is no easy way to tell you this—Kai Sanders is your father, Brooke, not Charles Barrington."

Brooke slammed the top of her laptop down. "I'm going to be sick." She stood up in a rush, bolted into the bathroom, and slammed the door behind her.

Seconds later, Quill's deep voice drifted up from under the door. "Come on out, baby. You're going to be all right, I promise. Look at the bright side, Dr. Psycho isn't your father."

Cracking the door open a drop, Brooke put her mouth up to the crevice. "How can any of this be real? I'm Brooke Kylie Barrington—holy shit! Kylie, like Kai, oh my God, she did that on purpose." She ran to the sink blasting the cold water, splashing her face until she couldn't see.

Two large, warm hands wrapped around her from behind, dragging her back. Quill grabbed a towel off the rack patting her dripping face. He turned off the rushing water. "You're all right. I've got you." He scooped her up, carried her out of the bathroom, returning to the couch, and deposited her onto his lap. "We're going to rip the entire Band-Aid off all at once this time. No more stopping, it's only prolonging the agony." He held her gaze, making no move to touch the laptop. She opened the computer and restarted the recording.

Olivia wept quietly. "Charles was completely obsessed with Kai ranting on and on about his strange magical powers. I thought he was delusional until I found a file in his office last week. I've copied all of the information and added it to this thumb drive. Brooke, listen to me, I don't have much time." She threw a quick look over her shoulder again. "I tried for more than thirty years to find Kai. I even hired a PI, but he disappeared without a trace. Charles swore he would take you from me if I ever left him and when you were grown, he threatened to kill you if I ever tried to leave.

"But now you know the truth, and I want you to run. Get away from Charles. The information on this drive will lead you to Kai. I know he's special, and so are you, Brooke. You were born with a strange birthmark on your palm, and I told you it was a burn, but that was a lie. I don't know what it means, but my gut tells me it's important. Find your real father. Stop Charles. I hope one day you'll find it in your heart to forgive me. I've never loved anyone in my entire life the way I love you."

Olivia hung her head again. Charles Barrington's harsh voice broke through the silence of her mother's reflection. The rage-filled tone shouting Olivia's name sent a chill up Brooke's spine. Her mother's fragile image filled the screen, a panicked look written all over her face, before all went dark, dousing Brooke in fear.

Chapter Six
Marina

Hiding behind her feminine guise, Marina had gone through the motions of dressing up and even put on a drop of makeup, but she still couldn't bring herself to push her way into the pub. She stood frozen outside the door for the longest time, her hands hovering over the wooden surface. Laughter floated through the air, and Marina caught sight of Laurel and Lily rounding the corner.

They waved to her, and she returned the greeting. "Hi, girls. Good timing, I was about to go in," Marina lied.

Lily looked her up and down. "Stunning as usual."

Heat rose to Marina's cheeks. "Stop it. You girls look great, too."

"What do you say we get this party started?" Laurel shoved the door open, and a blast of noise hit them.

Marina locked her shields in place, preventing the emotions around her from intruding on her senses. Her own feelings were more than enough for one person to bear. She pulled her shoulders back and followed her friends across the crowded bar. Greeting people as they made their way, Marina plastered a well-practiced smile on her face. Reaching the table, they slid into the large booth.

Marina stared off into space, the loud murmur of voices penetrating the air. The low thrum of bass sent vibrations drifting up from the floor beneath her feet. She wasn't fool enough to believe this little get together was only about Lily. Her well-meaning friends pushed and prodded to keep Marina from disappearing altogether. Resigned to living a lonely existence, she continued to keep her distance from everyone. Now, Lily was the one who needed support to cope with the tragic loss of River. Marina's time to grieve had come and gone.

After Landon's death, her grandmother had been the one who helped her get through the initial shock. Both endowed with the gift of empathy, the Guardian and her grandmother, the Water Elder, shared a special connection. Bey showed up, bags in hand at the West Tower prepared to care for her granddaughter, but Marina erected tall walls around her heart. Not even her grandmother's special brand of magic could remove the barriers she'd built. The Elder couldn't exactly be described as subtle, and the search of her granddaughter's secret memories unearthed hidden feelings Marina had long ago buried. Bey believed Marina had been mourning a different kind of loss altogether, and it had nothing to do with Landon. Repressing her grandmother's insight and interference, she focused her attention on the present.

Had the music gotten louder? Her head throbbed, and she fought the impulse to cover her ears. Spending most of her time alone, secluded in the stillness and quiet of the Grand Lake, her senses had become dulled to the normal sights and sounds of life. Maybe a little noise and fun would be a good escape for the night.

Marina sipped her wine in silence. Ashlyn and Laurel talked animatedly, their hands moving almost as fast as their mouths. Marina listened but didn't join in the conversation. The picture of the stoic widow, Lily ran her finger around the rim of her water glass with the concentration of a surgeon. Brooke fidgeted in her seat, her gaze darting from person to person before draining her glass like a pledge in a frat house. Marina sensed something special in Brooke but refused to use her powers to invade her new friend's emotions.

Marina looked away trying not to laugh and caught sight of Coal watching her from across the room. The man had a seductive, dark edge. His molten gaze bore straight into her, heightening her awareness and sending her pulse skyrocketing. These days he wore his onyx colored hair in cool, soft-looking spikes. His tattooed biceps bulged beneath his white T-shirt, defining the outline of every muscle across his broad chest. Multiple piercings ran along the outer rim of his ear, and Marina wondered if he had any on the rest of his body she didn't know about. The enigmatic Protector, a combination of scrumptious bad boy, with a sweet side few people ever saw, lived by his own rules. He glanced back her way, giving her an odd, knowing look from across the bar. The intensity in his gaze brought her back to a memory from long ago.

****

Marina shouted across the clearing, "Come on. They're going to start soon." She tapped her foot up and down waiting for her best friend, Lily, to get a move on.

At the end of each summer before school began, the high school students of Aether gathered together and camped out by the Grand Lake. Everyone pitched in to build a giant bonfire on the beach. Most of the kids were combing the forest for firewood, and Marina's irritation with Lily mounted. Freshman year had taken forever to arrive, and excitement churned in her belly at the chance to hang out with the older, cooler kids. This special night was all she and her friends had talked about for weeks.

"I'm coming. Hold your horses." Lily left the small cluster of boys surrounding her and ran up to Marina. Sounding positively giddy, Lily's words rushed out. "I was talking to River and a couple of his friends. Dear Goddess, he's handsome. Anyway, they offered to help us carry the wood we collect."

"My dear friend, I think we need to have another chat. You're the smartest person in our class, but to be honest, when it comes to boys, you're clueless. River likes you. I mean *likes* you *likes* you, not as a friend."

Lily's brow furrowed, and her nose gave a tiny twitch. "Really?"

"Oh, you know it's true. Stop looking at me like that."

Her friend's sweet blue eyes opened wide. "Do you really think so?"

"Absolutely. I think everyone knows but you. Senior boys don't offer to help freshmen girls. He's got a crush on you, and since I already know how you feel—"

"Stop right there." Lily thrust her palm out toward her friend. "I'm not going to date River. He's going to be a Protector. He's not interested in me. Just because someone is nice to you doesn't mean he *likes* you, *likes* you."

"Whatever you say, but I'll be the one laughing on the day of your Joining."

"Haha, very funny." Lily's hands moved to her hips, a smirk on her face. "You're not one to talk. What about Coal and Landon following you around all the time? They're like two loyal little puppies nipping at your heels. Which one of them are you going to Join with?"

Marina brushed off her friend's comment. "Don't be ridiculous. You know we've been friends forever. It's not like that with either one of them. Now stop teasing me and changing the subject."

"Fine, then let's go get some more wood. I'll go this way—" Lily pointed up toward the ridge. "—and you go up there. We'll meet back here in a little bit."

They headed off in opposite directions, Lily's joke lingering in Marina's head. Did Coal or Landon *like* her, *like* her? The two boys, polar opposites, each brought something different to their friendship with Marina. Landon looked and acted like the typical boy next door, a rock of dependability. Coal, the original wild child, possessed an undeniable spirit and thrived on pushing limits and taking risks. While most of the guys in their group wore their hair short, Coal's inky black hair touched his shoulders. His piercing midnight blue eyes always twinkled with mischief. She'd be lying if she didn't admit she'd fantasized about what it would be like to kiss Coal, way more than once.

Coal concocted mischievous plots, of one sort or another, keeping life interesting and often roping Marina and Landon into his brainchild of the moment. Somehow, she and Landon wound up taking the blame, and Coal managed to avoid getting caught altogether.

He always said the same thing, "You two were already in trouble, so I didn't see any reason for all of us to be punished." After a while it became a private joke among the three of them. Their innocent childhood adventures built the foundation for a lasting friendship. Coal and Landon remained her closest friends and each held a piece of her soul.

Gathering kindling, Marina strolled along placing the pieces she accumulated on a burlap cloth she arranged under one of the tall oaks. Her arms overflowing, she returned to her collection, depositing her latest bounty. The crack of a twig snapping echoed in the quiet woods, and Marina jumped. Her gaze darted from side to side searching between the trees. The sun dipped down in the sky while she'd wandered through the woods. Soon darkness would consume the forest, and even her lantern wouldn't help her find her way back to the campground. A shiver ran down her spine, and she clutched the branch she held with a white-knuckled grip.

Two strong hands grabbed her from behind, knocking her off her feet and into her attacker's chest. The high-pitched blood-curdling scream she let out could have peeled the bark from the trees. Heart pounding, she struggled to break free. A huge guffaw broke out behind her.

"Coal! I'd know your stupid laugh anywhere." The urge to punch him overwhelmed her, but she gritted her teeth instead. He released his hold on her a little at a time helping her regain her balance with a steadying hand.

"You should've seen your face. It was priceless." Cackling, Coal bent at the waist holding his stomach, his eyes watering.

"You are a complete and total jerk! I can't believe you did that. You scared me half to death." Marina shoved him with all her might.

"Sorry, I couldn't resist. You were so busy with your little kindling pile; you didn't even hear me. I thought Landon and I taught you to be more vigilant."

"You play dirty, and you can be sure I'm going to return the favor when you least expect it." Marina's eyes narrowed. "I will get you, Coal Idris, you can count on it. Now where is everyone else?"

"The others are all back at the campsite. I volunteered to look for you when it started getting dark. Lily was worried you got lost. Where's your lantern? I dropped mine back by the trees over there, and I can't see a thing. It got dark so fast."

"Hmm? I know I put it down near my woodpile. Help me feel around, okay?"

Irritation laced his voice, "Fine. Where are you? Put your hand out."

Marina groped around in the darkness finding his hand and latching onto his warm flesh. He yanked her toward him, an odd yearning spreading through her from the contact. Her stomach fluttered with the wings of a thousand butterflies. Inches apart, his hot breath mixed with hers, and heat flooded her body.

A gentle touch stroked down the length of her hair. She shuddered, goosebumps rising on her skin. Her name, a gasp on his lips. "Marina."

Before she had a chance to react, Coal's lips descended on hers, soft and tender, not what she expected from her wild child friend. He tasted glorious, and she wished the kiss would go on forever. The subtle sweep of his tongue invaded her mouth, and she responded in turn. Marina's mind whirled. *I can't believe this is happening. I'm actually kissing Coal.* His hands dropped from her heated skin, and he took a quick step back. Head spinning, she swayed on her feet, her lips suddenly cold.

"Dear God and Goddess, what am I doing? I'm so sorry, Marina. I always wondered what it would be like to kiss you, but I can't, no matter how much I liked it."

"You liked it?" she whispered, unsure.

"Of course, I did. You're the prettiest, smartest, most fun girl in school, but Marina, my cousin has a huge crush on you. He would kill me if he knew I kissed you. We can't be a couple. You should go out with Landon. He's perfect for you. Just ask my parents. He's smart and always does the right thing. You're going to be the next Guardian of The House of Water. You can't have a troublemaker for a boyfriend."

"What if I like troublemakers?" She reached for him.

Coal caught her hand. "Please, stop. You're the best, Marina, truly, but this can't ever go any further. I'm nowhere near good enough for you, and besides, Landon would be devastated. Let's go back to the campsite and pretend this never happened. I'm begging you." Coal may have been saying no, but his warm blue eyes said yes. Gripping her hand, he tugged her along leaving her speechless, and her pile of wood discarded in the dark forest along with her heart.

****

The images clung to her like a cobweb trapped on the ceiling dangling in the breeze. She waved her hand through the air brushing away the lingering haze of

memories. Things had changed the night of the bonfire, and Marina and Coal locked away their feelings for each other. He stared at her from across the room boring holes straight through her. Had she made the right decision that night, or should she have pushed Coal for more?

Doused with a splash of water, Marina's attention returned to her friends. She chuckled at Brooke's drunken lack of coordination and grabbed a napkin, toweling off. The men descended on their table, and Quill honed in on the adorable human scientist. A whole new side of him emerged. His eyes widened, and he took on a protective tone. Had someone replaced her easy-going friend with this serious, tense guy? She wasn't sure who was cuter, Brooke or Quill. Hiding her amusement, Marina enjoyed the banter unfolding more than she'd enjoyed anything in a long time. Quill slung Brooke over his shoulder, caveman style, and carried her out the door. The room filled with riotous laughter. The distraction masked the cloud of sadness hovering over the group of friends.

A full belly laugh rose up sneaking out of its own volition, and Marina turned to Ashlyn sputtering out between snickers. "I don't remember the last time I really laughed. It feels so good."

Her friend squeezed her hand. Marina held onto the comforting sensation, allowing it to wash over her. She was so tired of being tired, tired of grieving, just plain tired. Hanging out with her crew at the pub turned out to be a great idea. Laughing again lightened her spirit, but Lily's slumped shoulders and downward-cast gaze dissolved Marina's upbeat mood in an instant.

Lily didn't join in the merriment, instead, she sat

quietly, an empty sadness reflected in her eyes. Claiming pregnancy fatigue, she excused herself, but the grief she wore could not be camouflaged. Marina's heart broke for her best friend. River should be here with them, laughing and having fun, and she vowed to support Lily the way she had supported Marina after Landon's death.

Ashlyn, Hawk, Kai, and Laurel stayed to chat, and of course, Coal. His gaze persisted but now from across the booth instead of across the room. Tangible passion penetrated her shields, pulling her away from the intensity of Coal's stare. The heat generated by the two couples sitting in front of her threatened to overwhelm her powers. Marina crossed her legs under the table. She slipped her armor firmly back into place, but cracks formed allowing fragments of her friends' desires to seep through, bringing her suppressed memories to life. The reminiscent tingle of Coal's lips touching hers all those years ago resurfaced. The heat and electricity generated by a single kiss in the woods with Coal had left an indelible mark on her. She'd had a happy life with Landon and cherished him, but their physical connection stayed on simmer, never coming to a rapid boil the way it had with Coal.

****

Coal

A flurry of chatter burst out among the group the moment Quill swept Brooke away. Their friend's uncharacteristic behavior released a wave of speculation, and bets began as to the outcome of the night's entertainment. A grin spread across Coal's face. It seemed Quill and the adorable human had more than a few issues to work out.

Hawk entertained the group. "Quill's been obsessed with Brooke from the second he set eyes on her picture. You should've seen them when they met in person for the first time. The sparks nearly caused a fire. None of you are allowed to make fun of the way I look at Ash anymore. Quill is a thousand times worse."

Kai snorted. "Sorry, buddy, but no one is worse than you."

Coal rested his elbows on the table enjoying the moment. It felt right being around his friends again, like everything was clicking back into place. At times like these, Landon, and now River, permeated his thoughts. Their tight knit group had spent many hours hanging out together over the years. Good times and bad, they'd always had each other's backs, except Coal hadn't been quick enough to save Landon. He also hadn't been on the mission to rescue Ash, which cost him one of his closest friends. Regret gnawed at him, but he couldn't go back in time.

He gazed at Marina and vowed to change things between them. Coal believed his destiny waited for him with the beautiful Guardian. The time had come to confess his true feelings, but she looked so damn hot, and the idea of having a heart to heart with her seemed impossible. She leaned forward against the table, and her breasts lifted, the tempting swells calling to him. Her sexy, blue dress pulled taut and the outline of her hardened nipples peeked through the fabric. No way she was wearing a bra. Fire crackled under his skin. He ordered it back, leashing the flames and locking them deep inside.

Hawk called to him, dislodging his erotic thoughts. "Yo, Coal, you with us?"

"Yeah, sorry. I spaced out there for a minute. What did you say?"

"I said we're leaving. You?"

"I'm going to finish my beer," he answered. Marina slid her way toward the end of the oversized booth. Coal's hand covered hers. "Marina, why don't you stay and finish your wine. Then I'll walk you home." The order, cloaked as a request, halted her progress.

"Fine," she huffed out, scooting back toward her previous seat.

Marina lifted her wine glass bringing it to her pouting lips. The full, luscious bows glistened with the remnants of the fruity liquid, and he longed to lick the droplets off, one by one. The heavy weight of a hand on his shoulder surprised Coal, and he glanced up to Hawk's looming figure.

The lead Protector shook his head shooting him an uncertain look. "Um, have a good rest of the night. We'll see you tomorrow." Hawk clapped his hand on Coal's back a bit harder than necessary.

Ash kissed Marina on the cheek, and Laurel followed suit. The guys simply nodded their farewells, and the two couples headed out the door. Coal stared at Marina across the enormous table drinking her in. Even though he could reach out and touch her, the emotional distance between them grew like an abyss threatening to keep them apart forever.

"What do you want, Coal? You basically order me not to leave, and then you sit here gawking at me." Marina crossed her arms over her chest searing him with an irritated look. "Well?"

Her breasts heaved upward at the sudden

movement, and it took all of his self-control not to fixate on her chest. When it came to Marina, he had no self-control. Inappropriate images of the sexy Guardian bombarded him at every turn. She frowned at him, her brow scrunched up adorably, and in return, he simply ogled her. The fire blazing in her eyes only intensified his cravings. The impulse to kiss her in front of half of the village burned in him.

His voice scratched out, sounding like gravel. "You've been avoiding me again, and I want to know why. You can't keep shutting me out."

Marina's mouth popped open, but then she shook her head, and her mouth snapped shut again. She glared at him, her jaw clenched, the muscles in her cheeks straining. Coal almost smiled, but self-preservation kept him in check. The feisty Guardian would not tolerate being mocked at the moment.

"What did you want to say to me, Marina? Let it out."

She expelled a breath, and her gorgeous blue eyes sparkled with anger. "You have some nerve saying I'm shutting you out. Who do you think you are? Mr. Open? Please. It's a two-way street, you know." Marina's volume rose, and heads turned in their direction.

"We can't talk here. We're attracting attention. Come on, let's go for a walk."

Grumbling under her breath, Marina made her way toward the end of the booth. Her dress shimmied up her legs along with her movements across the length of the bench. Coal's gaze fixed on the expanse of her sexy, long limbs. His mouth went dry, and he swallowed around the lump in his throat. Taking her by the hand, her soft skin brushed against his palm, and he tugged her to her feet. The crowded bar suffocated him, and he hurried to get her outside where they could be alone. He didn't acknowledge anyone along the way to the door. He simply marched her right out of the pub. Picking up his pace, he dragged her along.

"Will you slow down?" Marina's winded voice interrupted his single-minded purpose. "I'm going to fall on my face. What's with you tonight?"

He didn't answer her right away, but he did relax his strides. Reaching the West Tower, he skidded to a stop. Spring inched toward summer giving way to warmer nights, and he inhaled deeply filling his lungs with fresh air. "Can we sit outside and talk?" Being alone in the empty tower with Marina would be too tempting for Coal to resist the magic of her allure.

Marina shrugged her shoulders. "Sure."

She led Coal around to their usual spot behind the tower without speaking. Nestled among a group of trees at the very edge of the forest, an A-frame swing stood partially hidden from view. He and Landon had built it from limbs which had fallen during the heavy winter snows. They'd also constructed a bunch of Adirondack chairs and circled them around an enormous fire pit. Landon turned the clearing behind the tower into an oasis for their friends and family.

Marina took a seat on the swing, staring off into the forest. Coal stood for a moment, running his hands over the timbers. Together, he and Landon had sanded the wood smooth and put on so many coats of polyurethane, it shone like glass. He took a seat next to Marina, and his weight shifted the swing, sending them rocking. Without thinking, he reached out, wrapping his hand around her upper arm to steady her. The tips of his fingers skimmed the bare flesh exposed from her sexy dress, and the front of his jeans tightened in response. Here they sat, the two of them. No Landon. He closed his eyes for a second, building up his courage to reveal the depth of his feeling for this incredible woman.

He cleared his throat and blurted out, "I can't do this with you anymore. It's been almost two years. I know it's different for you, but I lost him, too. There was a second tragedy the day Landon died that we never talk about. You vanished from my life. But we're both still here, Marina. Please, come back to me." He lifted her hand and intertwined their fingers.

Marina's expression softened. "I'm sorry. I know I've been pushing you away, but I can't help it." She dropped her head avoiding his gaze.

"I don't get it. There's a history between us. You know you can count on me." Coal leaned toward her and with a gentle hand raised her chin. "Please, look at me. Why are you doing this?"

She took a deep breath and looked him straight in the eye. "Okay, here it is—every time I look at you, I relive that day. Every night, I have the same dream. The forest is alive, and I'm struggling to get through it. I don't know where I'm going or what I'm looking for." Marina rubbed her temples. "And then suddenly, I see you sprawled out unconscious, and I can't find Landon anywhere. The emotions of every Protector are flooding my empathic senses, but I'm powerless to help either one of you." She brushed away a stray tear. "When I wake up, I'm in a pool of sweat, shaking. I miss Landon, but I'm terrified of losing you, too. I know I've been shutting you out, but I don't know what else to do."

"Why didn't you tell me about this? You know I would do anything to help you. Secrets aren't good for anyone. I should know."

"What is it you're trying to say?" Marina placed a hand on Coal's forearm.

This conversation wasn't going as he'd planned, and he supposed he'd have to spell it out for her in plain English. "Remember the night of the big bonfire our first year of high school."

"Of course, I remember—the first year was very special."

"Come on, Marina, you know what I'm talking about. When I went to find you in the woods. You have to remember our kiss. I know I will never forget it, ever." Coal ran his fingers through his hair. "I'm in love with you, Marina. I always have been. I'm tired of denying it, to you, and to myself."

"What are you saying? You-you can't love me. You're confused."

"I'm a lot of things but confused isn't one of them. Search your heart, search mine for once. I know you control your gift around me. You said it was out of respect, but I think it's because you're afraid. You recognize what's between us, the electricity, the intense attraction. I know you do. The night we kissed I sensed it. *We* were the ones destined to be together, but Landon was so crazy about you, and I was always getting into trouble. My cousin was the best. Everyone loved him. I'm not like him, and I never will be."

"Don't be ridiculous, you're an amazing person. Why don't you let people see that?"

"I guess I want to live up to my parents' expectations of not ever being as good as Landon. But you're not getting what I'm trying to say here. This isn't about him; it's about us."

"No. No, you're upset and lonely. You don't love me. The kiss we shared is a sweet memory. We need to make some new ones, both of us."

Coal raised his palm to her cheek, caressing her with a gentle touch. The sparkle of her blue eyes, mixed with her unshed tears, broke him. The time had come to take the chance he should have taken all those years ago. One hand slid to the nape of her neck and the other gripped her shoulder, bringing her closer. "You want some new memories. Here's one for you—"

He touched his lips to hers with the faintest contact, waiting for a response. She froze but only for a second, her mouth softening beneath his. Coal plunged his tongue between her lips savoring every bit of her gorgeous mouth. The sweet flavor of Marina's kiss lingered on his tongue. She tasted even better than he remembered. His hands wandered down her back, the delicate skin heating under his touch. In return, her fingers thrust into his hair, tugging him closer, and leaving no space between their bodies.

Releasing the tight grip on his hair, Marina jumped back. Inches from one another, eyes locked, they took in each other's very breath. Long, silent seconds passed. Her voice cracked. "We can't do this—I can't do this. It doesn't make any sense. I'm sorry, Coal; I have to go."

She flew off the swing, breaking into a full sprint and dashed into the tower slamming the door behind her. Coal sat there for a moment, frozen. Flames burst from the tips of his fingers and climbed up his arms with a whoosh. Calling his Fire back, he prayed she'd come to her senses soon, or he would surely lose his mind.

Chapter Seven
Quill

Nestled in Quill's lap, Brooke collapsed against him. A stream of tears flowed down her cheeks. Quill didn't say anything; he simply held her. After a few minutes, her sobs subsided. Her tears intensified the color of her eyes, the vibrant blue, sadly beautiful. His heart broke at the depth of her shock and pain.

Brooke's voice shook. "You were right all along. I can't believe this. Kai Sanders is my father not Charles Barrington. Oh my God, Quill; I guess I am an Aetherian after all or at least half Aetherian."

"Of course, you're an Aetherian. You're the Guardian of The House of Water. I've been telling you that since I saw your mark." Picking up her wrist, he peeled the glove from her hand revealing the bold triangle etched in her flesh. He tossed the glove aside and said, "You don't need to hide anymore."

"I know, I know, you've been saying it the whole time, but it's just too weird."

"You think this is weird? Wait until Kai finds out. The shit is about to hit the fan."

"Okay thanks, now I'm totally freaked out. Your best friend is my father."

Quill gave her a squeeze. "Don't worry about that right now. It's all going to work out. You'll see." She wiggled settling more fully in his lap. Rearranging

Brooke's body so she wasn't pressing against his erection, Quill reminded his overenthusiastic accessory to remain in check. He rubbed slow circles on her back whispering warm words of comfort. "You're okay, baby; I've got you." Her breathing evened out, but her entire body shuddered every so often, a stab to his gut. His warrior princess recovered bit by bit from the impact of her mother's bombshell, and pride filled him.

She spoke in a hushed tone, her soulful eyes brimming with emotion. "This is the most incredible feeling." Her cheeks glowed, and the corners of her beautiful mouth lifted. "I never felt like I fit in before, and now I know why."

"You were born to stand out. You're a Guardian, Brooke. I'm sorry it's taken you so long to find your way home."

"I'm not sure I can forgive my mother." Her look turned dark. "How could she have kept this from me? Did she really think my father, oh my God, I mean Charles, would kill me?"

"Seriously, Brooke? You're asking that question? Look what he did to you, and to Ash. It's hard to imagine what it must've been like for your mom. I agree she should've told you, but you need to put it behind you, so you can embrace the truth. Your mother believed she was protecting you and had no other choice. It seems to me she loved you very much, and maybe in time you'll be able to forgive her."

Brooke's shoulders drooped, and she stared down at her feet. "You're right, but I'm still hurt. We could've run together."

He cleared his throat, putting a bit of command in his voice. "Look at me, Brooke, and more importantly, listen to me." Her gaze lifted, meeting his. She nodded in silence flushing a pale pink. "We're going to get through this together. You'll see; once you get used to it, you'll love Aether. You belong there. Please give it—give me—a chance. I want to make all your dreams come true." Dropping his hands, he relinquished control to the Air, letting a small breeze fill the room.

Brooke moved in closer, her lips barely an inch from his own. Their breaths mingled, and her eyelids fluttered down. The open invitation to take her mouth tugged at Quill's resistance, and he stroked his hand down her cheek instead. "Once again, my sweet girl, you've put me in a position which is almost impossible to resist. You're in a vulnerable state, maybe for a different reason this time, but my judgement is still in conflict with my heart. What am I going to do with you?"

A renewed sparkle gleamed in Brooke's eyes. Quill fought to keep his expression serious. Her seductive invitation lured him like hunter to prey, and she had no idea of the power she held over him. His adorable scientist nuzzled into his touch, and his muscles tensed. Gazing up at him, she batted her eyelashes in a sweet, awkward manner.

"I know what I want you to do with me. It's all I can think about when I'm not preoccupied with what Charles Barrington is up to. When I close my eyes at night, I feel your hands on me, your lips on mine. I'm not drunk this time, and it's not because I'm feeling vulnerable. I'm doing what you said. I'm embracing who I really am. And who I really am, wants you so badly it hurts."

Quill let out a breath. "You know, we can only

have one first time. If we're together now, there's no going back. I have never, and I mean never ever, wanted any woman the way I want you. But after what you just learned—I know how shocked you are, and I need you to be sure about this because once we start, I don't think I'll be able to stop. Please, tell me this is as real for you as it is for me."

Reaching out, she raked her hands through his hair. It had gotten longer. He'd meant to cut it, but his mind had been hijacked by images of this maddening blonde woman. Quill leaned into the scratch of her nails against his scalp, and an involuntary "mmm" escaped from his lips. A rough tug on his hair startled him out of his haze. He lifted his brow. "Excuse me. You did not just pull my hair because if you did, I would definitely consider it a challenge." His voice dripped with lust.

Brooke smirked at him. "You know I did. I wanted to be sure you were listening." The heat in her eyes melted him. "What's between us is as real as it gets. This isn't a one-time thing for me, Quill. I'm tired of fighting my feelings. Please, kiss me."

Instinct took over. His cock hardened, and his heart pounded in his chest like thunder. Bringing his mouth to hers, he licked at her lips tasting the sweetness. Fighting his impulse to pounce on her, he slowed things down a bit. Quill intended to savor every moment of his first time with Brooke. Moving away from her soft mouth, his lips meandered down her neck, leaving a path of goose bumps in his wake. His powers surged, kicking up the breeze in the room.

Pulling back breathless, he struggled to form words. "Brooke, where's your bedroom?"

She stood and offered him a hand. "Come on, I'll

show you."

He relented to her control allowing her to tug him along toward the back of the apartment. They stepped through an open doorway. The room was cloaked in shadows; the sole illumination emanated from the hallway. With a click of a switch, light flooded the entire space. Quill blinked and shaded his eyes, adjusting to the brightness. He focused on the wall in front of him. Shades of turquoise, emerald, and aqua bathed the room, giving it an underwater feel. His mouth fell open. An awe-inspiring mural, depicting a magnificent lake, covered one entire wall. Surrounded by towering trees; the vast shoreline displayed rocks of varying sizes and shapes scattered along its edge. The colors, alive with fluidity and vibrancy, gave the painting an incredible and realistic feel. There it was, Aether's Grand Lake, captured in great detail on Brooke's bedroom wall.

Laughter erupted from deep within his belly, and he shook his head back and forth. "You little faker. When did you paint this, Brooke?"

Averting Quill's gaze, her voice dropped low. "When I was fifteen. I came home from school for a few days, and I kept having this vision over and over again. I was standing on the shore of this lake." Sweeping her hand through the air, she gestured toward the wall of color. "I couldn't get this image out of my mind until I painted it. My mom let me go to town, and I loved it so much. Charles, as I remember, was livid."

"All this time you were searching for us without even realizing it. Why didn't you tell me once you knew?"

"I guess when I got to Aether, it may have occurred

to me the Grand Lake resembled my mural, somewhat." Sarcasm dripped from her tongue. "To be honest, it didn't feel real. Aether is so magical; it's hard to accept that I belong there, and at the time the whole thing felt like a bizarre dream."

Wrapping his arms around her shoulders, Quill cradled Brooke against his chest. "How about now, baby? Search your heart. You belong with me. You know it's true."

"I want to believe I belong with you in Aether more than anything. I ache for you, Quill. From the moment you swept in and saved me from Devlin's knife, I knew it. I looked into your eyes, and I felt something I didn't even recognize, but I'm scared of disappointing you."

"You could never disappoint me. I love you. I know there will never be anything better than you and me together. I promise to make you feel good, baby, trust me."

"God, Quill, I'm not worried about you making me feel good. Kissing you is the most amazing thing ever and the rest, well, I can't imagine—" Brooke flushed bright red. "—but what if I don't know how to do certain, you know, stuff. My ex-boyfriend said I was horrible in bed, and that's not something a girl forgets. I've never even been with anyone else."

With a practiced hand, Quill reached behind her and released her tightly wrapped bun. Running his fingers through the silky strands, he gathered them together, grabbing the length in his firm grip. He bent low placing wet kisses down her neck. "Well it's obvious your ex is a complete moron. Look at you. You are the most beautiful, sexy women I've ever seen. Try to relax. We were made for each other."

She raised her head, and her uncertain gaze held his. The cutest little crease formed between her brows. "How do you know he's a moron?"

"Because, only an idiot of epic proportions would ever let you go." Electricity surged between them. Her satiny lips met his in a fierce kiss setting his entire body alight. Breathless, Quill pulled back, injecting dominance into his voice. "I want you to undress for me. I need to see you." He released her, placing a gentle peck on her lips.

Her fair skin pinked up the moment the order left his mouth. Brooke reacted to his Protector's tone, her head dropping. Her submissive posture ramped up Quill's already heightened lust. He leaned over, unbuttoning the top two buttons of her blouse. His voice, dark and husky, held a commanding bite. "You do the rest."

Hands shaking, Brooke's slender fingers moved to her shirt. She swallowed audibly, and one by one, she popped the buttons on her top, draping it over her milky white shoulders. She may not have realized it, but she had the whole seduction thing down pat. Quill didn't hesitate. He slid his hands beneath her blouse, and the feel of her soft flesh notched up his libido. Pushing the material off her shoulders, it slipped down her body. He traced the path of silky material with the tip of his finger. The swells of her perfect breasts, encased in a lacy, blue bra, made his mouth water. Adjusting the arousal growing beneath his jeans, he took a seat on the edge of the bed. His gaze traveled the length of her partially clothed body.

"Now your pants. Do it slowly." Peeling her jeans

down her legs, her gorgeous ass shimmied in the air. Her pants pooled at her feet, keeping her bound. Quill licked his lips. He kneeled at her feet and looked up into her eyes. "Hold onto me."

Brooke grabbed onto his shoulders. His hand grazed the back of her knee, and he lifted her leg placing a kiss on her thigh. Tugging her pants down one leg and then the other, he helped her step free of her confinement. She stood before him in a high-cut pair of matching lace panties.

Quill's eyes nearly popped out of his head. "Holy crap. Are you trying to kill me?"

"What? You like these?" she asked, sounding uncertain. "Ashlyn helped me pick them out." A sexy, little blush flooded her cheeks.

Quill ran his tongue across his lips. "If you looked any better, I might collapse. Remind me to do something extra nice for Ash."

The talking ended then and there. Quill had to touch her. It wasn't a choice. He reached out and let his hands roam down her arms. Brooke erupted in a series of shivers. Satisfied with her reaction, he tugged his shirt over his head and tossed it aside. Her heated gaze traveled over his shirtless body ramping up his arousal. Wrapping her in his arms, Quill fused his lips to Brooke's. The world melted away, and all the pieces which made up his life clicked into place. An awkward fumbling at his zipper interrupted the moment.

Taking hold of her wrists, Quill halted her motion. "Baby, I don't want to scare you, but I rarely wear underwear. I, um—I'm so hard for you. I don't know how much Ash told you about Aetherian men, but we're kind of, well, bigger than regular men."

Nudging his hands aside, she made quick work of removing his jeans. Her eyes widened, and a tiny gasp escaped her parted lips. Quill chuckled. Scooping her up, he deposited her on the bed, and came down alongside her.

His voice was rough with lust. "As much as I'd love to let you keep exploring, I need to see all of you. Sit up for me, baby."

Following his command, she rose to her knees. The golden strands of her hair fell forward resting above her scrumptious breasts. Quill pushed himself up, mirroring her position. He reached out brushing her hair aside, skimming his palms over the milky white swells of her breasts. "I am the luckiest man on the entire planet. You're stunning." He found the front clasp of her bra, and with an agile snap of his fingers it popped open.

"Hey!" she protested crossing her arms over her chest.

"I said I wanted to see you, and I meant it. Don't hide from me. I've been waiting so long for this moment." Quill dragged her hands away, drinking in the sight of her. "Much better. Now about these—" Tucking his fingers into her panties, he slid through her heat, teasing her intimate flesh.

Brooke moaned, thrusting her hips toward him. "Please, Quill. More."

He tugged on the thin strip of fabric she considered panties, the material breaking away with an audible tear. He pulled his hand away holding up a shredded piece of blue lace. "Oops."

"Aw, come on. Those were new." Brooke pouted.

"Don't worry. I'll get you more, as many as you want." Quill grinned. "Even though you looked spectacular in those, you look even better without them. Seeing you like this, touching you, it's more amazing than I imagined."

Brooke knelt on the bed wobbling on the unstable surface. She pitched forward, arms flailing, and Quill seized the opportunity taking hold of her shoulders, easing her down onto the pile of fluffy pillows. He lowered his body inch by inch, never taking his gaze from hers. Lovely pink nipples jutted out, abrading his chest. Need consumed him. His hands settled on her breasts, kneading the supple flesh.

"I can't wait to taste you." He leaned down, capturing one peak in his mouth, sucking, nibbling.

Brooke writhed beneath him, and he doubled his efforts. Her nipples darkened, hardening to sharp points under his attention. He licked his way down her body, bathing her tender skin; his hands and mouth exploring to his heart's content.

****

Brooke

She clutched his hair, digging her fingers into his scalp. "Quill, please, you're making me crazy." She arched her back, angling her needy body closer to his teasing mouth. "I've never felt like this before," she gasped out. "Oh God, what are you doing to me?" The whirlwind of Quill had barreled into her life setting it on its axis from the moment she'd first laid eyes on the handsome Protector. The contrast from her fast-talking hottie to this slow moving seducer sent currents of electricity through her entire body.

"Never have I tasted anything as sweet as you." His strong calloused hands crept up her thighs, the rough scratch lighting her on fire. He urged her legs open, further exposing her most intimate parts to his searing gaze. "I need my mouth on you again." Without giving her a chance to react, Quill lowered his head and dipped his tongue in deep, vibrating against the sensitive flesh with an "Mmm." A strangled moan escaped her lips.

The instinctive flex of her hips drew her body closer, seeking more of him. He added his fingers, relentless in his pursuit of her pleasure. She tugged him closer, exploding, crying out his name, riding out the wave of passion. Crawling up her body, he rained slow kisses on her neck and face. A small tear trickled out of the corner of her eye.

"My God, baby, did I hurt you?"

"No, of course not. It was mind-blowing." She pressed her lips to his and hugged him around the waist giving him squeeze. "This has never happened to me before. I feel so—connected to you."

"You mean you've never had an orgasm before?" he asked, shock and horror lacing his voice.

"Well, I'm pretty sure I had one once, maybe." Heat rose to her cheeks. "I was by myself. Please, never mind. Anyway, after this—" She trailed off, lowering her head.

Quill lifted her chin and gave her a sweet peck on the lips. "Don't be embarrassed. I plan on giving you all of your pleasure from here on out." He settled his hands on her hips, a sexy leer plastered on his face. He threw her a quick wink and flipped them both, exchanging their positions with one swift motion. He wrapped his large hands around her thighs, splaying her legs, and settling her on top of him.

A laugh bubbled up and burst out of Brooke of its

own volition. "Is sex supposed to be this much fun?"

"Baby, if you think that was fun, I'm just getting started."

She leaned down and kissed him, whispering in his ear. "I'm looking forward to it." She brushed back a lock of hair which had fallen across his forehead. "I look forward to everything with you." She brought her lips to his again.

It didn't take long for Quill to seize control. His tongue invaded her mouth, lashing against her own in a glorious duel. Breathless, he leaned back, the muscles in his biceps straining. His voice going husky, "You're in charge, now." Her dominant Protector's green eyes met hers, and he surrendered his command. "I'm all yours. Let's take it nice and slow. I don't want to hurt you."

Brooke reached down, timidly stroking him. He grew harder, lengthening in her grip. Butterflies danced in her belly. "Oh my God, are you kidding me with that thing? It's never going to fit. Do they even make condoms that big?"

He exploded into a fit of laughter almost toppling her over in the process. "I promise, it will definitely fit, and you don't need to worry about condoms. Aetherians don't carry typical human diseases." He turned serious, stroking her cheek with a tender caress. "Remember, we were made for each other, and if we conceive a child today, I'll be the happiest man in the world."

"Not going to happen, buster. I'll forgo the condom, but I've been on the pill to regulate my cycle since I was sixteen. So, no babies right now, but I'm looking forward to practicing."

Wiggling her way forward, her body pliant, Brooke rose to her knees. She hovered inches above him, reading the sexy ache in his stare. Her body heated. Lowering herself with slow, tentative movements, she eased her way onto his arousal. Lightheaded and breathless, the burning pleasure consumed her. She took a moment to adjust to the tight fit of his girth, then sinking down, she took him to the hilt. Quill gripped her hips, his fingers biting into her flesh. She was certain she would wear his mark tomorrow.

A wanton look crossed his handsome face, amping up her desire. He paused, his chest rising and falling in a rapid rhythm. Meeting her gaze, he asked, "Are you okay?"

Her words panted out. "Amazing—so full—oh, God—need to move."

Quill's gaze sizzled, and he took complete control, flipping her onto her back. She would surrender to her sexy Protector any day. Brooke sank into the soft pillows, her arms falling helplessly to her sides. Quill was a master at giving pleasure. His fingers dug sharply into her thighs, his power and dominance leaving her breathless. He rubbed his arousal along her slick heat eliciting a low moan from the back of her throat.

Carnal need surged through Brooke's taut body, her passion building. Quill penetrated her, only a fraction of his length entering, allowing her time to adjust to his size. Thrusting her pelvis upward, she drove him deeper, encouraging him to answer her silent demand. He countered with a deep thrust of his own, pounding into her over and over. Together they moved in perfect harmony, rising and falling as one. Brooke's body tingled, her nerve endings alight with sensation.

He reached down between them, his talented fingers dancing along her most sensitive flesh, sending her hurtling over the edge. Quill fell right behind her riding out their wave of ecstasy.

They collapsed in a heap of limbs. Quill's strong arms encircled her, all the while, stroking her heated skin with soothing caresses. He placed a gentle kiss against her temple. "I love you, Brooke." Lifting himself up on his elbows, he looked down at her. "And, by the way, I knew I was right. Your ex is an uber moron. I've never had hotter, more incredible sex, ever."

The heat of her blush warmed her cheeks. "I love you too, Quill. I never knew it could be like this. You make me feel special, and beautiful, and even sexy. I've never felt sexy before."

Quill nuzzled her neck. "You're the sexiest woman I've ever set eyes on. Being inside you is like a dream come true." The talking stopped, except for his whispered promises of more to come.

They made love throughout the afternoon until the sun began to dip low in the sky, filling it with glorious color. A magnificent array of shades bloomed across the heavens draping the city in burnt oranges, copper, and gold. Quill stood in front of the living room windows admiring the skyline. Brooke loved the childlike wonder with which he viewed the world. He plopped down next to her on the couch snuggling her close. His fingers danced up and down her back in lazy circles. She curved into his embrace, a contented sigh on her lips.

The truth of her paternity melted away the small sliver of guilt she still carried regarding Charles

Barrington. She swelled with determination to find the narcissistic psychopath she used to call father. The Aetherians were her people now, and nothing would stop her from protecting them.

Quill's sexy voice pulled her from her introspection. "I think you should feed me before I can't function anymore, and you know you want me functional." Brushing the hair back from her face, he leaned in, and placed a soft kiss on her lips. "Plus, you're going to need your strength for later."

"I'm afraid that ship has already sailed. I may never walk again." She tossed him a saucy smile. "I'm spent. Though I am starving. How about some pizza or Thai food? What's your pleasure?"

"You're my pleasure." Quill ran his finger between her breasts.

Laughing, she pushed his hand aside. "Sorry, I'm off the menu until I recover a bit."

"Okay, if I can't have you, I'd love to try Thai food. I've never tasted it before."

"Well you, my friend, are in for a treat. The best Thai restaurant in the city is around the corner, and they happen to deliver."

"Friend, huh? You get naked with all your friends, do you?"

Brooke elbowed him playfully. "Only the hot Protectors with amazing green eyes. And ones who possess magical gifts, both inside and outside of the bedroom."

Quill chuckled. "Okay, wiseass, let's get the food."

Brooke phoned in their order, and the food arrived a short time later. She piled her plate high, taking a huge forkful of her favorite noodle dish, popping it into her mouth. Moaning around the bite, she managed to mumble out a few words. "Sorry, so good. I'm starving."

"I guess orgasms make my girl hungry."

Brooke tossed a paper napkin at Quill, hitting him on the cheek. The conversation flowed with ease between indulgent bites and soon the inky sky bathed the room in shadows. Brooke leaned back, rubbing her stomach. Quill popped the button on his jeans proclaiming himself stuffed but continued to pick at a small pile of noodles on his plate. They lounged by the table sipping wine, exchanging long, slow kisses, and talking for hours. Brooke zoned out, swirling the ruby colored liquid in her glass, the waves of red mesmerizing.

Quill's voice brought her back. "Hey, what's going on? Talk to me. Your cute little brow is furrowed again. I can always tell when you're concentrating."

Brooke shrugged. "Just thinking."

"You know, I have ways of making you talk." He tickled her ribs, a lascivious gleam twinkling in his eyes.

"Cut it out." Laughing, she pushed him away.

He feigned injury in typical Quill style, grabbing his arm and falling over. "Ouch! You're such a bully."

"You are so full of it." Brooke took his hands, tugging him to his feet. "Come on." She rolled her eyes. "I'll tell you what I was thinking about. Let's go into the living room."

Quill sat on the couch pulling her into his lap. "Okay, shoot."

"So, we have the flash drive my mom left, and I know it's late, but let's go back to Aether now. We need to talk to Ash and Hawk, and God help me, Kai. I have absolutely no idea what I'm going to say to him. My stomach hurts thinking about it, but I owe it to him, and frankly, to everyone in Aether. It's time to embrace my inner Guardian." An awkward giggle escaped her lips.

"Whatever you want, baby. As long as the leftover Thai food comes with us."

His sense of humor never ceased to amuse her. "Of course, it's coming with us, but you're going to have to share your Pad Thai with Hawk or we'll never hear the end of it. Let's get our stuff and get out of here."

"I'll pack the food and grab our bags. Why don't you take a look around and see if there's anything you want to bring home."

Brooke strolled through the apartment, checking each room, basking in the memories. Returning to her mother's room, the door stood ajar. She pushed it open, taking a tentative step into the space which smelled like Olivia Barrington. Approaching the dark, walnut dresser, she ran her hand across the surface, lingering on a bottle of her mother's favorite perfume. Her fingers drifted to the tall jewelry chest placed on the end of the large wooden piece of furniture. She gripped the tiny brass knobs, opening the doors. Necklaces hung in rows, and Brooke zeroed in on the one she wanted, plucking it free. Leaning closer to the mirror, she clasped it around her neck, her eyes misting over. She scooped up the bottle of perfume, turned on her heels, and headed out the door.

She met Quill at the front of the apartment and stuffed the bottle into her bag. She looked up at him, unshed tears filling her eyes. "I'm ready."

"We can come back anytime you want, baby. It doesn't have to be forever."

She thrust her shoulders back, standing tall. "There's nothing here for me anymore. Let's go home." Brooke closed the door to her childhood home, ending a chapter in her life, and leaving her mother behind.

Her sexy Protector took her by the hand yanking her into the elevator. He dropped their bags with a loud thud shoving her against the wall. Lust burning in his eyes, his lips descended, searing her with a kiss. He devoured her mouth overwhelming her with his need. The elevator stopped, and Quill pulled back. Brooke panted helplessly as a look of satisfaction crept across his handsome face. The door opened, and lightheaded, Brooke steadied herself leaning against the wall.

"I've seen guys do the elevator thing in the movies and thought we'd try it out. It has definite possibilities, don't you think?" Smirking, Quill picked up their bags.

"You're going to be the end of me, you know that, right?" She let out an exasperated breath walking toward the door.

Quill stuck out his arm halting her progress. "Listen to me. I go first. You stay behind me and do exactly what I say, or I will spank your gorgeous ass until it's bright red. I have to keep my head in the game here, and I need to know you're safe. The guy in black could still be out there. Got it?"

"Yeah, I got it. I totally forgot you were obsessing about that guy. You did a great job of distracting me. Do you really think he's still lurking around out there waiting for us?"

"I'm not sure, but something's off here. I can sense it in the Air. There's a strange low-level vibration."

Quill reached back producing the gun he'd tucked in his waistband earlier. Clicking off the safety, he raised the weapon, pushing Brooke behind his back. "Stay right up against me so I know where you are the whole time."

Brooke pressed in close and whispered in his ear, "Okay. Let's do this."

The echo of their footsteps resonated off the concrete walls and floor, filling the cavernous space. A strong breeze picked up blowing the ends of her hair in the stagnant air. Quill put his finger to his lips, motioning silence. He kept her tight at his back directing her along between the cars filling the crowded lot. They made their way to the sedan slipping inside without incident. He tossed their bags into the backseat. Quill's jaw clenched, and his eyes narrowed.

"Wow. You're scary. Sexy, but scary."

He winked. "You ain't seen nothing, baby."

The slow-moving, metal door in front of them squealed, shaking on its tracks, returning their attention to its ascent. They waited, the car idling like an inpatient toddler hoping for a turn on the swings at the playground. At last, the door rose three-quarters of the way up, and Quill managed to whip beneath the narrow passage. Tires screeching, the car sped off into the night. Brooke's body flew back into the seat, and she gripped the armrest, white-knuckled.

Quill whipped his head from side to side scanning the dimly lit street. His eyes glistened with anger. "Oh shit, I knew it. There's the bastard who was watching us."

Brooke turned in her seat, straining to see in the darkness. "Where? You mean the guy standing by the motorcycle?"

The mysterious figure climbed onto a Harley parked across the street, kick starting the engine with a loud roar. Dressed in a black leather jacket, jeans, and boots, he blended into the inky night. His features remained obscured in shadow. Bright orange and red flames shot out from the tips of his fingers and whooshed up his arms, the brilliant glow illuminating his face.

"Oh my God. The motorcycle guy, he—he's got Fire power like Ash. And he's getting closer."

Shoving her onto the floor in front of her seat, Quill shouted, "Get down, now!"

His gun, gripped in his tight fist, pointed out the open window. Fighting her way back up to her seat, Brooke struggled against the never-ending thrashing of the shifting car. Swaying from side to side, at last, her butt touched down onto the leather seat. A thunderous crack filled the car, and popcorn-sized pieces of glass rained down on them.

"Oh my God, that lunatic shot out the window!" Her voice sounded shrill even to her own ears.

Quill weaved his way through the city streets at record-breaking speeds. "Stay down or you'll be getting the spanking I promised you for sure."

Brooke had the good sense not to answer him. Brushing a few shards of glass from her hair, her hand came in contact with a droplet of moisture trickling down her face. "What's this?" Pulling her hand back, she turned it over it in front of her eyes, startled to see it coated with a sticky red substance. "Blood, there's blood on me. I've been shot."

Chapter Eight
Marina

The door slammed with a loud shudder, piercing the silent night. Marina leaned her back against the rough wooden surface and little by little slid to the floor. Her chest rose and fell in a rapid rhythm, and the sound of rushing air escaping her parted lips echoed in the quiet room. Marina pressed her hands to her cheeks. They flamed beneath her touch.

She spoke to the empty room. "Dear Goddess, what was I thinking?"

Brushing her fingers over her inflamed lips, tingles scattered across the delicate skin and settled between her legs. The reminder of Coal's mouth on hers did crazy things to her body. His taste lingered on her tongue, and her head reeled with a flood of conflicting emotions.

"The man can definitely kiss, that's for sure—no way—I can't do this." She shook her head. Squinting up from her position against the door, a brilliant glow outside her window cut through the darkness. Brightly colored crimson and gold flames filled the black sky dancing in the moonlight. *Coal*. "Has he gone crazy? He told me to search my heart, but I think my heart must be frozen." The radiance of his Fire blazed through her windows.

Marina closed her eyes digging deep and reached

for her inner Guardian. Seeking her connection to the Water, power rippled inside her, building momentum. Opening the heart she'd been protecting with such intense control these past few years, she let go, summoning her empathic gift. It started off small at first, but swelled, growing until the sensation of Coal's Fire threatened to overwhelm her. Its scorching intensity ran through her veins sending shivers down her spine. Marina's entire body burned with arousal, desire, and passion. Yet, hidden away buried under his feelings, a trace of something secret seeped through, crashing over her. Love. Coal loved her. Her heart ached with it, and it surrounded her, enveloping her in a blanket of rapture.

"I can't handle this," Marina blurted out, springing to her feet.

Placing both palms on the timeworn door, she pushed her way through, bolting off into the night air. Coal was gone, but the smell of fire lingered in the air tickling the inside of her nose. She surged through the forest behind the West Tower. The ground rushed by under her feet as the scenery whizzed past. A fine sheen of sweat clung to her back. Her breathing grew heavy, but she couldn't stop running. She moved across the rough terrain. Her feet throbbed, protesting the fancy heels pinching her toes. Legs burning, Marina continued until she reached the Grand Lake.

She skidded to a stop on the sandy beach and bent at the waist to catch her breath. The rush of adrenaline cut off, and she dropped to her knees, sinking into the soft, damp sand.

Shaking her head in utter disbelief, Marina muttered, "No it's not true. This can't be happening.

Coal can't be the one; he can't be."

The gentle sound of water lapping onto the beach centered the Guardian, but the emotions swelling from within her threatened to spill over. The normally calm lake turned dark and turbulent, reflecting the storm brewing inside Marina. White water crashed against the rocks scattered across the shoreline. Tossing her dreadful shoes aside, she inched her way along the ground immersing her toes in the cool water. The contact with her Element produced a surge of power in her bloodstream, fortifying her with renewed strength.

For the longest time, Marina sat on the beach with the tide coasting in and out over her bare feet, burying them in the sand. With each pass, her toes sank deeper, obscuring them from view. "That's what I'm going to do," she declared to no one, "bury my feelings."

Exhausted, she crawled back from the water's edge and curled up into a tight ball on the sandy shoreline. She didn't remember falling asleep, but she would never forget waking up to the irritating coos of mourning doves. Rolling over, she tucked the blanket tighter under her chin. A distinctive fragrance tickled her nose. Confused, she bolted upright, rubbing the sleep from her eyes. It wasn't a blanket she'd pulled up to block out the chill in the air, but Coal's favorite jacket, the one he'd been wearing last night. Hugging the material close to her face, Marina breathed in, savoring his lingering scent.

"Wait a minute." She dropped the jacket onto the sand. "I can't believe he followed me." Marina scanned the beach and tree line searching for the Protector. She shouted out, her voice echoing in the stillness of the morning. "Coal, are you still out there? Don't you know

I can take care of myself?" Marina kicked at the sand sending a spray up in the air, covering Coal's leather jacket.

Determined to put last night behind her, she pulled her shoulders back. Looking up, she marveled at the sun's golden rays scarcely visible above the reflective surface of the crystalline lake. A warm glow bathed the surrounding area, and Marina's reconnection to her Element grounded her once more. "I'm not going to spend another minute thinking about Coal Idris. Even if he smells amazing and is an incredible kisser. And even if he is the sexiest man alive. So what! I don't care. I'm going home to shower and change. And then I'm going to see Lily."

Marina tilted her head from side to side cracking her neck with a loud pop. Stretching her arms up toward the sky, she let out a boisterous groan releasing the tightness in her muscles. Scooping up her shoes with disdain, she dangled the delicate straps from her finger, spinning them around and sauntered back up the beach. Reaching the edge of the sandy ground, she stopped and turned, eyeing the discarded jacket. She rolled her eyes grumbling, marched over, and scooped it up. Shaking the jacket out, she slipped her arms into the Protector's prized possession, and cuddled into the warm leather.

Taking a seat on the sand, she squeezed her swollen toes back under the band of the offending high heels. She winced the moment she stood. Her feet, puffy with red blisters, burned with every step she took. Last night, she ran all the way from the Tower in those miserable shoes, and now the throbbing pain lingered.

"If shoes only look great but kill your feet, why do

we women continue to wear them?" She laughed. "I know why I wore these torture devices. Coal. But I'm done with those urges. Note to self: no more thinking about kissing Coal. Or anything involving his body. Or his muscles. Or his eyes." Marina massaged her temples. Looking up to the heavens, she shook her head at her foolishness. "Dear Goddess, I'm hopeless." Trudging toward the West Tower, she blocked out everything except helping Lily.

Returning to her backyard, Marina lowered her achy body onto one of the Adirondack chairs Landon and Coal had built. She pried her shoes from her swollen, blistered feet and let out a groan. Rising on her tiptoes, she shuffled back to the tower cringing the entire time. She hobbled straight into the kitchen, popped the lid on the trashcan, and tossed her expensive heels into the bin with a farewell salute.

Marina made her way to the bedroom, each step tentative and slow. Removing Coal's jacket, she set it on her bed. With a slow, tender caress, she ran her hands down the worn leather. She sighed, shaking her head, retreating into the bathroom. Dropping her soiled dress onto the floor, she stepped under the warm spray of her shower. Marina mindlessly shampooed her hair. Suds dripped down stinging her eyes, but she welcomed the pain instead of her treacherous feelings. *Get the man out of your head. Lily, focus on Lily.*

Scurrying into her closet, Marina threw on the first pair of jeans and top she could find. She put on her fuzzy-lined slippers, cushioning her sore feet. Water trickled from the ends of her saturated hair leaving two dark, wet circles soaking the front of her shirt. Huffing out a breath, she yanked her towel from the floor and rubbed her hair with vigor. Returning to the bathroom, she hung her towel in its proper place. Approaching the mirror, she stared at her reflection. She looked the same as always, didn't she? She leaned in closer, transfixed by the unfamiliar sparkle reflected back in her eyes. Frowning, she looked away.

She ran a brush through her hair while her thoughts focused on Lily. She practiced what she might say to her oldest friend. "I know I'm not exactly a shining beacon of hope, but don't mind me. You know the old saying? Do as I say not as I do." Marina rolled her eyes. "Yeah that will definitely work. Not." She ignored the voice in her head and walked right out the door.

****

Coal

A tiny crescent of the moon brightened the sky surrounding it. The amorphous shape which remained glowed diffused in shadow, creating an ominous feel to the night. Coal paced the wooded area around the tower. The door flew open, and Marina fled toward the Grand Lake. It had always been her way to let things marinate for a while. The woman was never hasty, or impulsive, unlike him.

At odds with his instincts on a daily basis, Coal fought his intuition. It had been hammered into his head for too long that he wasn't good enough. As his parents often reminded him, he was no Landon. His cousin had been practically perfect; every woman wanted him, and every man wanted to be him. If he'd listened to his gut all those years ago, Coal would have Marina in his arms right now instead of watching her like a deranged stalker.

Marina sat by the lake composing herself, and he

remained out of sight ever watchful of her. The hours ticked by, and at last, she crawled back from the water to the sandy beach. Relief washed through him when she promptly fell asleep. Her long limbs contracted, and her frame remained tucked in a fetal position. Coal's heart broke. He shrugged out of his jacket, approached the Guardian, and placed the warm leather over her. He headed home, leaving his heart on the beach.

Sleep eluded him. Two opposing visions played on a loop in his mind: Marina locked in his embrace, her pliant lips sealed with his, the other, a painful image, Marina curled up on the beach emotionally exhausted. Coal tossed and turned, tangling with his bed covers. Shouting at the blankets, he swatted at them combatively. With a final grunt, he tore free, sat up, and slammed his head back against the wooden bedframe with a thump.

"Ouch!" Coal pressed his hand to the back of his head and hissed from the contact. "Maybe a good smack in the head is exactly what I need. What the hell was I thinking kissing her like that? What an idiot. Landon always said Marina could never love me." Rubbing the sore spot, he huffed out a breath and stomped to the ground. "I've got to get out of here."

Coal grabbed the pair of shorts he'd discarded on the floor sometime earlier and yanked them on over the boxer briefs he'd been sleeping in. Pulling a T-shirt out of his drawer, he slipped it over his head, and shoved his feet into a pair of sneakers. He sprinted out his front door without closing it. Running with no particular destination in mind, his lungs burned from his relentless pace. Sweat ran down his back, soaking the T-shirt clinging to his body.

The spring morning dawned with a beautiful array of warm tones which bloomed like a field of wildflowers. Amber, burnt copper, and amethyst hues warmed the sky and kissed everything they touched, but Coal couldn't appreciate the splendor. Fire coursed through his body, and he fought to maintain control. The forest stood as a barrier he needed to break through. With a fierce cry, he breached the entrance. The sun radiated between the trees, illuminating a path for him to follow. He forged ahead, the flat terrain growing in pitch at a steady rate, but Coal took the steep incline without slowing. Pumping his arms with urgency, his biceps flared, and the muscles in his thighs protested.

His chest constricted, and he gave into the pain. Stopping at the top of a ridge, his breath rushed out in heavy pants. Coal's stomach dropped when he realized where he had come to a standstill. He stood in the exact spot he'd been standing in during the explosion which decimated so many lives. The accident had been an all-consuming loss for the people of Aether, especially for River, who blamed himself for Landon's death until the day he died. Brack may have escaped physical injury, but the young Protector bore emotional scars which could not be erased. Coal lost more than his cousin the day of the accident; he'd lost Marina, too. Guilt festered within him, ravaging his system. Why hadn't he been meant to save Landon? The single moment in time had created a domino effect steamrolling everyone in its path.

Coal mopped his brow with the bottom of his shirt and stared down the hill at the cave below. He took one tentative step forward and coasted another few feet.

Gravity took over, and he accelerated from the flow of rocks and debris beneath his shoes, surfing his way along. Skidding to a halt, he reached the base of the slope, haunted by the familiarity of this place. His memories had always been a bit scattered regarding the day of the accident, but there was one thing he would never forget, the percussive sounds of the earth descending upon Landon, devouring him. Coal shuddered, an eerie sensation traveling through him.

He looked around the quiet forest before speaking aloud, his voice rough with emotion. "I'm so sorry, Landon. For everything. For not saving you. For lying to you about how I felt about Marina. But you made me think I didn't stand a chance with her, and then you swooped in and took her for yourself. How could you have done that to me? You knew I loved her." Coal gazed up at the blue sky peeking between the trees and shook his head. "Great, I'm talking to a dead guy. I think I'm losing my mind." Hands on his knees, he bent at the waist taking a cleansing breath.

A deep voice pulled him from his one-sided conversation. "You haven't completely lost your mind—yet."

He rushed to stand, and his head spun. "Am I crazy? Landon, is that you?"

"No, you idiot. It's me." Hawk stepped out from between the trees dressed in shorts and running shoes. His chest bare, the lead Protector looked like a Native American warrior, statuesque and proud. His muscular body glistened with perspiration further defining his toned physique. If Coal didn't know him so well, he might have been intimidated by the large man's presence.

"What are you doing here, Hawk? Are following me?"

"Um, no. Paranoid much? I run here all the time. What's going on with you, Coal? You're acting more nuts than usual."

"Guess I'm busted, huh?"

"It's always been obvious the accident took a toll on you, but I didn't realize how much until I overheard your little chat with Landon. You know, you could've talked to me, right?"

"No, I couldn't. What was I supposed to say? Hawk, I love Marina. I've always loved her. I never should have let her Join with my cousin, who by the way, also happened to be my best friend. Well, now he's gone on to Arcadia and I'm here with the woman of my dreams, and she can't see beyond our past. She can't see me."

"Okay, so things are a little complicated—"

"Are you kidding? Complicated. That's the best you've got?"

Hawk glared at him, and Coal fought the urge to flinch. "You didn't give me a chance to finish. She sees you, Coal. I know she sees you. I'd recognize the look in her eyes anywhere. It's the way Ash and I looked at each other before we got together. It's the look of longing and unrequited love."

"Unrequited love? Are you kidding me? I can't believe that came out of your mouth. And you think I'm the one acting nuts. Do you hear yourself? I never would've thought—wow."

Hawk shrugged. "Go ahead, make fun of me if you want, but I know what I see. By the way, everyone else sees it, too. That is, everyone but you and Marina."

Without a doubt, Hawk hit a nerve. The heat of Coal's Fire rushed through him. *Reel it in, dude.* A few solid, deep breaths cooled his escalating temper. "Look, I know you mean well, but I think you're wrong about Marina. Last night she ran from me like I burned her."

"I think that's the exact problem, maybe you did. It seems clear she can't deal with her feelings of attraction for you. You two have a history, a connection. Believe me; no one gets it better than I do. You need to show her how great you can be together. Keep trying. I promise it will be worth it in the end."

"I know you're right, but it's been forever." Coal lowered his chin. He couldn't maintain eye contact with his lead Protector a minute longer.

"Look at me, man." Hawk waited until Coal lifted his gaze. "Give her a little time, but not too much, then go see her. If you can't tell her how you feel, show her." Hawk wiggled his eyebrows in a suggestive manner.

Coal shook his head. "You know, I'm worried about you. One minute you're practically spouting sonnets and the next you're being a wise ass. I'm not sure which one I hate more. And I think you're spending way too much time with Quill, because the eyebrow thing was exactly like him."

A broad smile crept across Hawk's face, relaxing his harsh features. The brawny man was a softy deep down, and Coal couldn't help but smile back.

Hawk's brows slashed downward, and his tone grew serious. "I'm still your lead Protector, so you have to follow my orders. Stop talking to Landon. He can't answer you from Arcadia. Come to me or any of your brothers, but the most important thing is, don't let

Marina slip through your fingers. You both deserve happiness."

Without saying good-bye, Hawk simply jogged off between two towering pines. Coal stood there replaying the strangest conversation he'd ever had.

****

Marina

Poised to knock, her knuckles hovered over the peeling red paint of Lily and River's front door. River mentioned he'd wanted to repaint it before Lily's birthday next month. A sadness filled Marina. "Oh God, I'm stalling. Lily's door, really? What is wrong with me?"

She squared her shoulders, dropping her hand against the wooden surface in a barely there knock. Chuckling at her lack of effort, her small snickers swelled into a full-on laughing fit. Tears trailed down her cheeks. She struggled to catch her breath from the gush of her irrational, uncontrolled amusement. A quick breeze swept over her, drawing her attention to the open door revealing a perplexed-looking Lily. Her friend's sparkling blue eyes scrunched up, and her head canted. Marina laughed even harder at the confused expression on Lily's face.

The mom-to-be practiced her maternal posture, hands planted firmly on her hips, wearing a scowl on her pretty face. "Are you done cracking yourself up? What are you doing here so early, and what in the name of the God and Goddess is so funny?"

Sputtering out the remnants of laughter, she managed to utter her first few intelligible words. "I'm sorry, Lil." Marina wiped her eyes using the back of her hand. "I'm not sure what's gotten into me. I had a

pretty strange night. I guess this is the after-effect."
Regaining her composure, she placed a hand on Lily's
shoulder. "But that's not why I'm here so early. I'm
here because I didn't want to let another minute go by
without telling you how sorry I am. I've been an awful
friend. Please forgive me."

Lily stepped back from the door gesturing with her
outstretched arm for Marina to enter. "Don't be
ridiculous, there's nothing to forgive. You're like my
sister. I know this isn't easy for you either." They
gravitated to their usual spots at the kitchen island.

"Come on, it's no excuse, and we both know it.
You were there for me through every bad moment.
Even when I thought the grief would consume me, you
held me up, and I haven't done the same for you. We
haven't even had a chance to really talk since you lost
River. Please, I'm here now. Let's talk."

Lily blew out a forceful breath sending blonde
wisps of hair flying around her face. Her lovable friend
ignored Marina's confession of guilt and spun around
with her usual grace, moving to the stove like nothing
was ever mentioned. Lily lifted a silver kettle and shook
it next to her ear. Satisfied with its contents, she placed
it back on the burner, flicking the knob with a twist of
her wrist. Gas hissed out, and the flame ignited with a
whoosh.

Lily plopped down on the stool next to her. "If it's
going to be one of *those* talks, I have to warn you,
herbal tea will have to suffice. Since A, I can't drink"—
she rubbed her adorable baby bump—"and B, it's way
too early." She chuckled, but her eyes brimmed with
sorrow. Even in the midst of all her suffering, Lily
handled her grief with her usual grace. Small but

mighty, she held her own against the toughest of Aetherians.

Marina laughed. "Take it easy. It's not one of *those* talks. I wanted to tell you how sorry I am. I plan on spending all of my free time with you from now on." She put every ounce of strength she could muster into her voice. "I'm turning over a new leaf."

"Oh please, you seriously expect me to buy that? You're using me to avoid Coal, and I want no part of it."

"You're way off base. I'm—"

"You're what, Marina? Give me a break. I see the way you two look at each other. Having feelings for Coal doesn't mean you didn't love Landon. He's not coming back, honey. You need to move forward. Coal has always loved you, and we all knew it, especially Landon."

"Don't be ridiculous. Landon never said a word to me and besides, Coal only wants what he can't have. If we were together, he'd be sick of me in no time. It's the way he is."

Lily's lips formed a thin line. "How can you say that about Coal? You've been acting nuts from the minute you laughed your way through my door. What's going on with you? Spill, now."

Throwing her head back, Marina looked to the ceiling seeking divine intervention. What could she say to Lily? Her best friend had turned the tables on her. She met Lily's eyes. "I don't want to burden you with my crap right now. It's the last thing you need."

Lily's tone was soft and warm. "To be honest, I'd love something else to think about."

If her best friend faced raising her child alone,

shouldn't Marina be brave enough to confide in her, including her history with Coal? Lily busied herself making the tea while Marina sat with the idea a bit.

"Okay, but I think I need the couch for this conversation." Marina grabbed both mugs of tea and headed into the living room without waiting for a response. Lily let the comment roll off her back and followed in silence. The mugs teetered in Marina's hands, clinking together, and sloshing over the sides. She narrowed her eyes, targeting the overflowing liquid, and called it back where it belonged. "I wish every mess was this easy to avoid," she muttered under her breath.

A brown leather recliner, which matched nothing else in the room, sat noticeably empty. River loved the "hideous brown beast" as Lily called it. The couple had the funniest little spats about getting rid of it. Her pint-sized friend, belly protruding, climbed into the oversized chair curling her feet under her body. Taking in the image, Marina's heart broke. Lily had always hated the monstrosity, but Marina understood her friend's need to feel close to River right now. She'd spent many nights after Landon died wearing his favorite shirt in a desperate attempt to connect to him even in the smallest way.

Lily stared Marina down. "I'm waiting." She tapped her fingers on the chair's armrest. "Hello? Still waiting here."

She'd never told anyone what had happened that night in the woods, and Marina didn't know where to start. Finally, the words fell from her lips, and she confessed the details to Lily. She started with the story of her first kiss with Coal and ended with the giant emotional storm of last night.

Lily remained quiet, too quiet. Marina sat in the silent room, waiting. Lily crossed her arms over her tiny, rounded belly and raised her eyebrows. "Well now, what are we ever going to do about this?"

"Dear God and Goddess, please help me. You're formulating a plan, aren't you?" Marina shook her head exhaling a loud breath.

Chapter Nine
Quill

The sound of shattering glass echoed through the car, and an instant blast of heat hit the back of Quill's shoulder. The familiar sensation of searing pain radiated down his arm. Pressure built like a giant blister about to burst. His right arm drooped, and his forty-five fell to his lap, too heavy to grip. *Oh shit, this isn't good.* With a shaky hand, Quill reached over, exploring his shoulder with the tips of his fingers. He glanced over at Brooke. Frantically, she patted her body from head to toe.

Her panicked tone rang in his ears. "Oh my God, Quill. I'm bleeding. I think I've been shot! But I must be in shock because I don't feel any pain yet."

Quill kept his voice steady hoping his calm tone would soothe her. "You're okay, sweetheart. It's my blood. Please, stay down." Pitching forward, Quill slumped against the steering wheel gripping it one handed. He broke out in a cold sweat.

Brooke grabbed the hem of her shirt tearing it along the seam. Wadding up the material, she faced Quill. "Where did he get you?" Her voice quivered, but her hands remained steady.

The car jolted over the curb racing along on the edge of its tires. Sliding down the seat, she hit the center console with a forceful thump emitting a painful cry. The impact sent Quill's cell phone sailing through the air and smashing into the dashboard. Brooke groped around picking up the pieces of the demolished phone.

"Don't worry about the phone. Get your seatbelt on right now! And God damn it, keep your head down!" Quill growled, no longer able to maintain his composure.

Brooke threw him a dirty look, but she took no time in buckling up. The familiar click of the restraint snapping into place gave him a small measure of relief, yet tight knots still twisted his stomach. Under normal circumstances her reaction to his dominant command would've pleased him, but even Quill knew when it was time to wear a poker face. She twisted around glancing into her side view mirror. Following her gaze, he read over her shoulder. *Objects in mirror are closer than they appear. Well that's damn for sure.* Quill pressed his foot on the accelerator. "This asshole is way too close for comfort. I wish this piece of shit would go faster. He's gaining on us. Keep your head down."

Odd vibrations surged through Quill's powers, and he could sense the change in the Air. The mercenary barreled down the sidewalk toward them, his image growing larger by the second. Quill's heart pounded like a beating drum. The car bounced leveling off and picking up speed at the same time. Like a driver on a NASCAR track, the Protector weaved around parked cars, racing down the city streets. The small sedan squealed and shimmied in protest to Quill's rough handling. Devoid of traffic and pedestrians at this late hour, they flew through the neighborhood.

"If you don't take it easy with your driving, we're not going to have to worry about the crazy man chasing us because you're going to kill us."

He ignored her comment, keeping his focus on the road. "Can you reach the duffle I tossed in the back?" Her hand hovered over the seatbelt, and he said, "I can see you thinking about unbuckling. Go ahead and do it, but make it quick." Brooke reached over and released the metal plate with a click. The car bounced over a pothole, and she bumped his wounded shoulder. He gritted his teeth suppressing a groan.

"Are you okay? If you would slow down a little maybe I can get the stupid bag without hurting you in the process."

"Sorry, baby, can't slow down. Do your best, and don't worry about me."

Brooke arched her back contorting her body while reaching down. "My fingers keep slipping off the stupid straps, and I can't get a grip on it." Hitting another bump, the car jerked to the right, and she shouted, "I got it!" Brooke grunted, yanking the heavy load onto her lap.

"Good girl, now get your seatbelt back on."

"Okay, okay. I'm doing it." Rearranging the duffle, she followed his instructions. "What's in here? This bag weighs a ton."

Unzipping it, her eyes widened taking in the extensive collection of weapons contained inside. With the black bag balanced on her legs, she reached in withdrawing a forty-five millimeter, a mirror image of the one Quill had been holding. He'd trained Brooke with guns and knives back in Aether. During the last couple of weeks, she'd made tremendous progress. She had quick reflexes, not to mention she looked hotter than sin with her hands wrapped around a gun. Pulling out a seven-round magazine, she checked the weapon before slamming the clip into place with a resounding click.

Brooke straightened her shoulders. "Okay, I've got your traveling arsenal in my lap, but I'm not doing another thing until you let me see your wound."

"I'm fine. Get your shot lined up like I taught you. I'm not sure I can shoot lefty and steer the car at the same time. Do what I say, Brooke, and shoot the son of a bitch."

Her gaze ping-ponged between Quill, blood oozing from his shoulder, and the maniac pursuing them. "All right—" She passed him the piece of her ripped shirt, and her hand lingered in his. "—but keep this on your wound, and put some pressure on it." Fear burned in Brooke's eyes. "Your hand is ice cold, and your color looks awful. We have to stop. You need a hospital."

"No! No matter what happens don't take me to a hospital. Aetherians have a different genetic makeup, and the doctors would know something is off about me." Even with the possibility of him bleeding to death in this stupid little sedan, Quill shot her a stern look. "Tell me you understand what's at stake here. I know you hate the idea of doing nothing, but this isn't only about me. It's about everyone in Aether. Please, promise me."

A tear slid down Brooke's cheek. "All right, I promise," her voice choked with emotion, "but please, you have to be all right. I need you, Quill."

"Don't worry, baby, I'm not going anywhere." He raised his knee steering the car with it. He waded up the material she'd given him and stuck it under his shirt pressing it to his wound. Wincing, he forced a smile.

"See, good as new. Now shoot the damn gun."

Brooke hit the button on her armrest, and her window descended with a slight squeak. She used the headrest as a makeshift shield. Transferring the gun to her other hand, Brooke wiped her palm down the front of her jeans. Re-gripping her forty-five, she pointed the weapon out the window, taking aim. She fired off several rounds, yet their assailant continued his relentless pursuit.

"Ugh! This is impossible! He's moving all over the place, and we're going too fast. I can't hold the gun steady enough."

A spark glinted in Brooke's eyes, and a wave of unease surged through Quill. "Whatever you're thinking, don't do it. I'll lose him. Keep shooting. You don't need to hit him. Just let him know who he's dealing with."

"Exactly, you keep saying I'm a Guardian. I'm supposed to have powers, right? Maybe I can stop this guy without killing him. Trust me." She retracted the forty-five from the open window and placed it in the console between them. "I know what I'm doing—I think." Brooke's hands came up without further warning. She took slow, shallow, controlled breaths, a pink blush rising in her cheeks.

The pain from his gunshot wound throbbed. Quill's arm tingled, and his motor responses grew more limited by the minute. No matter how he shifted his body in the seat, he couldn't find relief. The distinctive scent of copper permeated the small space. His shirt, sticky with blood, adhered to his back. Quill struggled to keep his eyes open, fighting the blackness which threatened to overtake him. He took a hard left, the car careened, and he expended most of his remaining strength to keep it steady.

"I have no idea what you're thinking, but you're scaring the crap out of me. Can you stop being so stubborn, and shoot the mother fucker." Brooke ignored him, and he huffed out an exasperated sigh. "I know you hear me." Quill's useless arm rested like a dead weight against his side, and he watched on helpless. If only he could shoot, he'd take this asshole out once and for all.

Brooke's eyes scrunched into two tiny slits, and her chest rose and fell in an accelerated cadence. Her hands shook, and she opened and closed them into tight fists. With one final emphatic shout, his beautiful Guardian emerged, strong and confident. Her shimmering blonde hair flowed loosely around her shoulders. Man, it was good to see her unwind her tightly wrapped bun and embrace her true self. She had never looked more magnificent. Brooke muttered quietly, concentration written across her stunning face.

The roar of the mercenary's engine vibrated alongside the vehicle. Quill swerved ramming the edge of the sedan into the bike and sending their attacker sailing along the sidewalk. The soldier recovered his balance way too fast and continued forging ahead on a path straight toward them. Bullets pinged off the car's body. A chill ran down Quill's spine, and he wasn't sure if it was from their impending doom, or a result of his injury.

Brooke's mumbling shifted into a full-on chant. An explosion rocked the car, and Quill straightened glancing in the mirror. The bright yellow cap of a fire hydrant shot straight up in the air. The flying metal crashed down on the pavement filling the quiet streets with thunderous clatter. A rush of water burst from the hydrant like a geyser. The bolts on either side of the fireplug followed popping off in succession, the liquid shooting out like a cannon.

Her hands swept back and forth directing the gusts of water, and Brooke shouted, "Quill, look, I did it. Wait—watch this. I'll show that jerk who's boss."

Brooke's entire body undulated in a beautiful dance, and Quill fell under her spell in complete awe. Water rose up and pooled all around them. A giant wave crested, swaying in time with Brooke's movements. It chased the Harley overtaking it along with its rider, sending them both hurtling through the air. The sound of the leather-clad man crashing into a nearby dumpster reminded him of a giant gong. The guy bounced off the metal bin rolling headfirst into a parked minivan landing in a motionless heap. Quill cringed. The stranger's Fire had gone dark, extinguished by the power of Brooke's Water. The motorcycle had fractured, the sum of its parts scattered across the roadway.

With the soldier out of commission, Quill slumped forward succumbing to the pain of his injury, his body's healing ability failing to stem the heavy bleeding. The compact sedan he captained at the moment coasted along like a log on a flume jostling his wounded shoulder. Spasms of searing agony ripped through him. Quill's white-knuckled grip held steady against the surging current. Sweat rolled down his forehead, and the last of his remaining strength quickly drained away. The car lurched to the right taking out the side view mirror of a fancy sports car. Metal scraped against metal, and Quill shuddered. The shrill alarm of the damaged vehicle blared filling the quiet night.

They reached a dip in the road, and water rushed passed them on both sides of the car, the tide gradually flowing away. Bringing his foot down on the brake pedal like a hammer, Quill sent the car hydroplaning along the slick surface. His vision blurred, and the wheel jerked away from his hand in a violent motion sending his body into the door with a thud. The ear-splitting screech of tires and the smell of burnt rubber filled the vehicle. Quill stared at Brooke; his beautiful Guardian resembled a superhero straddling the console. He would have laughed except for the fact she'd rammed her shoe into the top of his foot, slamming their feet and the brake pedal to the floor in the same instant. The wheels of the car locked up, and a harsh squeal echoed in the night. His shoulder whiplashed back into the seat, and he fell forward in a helpless mass. The car bumped to a stop riding up on the curb before dropping back down.

Panic filled Brooke's voice. "Quill! Oh my God. Can you hear me?"

Using the last of his depleted strength, he reached out to Brooke taking hold of her arm. His words eked out, distant and sluggish. "It's okay, sweetheart. You were amazing. He won't be following us anytime soon. I need a minute to rest, and then we'll get going." Quill listed to the side, resting against the door, blood staining his T-shirt a dark crimson. The choppy airflow in the car mirrored his labored breathing. Brooke leaned down, her soft hair brushing against his heated skin. Quill struggled to speak, his voice a mere whisper. "Save yourself. Get back to Aether. Tell my parents I'm sorry. Lo-ve-you." The breeze in the car cut off fading along with his powers. Quill's vision dimmed, and Brooke's beautiful face dematerialized before his eyes.

****

Brooke

"I love you, too. Please, stay with me. I can't do this without you." Brooke's clammy hands clutched her pounding heart, adrenaline still surging through her body. "This can't be happening. Quill, come on, wake up." Shaking him with a gentle motion at first, the large Protector remained unresponsive, and she grew more forceful.

A single tear trailed down her cheek before she squared her shoulders, wiping away the droplet of moisture. "Okay, Brooke, get yourself together. Quill needs you. You're the Guardian of The House of Water. You can do this." She rambled on unable to curb her chatter.

Pulling Quill away from the door, Brooke brushed the damp hair back from his face. "I need to control your bleeding—I wish you could help me. You are way too heavy for me, but here goes anyway. I sure hope my new powers are still working."

Climbing over Quill, she reached blindly for the controls to his seat back. Relief set in when the seat vibrated lowering into position. He descended until his headrest touched the backseat, and she crawled behind him. "Sorry, this is probably going to hurt." Brooke looped her arms under Quill's armpits, took a deep breath, and tugged with all of her might. He didn't budge, but she would not be deterred. Clenching her teeth, she channeled her newly discovered Guardian. The muscles in her body cramped contracting all at once from the exertion. With one last grunt, she yanked his bulk, throwing all of her strength into the effort. The deadweight of Quill's body gave way, hitting the leather upholstery with a blatant smack. Brooke winced, her eyes snapping shut. "Oh my God, I'm so sorry."

She opened her eyes to the sight of his motionless form sprawled out. Quill's upper half now occupied the back seat while his legs remained draped across the driver's seat. Groaning, she grabbed hold of his feet and hauled them across the back seat. "I'm sick to my stomach that this is going to hurt you again." Digging her hands into the fabric of his shirt, she hoisted him to the edge of the seat. Wedging into the cramped space between Quill and the front seats, she used her legs as a lever, yanking his shirt at the same time. He flipped over hitting the seat with a loud thud. The sound of his T-shirt ripping rang out in the small space. Torn at the collar, she shoved the bloody fabric aside revealing his oozing bullet wound.

Pressing her fingers to his neck, she let out a sigh of relief. "Thank God, you're alive." She probed the area around his wound with a delicate touch. The side of his handsome face pressed into the leather seat, and a low moan escaped his lips. Brooke placed a soft kiss on his forehead. "It's going to be okay. I'm going to help you."

Grabbing her bag, she began rummaging through it. Discarding items haphazardly, she sent them flying through the car. Her gaze settled on a blue and pink package of maxi pads. To Quill's unconscious form, she said, "You're definitely not going to like this, but it's the best we've got." She pulled a handful of pads from the box and dumped them onto the seat beside him.

Taking a water bottle from the console, she twisted off the cap, and poured it over Quill's wound. Blood mixed with the liquid creating a stream of red, and Brooke forced down the wave of nausea rolling through her stomach.

Plucking a pad from the pile, she blotted the area. "I wish your magic healing powers would kick in already, but in the meantime, I'm really sorry, but I need to put some pressure on this to stop the bleeding."

Fishing around in her bag, she pulled out her running shoes tearing the laces free. Tossing the sneakers aside, Brooke stuck two more pads together and with a firm hand, held them to his open wound. Gripping one of the laces between her front teeth, she tied the two ends together, and threaded the length underneath his arm securing it with a knot. Quill twitched a bit but didn't wake.

She slid a fleece sweatshirt under his head and placed a light kiss on his lips. "I'm going to get you back to Aether, and Kai will fix you up. You saved me once, now it's my turn to save you."

Brooke jumped into the driver's seat and sped off, her tires screeching. Quill's body was so still she feared he might've stopped breathing. She hit a pothole, and his soft moan sent relief flooding through her. Angling the rearview mirror, she checked behind her swearing she caught a glimpse of flames over the horizon. Hitting the gas with a bit more gusto, the sedan lurched forward, and the colors faded into the distance.

She raced through the night, away from the bright lights and noise of the city, toward the serenity of

Aether. The light pollution dissipated, and total darkness crept across the sky consuming any remaining illumination. She couldn't remember ever seeing the sky appear so shadowy before. A heavy cover of clouds obscured the natural glow of the moon and stars, camouflaging them in a thick layer of fog. The farther away from the city she traveled, the more her heart rate slowed, but Brooke's stomach remained tight with knots. Every thirty seconds, she tossed glances over her shoulder, checking the mirrors for the motorcycle riding lunatic. "What is Charles Barrington up to now? I have to find him and stop this craziness."

The long drive seemed interminable, the hours passing as slowly as watching grass grow. Gnawing on the corner of her thumbnail, she rolled her head on her shoulders releasing the tension in her neck with a loud crack. Her nerves were shot as images of Quill meeting his demise permeated her thoughts. His breathing remained even, and his face appeared relaxed in slumber, yet fear niggled inside her. She worried he might never wake up. White-knuckled, her hands gripped the steering wheel, and sweat rolled down her back even with the AC blasting. The need to see his incredible green eyes open, sparkling with life again, consumed her. She glanced back one more time at the man of her dreams. "Come on, Quill, you have to be okay. Now that I found you, I can't imagine my life without you."

Chapter Ten
Coal

Lily sat on the steps of Coal's front porch, her petite legs stretched out in front of her. The floral sundress she wore draped gracefully over her lovely new shape. The blonde beauty rubbed her belly in slow circles. Her head dropped low, and Coal caught wind of Lily's hushed whisper but couldn't make out what she was saying. A lump caught in his throat. River should be here watching his Adara grow round with his child. They should be sharing this experience together. The image of Lily all alone made a heartbreaking picture, even to a miserable, lonely Protector like himself. He knew River would be proud of the way she was handling things. She carried herself with strength and grace wrapped in an indomitable spirit.

He mumbled under his breath. "Well this is a surprise. What is Lily up to now?" Coal dragged his feet nearing his friend. While she may have appeared meek and docile, she possessed an attitude as feisty and tough as they come. He nodded. "Good morning. What brings you here so bright and early?"

"Oh, please, like you don't know. Come on, Coal, let's not bother with the niceties. I want to talk about Marina. She told me everything, and I mean everything, so there's no point in acting like you don't know what I'm talking about."

"Alrighty then. No mincing words here. Got it. What's on your mind, Lil?"

"Well, I thought you'd never ask." A mischievous look twinkled in her eyes, and a slow, sly smile spread across her lips. "I want to talk about what we're going to do to convince Marina that you two belong together. Everyone can see the way you look at each other." She stood facing him, and her hands moved to her hips, thrusting her protruding belly in his direction. "Marina and I are best friends, but what she shared with you and Landon growing up was special. I understood the connection was unique in ways the rest of us couldn't even fathom. You both loved her with equal measure, but I guess I thought you'd be the one to Join with her, not Landon. I could always see how much he wanted to win Marina and beat you."

"What are you talking about? It wasn't a competition. You know we were more like brothers than cousins." Coal's head spun. "It can't be true. I mean, I know we were competitive, but he wouldn't have gone that far, would he?" He dropped to the top step taking a seat, resting his elbows on his knees.

Lily sat beside him. "Listen to me. I adored Landon. He was a great guy, but both you and Marina have created a version of him in your heads that didn't exist. Think back. Winning Marina was the ultimate prize. Don't get me wrong, I'm not saying he didn't love her, it's only—Marina never looked at him the way she looks at you. I've always wondered why you stopped fighting for her. You practically gift wrapped her and handed her to Landon on a silver platter. Please, tell me why. I'm not only Marina's friend you know. I'm yours, too."

Coal shook his head and huffed out a breath. "I've already had the strangest conversation with Hawk today. Now you want to grill me. Give me a break here, will you?"

"Sorry, my friend, but I think you've had enough of a break. It's time to talk." She placed her delicate hand on his forearm and gave him a squeeze. "Please."

He couldn't resist sweet-looking Lily, who in truth, was a little terror. Her sad blue eyes met his gaze, and Coal hung his head admitting defeat. He adored Lily beyond measure and would do anything to help distract her from her pain. "Okay." Coal put his hands up in surrender. Clearing his throat, he blurted out, "You're right—I love her—I've always loved her."

"Aha! I knew it." Rising to her feet, she pumped her small fist in the air, her expression triumphant.

"If you already knew, then why did you make me say it?"

"I needed to hear you say it out loud. It makes it more real when you say the words."

"Believe me, it's real no matter what I say aloud, but Marina can only see the past not the future. She'll never be able to think of me as more than a friend. That is, if she ever talks to me again."

"That shows how much you know, aka, nothing. You're wrong about Marina. Give her some time. I know she loves you. I asked you before; why did you stop fighting for her all those years ago? She lights up whenever you're around, and neither one of you even realizes it. Landon didn't bring out her passionate side the way you do. She told me about your kiss in the woods when we were kids and that you wanted to pretend it never happened. Why?"

"Lily, I know you're trying to help, but that's ancient history."

The spunky, little woman wouldn't let it drop. "Apparently not. I heard you practically kissed her lips off last night. I'm pretty sure she used words like devoured and consumed."

Groaning, Coal ran his fingers through his hair, and got right to the point. "Face it, Lily. I'm not good enough for Marina. I never have been, and I never will be. Landon was the right choice for her. He was the guy everyone counted on. Not to mention, he worshiped the ground Marina walked on. I couldn't hold a candle to him no matter how hard I tried."

"You're right. He was a really good man, but he was far from perfect. You need to do yourself a favor and take Landon down from the imaginary pedestal you've put him on. Besides, you're pretty wonderful yourself. You should let people see the real you more often."

"This is the real me, Lil. What you see is what you get." He kicked the dirt beneath his feet. "And believe me, I wish you were right about Marina. But I'm not sure if she'll ever be able to let go of the past." Pacing back and forth, he looked to Lily, who stood there grinning at him.

She gave him a saucy, little wink. "Okay, here's what we're going to do."

****

Marina

Approaching the Grand Lake, she sensed Coal before she saw him. Marina's empathic gifts prickled with his anxiety and frustration, but she also sensed the warmth of his love. He stretched his long legs out on one of the enormous, flat rocks by the water's edge, her fantasy come to life. Gone were the soft spikes, instead his dark hair was brushed back from his chiseled face making him appear younger. She longed to stare into his incredible cobalt eyes which sparkled with intelligence and passion. He leaned back braced on his hands, showcasing his triceps in a spectacular fashion. Each line of muscle flexed with his movements, and Marina swallowed, fighting the sigh threatening to escape. His black T-shirt pulled tight across his broad, muscular chest, and her hands itched to stroke him. The man was hotter than sin.

In silence, she edged her way closer. Coal bolted upright, and Marina froze in place. She said a little prayer of thanks when he didn't notice her. A glint of sunlight flashed in her eyes from the row of shiny earrings hugging the rim of his ear. The low rumble of his voice drew her closer. *Who's he talking to? There's no one around—Dear Goddess, does he know I'm here? Don't move. Don't breathe.* The need to hear Coal overtook all rational thought, and she crouched low tiptoeing in right behind the rock he occupied. Scrunching her eyes, she canted her head poised to listen.

"I know I told Hawk I would stop talking to you, but there are some things I need to tell you even if you can't hear me."

Marina's hand flew to her mouth repressing a gasp. *Is he talking to Landon?* Her Kanti had been dead for almost two years, and she still talked to him often, but she also suffered from debilitating nightmares and lusted after hot Protectors she shouldn't.

Coal cleared his throat. "Lily came to see me."

I'm going to kill her. I told her I would handle things with Coal. I should've known the minute she got that look in her eyes she wouldn't let it go.

"She seems to be under the impression Marina and I were meant to be together. The little trouble maker also told me you wanted Marina simply to beat me at something. That can't really be the reason you went after her, can it? I know you loved her." Coal shook his head and let out an audible breath. "But you knew I did, too. I told you right before the big bonfire freshman year. It was so long ago, but I always wondered if Marina really told you she could never be with a guy like me, or were you just trying to psych out the competition?"

Dear Goddess, why would Landon say that? Her stomach churned. *I never said any such thing about Coal.* Hovering in her awkward position, her thighs burned, but she didn't dare budge.

"I never told you, but she and I kissed one time. You weren't dating yet. The minute our lips touched, my Fire shot straight through my body. I knew then, she was the only one I would ever love."

Marina's stomach dropped. *How could I have been so stupid? He did feel it, too.*

"But I heard my parents' voices in my head telling me I needed to be more like you. Selfless. You were always way more deserving than me, so I pushed her away—and straight into your arms. But you're gone now, and I need to see her happy again. And more than that, I need to be the reason she's happy. Please forgive me, cousin, but I can't walk away this time." Coal stood, picked up a small stone, cranked his elbow back, and skipped it across the lake. It ricocheted along the surface several times before sinking into the water.

Her heart constricted. Sorting through the overwhelming influx of emotions within her, Marina couldn't tell where her feelings ended and Coal's began. Her legs trembled, and she wobbled falling flat on her butt with a loud thud. He spun around with a flash of Fire. The Protector's powerfully built body stood poised to fight. His eyes locked on the uncoordinated tangle of her limbs, and his expression softened in a heartbeat. Scooping her up into his arms, he placed her gently on a nearby rock.

"Marina, what are you doing here? You took me by surprise. I could've hurt you. Are you okay?"

"I'm fine. Lily, the scheming little fox, set us up. She told me to come here by myself, to relax, and think things through."

Shaking his head, he grinned. "She's a sneaky one."

"Listen, Coal, I'm sorry. I didn't mean to eavesdrop. It—sort of—happened. One minute I was standing there, and the next minute I was spying on you like some kind of crazy stalker." She focused on his feet afraid of what she would see in his eyes.

"It's okay. I wanted to talk to you anyway. How much did you hear?"

She looked up at him feeling the heat rise in her cheeks. "Pretty much everything, I think."

"Good. I'm glad. You need to know." He bent at the knees taking her hands in his much larger ones. "I've been sleepwalking through life since the moment I kissed you and made the mistake of pushing you away. I know you don't believe me, but we were the ones meant to be together. I feel it deep inside. My mind. My soul. My body—" His voice trailed off and his eyes burned into hers with a covetous stare.

Touching Coal, even in such a simple way, sent goosebumps racing up and down her flesh. Her blood heated, and her heart pounded.

He released her name on a sigh. "Marina." Brushing the hair back from her face, his fingers lingered, toying with the loose strands. His sensual gaze locked onto hers. Marina's palms grew moist, and her stomach flip-flopped.

Her voice squeaked out, "I'm not sure what to say, but I want you to know that I never told Landon I couldn't be with a guy like you. Why would he lie and say such a thing?"

"Come on, Marina. Lily is right. Think about it. He wanted you, and he didn't want me to have you, plain and simple. Landon was my best friend, but he could be manipulative. Yet, he always managed to come out looking like the good guy—"

"He was a good guy!"

"Of course, he was. He simply wasn't as perfect as we remember. He loved you very much, but so do I." Coal grabbed her hands pulling her to her feet until their bodies were almost touching. "If Landon hadn't interfered all those years ago, who knows what might have developed between us."

"Don't blame Landon. You were the one who walked away after our first kiss back then. No one made you do that. You had to know I didn't want it to end."

"You're right. I was a stupid, insecure kid. I never considered myself in the same league as you. Not then, and not now. The difference is I don't care anymore.

My feelings for you are too strong to fight. I should've listened to my gut all those years ago, and not Landon. I never should've stopped kissing you, ever."

One of Coal's capable hands found the nape of her neck and the other reached behind her, settling low on her back. With a gentle tug, he brought her body against his own, wrapping his arms around her. Sparks ignited, and her eyes closed of their own volition. The hard line of his erection pressed against her heated body. Inhaling, she took in his scent of dark spices and sex. His tantalizing fragrance filled her nose, and her knees gave way. She grabbed onto his broad shoulders, her fingers digging into his firm muscles.

Marina didn't have a chance to think. Coal's lips descended on hers, gentle as a whisper, covering every inch of her mouth with delicate kisses. If he hadn't been holding her so close, she might have dropped to her knees. He amped up his efforts, showing no mercy; his tongue sweeping into her mouth, devouring her. Marina's body softened, succumbing to the rush of heat. Her head spun in dizzying circles.

He slipped his hands under her top, setting her skin ablaze. She hadn't worn a bra and was instantly aware the moment he realized it. His hands, everywhere at once, stroked her breasts grazing her nipples again and again. A strangled cry escaped her lips. Coal's mouth traveled down her neck, nipping her collarbone, and licking his way to her breasts. Marina's shirt wound up over her head, and Coal latched onto her nipple, circling it with his tongue.

Looking up at her with fire gleaming in his eyes, he spoke, "I knew you would taste sweet, but reality is so much better than my fantasy."

He palmed her breasts and rose up kissing her with abandon. Marina tore at his shirt, and he ripped it over his head tossing it aside. Smooth skin blanketed hard-ridged muscle, and she reveled in the sensation of her hands on his warm flesh. Coal reached for the button of her jeans, and Marina jumped back grabbing his hand, halting his movement.

Her voice quivered laced with panic. "Don't, please." Her breath panted out, and her hands shook. She scooped her shirt up off the ground yanking it back over her head. "I'm so sorry, Coal. I want to, believe me I want to—I'm not ready for this." She backed away from him taking a few steps down the beach, but kept her gaze locked on his.

"Please, Marina, don't go. I love you. We both need to let go of the past—to move forward—please, we belong together."

"I'm sorry, Coal. Sometimes love isn't enough." She turned away and headed off, this time without looking back.

Chapter Eleven
Brooke

In and out of consciousness the entire ride back to Aether, Quill roused again calling out Brooke's name. His long legs contorted in the way too small space, and he thrashed around bumping her seatback every so often. Her maxi-pad bandage seemed to have done the trick because Quill's bleeding had slowed. For the past hour his chest rose and fell in a steady cadence, and now she prayed they would make it back in time to save his life.

Wiping her sweaty palms down the front of her jeans, Brooke traversed the road along Aether's border. "Oh God, how am I going to get through the mystical protections around the village?" She picked up a piece of Quill's broken phone, shook her head, and tossed it aside. "Stupid, useless piece of—"

Row upon row of tall trees lined the winding country road standing out in the darkness. Like soldiers guarding the entrance to an enchanted castle, they taunted her, their uniformity cloaking the gateway to Aether. The combination of adrenaline and fear had kept her going during their escape from the fire-wielding, motorcycle-riding lunatic, but now the monotonous hours of driving had worn her down. Every muscle in her body ached in protest.

Exhaustion crept its way through her system, and

her tired eyes itched and burned as if someone had dumped a bucket of sand in them. Her lids grew heavier by the minute. Slapping her cheeks a few times, she forced herself to wake up and focus. Brooke scanned the side of the road searching for a familiar tree or rock, anything to guide her. Nothing. A pounding headache took up residence behind her eyes, throbbing and pulsing. She rubbed her brows with the tips of her fingers to alleviate the pressure, but it was pointless.

"This is absurd." Brooke cranked the wheel to the right sending the small sedan skating along the sand and gravel which made up the highway's shoulder. Rocks pinged off the side of the car, and a cloud of dust enveloped the vehicle. Brooke scowled, her words huffing out laced with frustration. "Everything around here looks exactly the same."

Shifting the car into park, Brooke sat for a moment composing herself. "Okay, I can do this. Quill said I'm the Guardian, so I have to be able to find Aether, right?" She shut her eyes tight and stayed that way for quite a while—then, one eye squinted open a bit—still nothing—the other eye joined the squinting contest. "Oh, for heaven's sake, this is ridiculous!" She popped both eyes open wide, confounded. "Maybe they're all living in crazy town, and I drank the Kool-Aid or something." Brooke's hands hit the steering wheel with a furious slam. She brought her head down on top of her white-knuckled grip, deflated.

She concentrated, taking a deep breath. The air around her turned hazy and warped before her eyes, the beginnings of an image forming. The sensation grew more familiar with each successive vision, and she embraced her gift encouraging the impressions to flow freely. She straightened up peering out the window, her instincts kicking in.

Bright light illuminated a small opening between two gargantuan trees framing an entryway. "I've got to be imagining this." Brooke rubbed her eyes attempting to bring back some measure of reality. Reopening them, she squinted through the window. "Nope, still there." She shook her head, her voice a mere whisper, "I can't believe this."

A magnificent arbor stood fifteen feet tall entwined with beautiful greens and hundreds of flowers bordering the entire expanse. It glowed with more lights than the Rockefeller Center Christmas Tree. Brooke gasped bringing her marked palm to her mouth. Her ears perked up at the sound of running water whooshing by, and she zipped the window down searching for the source.

Her brows lifted, and her head canted. "What on earth? I hear water. It's all around, but there's nothing here. This might be the strangest day of my life, but I'm going to go with it."

Brooke honed in on the rush of Water which clearly existed only in her head. The Water infused her with a wave of confidence. Twisting around to face Quill, still bent like a pretzel in the backseat, she shouted over her shoulder. "Don't worry; I know exactly what to do now."

Compelled to let the music of her Element guide her to Aether, Brooke threw the car into drive and followed the curious sounds of rushing water. Like riding a current down a fast moving stream, she allowed the ebb and flow to navigate the way. Steering with a mindless focus, Brooke's connection to her Element was as natural as breathing. Reaching the familiar surroundings of the village's parking area, gravel crunched under the car's tires. "I did it!" She shifted into park, cut the engine, and let her hands fall to her lap.

"Alrighty now, time to get things in motion here." She climbed over the console and squeezed into the backseat next to Quill.

All the color had drained from his face; even his lips had gone milky white. Stretching his torn shirt back, she peeked under her makeshift bandage examining his shoulder. A gaping wound oozed where the bullet remained lodged. Heat radiated from the red and inflamed area surrounding the injury. Soft moans fell from his lips, and Quill's handsome face scrunched up in a grimace.

Reaching out a gentle hand, she caressed his cheek. "Quill? Can you hear me?" Brooke brought her lips to his giving him a gentle peck. "Come on, Quill. I need you to wake up."

His eyelids fluttered. "Brooke?" He tried to sit up too quickly and ended up flat on his stomach.

"Whoa, take it slow." She placed her arm around his shoulder and helped ease him into a seated position.

Reaching for her, Quill's voice cracked, "Are you hurt? Where are we? The guy on the Harley—"

Brooke met his beautiful emerald gaze the way she prayed she would all those hours he lay unconscious. "Thank God. I knew you'd be okay. Relax, we lost him back in the city. We're in Aether, but your cell is smashed to bits. You need to get up so we can get you to Kai. Do you think you can walk?"

Quill's head spun around, as if on a swivel, and his

eyes darted back and forth scanning the surrounding area. "You're sure we weren't followed?"

"I'm sure. I took him out with the fire hydrant. Don't you remember?"

He beamed with pride. "You bet your sweet ass I remember. My tough little Guardian showed him who's boss. It was awesome, but I have to admit, I don't remember anything after watching that dickwad crash and burn out. I'm sorry I left you alone like that." Quill bowed his head and looked away.

"Stop. It's not your fault. You were shot for God's sake. Besides, I did fine all by myself."

Quill's eyes locked on hers, love swimming in their depths. Her pulse quickened, and warmth radiated through her hitting her square in the chest. She could've lost this infuriating and beautiful man. Right this minute, she was more than grateful he was sitting up and talking to her.

****

Quill

"I'm so proud of you. You're such a little badass"—he stroked his hand down her cheek—"but we need to wake Hawk up and tell him about this new threat to the people." Quill attempted to work his way out of the tiny backseat, but his body remained uncooperative. His long legs spasmed with cramps, and a warm trickle of blood flowed down his back.

"Hold on there, big guy. You're not doing a thing until we get you over to Kai. He needs to patch you up. You do realize you could've died back there—" Her voice trailed off choked with emotion, and she wiped away a few stray tears.

He'd almost forgotten how frightening Brooke's

157

reality had become since meeting him. Finding out you're from another world and then having to run for your life, all in one night, was a lot to absorb. "Okay, honey. We'll go see your daddy." He chuckled under his breath.

"Very funny. I almost forgot for a minute. Thanks for that." She gave him the stink eye, a half smile sneaking across her lips. As far as smiles went, it was still a heartbreaker. The woman couldn't do nasty to save her life. Even her voice carried a softness. "If you weren't hurt, I'd probably punch you right now, but since you were shot, I guess I'll give you a break. Come on, let me help you."

She climbed over him unlatching the door. Like a spring releasing, his bent legs uncoiled from their contorted position, and his size eleven sneakers flew out the open door with a loud bang. A mix of pain and relief ran through his entire body. Brooke raced to his side, the smell of summer rain filling his nose as she leaned in close. Her blonde hair, hanging loose around her shoulders, brushed his face in feather light strokes. The wild flowing mass had finally been set free from the confines of her tightly wrapped bun, and she looked like a rebellious angel.

"Sorry." She winced. "Did that hurt? I wasn't thinking." She hoisted him up until his feet touched the ground, and his butt rested on the seat.

He ducked down in the tiny opening to fit inside the doorframe. "I'm all right, but do you want to tell me how I wound up in the backseat, and why I feel like one of those contortionists in the circus?"

"Yeah, um, sorry about that, too. I kind of dragged you back there and flipped you over."

A bit lightheaded, he managed to throw a small smirk her way. His shoulder burned like a bitch, but he wore a mask of stoicism to protect Brooke from any further worry. "I would've loved to see that. I'm sure it was quite the sight." Quill gripped the cool metal on both sides of him and pulled up, straining to stand. "I'm fine. Let's go." He locked his knees to keep them from buckling under his own weight.

"Ash was right about you Protectors. You're all as stubborn as the day is long." Brooke shoved her shoulder under his good arm supporting him. "Now move out, soldier."

"Aye, aye, Madame Guardian." Quill raised his arm to salute her and regretted the action the minute searing agony jolted through his shoulder. He couldn't hide the pained expression on his face, but she must've taken pity on him because she ignored it.

The woman had transformed into a true Guardian right before his eyes. She dragged his heavy ass along the gravel pathway from the parking area all the way through the woods toward Kai's house without a single complaint. Dawn broke and splintered light peeked out from between the trees as they reached the Village Square. Warm hues kissed the sky with dazzling color filling Aether's center with a magical aura.

Quill slowed his pace. "That Dorothy chick from The Wizard of Oz was right. There's no place like home. I have to admit I was a little worried that I might never see Aether again—" He stopped in his tracks and caught her gaze. "—but the thought of never seeing you again, or kissing you, or touching you filled me with complete terror."

"I was pretty terrified myself. You don't know how

good it is to see you up and moving around." She wiped a tear from the corner of her eye.

"Don't worry, baby. I'm going to be fine." He kissed her temple, and they shuffled forward toward Kai's place.

Their footsteps echoed in the deserted Village Square, and they reached his friend's door behind the Medical Center without incident. Sweat soaked Quill's back. He leaned up against the side of the house, his chest heaving. Brooke balled up her fist and pounded on the door. A minute later, a flash of light sparked, and Kai's living room glowed. The front door swung open, and Laurel greeted them, wrinkles tightening her brow. Quill edged his way out from behind the house holding onto the shingles. Laurel gasped, her wide-eyed stare glued to his bloody, tattered clothing.

"Oh, dear Goddess. Come in." She stepped away from the open door allowing them to enter. "Here, Quill, come sit. I'll go get Kai." She turned toward the bedroom, and a loud voice rang out from the hallway.

"No need to get me. I'm right here." Kai's gaze traveled up and down Quill's disheveled body, and he shook his head. "What in the name of the God and Goddess have you gotten yourself into now?"

The Protector plopped onto the couch, blood dripping down his incapacitated arm. Brooke moved in front of him, using her body to shield him from Kai's accusatory tone. "He's been shot in case you didn't notice, so be nice to him."

Kai put his hands up in a gesture of surrender. "I'm always nice. My brother, Quill, on the other hand, has the reputation of being a wise-cracking pain in the ass. But did you need to shoot him?"

Quill's good hand tightened into a fist. He would wipe the smug look off his old friend's face if he didn't watch his step, but Brooke jumped back into the mix. Her cheeks flooded with color.

"I'm not the one who shot him!" Standing tall, Brooke thrust her hands onto her hips stepping into Kai's space. "Actually, he was shot by a motorcycle-riding, fire-throwing lunatic." An imperceptible growl rumbled out of Brooke.

Wait til my buddy finds out about his little girl. Quill suppressed a laugh. *This is about to get good.* Laurel wedged between Brooke and Kai. The petite woman, dressed in one of Kai's T-shirts, placed her hands on the doctor's chest pushing him back. Tangles of long, dark hair fell in Laurel's face. Quill surmised they might've interrupted the couple in a private moment. *No wonder Kai is cranky as hell.*

Using her authoritative teacher's voice, Laurel shifted into command mode. "Listen up. Calm down and stop fooling around this instant." She turned to Brooke. "Please forgive Kai." Laurel shot her Kanti-to-be the evil eye. "He's, um, a little—tired."

Kai's eyebrow quirked up. "Tired, huh? Is that what we're calling it now?" Grabbing Laurel around the waist, he nuzzled her neck, and she squealed.

She elbowed him playfully. "Knock it off. Quill's hurt. You need to put on your doctor clothes, and do your job."

"Yeah, yeah, yeah. I'm going to get dressed." He headed toward the back of the house calling out over his shoulder, "Hey, Quill, try not to bleed all over my couch."

"Sorry about him. I'll go get dressed, too, and then

we can all head over to the Medical Center." Laurel followed Kai out of the room.

They disappeared from view, and Quill laughed. "Well that went swimmingly. Don't ya think? Big Daddy is in a great mood. Want to spill the beans now, or wait until the shit really hits the fan?"

"You know you're not helping, right?" She crossed her arms over her chest giving him a pointed look.

"I can't help myself. Besides, I'm wounded and confused." His lower lip jutted out, and he conjured up his best puppy dog eyes directing them at his pissed off girlfriend.

"Being cute only gets you so far. I'm warning you. I don't think you're funny."

Kai and Laurel walked back into the room hand in hand, cutting off his response. The doctor had donned a pair of dark blue scrubs with fluorescent orange sneakers. Laurel's "you just pulled me away from sex" look had been transformed into her usual polished shine.

"We're ready. Quill, can you make it or do I need to carry you to the Medical Center?" His friend's false sounding concern didn't go unnoticed by the two fierce women in their company.

Laurel grabbed his forearm, her fingers sinking into his flesh. "Kai, that's enough. You're both upsetting Brooke."

The doctor muttered, "Fine. But you owe me, Robbins." He moved to Quill's left side and ordered, "Put your good arm around me."

"Sorry, buddy, but you're not my type. Especially in those sneakers." Quill nodded toward the offending footwear. "Laurel, how can you let him go out in those ridiculous things?"

Brooke's eyes narrowed, and her teeth clenched. "Quill, if you say another word, so help me." Turning, she shot daggers at the doctor. "That goes for you, too. Now start walking before you both regret it." She stormed over to the door, whipped it open, and gestured for them to proceed. "Go."

They were both too smart to talk back to this tough, new Guardian version of Brooke. While the typical banter between his old friend and himself lightened Quill's mood, it wasn't helping Brooke deal with the situation.

Kai supported his weight, and Quill held in his next sarcastic comment, changing the subject. "Wait, I need to call Hawk and tell him to meet us at the Medical Center. He has to be updated on this new threat. Seriously, Aether is in danger."

Brooke held out her hand to Laurel. "Can I please borrow your phone? I forgot mine and Quill's got smashed." To Quill, she said, "I'll call. You start walking."

The noisy group burst into the Medical Center, Hawk and Ash arriving on their heels. Kai and Hawk lifted Quill, settling him on an exam table, the paper beneath his body crinkling. Brooke kept close to his side; her warm hand encased in his.

Kai checked Quill's vital signs and then announced, "I'm going to call my dad to come help. You guys keep an eye on him. I'll be right back."

Returning a few minutes later, cranky Kai had vanished and shifted into professional mode, taking on an authoritative tone. "My father will be here soon. In the meanwhile, I need to examine your wound and run some tests."

"It's going to have to wait." Quill nodded to Hawk. "I have to tell you what's going on. There's no time to waste."

Brooke's grip on his hand tightened. He met her gaze, and her eyes clouded with tears. "I almost lost you today. You have to let Kai examine you."

Hawk stepped up to the end of the bed doing his best impression of a terrifying dictator. "Whatever it is, it can wait. I'll be out in the hall until Kai is done. Come on, Ash." His best friend took Ashlyn by the hand and headed toward the door.

"No! Don't you dare walk out of here." Quill rarely raised his voice, and it got everyone's attention in a hurry. "Kai, can you work while I talk?"

"Sure. I can do that for now, but make it snappy. I told you I have tests to run."

No one spoke while the doctor cut the remainder of Quill's tattered, blood stained shirt away. Kai backed up with a giant grin plastered across his face. He motioned the others over to Quill's bedside pointing at his wound. The quiet room erupted in riotous laughter. Kai held his stomach, tears streaming down his face. Everyone joined in the mix, except for Brooke, whose eyes dropped to her feet.

"What the hell is wrong with you people?" Quill stretched his neck over his shoulder catching a glimpse of the source of everyone's amusement. His gaze locked onto a couple of red soaked sanitary thingies tied to his shoulder with shoelaces. He narrowed his eyes glaring at Brooke. "Babe, really. Lady pads? What were you thinking?"

Color crept across her cheeks, and he instantly

regretted his harsh tone. Her soft voice filled with remorse, "I'm sorry. I had to improvise. You were bleeding so badly, and it was the only thing I could think of."

Kai jumped to her defense. "It was absolute genius, Brooke. Not only did you stem the bleeding with your brilliant plan, but you managed to make Quill look like a total idiot at the same time."

Her lips pulled into a tight line, and she shook her head emphatically. "It certainly wasn't my intention to make Quill look like a fool. I was trying to save his life."

This time, it was Kai, not Brooke, who turned a bit red. "I'm sorry, Brooke. I keep putting my foot in my mouth. It happens when I'm—frustrated—"

"Kai, seriously, if you don't stop talking and start taking care of our friend"—Laurel nudged his shoulder—"you're going to be frustrated in more ways than one. And it will last for a long, long, long time."

Hawk covered a snicker with a cough, and Ash elbowed him in the ribs. Kai didn't say another word instead he focused his attention back on his patient. Clipping the ties, which kept Brooke's handiwork in place, he tossed the blood-covered mess onto a silver tray. Kai irrigated the wound. Quill grimaced through the pain and set about explaining to the group all he and Brooke had endured. Of course, he left out the parts about her lineage and her visions; that news was Brooke's to share.

She picked at her cuticles and remained quiet during his entire briefing, but the minute he finished she piped up. "Okay, you told the story, now let Kai do his job. And I need to call your parents."

"Um, honey, isn't there something else we need to discuss—"

"Nothing else is being discussed until after Kai takes care of you, and that's final. I suggest you cooperate." Brooke's hair still hung wildly around her shoulders, and she stared down at him, her look fierce.

He nodded. "Okay, I hear you loud and clear. We'll talk after. Kai, let's get this shit over with."

****

Brooke

Pacing around the tiny room, Brooke waited. Nobody spoke. Hawk typed furiously on his phone. Laurel and Ash sat leaning against one another in the uncomfortable-looking guest chairs propped against the wall. The door flew open, and Willow and Van Robbins burst into the room, winded and disheveled. Relief flooded Brooke, and she raced to Quill's mom, embracing her.

Willow's soft, lilting tone soothed her. "It's going to be all right, honey. We're here now."

Van, built tall and thick with a booming voice and a personality to match, filled the room with his presence. The carpenter was the epitome of a gentle giant. His work-roughened hands stroked her cheek with a delicate touch. He was one of the kindest people she had ever met, and his tenderness melted away a bit of Brooke's tension.

"Not to worry, sweetheart, my son is as tough as they come. You'll see, he's going to be absolutely fine," he said, placing a kiss on the top of her head.

He squeezed into a seat, way too small for his oversized frame, and Willow settled next to him taking his hand. Brooke examined Quill's parents more

166

closely, and signs of distress emerged from beneath their masquerade of composure. Van's right knee bounced up and down like a teeter-totter in perpetual motion. Willow's normally free-flowing hair had been secured on top of her head with chopsticks, wisps escaping in every direction.

An amalgamation of his parents, Quill possessed qualities from both of them. Van's large stature fit his boisterous personality. When she looked at Quill, glimpses of his father peeked through at every turn, but the Protector's physical appearance was all Willow. From the sandy coloring of their hair, to the dazzling green of their eyes, mother and son could grace the cover of any fashion magazine. Glad to have them here by her side while they waited, Brooke had learned to love this quirky pair from the first moment she'd met them.

Kai wheeled Quill back into the exam room. Brooke rushed to his side giving into her urge to kiss him. His hand came up to cradle her nape deepening the kiss. All thoughts faded away except the ones involving the handsome Protector currently kissing her lips off. For once she didn't care what her new friends, his parents, or anyone else thought.

"Well it's about bloody time you two got together," Hawk's baritone broke through the drugging haze of Quill's kiss, and they separated breathless.

"Amen to that," Kai chimed in.

Ashlyn's voice carried a dream-like quality. "Hush up both of you. It's beautiful to see you two finally come together. It's meant to be."

Quill piped in, "Speaking of meant to be—"

"Not now, Quill." Brooke delivered a scowl of epic

proportions in his direction and turned to Kai. "What did the tests show?"

"The bullet fractured his clavicle and is lodged in the bone. His brachial plexus is damaged. This is affecting the cutaneous sensations and movements in his upper limb."

"Dude, if you're telling me I can't move my arm, I think I got that."

"I'm not sure why your healing powers haven't extracted the bullet at this point. I don't think you understand the ramifications. Your body is acting typically human in regard to this injury. In non-Aetherians, most penetration wounds require immediate treatment and aren't easy to repair. A gunshot wound to the brachial plexus can damage, or even sever the nerve. The placement of the bullet can inhibit action potentials needed to innervate that nerve's specific muscle or muscles. Until I can develop a plan to correct your body's regenerative qualities, I will be forced to treat you as if you are not enhanced."

Quill rolled his eyes huffing out a breath. "Can you repeat that in English please?"

Brooke took his hand. "What Kai is trying to say is your healing powers are on the fritz. He needs to do surgery to repair your nerve and fix your fractured collar bone."

Quill turned to Kai his brows furrowed. "Why the hell didn't you say that?"

"I did, and I also want to remind you that the procedure is going to be quite painful." Kai put his hand on Quill's good shoulder. "You really should let me put you under. I'm saying this as your doctor not your friend. You won't be happy with me if you're awake."

"Buddy, I'm not happy with you now. I only have one very important question before we start. Did that prick get my Protector tattoo? Because if he did, I'm going to hunt him to the ends of the Earth."

"Nah, he missed it by a few inches. The surgery won't interfere with it at all."

"Well then, let the games begin."

Willow bent down and kissed her son's cheek. "We'll be waiting right here when you get back."

Van tousled his hair. "Hang in there, buddy."

"Thanks, guys, I'm fine, really. You don't need to worry. Take care of my girl while I'm gone."

Quill winked at Brooke, and Kai wheeled him off to the operating room. Her stomach tightened in knots. What if her new father couldn't help him, and Quill lost the use of his arm? Embracing her newfound heritage, she closed her eyes and prayed to this elusive God and Goddess she'd been hearing so much about for the past few weeks.

The distinctive squeak of rubber on linoleum interrupted her silent prayer. Cassy Sanders rushed into the room. Brooke marveled at the beautiful woman. Tall and slender, Cassy wore her long blonde hair tied back in an intricate French braid. She didn't look like any grandmother Brooke had ever seen before. In fact, her wrinkle free skin glowed with a youthful vibrancy. Cassy offered everyone in the room a warm smile, the dimple in her left cheek winking exactly like Kai's.

Willow stood, and Cassy bolted straight toward her best friend, wrapping her in a tight hug. "Don't you worry, Kai and Rayne are taking great care of Quill. He's going to be fine."

Willow dabbed her eyes. "Thanks, honey. I have to admit my nerves are shot. This waiting around is absolute torture."

Cassy addressed the entire group, "I think I can make your wait a bit more comfortable. Why don't you all come with me?"

They followed Cassy into a lovely room which resembled a hotel suite more than a hospital room. Sophisticated shades of gray and blue, coupled with modern design features, adorned the space. A plush couch and matching loveseat sat nestled into the corner. The center of the room featured a motorized, queen-size bed draped with a fluffy comforter and matching shams. A flat screen television hanging on the wall completed the look.

"We thought it would be nice to have a room that combined modern medical technology with the warmth and comfort of home. Do you ladies like it?" Cassy asked, presenting the space.

"It's gorgeous, but if you don't mind me saying, it needs some plants. I'll bring some by as soon as Quill is feeling better," Willow answered.

"Thanks, that would be great."

Laurel brushed her hand over the comforter. "This place is incredible. Even better than drawings Kai showed me a few weeks ago."

"I'm so glad you think so." Cassy approached Brooke placing her hands on her shoulders. "Try not to worry, sweetheart. Kai is going to take excellent care of Quill. They may joke around a lot, but they really are like brothers."

Hawk dropped down onto the couch which creaked under the weight of the large man. "Brothers who fight like twelve year olds." The biggest pair of boots Brooke had ever seen hit the coffee table with a loud thud, along with Hawk's snarky comment.

Cassy shook a finger at him. "Hawk Crane, you take those filthy boots off my new table, or you'll be sharing this room with Quill."

His feet hit the floor in an instant. "Sorry, Cass, I forgot my manners there for a second."

Ashlyn took a seat on his lap. "He's a work in progress, but I'm doing my best to housebreak him."

"I'm lead Protector of Aether. You'll never break me, hot stuff."

"You sure about that? Remember, I know your weaknesses." Ash cuddled closer to Hawk.

"You're my only weakness." Hawk tightened his hold on her and planted a passionate kiss on her lips.

"You two are so perfect for each other." Cassy placed her hand on her chest. "It does a mother's heart good."

"Indeed it does," Willow agreed.

The love Ashlyn and Hawk shared radiated off them in waves. It only served to remind Brooke how much she needed Quill in her life. His voice, a constant in her head, fell silent. The spark of his green eyes dimmed, and his touch vanished from her skin. Brooke closed her eyes longing for Quill.

The hours ticked by slow as a rain cloud on its journey to the desert. Their friends came and went, but Brooke and Quill's parents refused to budge. Willow and Van snuggled together dozing on the couch. Brooke curled up in the comfy loveseat, her legs tucked beneath her. *What am I going to tell Kai? Oh hey, Kai, just a heads up, you're my dad—This whole thing is nuts.*

Cassy took a seat beside her and handed her a cup of steaming liquid. "You look more like a tea kind of girl to me than coffee. I brought you my favorite, English Breakfast, with a drop of honey."

"Thank you. English Breakfast is my favorite, too." Brooke warmed her hands on the cup before taking a small sip of the aromatic elixir. Her mother had always made her tea when she was out of sorts, and the memories came flooding back.

Brooke's lips quivered, and Cassy wrapped an arm around her shoulder holding her close. "Oh, you poor baby. You've been through so much. It's going to be all right. You'll see."

Collapsing into Cassy's comforting arms was like coming home again. Brooke ached for one of her own mother's signature hugs. Her new grandmother reminded her of her mom in so many ways. She may not have looked like Olivia Barrington, but Cassy had an air about her which went beyond familiarity.

Kai and Rayne interrupted the moment by wheeling Quill back into the room on a gurney. Brooke rushed to his side taking his hand. Van and Willow situated themselves on the other side of his bed. Quill's fingers tightened around hers, and relief flooded her. Brooke looked to the doctors and asked, "How did the surgery go?"

Rayne laid a comforting hand on her shoulder. "It went great. Kai's an outstanding surgeon. Quill will be back to his old tricks in no time."

Kai's gaze met hers. "The extraction of the bullet, and the repair of the brachial plexus went smoothly, but I have some concerns about the bullet we removed. The surrounding tissues were oddly affected. I've taken out many bullets in my day, but this one was strange. As soon as it came out, Quill's healing cells began functioning at their normal capacity. I'm concerned the bullet may hold special properties meant to inhibit our natural healing abilities. I'm heading to the lab to run some tests on it." Kai turned to leave, but Brooke stopped him grabbing his arm.

"Kai, wait, please. I need to talk to you about something first, and it's personal." Sweat coated her palms, and her heart pounded.

Cassy stood, and to the rest of the group she said, "Come on you guys, let's give them some privacy."

Brooke's voice shook, but she knew what she had to do, "No, it's okay. You can all stay. You all need to hear this anyway." She walked over to her tote bag, pulled out her laptop, and placed it on the bottom of the bed by Quill's feet. Fishing inside the front pocket of her jeans, she withdrew the flash drive her mother had hidden. Curious stares followed her movements, and one by one the others gathered around the bed. Swallowing audibly, Brooke flipped the computer open and shoved the flash drive into the slot on the side. "It's easier to show you this instead of trying to explain. I'm sorry, Kai, I don't know any other way to break this to you."

Brooke returned to Quill's side. Olivia's face filled the screen, and Kai's eyes lit up with recognition. As Olivia's message became clear, Kai backed away from the foot of the bed, white as a sheet. Quill's large hand encased hers, and she gripped it like a life raft on a raging sea. He repeatedly swept his thumb across the back of her hand in a soothing motion. Warmth and gratitude filled her heart.

Even watching it for the second time, Olivia's video confession slammed Brooke in the gut. Kai's eyes popped wide fixating on the computer screen, his chest heaving. Everyone in the room froze focusing on the laptop at Quill's feet. Time passed in an odd rhythm.

The loud boom of Charles Barrington's voice smothered Olivia's, cutting through the silence in the hospital room. Ashlyn shuddered, all the color draining from her pretty face. She leaned into Hawk. Wrapping a protective arm around her, he whispered in her ear stroking her beautiful red curls. A close-up image of Olivia reaching forward filled the display, panic brimming in her hollow, blue eyes. The screen plunged into darkness kicking Brooke's anxiety into high gear.

Kai's eyes remained glued to the monitor. Ashlyn and Hawk moved in behind Brooke. Ash didn't utter a single word but enveloped her in a loving embrace. Cassy and Rayne flanked Kai. His mother rubbed slow circles on Kai's back, and his dad's hand rested on his son's shoulder. Kai's eyes darted around the room, and his face fell. Brooke followed his line of sight glimpsing Laurel slipping out of the room.

Brooke cleared her throat. "Um, there's one more thing." She pulled off her compression glove and turned her hand toward the gathered crowd.

Cassy gasped loud enough for everyone to hear, and Rayne stood silent, still as a statue. The impact of the shocking news filled the room with tension thick enough to cut with a knife. Kai's eyes lifted and honed in on Brooke. He looked at her the way she'd always wished Charles Barrington would have. No one knew what to say to the stunning news, except for Quill, of course.

Groggy from the anesthesia, Quill reached out a shaky hand, grabbed the bed's remote, and raised the head into a seated position. Brooke leaned in, putting her ear to his lips. Quill's gaze shifted to Kai, and the doctor edged in closer to his friend's bedside.

"Kai man?" he croaked out. "Your—"

"Yes, my brother, I'm here. Are you in pain? What is it you're trying to say?"

Doing his best impression of the dark, masked villain from the Star Wars movies, Quill's voice deepened into a raspy, mechanical tone. "Brooke, I am your father."

Brooke rolled her eyes and blew out an exhausted breath. "Oh God, you did not just say that, did you? You're going to be the death of me."

Chapter Twelve
Marina

A week had passed, and the village still buzzed with the shocking news. Not only was Brooke Barrington the daughter of Kai Sanders, but she also wore the mark of The Guardian of The House of Water. Since finding out about Brooke, time progressed at a glacial pace for the current Guardian. Marina had expected to bond with an infant and teach her the ways of being a Guardian, not to have to crash train a thirty-six-year-old human-raised woman. She kicked off the ground beneath her feet, and the A-frame swing under her swayed in time with the rhythm of her shoes smacking the dirt. No more worrying about Coal Idris and his hot kisses. Protecting and mentoring the pretty young scientist just jumped to the top spot on her list of things to do. Gossip spread like raging rapids, bouncing and leaping all around the village. Poor Brooke. Welcome to Aether.

"Marina?" Lily's voice rang out. "You back here?" She breezed around the corner wearing a pale, blue denim sundress tied at her shoulders, accentuating her expanding baby bump. Her long, wavy, blonde hair flowed down her back, and a luminescent glow radiated all around her, giving her an ethereal quality.

Marina stared at Lily in awe. "You look so beautiful—and strong. I wish I were more like you.

What kind of Guardian am I anyway?" Her feet slammed to the ground bringing the swing to an abrupt halt.

Lily stood in front of her eyeing her up and down. "What's that supposed to mean? You're a perfect Guardian and one of the strongest people I know." Lily's hands moved to her hips, and her toes tapped the ground. Marina shrugged, slapping a look of innocence on her face. Her friend's brows lifted, and her gaze pierced Marina like a dagger. "Really? I know that look. You're still hung up on this Coal thing, aren't you? I thought you two worked out your ridiculous issues and decided to live happily ever after."

"Can you please give me a break here, Lil? I'm kind of handling a lot right now. Do I have to remind you the baby Guardian I expected turned out to be a thirty-something-year-old human and is our friend's long-lost daughter to boot?"

"You give me a break. This isn't about Brooke. This is about Coal. I really don't see the problem. He loves you. You love him. End of story."

"I wish it were that simple—"

Lily took a seat on the swing. "Actually, it is that simple. You're complicating it for no reason. I sound like a broken record here—but—Landon is in Arcadia." Her friend's tone grew sarcastic. "You remember Arcadia, don't you?" Taking Marina's hands, her manner relaxed, and her voice softened. "The amazing place we Aetherians strive to reach when we leave the physical world. Landon is there. Living in tranquility. In a world without boundaries. How do you think he would feel if he thought you were existing day to day? I get it. You miss him, but you have to open your heart to

Coal. I know it's weird right now, but you two were meant to be together. I'm absolutely positive."

"It must be nice to be so sure of yourself all the time. I hear you, I do, but I can't help how I feel."

Lily pushed off the ground setting the swing in motion again. "How do you feel?"

Marina closed her eyes rubbing her temples. She looked up, a small sigh escaping. "Conflicted—yes, conflicted, that's the word du jour. I'm thinking of having it tattooed on my ass."

The sassy little blonde laughed grabbing her tiny, rounded belly. "Fair enough," she managed to choke out between giggles. "Okay, let me ask you this? What does your heart tell you about Coal? Because I think your brain is interfering here. One's brain should never be involved in matters of love."

Marina placed her marked palm square on her chest, her heart pounding from the mere mention of the Protector's name. She nodded and pulled her lips into a tight line. She was forced to admit the truth. "My heart wants him. It always has, and I guess it always will—but every time I think—"

Lily's hand came up cutting off Marina's words. "Stop! From this moment on, no thinking, only feeling. I'm your best friend, so that means you have to listen to me. Please, take my advice, and follow your heart."

"Fine. No more thinking. Besides, it hurts my head way too much anyway," Marina acquiesced. Lily dragged her feet across the ground stopping the A-frame mid swing and gave her friend the once over. Marina knitted her brows together. "What's with that face? I promised not to think."

"Um, sweetie, what happened to your hair? You

look like hell. Let's go get you cleaned up before everyone gets here." Lily got to her feet offering Marina a hand up.

A few of her girlfriends would be arriving shortly to get ready for tonight's extravaganza. The women of Aether were hosting a celebration for the newest Guardian of The House of Water. The unique situation with Brooke prompted Ashlyn to set up a ladies only party to welcome the Guardian in style. Acting on an impulse, Marina had offered to host a small gathering at the West Tower to primp and pregame before the festivities.

Her best friend dragged her into the bathroom. The Guardian caught a glimpse of her reflection and cringed. "Dear Goddess"—she leaned into the mirror pushing the messy nest of hair out of her face—"you weren't kidding. I look like total crap."

Lily wrinkled up her nose. "I've definitely seen you look better. Now get undressed and get in there." She cranked the faucet on while Marina stripped, leaving her clothes in a heap on the floor. Lily shoved Marina beneath the warm spray of the shower, grabbed the pile of discarded clothes, and turned on her heels leaving the Guardian alone with her jumbled thoughts.

The water penetrated her skin, sinking deep into her tense muscles. The warm stream of liquid infused her body with the power of her Element. Marina stood beneath the spray until the water cooled and her fingers resembled raisins. She jumped out reaching for the towel she'd left nearby. Pulling on her robe, she tied the sash around her waist, and got down to the business of getting ready. Glossing on some lipstick, she almost escaped before Lily stopped her.

"Oh no you don't. You're not getting away without wearing any makeup. Don't you move, young lady." Her friend entered the bathroom carrying her bag of tricks, as she liked to call it. Lily put the finishing touches on Marina's makeup, and Marina stared into the mirror amazed. The dark circles under her eyes, a constant reminder of her sleepless nights, had been camouflaged with the skill of an artist.

The sun dropped down in the sky. The lengthening spring days kept the sun shining well into the evening. Marina glanced at the clock across the room and picked up her pace. Shouting over her shoulder, she dashed into her room to slip on her dress. "Lil, I'll be back in a sec. I don't want to be in my robe when the girls get here."

Five minutes later, she entered the living room, and a beautiful array of hors' d'oeuvres sat on her oversized coffee table. While she'd shimmied into her too tight dress, Lily had managed to set the most stunning table. Not only did the food look amazing, but so did her friend. She wore a silk organza maxi-dress. The fabric flowed in a striking ombre pattern in descending shades of light lavender moving down to deep purple at her tiny feet. Her hair, arranged in an elegant twist, completed her look.

Lily caught her eye and twirled around in a circle exactly like when they were little girls. "You like?"

"You look gorgeous." Marina couldn't wrap her brain around her friend's light and happy manner. Would Little Miss Cheerful's façade crumble soon? "I can't believe you did all this while I was getting dressed."

"And I can't believe you invited all these people

and didn't make anything. You're lucky I came prepared." Lily tweaked one of the already perfect looking trays.

Pointing to the table, Marina asked, "Where did all this food and stuff come from?"

"While you were outside pretending not to pine for Coal, I brought everything over from my place. I dropped it off here before I found you in your thinking spot. It's all good, no worries. The champagne is chilling in the fridge. We need to grab it and the glasses from the kitchen when they get here for *your* festivities," A hint of sarcasm leaked out in Lily's tone.

The Guardian's talents didn't extend to the kitchen. Marina and Julia Child only had one thing in common, they were both female. Lily, on the other hand, probably could have given the famous chef a run for her money. She always stepped up to help no matter what Marina needed from her best friend.

Marina laughed. "I appreciate everything you did, really." She planted a kiss on her friend's cheek. "You're so much better at this kind of thing than I am, and I've been way too overwhelmed to even think about it. I wanted to do something nice for Brooke. It's important to all of the Guardians that we make her feel welcome. And besides, you know I could never make it look this good." She gestured toward the artfully arranged platters on the table. "Your skills are way more impressive."

"You're very sweet. You know that, don't you?" Lily blushed. "So, who's coming to this little soiree of yours anyway?"

"Well, Brynn called earlier and said she'd met us at the party. She didn't say why. But all the other

Guardians are coming. Plus, Zephyr is bringing Skye, of course. Cassy and Willow have both been super supportive of Brooke since the big news broke, so I invited them, too. Cassy promised to drag Laurel along. Ashlyn didn't have any luck trying to convince her to come."

"I take it she's still a little freaked out about Brooke being Kai's love child, huh?" Lily questioned.

"You think? I can't really blame her. Laurel and Kai weren't together at the time, but still, it must hurt. Knowing how hard it is for Aetherians to conceive, and the good doctor manages to knock up the first ordinary human in the history of the people. I'm sure she's wondering if the God and Goddess will bless her and Kai with a child of their own. I know I would be."

A knock sounded at the front door, and they didn't have a chance to get into the conversation any further. One by one, their friends filed into the open space of her great room looking like a queue of models walking down a runway in a Paris fashion show, each in her own unique style.

Marina mumbled under her breath, "Gotta love online shopping."

The first to enter, Quill's mom, Willow, floated into the tower dressed in a floor length floral gown. Layer upon layer of flowy chiffon danced around the stunning woman. Her sandy colored hair flowed down her back, wild and a tad frizzy. A wreath of flowers rested on the crown of her head.

The Anani sisters, Zephyr, Guardian of The House of Air, and Skye, the sharpshooting Protector, looked stunning. The girls, fraternal twins, still shared a striking resemblance. Tonight, dressed in opposing styles, the sisters looked nothing alike. Zephyr wore a mermaid cut, form-fitting lace dress in an elegant cream color which showcased her sexy curves. Her raven-colored hair hung down around her shoulders in soft waves.

In contrast, her sister, the Protector, donned a fashion forward jumpsuit in jet black. The top draped across one shoulder and fit her as if it had been tailor-made for her incredible athletic build. The pants flared out giving the outfit graceful movement. Skye's midnight black hair, pulled back in an elegant, high ponytail, accented her gorgeous cheekbones.

Cassy arrived seconds later, dragging a fidgety Laurel into the room. Relief flooded Marina, and she rushed to Laurel's side enveloping her in a bear hug. Lily moved in right beside her, joining in the embrace.

Laurel's good-natured smile lit up her pretty face. "Hi, girls, good to see you, too."

Marina marveled at the eclectic group of beauties standing in her living room. "You all look absolutely gorgeous. But where's Ashlyn—"

The door burst open, and Ash poked her head in. "We're right here." She turned back tugging Brooke through the doorway.

Marina's mouth dropped open. Brooke was unrecognizable. Her tightly twisted bun and conservative clothing had vanished, replaced by a sheath of shimmering silver. The gown wrapped around her body forming a plunging V in both the front and back of the dress. A slit ran up on one side reaching the top of her thigh, exposing her toned legs. Her shoulder-length, blonde hair had been expertly styled and curled to perfection. The normally fresh-faced young scientist wore a full complement of glamourous make-up including a smokey eye done in shades of gray.

The room fell silent, and Brooke backed up toward the door. "I know, I look ridiculous. I'm going home to change."

Cassy took hold of Brooke's arm. "Sweetie, please don't go. You look anything but ridiculous. It's—we aren't used to seeing you this way. You're the most beautiful, radiant woman I've ever seen." A blush crept up Brooke's neck filling her cheeks with a rosy glow.

Willow rose from her seat. "I wholeheartedly agree."

Ashlyn came up on Brooke's other side. "That's what I've been telling her for the past hour." She took the newly revealed beauty and spun her around. "Did you guys know she had this awesome cleavage?"

Brooke's cheeks brightened from their rosy glow to a deep crimson. "Ash, remember what I said about embarrassing me? You're doing it right now."

"Sorry, I can't help myself. You're my masterpiece."

Brooke rolled her eyes and laughed off Ashlyn's comment. Fate had brought the pair together and their tight bond shone through their banter. A twinge of jealousy found its way inside Marina twisting her gut in knots. *I should be the one bonding with Brooke, not Ash.*

Picking up a glass of champagne, Marina clinked her fork against the side, and raised it in the air. "Ahem. Ladies, I'd like to make a toast." Everyone stood holding their glasses high.

"Wait a sec. I'm coming." Lily quickly poured some sparkling cider and raced to rejoin the group.

Marina gestured toward Lily with her glass. "First, a word of thanks to my dearest friend for making this little gathering so lovely."

"Like we ever thought you could pull this off." Ashlyn snorted back a laugh, and the others joined in.

Marina shot her a dirty look. "Anyway, as I was saying before I was so rudely interrupted, thanks again, Lil."

"It was no big deal." Lily shrugged off the compliment.

"It really was, but let's get back to the reason we're here tonight. Brooke. I know I speak for everyone in this room when I say, we are thrilled that you've finally found your way home. You're going to make an amazing Guardian, and I can't wait to start sharing this special journey with you. Welcome to Aether, my little sister Guardian. To Brooke!"

They formed a circle clinking their glasses together and shouted in unison. "To Brooke!" Their flutes crashed together in a symphony. Golden liquid splashed everywhere, and laughter erupted from the group.

****

Coal

Same music, same seats, same food and drinks, but the vibe in their favorite gathering spot suffered without any women in the room. The last time Coal hung out at the pub he'd left with Marina. Memories of the beautiful Guardian wearing a sexy, blue dress, wrapped in his arms, their lips joined together, consumed him. The Protector surreptitiously adjusted his arousal under the table, while his buddies sat across the way, oblivious. It was going to be a long night.

Hawk's fist landed on the hard, wooden surface in

front of him jolting Coal back to the conversation. Their lead Protector's voice sounded more frustrated than angry, "I don't care how many times you've told me the story already. I want to hear it again. How the hell did this guy get my Ashlyn's powers?"

Quill blew out an exasperated breath. "Listen, buddy, no matter how many times you ask me, the answer is going to be the same. *I...don't...know*. Is that plain enough for you? We didn't exactly stop and have a chat with him. He was shooting at us in case you forgot that part." Quill rubbed his shoulder, which had come out of a sling only yesterday. "He's lucky he got me instead of Brooke, or he'd be dead right now."

Kai piped in, "The fire-throwing guy isn't the only mystery we need to solve. There's something very strange about the bullet I removed from you. I've been a bit—overwhelmed, but I've been working on it without any success so far. I'm not sure what I'm going to do next, but I know I'll figure it out."

"You need to let Brooke help you," Quill added. "I know this has been a shock for you, but imagine how she feels. Charles Barrington took everything from her. She deserves to be a part of this. Besides, no one knows their way around a lab better than your daughter."

"For once, I think he actually has a point." Hawk bumped Quill's shoulder.

"Hey"—Quill reached out, soothing his injury— "watch it will ya?" He shot Hawk a dirty look and scoffed back, "It's been known to happen on a rare occasion."

Hawk ignored Quill's remark. To Kai, he said, "Brooke is seriously a genius. I can hardly understand a word she says when she talks about all this science crap." The lead Protector took a swig of his beer. He wiped his mouth with the back of his hand and continued, "She's obsessed with figuring out how the Harley guy got Ash's powers and also about the tainted bullet. You need to work with her on a solution. This is common ground for you guys and a great way for you to get to know her better."

Coal couldn't stay quiet. "No one is denying this situation is awkward, but take it from someone who knows about wasting time, you shouldn't miss another minute. Don't you want to know your daughter?"

Kai nodded. "Of course, I do." Shifting his gaze back and forth among his friends, he continued, "I have gotten to know Brooke. She's been in Aether for weeks, but you have to understand how crazy this feels to me. I barely knew Olivia. It was a one time—" The man closed his eyes mid-sentence shaking his head. They sat in silence until Kai spoke again. "I'm trying. I really am. Brooke is great, but it's not only about us. Laurel is crushed, and it's all my fault. She's been so quiet since we found out. She says she's not mad, but she stayed at her parents' last night. My mom keeps saying she needs some time to process everything, but I can't help feeling like I'm losing her again."

"You're not going to lose her. Cassy's right. Give Laurel some time. She'll come around. I'll ask Ashlyn to talk to her again," Hawk assured.

"I know the women aren't here tonight, but we're starting to sound like them. Let's do something macho, like shoot some pool, before we all get our man cards revoked." Quill's wisecracking comment managed to lighten the mood as always.

The loud scrape of Hawk's chair dragging across

the floor set the rest of the men in motion. They instinctively followed their lead Protector toward the pool tables set up at the back of the pub. Coal brought up the rear right behind Kai. He lowered his mug to the scarred surface of one of the high-top tables scattered among the sea of green felt, taking a seat. Quill grabbed the rack off the wall and corralled the colorful balls into a perfect triangle. The hard plastic globes spun around clanking together in a familiar timbre. Scenes like this one made Coal miss Landon even more than usual, but tonight he couldn't get River off his mind. The father-to-be belonged with his friends having a beer and shooting pool, not lost to his Adara and all of Aether.

"Stripes," Kai called out before lining up his shot. A loud crack rang out, and the balls ricocheted racing around the table. "Yes! Perfect break as usual."

"Doesn't matter, *Dad,* I'm going to kick your ass anyway," Quill replied in a snarky tone.

"Kai, if you want to beat the crap out of him, I'm totally fine with it." Hawk leaned against the table, his long legs stretched out. The imposing man shot Quill a look of warning, his muscular arms crossed over his broad chest.

"Neither of you guys possess even the smallest hint of a sense of humor. Am I right, Coal? Come on, that was funny, wasn't it?" Quill encouraged his friend to join in.

"Don't even think of dragging me into your bullshit tonight, Robbins. In fact, I um, have to run out for a few minutes. Hawk, you play winner of this game, and I'll play the next." Coal didn't give his buddies a chance to ask him anything. He headed to the door slipping out into the cover of darkness.

Coal stuck to the shadows slinking along the tree line adjacent to the banquet hall. Vibrations from the music escaping under the doors shook the ground. Strobe lights flashed through the fogged up windows casting oddly-shaped shadows. Coal crept closer. "I feel like a freakin' stalker," he mumbled. Crouching down alongside one of the oversized French doors, he peered around its edge. His voice whispered in the air to no one, "I need to see her." He'd rationalized the entire scenario in his head at least fifty times. "One little look, and I'll head back to the pub." A self-mocking chuckle escaped his lips. One look would never be enough. Just like one kiss hadn't been enough either.

He searched the crowded room zeroing in on his beautiful Guardian. Her golden blonde hair flowed down her back. Laughing, Marina's hand reached out playfully swatting at Brooke. The young scientist looked like a Hollywood starlet, her head thrown back, a glass of champagne in her hand, but Marina's beauty captivated him. Everything in its wake faded away until the world around him vanished and only she remained. His heart pounded in his ears leaving him breathless.

Skin-tight shimmering black material clung to every one of her curves. The front plunged down low exposing the gentle swells of her luscious breasts. His gaze locked on Marina, and lust slammed through him. A humongous hand dropped down on his shoulder. Flinching, his fist shot out ready to swing.

His lead Protector's deep baritone rang in his ears, "What are you doing out here acting like a peeping Tom? I told you to talk to the woman not spy on her."

Coal exhaled a deep breath. "You scared the shit out of me." He shoved Hawk's hand off his shoulder.

"Why do you keep sneaking up on me?"

Hawk scowled. "First of all, you need to be more focused on your surroundings. I'm thinking a few extra training sessions are in order. And second of all, you're kidding, right? You took off from the pub like the village was on fire or something. What did you expect me to do?"

"So, you followed me?"

"Duh, of course. It's my job to look after you boneheads."

"Hawk, you're lead Protector, not Dear Abby. I know you're trying to help, so please don't take this the wrong way, but fuck off."

The other man smiled, his bright white teeth glistening like a predatory animal. "Watch it, Idris. I—" Elevated voices came up from behind them cutting off Hawk's warning.

Coal rolled his eyes. "Quill and Kai, of course."

The two emerged from between the trees mid argument, Quill balking at the doctor. "My shot was perfectly legal. I guess you're not as smart as you act, or you don't know the rules."

Kai pushed by Quill, joining Coal and Hawk. "I know the rules perfectly well." He shouted over his shoulder, "You're a cheater."

"Face it, Doc; you've always been a bit of a sore loser. Right, guys?" Quill asked, coming up alongside Hawk.

Pulling his shoulders back, Coal took a step away from his friends. "Are you guys for real? Why are you all here?"

Quill gave Coal a small shove. "Same reason as you, brother. We want to see our ladies."

"Back off." Coal moved in front of the window blocking the others' views.

"Why should you have all the fun?" Quill pushed back again, and the others followed.

Bodies pressed in on Coal from all sides, giant boots crushed his toes, and the smell of beer made his eyes water. The oversized men crowded him, each struggling to get a glimpse inside at what they treasured most in all of Aether. He'd been making a concerted effort to spend more time with his friends, but this was ridiculous. Coal had only wanted to obsess over Marina in peace, maybe collect some more footage for his fantasy reel.

Hawk froze in place and closed his eyes. Quill held up a hand and said, "Hold on guys. Telepathic link in action." The others stopped battling for position and stood motionless.

Their lead Protector opened his eyes and flashed a broad grin. "Ashlyn says we should come join the party." Hawk muscled the rest of them aside like a little kid trying to be first in line for ice cream. "I'm going to dance with my girl. See you later, guys." Quill and Kai followed at his heels.

From the safety of his perch outside the window, Coal peered through the foggy glass. Pressing Ashlyn up against a wall, Hawk's fingers tangled in her mass of red curls. The big man lowered his head, kissing the daylights out of the stunning Guardian. Coal harrumphed. "That does not look like dancing to me. Hawk is one lucky guy."

Kai stood on the edge of the dance floor holding Laurel's hand and whispering in her ear. Her eyes lit up, and she nodded. With a hand on the small of her back, Kai led the beautiful teacher into the center of the crowd. Holding her close, they swayed in time with the music. Kai and Laurel had found their way back together once before, and Coal knew they would somehow work things out between them again.

Coal allowed the words and music to wash over him. The song spoke of a loving couple growing up and finding love together in their own backyard. It went on about kissing in the starlight, and his memories raced back to his lips joined with Marina's.

A flash of silver on the dance floor drew his attention from Kai and Laurel bringing his focus to the blur flying past. Quill, a force of nature, swept in on a current of Air twirling Brooke around in dizzying circles. Her head thrown back in abandon, the young Guardian's shoulders shook with laughter. Quill lowered her to her feet bringing his lips down on hers with an obvious hunger Coal recognized in the pit of his stomach.

Apparently, word had gotten out about ladies' night opening its doors to the men, because Coal found his view unexpectedly blocked by large bodies filing into the grand space. Craning his neck, his head bobbed and weaved scouring the crowd for a glimpse of Marina's incredible beauty. Coal ached to be beside her. His eyes narrowed. "Where the hell did she go?"

A light touch came down on his shoulder, and Coal stiffened jumping back. Caught off guard for the second time in one night, the Protector grabbed hold of a delicate appendage. The scent of sunshine and freshly cut flowers wafted up, and he inhaled deeply. "Marina," he whispered, his fingers tightening around her hand.

Her warm breath brushed against his ear. "I was

hoping you'd be here. I wanted to talk to you, but why are you out here all alone?"

Coal turned, meeting her eyes with his best glacial stare. "I was just leaving. Have a good night, Marina."

The same warm fragile looking hand landed on his arm this time. "Please, don't go. I'm sorry. I want to—"

"What do you want? Because I can't do this anymore with you. If you don't want to try and see what this is between us, well, I guess there's nothing I can do about it. I'll have to figure out a way to move on. Please, I can't be around you for a while, it's too hard." He spun on his heels and headed off.

"What if I want to try?" she called to him, her voice sweet and tentative.

A combination of shock and disbelief froze Coal in place. His heart skipped a beat and then jumped into a quick, pulsing rhythm. "Have you been drinking tonight?" He couldn't turn around. He couldn't look at her. "You can't be saying what I think you are."

Marina came around from behind him, her beauty even more evident without the window between them. "To answer your first question, of course I've been drinking, it's a party, but I'm not the least bit drunk. And as for your second question, I know exactly what I'm saying." She placed her hand over her heart, her eyes brimming with unshed tears. "I'm tired of fighting this attraction between us. The girls have been all over me about opening my heart. I'm not making any promises here—but I really want to explore my feelings for you." Her cheeks flushed a gorgeous pink.

Coal ran the back of his fingers down her heated skin. "Mmm, so soft. Am I dreaming?"

"Maybe you should kiss me and find out."

Marina's rosy lips parted.

Coal's hands flew to her shoulders, and in the next moment, he dragged her body against his own. Feather light kisses rained down his neck, and a rush of Fire surged through his veins. He lowered his mouth to hers, inch by slow inch. His tongue snaked out running along the full red bows of her lips, her moan music to his ears.

"Oh God, Marina. I need you so much it hurts. Are you sure you want this? Tell me now. Do you really want to be with me?"

"Yes, I do. Since I was sixteen, I've wanted to be with you. I gave half of my heart to Landon and hid the rest away, but tonight I'm taking the hidden piece back, and I want to share it with you. Let's start from the beginning this time." A mischievous look spread across her face. She stuck out her hand offering it up for him to shake. "Hi. I'm Marina. Do you live around here?"

Coal burst out laughing. Tucking a stray hair behind her ear, he leaned in close. "I'm Coal. And I happen to live a stone's throw from here. Can I offer you a nightcap?"

They both chuckled at the silliness of the little game they played, but it was freeing pretending they were meeting for the first time. There hadn't been a drop of lightness in their relationship since they'd lost Landon. Taking in a deep breath, the tightness in his chest loosened. Coal took her hand, placing a kiss on the back. Goosebumps rose on her flesh multiplying and spreading up her bare arms pleasing him to no end.

Marina squeezed his hand. "A nightcap sounds great." She nodded in the direction of his house. "Come on, let's go."

Neither of them spoke the entire way to Coal's

place. He was afraid if he said a single word she might disappear, and he would wake up alone in his bed realizing this had only been a dream. Marina stayed quiet, too quiet. Walking in step together, her gaze fixed on their feet. Her lips pressed into a thin line, and her posture turned stiff. Stopping at his door, nervous knots settled in his belly. "It's okay if you've reconsidered. I don't want to force you into anything."

She stroked his stubbled cheek. "You're not forcing me. We both want this. Need this."

Coal shouldered the door open and yanked Marina inside. He didn't stop to turn on a light, or for a drink of water, or even to use the bathroom. With the bright glow of the moon shining through his windows as a guide, he made a beeline for his bedroom. He towed the beautiful Guardian along with single-minded focus.

He ran his hand down her long, blonde hair. "Are you one hundred percent sure?"

"One hundred and fifty percent." She got up on her tiptoes and planted a firm kiss on his lips.

Her ethereal beauty was enhanced by the soft beams of light filtering into the room. Passion flared in her eyes, and he gave into his need to claim this woman once and for all. Scooping her up, Coal tossed her onto the down comforter. Coming down on top of her, he covered her face with kisses. Marina writhed beneath him, and satisfaction surged through his veins. She arched back giving him better access to her long, slender neck. Moving south, he kissed her everywhere, licking and nipping at her heated flesh. Coal grew frantic. His hands shook following his mouth's path, stroking her delicate skin. Spilling from the confines of her form fitting dress, her breasts thrust upward tempting his hungry mouth.

Breathless, he paused propping himself up on his elbows gazing down at her. "I've always thought you were the most beautiful woman I'd ever laid eyes on but seeing you like this is—I have no words." Coal's lips descended meeting Marina's with a fierce possession.

Her taste so sweet, he plunged deeper. Marina's kisses acted like a drug pulling him into the intense pleasure. Coal's head spun. Stroke for stroke, her tongue met his in a bewitching duel. He drew back from her delicious mouth. The ability to form coherent sentences escaping him, "Clothes...too many...off...now."

Marina's heavy breathing matched his own, and he eased off her with care. She shifted making her way to the edge of the bed, exposing herself with every shimmy of her gorgeous curves. Coal surged to his feet, grabbed her hands, and hauled her up onto her wobbly legs. Reaching back, he tugged on the zipper of her sexy, black dress. The slow rasp filled the quiet room, and Marina shuddered never taking her eyes off him. The silky fabric parted slipping down to the floor revealing a red, strapless bra. The lacey cups lifted her breasts in a glorious fashion, and he licked his lips in anticipation.

Traveling down her body, his gaze devoured every inch of her radiant form. Her matching high-cut thong stopped his vision quest in its tracks. A tiny triangle covered her most intimate flesh, leaving little to the imagination. Thin straps held the material in place accentuating her long, slender legs. "Dear God, Marina. I think I swallowed my tongue. You look so—"

Her cheeks flushed. "Please, Coal. I need to see you, too."

Taking hold of the tail of his shirt, she yanked it over his head. Her hands trailed down his chest, and his eyes closed of their own volition enjoying the warmth of her touch. Coal's body burned with passion. He hardened beneath his jeans, pulsing against his fly.

His voice lowered several octaves, and he placed Marina's hand on top of his growing length. "See what you do to me?"

She smirked. "Yes, I can see we have a situation on our hands here. But I'm pretty sure I can help you out." Marina flicked open the copper button at the top of his jeans.

Coal swallowed audibly, his mouth suddenly dry. He smoothed his hands down her fair skin while she worked his pants down his legs. They pooled at his feet, and he toed off his shoes and jeans his one swift motion. His boxer briefs tented. Marina's heated stare penetrated right to his core, and his erection stiffened further.

Slipping her fingers into his waistband, her hands slid down to the globes of his ass squeezing them in her firm grip. She dropped to her knees tugging his underwear down stopping at his thighs. Trapped by his own clothing, he couldn't do anything but breathe. Her sweet, pink tongue grazed the head of his shaft, sending sparks through his body. She grew bolder wrapping her hands around his cock and alternated between stroking and licking him with equal measure.

Coal's breath panted out, and he struggled to speak. "Sweetheart, you have to stop."

Big blue eyes sought his out with concern in their

depths. "Dear Goddess, did I do something wrong?"

"The exact opposite. If you don't stop, you're going to finish me off."

A lovely blush rose to her cheeks. "Oh, okay." Her gaze lowered to the floor.

He raised her chin with the tips of his fingers. "Please, look at me. You're amazing. Your mouth on me is better than any fantasy I've ever had. Well, except for this one—"

Coal kicked off his underwear, pulled her to her feet, and deftly unclasped her bra in one motion. Her nipples hardened to sharp points. He leaned down taking one of the pebbled buds into his mouth. Marina cried out, ecstasy lacing her voice. The thrust of her curvaceous hips in his direction propelled his libido into overdrive. Desire spread through Coal like a wildfire, controlling him, demanding he taste her. He lowered Marina onto the mattress coming down on top of her.

Tearing the strings from her panties, he tossed them aside. "Sorry, not sorry"—he laughed—"but doing that was on my bucket list. I'll buy you new ones tomorrow." Coal kissed his way down her body, reaching her most intimate flesh. He inhaled her heavenly fragrance. "You smell so good, and I bet you taste even better."

Marina's fingers channeled into his hair pulling the strands taut. Spurred on by her enthusiastic response, he spread her luscious thighs. Gently parting her folds, he ran his tongue through her moist heat.

"Coal," she moaned out her pleasure, his name a mere whisper on her lips.

He tasted her arousal on his tongue. "Wait for me, sweetheart. I need to be inside you. Come with you."

"Yes," she pleaded.

Coal crawled up her body and took her lips in a fiery kiss. Marina wrapped her longs legs around his back urging him closer. Coal obliged, thrusting forward, and entering her in one swift motion. Marina's lips parted, tiny whimpers and moans escaping. Her tight channel gripped him sending sparks through his body. Coal set a relentless pace, plunging deeper, stroking her inside and out. Marina countered each movement with one of her own. They fell over the edge together in a mind-bending climax.

Depleted, the couple rested in a tangle of limbs. Coal's heart pounded. "I love you, Marina. I always have, and I always will."

She didn't respond with words, instead, she pulled him down for a passion-filled kiss. He'd worry about hearing the words from her in due time.

Chapter Thirteen
Brooke

"The view from up here is incredible. I don't think I'll ever get used to it." Brooke leaned out of one of the cutout windows which lined the Atrium at the top of the West Tower. In awe, she gazed down at the village of Aether resting her palms on the rough, stone window ledge. Steeped in magic, the ancient village overflowed with age-old tales of Aether's history.

Marina came up alongside her and hopped up onto the wide sill, taking a seat. "I feel the exact same way. I never want to take this beautiful life, this special gift we've been given, for granted."

"I can't help feeling like this is all a dream or something. How can I be an Aetherian, let alone the Guardian of The House of Water? I really appreciate how much time you've been spending with me since I *came out.*" They both laughed.

"You have got to stop referring to your Guardian status as *coming out.*" Marina raised her foot playfully kicking her friend. "The God and Goddess work in mysterious ways which aren't always clear to us. You were chosen for a reason and given your powers to help keep balance. I believe in you, Brooke, but you need to believe in yourself."

Brooke nodded in acknowledgement. "I'm starting to." A satisfied smirk ticked up the corners of her mouth. "I did knock that psycho with Ash's powers off the motorcycle. I'm pretty sure it was pure Guardian power at work there."

"You're doing amazing. I'm really proud of how hard you've been training. I know you're anxious, but the Elders said there's no rush. Whenever you feel ready, we'll have the Guardian ceremony."

"I appreciate that, but I'm desperate to make up for lost time. I've never wanted anything so much before." Brooke paused, heat creeping up her cheeks. "Well, except for Quill, of course."

Warmth glowed in Marina's eyes. "I'm so glad things worked out for you two." She squeezed Brooke's hand. "Now you have to be patient with yourself. You're learning about a whole new world and all the power which goes along with it. Growing up away from Aether has put you at a bit of a disadvantage. Ashlyn and Ember are already bonding. The baby is learning to trust Ash as much as her own parents. It—"

"I trust you implicitly." Brooke walked away from the enormous window and headed over to the raised pedestal which held the Vessel of Water. "Please, you have to know it's not about you—you're the best. It's me. I'm not sure I can be everything the people need."

Her hands grazed the ancient stone Vessel. It represented all she strived for, a deeper connection to her Element and the ability to harness its gifts. Sitting in its position of honor in the center of the Atrium, the magical Waters contained within the Vessel bubbled up from the bottom, rising in a swell, and cascading down upon itself in a mesmerizing rhythm. The sound of rushing Water filled the space soothing Brooke, yet she longed to share the symbiotic relationship with her

Vessel the way the other Guardians had described it. They promised in time it would become part of her heart, and she would give anything to protect and preserve its essence.

"It's important to simply be yourself, and you are exactly what the people need. Don't forget for one single second that you've been chosen, by divine prophecy, to bear the mark of The Guardian of The House of Water. The God and Goddess don't make mistakes." Marina tossed her a no-nonsense look.

"I hear you. I'm working on relaxing and being myself around new people." She nodded at her friend, who was fast becoming the sister she'd never had. "It's hard for me. I've always been super self-conscious. Quill's helping me get through it by being his usual annoying self." Brooke twisted her ponytail around her fingers. "He gave me a hard time about wearing my hair up today. Ever since Ashlyn made me over for the party last week, he insists I keep it loose at all times. The man is exhausting. If I didn't love him so much, I'd probably strangle him."

Marina laughed. "Quill is only trying to get you to unwind a bit. Even you have to admit, you looked incredible that night."

"Yeah, well, Ash is a miracle worker."

"Oh no you don't. You're going to admit right this minute, you looked like a movie star on the night of the party. Everyone thought so. Quill couldn't take his eyes off you from the minute the guys crashed."

"All right, all right, I looked—pretty good." She changed the subject. "Speaking of the party, I've been meaning to ask you where you disappeared to. Right after the guys showed up you kind of vanished. Care to elaborate?"

The beautiful Guardian let out a quiet sigh. "I've been waiting for you to ask. I'm surprised it took you so long."

"I don't mean to pry, but you and Coal make such a gorgeous couple. I can't help myself. I'm sorry. I'm being a busybody. You don't have to tell me if you don't feel comfortable."

Marina shuffled her feet, avoiding eye contact with Brooke. "I left with Coal as I'm sure you already know. We spent, um, a beautiful night together. But then, I guess, I kind of freaked out. After he fell asleep, I snuck out and ran home. I know it was the coward's way out, but I don't know how to act around him, how to feel, what to say. He found me by the Grand Lake the next morning, and we talked a bit. But to be honest, I've been avoiding him like the plague for the past week."

"The village isn't very big, so where have you been hiding out?"

"I'm very creative." Marina winked.

"You know the man is hotter than hot, right?"

"Yeah, I noticed that." A blush flared to Marina's cheeks. "But it's—complicated."

"I understand you two have a long history together."

Marina muttered under her breath, "Lily has a big mouth."

"Actually, it was Quill who told me, not Lily. But it's good to know she'll be a reliable source for info in the future. Seriously, I know you're supposed to be guiding me, but can I give you some unsolicited advice?"

Crossing her arms over her chest, Marina nodded.

"Sure, go ahead."

"Stop hiding. Go find Coal. Tell him you're sorry, and that you love him. And don't try denying it, because it's written all over your face."

Marina exhaled audibly, her hands moving to her hips. "You're way more of an Aetherian than you think. Nobody around here can mind his or her own business. Speaking of business, we're supposed to go down to the Grand Lake to train today. Remember?"

"Yes, oh wise one, I remember, but love comes first. Besides, Cassy wants me to go into the forest with her today, so she can teach me about some of the botanicals they use in the Medical Center."

"You are aware of Hawk's orders, aren't you? No one is allowed to leave Aether, or even go into the forest, without a Protector escorting them." The older Guardian's maternal tone reminded Brooke of her mother.

"Don't worry. Cassy says we are sticking very close. We're only going directly behind the Medical Center. We won't really go into the forest."

"Fine. I'll give you a break for a few hours. You really are quite gifted when it comes to medicine and healing. Being of The House of Water isn't only about blasting bad guys with water cannons," Marina's voice held the slightest hint of sarcasm and pride blended together. "Generations of healers have been born to our house. Your affinity for chemistry proves it. From what Kai tells me, your work on the bullet has been brilliant. How's it been going?"

"I was positive from the start the bullet had been laced with a chemical." Brooke understood the way Charles Barrington's mind worked, so it wasn't too hard to figure out what he'd been up to. "The one we removed from Quill impedes the supernatural healing powers of Aetherians. Now, Kai and I are working on developing a reversal for the chemical's action. But hopefully the Protectors will find these guys and stop them before anyone else gets hurt. I need to find my fath—I mean Barrington's research and destroy it. I need to stop him. I'm worried the stranger with Ash's powers is only the tip of the iceberg."

"Okay, in that case, take the rest of the day off. Spend some time with Cassy, and then go to the lab, and use your brilliant Water Guardian powers to figure this whole mess out."

"Thanks for the vote of confidence. No pressure. I'll formulate a plan, set it in motion, and save Aether from Barrington. Easy peasy, no problem."

****

Quill

Since their run in with the Fire-throwing biker from hell, the Protectors had been taking on extra rotations of sentry duty. Today, Quill was teamed up with Skye, the young, sharpshooting Protector. The saying, "looks can be deceiving" must have been penned with Skye in mind. Her long, dark hair, tied back in two braids, gave her a much more youthful appearance than her twenty-five years. Her penetrating blue eyes shone with intelligence in their depths. The best sniper Aether had ever known, Skye might not look intimidating, but she could hit a target a mile out with one arm tied behind her back.

Skye leaned against a giant oak checking her weapon's safety for the third time. "Patrolling is a total pain in the ass, not to mention a complete waste of time. There's no way Barrington's men are getting passed Aether's protective shields."

"Really? How do you explain what happened to Ashlyn and Laurel? You were there when we rescued our Fire Guardian, you should know, anything is possible." Quill hated the way he sounded like the wise old Protector compared to the young soldier in front of him.

Straightening up, she tucked her gun into its holster. "Ash told me the only reason Devlin got them was because they walked far beyond Aether's borders. Plus, the entire village is on alert. People know they need an escort to go anywhere."

"Yeah well, rules are made to be broken." Quill smirked giving Skye a knowing look. She and her twin sister, Zephyr, Guardian of The House of Air, had broken more than their fair share of rules growing up, but when it came to being a Protector, Skye was altogether serious.

"I hope in this case you're wrong," Skye said. "It may be safe, but we don't need anyone out here unprotected, tempting fate."

"Don't worry, Hawk made it very clear at the village meeting. Let's start our perimeter run. Why don't you take point?"

"You got it, boss." She saluted taking off.

Quill followed behind staying vigilant. He didn't share Skye's confidence with regard to Charles Barrington's lack of ingenuity. Quill had no doubt, given enough time, the depraved doctor would find his way back to Aether. They jogged along keeping a steady pace. Skye skidded to an abrupt halt, her outstretched arm signaling him to do the same. The low murmur of voices penetrated the thick brush, and the Protectors moved in crouching low. Quill's senses kicked into high gear, and a gush of Air swirled around his knees. The other Protector reached for her weapon, and Quill shook his head putting his finger to his lips. Skye, of course, ignored him and held her SIG up to her chest shaking her head back at him. As a senior Protector, he'd deal with her defiance later. Right now, he had to focus on the intruders in their midst.

Quill tapped into his powers moving on a silent current of Air. Parting some of the greenery, he peeked through getting a glimpse of their intruders for the first time. He froze, his eyes widening. He dropped back. Drawing out his phone, he typed a quick text to Hawk. —*Follow the locator in my phone. We have a situation in the west end of the forest*—

Hawk responded within thirty seconds. —*What the hell is going on? Are you okay?*—

Quill ignored him running off a text to Skye instead. —*Follow my lead, no matter what goes down. And whatever you do, don't shoot*—

Her brows knitted with confusion, but her response came through as expected. —*Affirmative*—

Quill honed in on the voices choosing his target through careful deduction. Adrenaline pumped through his body. The trained Protectors moved in unison stalking their prey with silent precision. They crept low along the ground gaining purchase with every step. Holding his breath, Quill drew his weapon but didn't chamber the round. He ducked behind a tree keeping his body flat. Advancing further, the voices became more distinct.

He slipped in behind his victim and wrapped his

arm around a slender neck, while his Beretta came up to the person's temple. "Don't move a muscle," his voice barked out, scratchy and rough.

"Ahh—" A woman's scream rang out in the quiet forest.

The high-pitched wail pierced his eardrums. Quill released his hold holstering his weapon. Stepping back, he yanked a terrified Brooke around to face him. "You're okay, sweetheart, It's only me."

She held her hand to her heart, all the color draining from her face. "What the hell is wrong with you? You scared the crap out of me."

Skye lowered her SIG from the back of Cassy's head. "Sorry, Cass, just following orders. You all right?"

"I'm fine. Brooke, are you okay?"

"If I could get my heart out of my throat, I would be. What were you thinking sneaking up on us like that?" Brooke swatted him on the arm, and her cheeks flushed bright crimson.

"I was thinking that our lead Protector gave an order for all Aetherians to travel with an armed escort. Are either of you packing by any chance?" Quill's tone grew sarcastic.

Cassy came within an inch of his face. "Listen to me, young man, your mother and I have been best friends our entire lives. I know Willow would agree with me when I say you had no right to frighten us like that. We are perfectly safe here. I was only showing Brooke some of the botanicals we use in the Medical Center."

Skye came up alongside Cassy and placed a hand on her shoulder. "I'm sorry we scared you, but you shouldn't be out here alone. We have to follow Hawk's orders. He's trying to keep everyone safe until we find Barrington and eliminate the threat."

"I'm sorry, Cassy. I don't mean any disrespect, but you have to admit with everything going on, this was a really bad idea. I can't believe you'd take a chance like this with Brooke's safety." Reprimanding the woman who had been like a second mother to Quill filled him with remorse, but she had no right to take such a huge risk with the woman he loved. Cassy's gaze dropped to the ground, and the sliver of guilt he carried dug even deeper in his gut.

Brooke's beautiful blue eyes narrowed. "Don't you dare blame Cassy for this. I knew we were wandering too far, and I didn't say anything."

Cassy approached one of the great pines running her hands over the roughened bark. "No, sweetie, he's right. I do know better, but I wasn't thinking because I love spending time with you. Sharing the mysteries of our world with you means everything to me, but you're a Guardian of Aether. Even more importantly, you're my granddaughter, and I should protect you at all costs."

Quill had been playing up this entire scenario in order to teach both of the women a lesson. "It's okay, Cass. No harm, no—"

A dark figure swept in behind the unsuspecting woman, capturing her, and knocking her off balance. A Desert Eagle handgun came up under Cassy's chin. Her eyes widened, but she remained calm. The Israeli-designed weapon, one of the largest magazine-fed handguns in the world, packed a serious punch. Too pissed off to admire the sexy looking gun, Quill faced off against Cassy's attacker. The breeze grew stronger, debris swirling on the ground.

Quill grit his teeth. "Whoever you are, you'd better let her go, and back off."

The intruder grasped Cassy in a tight chokehold. He shoved the gun deeper into her flesh forcing her head back. Skye clutched her SIG easing her way toward the enormous man but halted on Quill's signal. The sharpshooting Protector dominated with any weapon in her hand, but he couldn't risk her hitting Cassy.

He glanced sideways at the imposing intruder. Quill's gut churned. The soldier's eyes appeared vacant. The man was huge, built like a brick shithouse, the kind the ladies went for, except for the creepy, silent factor. The last thing Quill wanted to do was to set this lunatic off.

Quill slowly raised his palms keeping his voice calm and even. "Listen, buddy, I think we got off on the wrong foot here. Why don't you let the innocent lady go, and we can talk man to man?"

Flames ignited in the whites of the mercenary's eyes, and his hold on Cassy grew more rigid. A small whimper escaped her lips. Tears leaked out of the corners of Cassy's eyes trailing down her cheeks. Her gaze met Quill's, and she mouthed the words, "I'm sorry."

Adrenaline pumped through Quill's system. Clouds of dust kicked up around his feet. The Protector wasn't known for his tactful negotiation skills, but he called on every one of his internal resources. Swallowing the lump in his throat, Quill turned on the charm. "Come on, you don't want to hurt her. She's a nice lady, a grandma."

The most pompous sounding voice he'd ever heard rang out in the peaceful forest, "That young woman is certainly no grandmother. Ignore everything these barbarians tell you, Mr. Heller."

Charles Barrington emerged from behind a tree, and Brooke gasped. "Oh, dear God, no."

The pretentious prick eyed her with disdain and continued polluting the air with his rhetoric. "Well, Brooke, it's no surprise to find you here. I hope you've enjoyed your time with your new friends." The doctor sneered, his lip curling up. "Look at you. You're positively unkempt. It seems I've arrived in the nick of time. Good thing I had Mr. Heller, here, staking out your apartment in the city. Sentimental fool, I knew you'd show up there eventually."

Brooke struggled against Quill's hold, her muscles tensing under his grip. Itching to release his gun from its holster, he was unable to grab the weapon without relinquishing his grasp on his irate girlfriend. He whispered in her ear, "Keep it together, baby."

She broke free of his hold, cheeks flaming, and charged toward Barrington. Quill caught her and pushed her behind him. Struggling, she shouted at the doctor, her voice dripping with venom, "What are you doing here? What do you want from us?"

Barrington wore pressed slacks, a starched button down, and shiny shoes. The uptight doctor stood out like a sore thumb in the forest surrounded by nature. His nose crinkled up, and he steepled his fingers in front of his chest. "What sort of infantile question is that? You have no business with these—creatures. I've come to collect you and to obtain more samples for my research. If anyone is going to control the Elements, it's going to be me. Now stop this absurd behavior at once, and let's go."

Rage filled Quill. Yanking his Beretta free, he gripped it in his fist pointing at Barrington. His voice turned dark and quiet, "She's not going anywhere with you. Now tell your goon to let the woman go before I shoot you in the head."

The Harley guy's fingers sparked, and Cassy cried out for the first time since being snared by the robotic mercenary. Skye didn't budge from where she stood but cinched up on the grip of her weapon looking to Quill. He gave a subtle shake of his head, and she nodded back.

Barrington thrust out his chest, his face a mask of indifference. "Mr. Heller, please demonstrate to these barbarians who is in charge here. Dispense with the woman. She is of no use to me."

"No! Don't! I'll go with you. Let her go," Brooke pleaded with the stone-cold man.

"Brooke, you stay right where you are." Turning to Barrington, Quill's jaw clenched. "I'm warning you. If you harm one hair on her head, I'll make you pay for the rest of your life."

The doctor turned his nose up. "I don't know your name, nor do I care, but you sound like quite the cliché. Your petty threats are of no consequence to me. I will do as I please, and no one can stop me."

Quill kept his eyes fixed on the vile man in front of him. The standoff continued. "That's what you think. I can, and I will stop you."

A raspy female voice followed Quill's promise drawing everyone's attention. "Speaking of clichés, you are the epitome of a villain, you know that, right? Now here's one for you, don't move, or I will skewer you." Zephyr stood behind Barrington bringing her crossbow to the back of his head.

Quill was sure he wore a matching expression to the stunned looked currently plastered across Skye's face. Cassy stood stock still, not resisting the mechanical soldier. He clutched her to his chest with one hand while flames danced around the gun in the palm of his other. Anger pulsed from Brooke in waves, and Quill had to keep an arm around her to prevent her from flying at the doctor. Zephyr poked Barrington with the bolt sticking out from the tip of her bow. The doctor's arrogant demeanor flickered, giving Quill a small measure of satisfaction. The pretentious ass had the good sense to raise his hands in surrender to Zephyr. A spark of pride ran through Quill watching the cunning, young Guardian in action.

Zephyr had been fighting to take on a dual role as both Guardian and Protector since coming of age. The Elders refused to permit her to participate in the Protector Trials due to their preconceived notions of each Aetherian's preordained path. Their firm beliefs had been set into motion by the God and Goddess since the beginning of time. Many of the Protectors, including Quill and his posse, disagreed with their leaders' decision. Why shouldn't Zephyr be given the same chance as any other citizen of Aether, simply because she's a Guardian? She exuded the same calm confidence he'd witnessed in his fellow Protectors many times. Quill didn't speak but laughed to himself instead. *I guess it's Zephyr's show now.*

Her biting sarcasm cut right to the chase. "Tell

Rambo to let my friend go right now. Trust me, you don't want to test my patience, because I don't have any."

Barrington swallowed audibly and cleared his throat. "Mr. Heller, call your flame back immediately, and release the woman."

The soldier's flame snuffed out, and his hands fell to his sides in an instant. Cassy ran into Brooke's waiting arms, and they clung to each other. Quill motioned Skye to follow him toward the unmoving man Barrington had called Heller. The mercenary's thick arms hung loosely, and his blank stare remained firmly in place. Skye took hold of his gun shoving it into her waistband. Running her hands up and down his massive frame, she checked him for hidden weapons. Quill grabbed a set of zip ties from his pocket securing the mercenary's hands behind his back. Heller didn't resist the Protectors' imprisonment.

Quill mumbled to Skye, "What the hell did Barrington do to this guy? He looks like someone erased his hard drive. Hang onto him. I'm going to have a little chat with the good doctor." He approached Zephyr whose tight grip dug into Barrington's forearm. Teeth clenched, Quill got in the other man's face. "How many others do you have with you?"

The loud stomping of boots trampling through the forest stopped Barrington from answering. Hawk crashed through the trees, weapon drawn, followed by Coal, Brack, and at least three other Protectors all armed to the hilt. Their imposing lead Protector wore several weapons strapped to his body. His chest heaved, and his eyes darted around the clearing.

Hawk's voice exploded, "What the hell is going on

here, Quill?"

"Glad to see you too, buddy. It seems our friend, Dr. Barrington, is under the false impression he can take Brooke, and our powers, and be on his way. He's brought this robot"—Quill gestured toward Heller— "with Fire power as a little gift. We were about to discuss his misinterpretation of the facts when you arrived."

Hawk's eyes flared. Storming over to Quill, he shoved his friend out of the way, and towered over the doctor. "How did you get in here, Barrington? This place is protected."

"Please regard my personal space, take several steps back, and then I will consider speaking to you?"

Hawk seized Barrington by the shirt lifting him off the ground. The man's feet dangled in the air kicking wildly. "You're lucky I didn't put a bullet between your eyes the minute I saw you. You may think you're the shit, but you're in my world now, so take a big whiff." Hawk's fist connected with Barrington's face, and the doctor collapsed in an unconscious heap.

Chapter Fourteen
Brooke

The familiar scent of chemicals wafted in the air around the lab. Brooke stood at the counter reviewing the same data for the third time in the past ten minutes. She'd been working with Kai on the enigmatic bullet since it had been removed from Quill's body. Today, however, she was in the lab for one reason and one reason only, to avoid a confrontation with Charles Barrington. Twenty-four hours later, and Brooke still couldn't bring herself to go visit the prisoner she once called father.

The whoosh of a Bunsen burner igniting drew her attention back to Kai. His eyes, cast downward, focused on a new amalgamation of chemicals they'd been busy decoding for the last week. As it turned out, her real dad was an incredible man. Brilliant. Kind. Talented.

She came up behind Kai tapping him on the shoulder. "Hey, how's it going with the new formula?"

"Meh. I'm not sure if we've synthesized the compounds correctly. But don't worry about it, I'll figure it out. How about you? Did you get a chance to start the analysis on Heller's blood?"

"Sorry, not yet. I'm kind of distracted today. I can't seem to keep my head in the game."

Kai set the beaker he'd been agitating down on the counter and put his hand on her shoulder. "Barrington?"

She nodded, and he continued, "It's strange for me, so I can only imagine how you must be feeling. Have you seen him since they locked him up?"

"No."

He gave her arm an affectionate squeeze. "Maybe you'll get some closure if you talk to him."

She shrugged. "I highly doubt that."

Kai laughed. "Or not. Why don't you take some time to think about it? It's not like he's going anywhere anytime soon."

"I've been thinking about it nonstop. It's not like he can hurt me anymore, but I don't want to face him alone, and I can't let Quill anywhere near the man. I'm afraid he'll kill him. In fact, he's ordered me to stay away from Protector Headquarters altogether. As I'm sure you're learning"—Brooke winked—"I don't take orders very well. I'm thinking of going to see Charles today while Quill's on patrol."

"Would you like me to go with you? I've certainly got a few things I'd like to say to good old Charlie."

"You-you wouldn't mind?"

"Of course not. You're my daughter, Brooke. We've lost so much time together, but I'd really like to make up for that. I want to be the father you deserved but never had." His face turned a subtle shade of red. "If you'll let me."

A lone tear ran down Brooke's cheek, and she wrapped her arms around his neck. "I'd love that—Dad."

"I can't tell you how happy I am to hear you call me that." Kai rose to his feet. His blue eyes, which matched her own, locked onto Brooke's. Tugging her into a full bear hug, he whispered into her hair, "Don't you worry, sweetheart, everything is going to be all right."

Kai's enthusiastic display of affection took her by surprise, but she fell into the warmth of his embrace with ease. Brooke didn't possess a single childhood memory in which Charles Barrington had rewarded her, with so much as a pat on the head, let alone something so ill conceived as a hug. He'd cultivated an environment which included a rigid no affection policy at all times. Kai's grip tightened around her. She guessed he didn't maintain the same rules regarding physical proximity. In the few short weeks she'd gotten to know her real father, he'd shown her more tenderness than her false one ever had in her entire life.

Brooke extricated herself from his embrace shaking her head. "I wish I shared your confidence, but you don't know Charles the way I do."

"I'm going to have to disagree with you on that fact. Charles and I are extremely well acquainted. Don't forget, I was his roommate in medical school. We may not have seen each other in more than thirty years, but clearly he hasn't changed much."

"True"—she laughed, but her smile faded fast— "but what do you think he's going to say when he sees you, and you haven't changed at all? How do you think he'll react to that little tidbit?"

"Good question. I can tell you one thing for sure"—he leaned in close, his voice dropping to a whisper—"I can't wait to find out, you?" Kai smirked.

Brooke gave him a playful shove. "Ha, ha. You might not think it's so funny when he realizes he has one more reason to steal our powers."

"Yeah but think about how great it will feel when

the pompous ass finally understands whom he's messing with."

"If you knew him as well as you say, then you'd know he'll never give you the satisfaction. The man wears a mask of stoicism and doesn't let anyone see him display anything as pesky as emotions. You're wasting your time, but maybe you're right about this whole closure thing. Part of me is dying to confront Charles Barrington. I want him to know I'm Brooke Sanders, Guardian of The House of Water, and I don't belong to him."

Kai's voice exuded comfort. "You let me know when you're ready to go, and I will be there right by your side."

Brooke twisted her ponytail around her fingers. "I guess there's no time like the present. Let's go now—I mean, if you're okay with that?"

Kai didn't answer. He cut off the gas to the Bunsen burner, draped his lab coat across the back of his chair, and stood to face her. "Now works for me."

Sweeping through the lab, they returned everything to its rightful place and headed over to PH. They walked in step, and Brooke wiped her hands down the front of her jeans. "It's lunchtime, do you think Protector Headquarters will be a bit less crowded. I don't relish the idea of Quill finding out I've been to see Charles before I can explain everything to him. You know what a hot head he can be, especially when it comes to my former dad."

Kai held the door to PH open for her and gestured her inside. "I'm sure most of the Protectors are at lunch or on patrol. It's going to be fine. Try not to worry. I can handle Quill."

She took a deep breath and stepped over the threshold. "I haven't been in this building since I first arrived in Aether. What do Quill and the other Protectors do here anyway, play poker or something?"

Kai chuckled. "I'm not really sure, but I think that's a safe bet."

Bear's booming voice rang out, and she flinched a bit. "Kai, Brooke, what brings you to our humble abode? Or do I even need to ask?"

Raising her chin, she met the ancient Protector's gaze. "We've come to see my—I mean, Dr. Barrington. We both have a few things we'd like to say to him."

"Yeah, what she said," Kai agreed.

"I understand. The truth must be released so healing can occur. Let me take you to him. We have Dr. Barrington locked in one of the rooms downstairs. Mr. Heller is being contained in the power neutralizing room we use for Protector training." Bear led the way, and Brooke and Kai trailed the massive man in silence.

They reached the end of a long hallway, and Brooke's stomach flip-flopped. She squeezed her hands into tight fists, adrenaline racing through her system. "Um, sir, has he said anything? Asked for me?"

"No, little darling, he has been quiet as a mouse. He has not eaten and will only drink bottled water."

Brooke and Kai both laughed. Hawk's grandfather held a genuine fascination for her. The Elder Protector looked like the Rock but sounded like Mr. Rogers, minus the sweater. The eclectic group of people who populated Aether possessed a rare beauty unlike any she'd ever encountered, and Bear was no exception.

She skidded to a halt, her hand covering her racing heart. "I'm not sure I can do this?"

The mountainous Elder turned and reached out stroking her cheek with the most unexpected gentle touch. "You have more strength inside you than you are aware of, young lady. You do not yet know how great you can be. How much you can accomplish. What your potential is. But the rest of us can see it quite clearly. Share what is in your heart with Dr. Barrington, and you cannot go wrong. Even if he cannot understand, you will be freed by letting go."

Kai put his arm around her shoulder. "We'll face him together, as father and daughter." He bumped her hip with his own. "It'll be fun. Charles is in for the shock of his life. Let's show him how much he doesn't know. It will make him even more crazy than he already is."

She laughed releasing some of the tension which had been building inside her. "You're right, I can totally do this."

Wrapping an arm around her father's waist, they made their way to Barrington's room, which the Protectors were providing in lieu of the cell he deserved. The peaceful community of Aether had never required that type of accommodation in the past. They stopped near the entryway. Nothing special caught her eye, just a plain, white six-paneled door, but inside, the man she'd once believed to be her father sat prisoner for his crimes against the people of Aether. One of the Protectors, whose name escaped her at the moment, stood guard, a weapon strapped to his beefy leg. His shoulders shot back the moment he spotted them approaching with the fearsome Elder.

Bear's voice echoed in the quiet hall. "Good day. Kai and Brooke are going to have a visit with Dr.

Barrington. Please give them some privacy by staying back a bit, but be vigilant, this prisoner is not to be trusted." The Elder nodded in their direction. "I will see you two later. Please let me know if you require any further assistance." Bear signaled for the soldier to unlock the room, and the obedient man jumped into action.

The Protector drew his weapon and flung the door open one handed. Charles Barrington sat on a twin-sized bed, one knee crossed over the other, and his hands neatly folded in his lap. Blood stained the collar of his starched white dress shirt, still buttoned at his wrists. His dark slacks, wrinkled and dirty, nevertheless bore the dry cleaner's sharp creases down the legs. His salt and pepper colored hair remained coiffed in its usual neat style, but stubble covered his normally clean-shaven face.

Brooke took Kai's hand, stepping further into the room, and stopped no more than two feet from Barrington's perch. The doctor's eyes drooped, and dark circles marred the skin beneath. His gaze zeroed in on their clasped hands, and his mouth fell open.

Kai didn't give Barrington time to process the situation. "Hey there, Charlie boy, how's it going?" The man froze, his ominous, dark eyes wide with shock. "What's the matter? Don't you recognize me?"

Stuttering, the doctor responded, "You-you, can't be. How-how is this possible?"

Brooke stood tall thrusting her hands on her hips. "Aether is a magical place with power someone like you could never comprehend. That's how."

Barrington found his voice, his arrogant manner slipping back in place. "Brooke, step away from that

222

man at once. Something is very wrong with these people.*"

"No. I'm right where I belong."

Charles' jaw clenched. "You belong with me, your father, not this mutant freak."

Kai dropped his arm around Brooke's shoulder. "I am her father. You pompous, cocky, pretentious ass. How could you think this beautiful, brilliant girl could be yours? She's everything you're not. You don't even deserve to breathe the same air as my daughter."

Charles Barrington's face went crimson, the shade nearly purple. His hands fisted, and the doctor's words crept out through gritted teeth, "That is a ridiculous theory, of course she is my daughter."

Brooke pulled her shoulders back. "My mother left a flash drive hidden in the apartment in the city. She told me the truth about you and my real father." Wrapping both arms around Kai, she continued, "Not only that, but she copied all of the information you've collected on the Aetherians. We have the computer you left in your house. Our experts are going through the data, and we will find every last scrap of stolen information. You're done hurting my people."

Barrington surged to his feet, a vein throbbing in his neck. Kai scooted Brooke behind him. The Protector from the hallway stepped in and raised his weapon.

Spit flew from Barrington's mouth. "Your mother was a lying, manipulative, trollop. You are not the daughter of this-this, thing." Charles poked his finger into Kai's chest. "Get your filthy hands off my daughter this instant."

Brooke jumped out from behind Kai descending on Barrington. "Stop it! I am not Brooke Barrington. I am

Brooke Sanders, Guardian of The House of Water." She lifted her left palm thrusting her Guardian mark in Charles' face.

****

Quill

One shrill voice rang out above all the others pouring from Barrington's room. Quill charged in shoving the Protector on duty out of the way and knocking him sideways to get to Brooke. His feisty little Guardian stood an inch from the doctor's face laying into him with both barrels. Barrington fisted his hand into a tight ball. In her wrath, Brooke didn't react to the movement of his arm cranking back ready to swing.

Quill saw red. "I'm going to kill you!" Diving at Barrington, he sent the unsuspecting man sailing backward.

An audible "oof" rushed from Charles' mouth as he landed on the bed in a heap. Quill's momentum carried him forward, and he skidded to a stop a foot from the downed man. Swirling in powerful gusts, the Air around the Protector whipped through the tiny room scattering its contents. Quill surged forward, his hands outstretched, reaching for Barrington's throat. Two beefy arms, he'd recognize anywhere, came around his torso yanking him back into a tree trunk of a chest.

"Damn it, Bear. This guy needs to be taught a lesson." Quill fought to break free of the Elder's legendary power. "Come on, let me go. How are you so strong anyway? You're what, like topping five-hundred? I thought I lost you back by the entrance. You're fast as lightning."

Bear's deep baritone made everyone stop and come

to attention. "Quill, that is quite enough. I believe your conversation with Dr. Barrington has come to an end. Brooke, Kai, you are included in that sentiment. Please depart at once."

Breathless, heat rose to Quill's cheeks. "Bear, he was going to hit Brooke. Give me one good swing. That's all I'm asking for. I promise I won't kill him—yet." Quill inhaled a series of controlled breaths forcing his rage to settle down to a low simmer.

The giant man met his gaze. "Quill, I do not like to repeat myself as you well know."

Quill raised his hands in surrender. "Okay, I get it. Don't poke the Bear, as the saying goes. We're leaving."

He threw Brooke a sideways glance, and she came up alongside him. Her small frame shook, and Quill's fury mounted. He tucked her into his side wrapping her in the safety of his embrace. Placing a gentle kiss on the top of her head, he led her to the door.

Charles' voice polluted the air. "Brooke, you will regret this decision. Disloyalty of any kind is not tolerated among Barringtons."

Brooke tossed her head over her shoulder sneering at the doctor. "Good thing I'm a Sanders then. You're a shell of a man. A machine with no heart. You were never my father, and I was never a Barrington. I have nothing more to say to you." She twisted around walking away from the contemptible man.

Barrington lunged for her, but the Elder took complete control of the situation. Bear's hands snapped forward pointing toward the doctor from across the room. Barrington levitated several inches off the ground, his eyes wide. The Elder's face reddened, and he waved his hands through the air. The helpless man bounced around like a ragdoll, his feet suspended in the air. This rare display of Bear's extraordinary abilities stunned the group.

With a small flourish of the Elder's wrists, the doctor froze midair. Bear's voice exuded a calm chilliness. "Dr. Barrington, I would like to remind you, at this moment, you remain a guest in Aether, but you are trying my patience. I do not believe you would enjoy experiencing a full display of my temper. I will release you if you agree to behave respectfully. I do not wish to hear the sound of your voice. It grates on my nerves like fingernails on a slate board. Simply nod if you are willing to comply."

Barrington's head bobbed up and down in silence, and Quill smothered a laugh. "You tell him, Bear." The Elder shot Quill a stern look.

Brooke's soft voice floated through the chaos. "Please, let's go. He's not worth it." She turned to Kai. "Come on, Dad, we're leaving, like Bear said."

Kai came around to Brooke's other side, and the trio sauntered out the door. The Elder didn't follow, and a strong wind slammed the door behind them leaving Barrington alone with a very angry Bear.

The moment the door closed, Brooke turned on Quill. "What the hell was that all about? I think I proved I can take care of myself. I'm the one who saved us from that Heller guy in the city. How could you barge in there acting like a maniac in front of that man? You realize, you reinforced every idea he has about Aetherians. He thinks we are sub humans who don't deserve the power we've been given. Thanks." Sarcasm dripped from her lips. She crossed her arms over her chest, her eyes narrowing into slits.

Quill shot back, "Well, if you had obeyed me in the first place and stayed away this never would've happened."

"You did not just use the word *obey,* did you? Because if you think I'm going to obey anyone, you can go jump in the Grand Lake."

Kai stepped between them. "Um, guys, I think you should take this conversation home before you bring every Protector in Aether out of the woodwork."

Quill pushed his friend out of the way. "Do you think I give a shit? You know what, shut up, Kai. This is your fault, too." Turning back to Brooke, he grabbed a hold of her hand. "Come on, let's go." The Protector marched them out of PH, Kai trailing behind. The spring breeze blew Quill's hair back but did nothing to cool his temper. He halted his steps rounding on Kai, his posture rigid. The Protector snapped at his friend. "How could you bring Brooke here and shove her in Barrington's face."

Kai lowered his head. "You're right. I have to admit I couldn't resist the urge to flaunt Brooke's paternity in front of Charles. I should've known how he'd react." He looked up meeting Brooke's gaze. "I'm so sorry. I never should've subjected you to that pompous ass."

Brooke yanked her hand from Quill's grasp and threw her arms around Kai. "Don't be ridiculous, none of this is your fault. I wanted to go see him. You were nice enough to come with me." She released Kai, and faced the Protector wearing a tight-lipped smile. "Quill may think he's my boss, but I can assure you he's not. I see who I want, when I want." Brooke jabbed her finger in the air pointing it in Quill's face. "You trained me to defend myself, and I was handling things fine. I knew he was about to hit me. I was waiting for the right moment to drop him on his ass, but then you stormed in like a hurricane, as usual. If you noticed, I wasn't alone. Kai would never let Charles hurt me. Isn't that right, Dad?"

Her father raised his hands shaking his head. "Yeah sorry, honey, not going there. That's my cue to leave. You two need to work this out alone. Brooke, again, I'm sorry for exposing you to this insanity. Quill—I'm just, sorry. See you guys later." Kai skulked away.

Stomping their way toward home, both huffing and puffing, Quill and Brooke looked like two bulls ready to face a matador. They reached the front door, and she shoved passed him storming into the house without glancing his way. He followed her in, closing the door behind them, and took a seat on the couch. A combination of fury and frustration mingled inside him. Quill's knee jittered up and down.

"Brooke, we need to talk about this. We're both upset, mad, but maybe neither of us is wrong. We merely see things differently."

She plopped down on the couch beside him. "No shit, Sherlock. You're a controlling, domineering madman. I am a grown woman and have been taking care of myself for quite some time. You don't own me, Quill. I love you, but I'm not going to take orders from you, or anyone else."

He took her hand. "I love you, too. That's why I need to take care of you, protect you, keep you safe. I don't mean to be so overbearing, but when it comes to you, I can't help myself. What did you hope to accomplish by talking to that asshat?"

Brooke's entire body buckled. She quivered in violent spasms, tears pouring down her cheeks. Quill pulled her into his embrace stroking her back in soothing circles. Her words choked out between staggered sobs. "I-I don't know."

"It's all right, baby. I've got you. I'll never let him near you again. We won't even use his name. It will be like that Voldemort guy from the Harry Potter books. Charles Barrington will henceforth be known as: The Nameless Asshole."

Brooke sat back. Sniffling, she wiped her eyes, her voice soft and sweet. "I know you don't understand because you grew up with Willow and Van for parents. You guys are like the Aetherian version of the Brady Bunch. I've spent my entire life trying to please Charles Barrington. I wanted to see him—to get some closure. But you were right, it was pointless. That man can't hear anyone. He's blinded by hate and greed."

"Baby, I—"

"Don't you baby me, Quill Robbins. Your charm won't work this time. I'm still pissed at you." Her nose crinkled up, and she crossed her arms over her chest.

"I really am sorry. I lost my head when I heard you were in Barrington's room. I love you so much, and I can't stand the thought of anyone causing you pain. Please, don't be mad at me." Quill conjured his sweetest expression. "Come on, you know you want to kiss and makeup." He waggled his brows suggestively.

Brooke rolled her eyes. "You're impossible."

Quill tugged her ponytail. "I thought I told you to wear your hair down from now on?"

"And didn't I just tell not to boss me around?

Besides, I was in the lab, so give me a break."

"Well, you're not in the lab now." His fingers slid through the silky strands of her hair freeing them from their confinement. "There, that's much better."

"Stop playing with my hair. You can't flirt your way out of every argument. I'm still mad."

"Well, I'm still kind of mad at you, too. I think I should take you in the bedroom and show you what happens when you defy me." He licked his lips waiting for her to react. Reaching out, he stroked a gentle hand down her cheek, and Brooke's skin flamed beneath his touch. "Hey, baby, I only have one question for you."

Brooke's chest heaved, and her pretty, pink lips parted. "Yeah, what's on your mind?"

"Do you like your handcuffs with or without fur?"

Chapter Fifteen
Marina

She sat at her kitchen island, steam rising from the mug cupped in her hands. Marina blew on the contents and took a small sip. Lowering her tea to the counter with a bit too much force, the warm liquid sloshed over the sides. She raised her hand over the spill, and it rose in a puddle hovering above the granite surface. With a flick of her wrist, the small mess flew back into her mug with a tiny plop. Checking the ticking clock on her kitchen wall for the second time in five minutes, she stood dumping her tea down the drain.

"I think Ash said eight, or maybe she said nine. Oh, eight is okay. It's not that early. I know she's up." Marina grabbed the coffee cake she'd baked at five a.m. off the counter. Her unnerving dream had woken her and falling back to sleep had been out of the question. Keeping busy helped her wandering mind focus on anything other than the strange images running around her head.

"Dear Goddess, I hope I don't poison Ash a week before her Joining. I'm the worst cook in Aether." Shrugging, she tucked the treat under her arm and flew out her back door slamming it behind her, along with the memories of her pesky dream.

Marina strolled down the cobblestone pathway leading away from the West Tower. Century upon century of travel had worn the bricks smooth leaving the surface with a reflective sheen. In the center of the Village Square, a beautiful mosaic compass rose guided the Aetherians to the four Elemental towers. Taking a moment, she bent down running her fingers across the timeworn stones. The springtime sunshine heated the surface, and she closed her eyes absorbing its warmth.

Marina looked up to the sky. "Time to stop stalling and go talk to Ash. Maybe she can figure out what my crazy dream means." She stood tall, pulling her shoulders back, and walked straight to the South Tower.

Knocking, she strode in calling out to her friend, "Ash? Am I too early?"

A mass of red curls poked through the kitchen doorway. "Hi, of course you're not too early. Come on in."

A delicious aroma wafted from the kitchen, and Marina followed her friend into the spacious room. She inhaled deeply, the tempting smell of coffee permeating the air. Marina plopped down at the massive farm table in the center of the room making herself comfortable.

Ashlyn held up a mug. "Coffee? Tea? What can I get you?"

"Coffee would be great, thanks. Where's Hawk?"

"Long gone. He went for a run and then was heading over to PH to see if he could get anything out of that Heller guy. It's totally creepy, you know, him having my powers and all." Ash slid a cup across the table and passed Marina the cream and sugar.

"It certainly is creepy. Barrington is a psychopath. Brooke says he turned that poor man into a killing machine, fueled by Fire."

"Believe me; no one knows how crazy Charles

Barrington is better than I do."

Marina reached across the table and took her friend's hand. "I'm so sorry, Ash. I can't imagine how hard this has been on you. I'm afraid to ask this question, but are you sure you don't want to postpone the Joining until the Elders straighten this entire mess out?"

"Absolutely not! That vile man has taken more than enough from Aether, and especially from me. I will Join with Hawk next Saturday, and nothing is going to stop me."

"I'm thrilled to hear that. I would hate for that horrible man to win. Now let's talk about this momentous ceremony. What can I do to help?"

"Nothing. Not one thing. Except you can tell me what's going on with you." Ash pointed to the brick of a coffee cake. "Since when do you bake?"

"Since I couldn't sleep and decided to hang with my new best friend, Betty Crocker."

"You're too funny. But really, it's barely eight-thirty, and you're sitting at my kitchen table looking like the world is coming to an end. So, spill. Now."

Marina forced out an exhausted breath. The endless number of sleepless nights marred her eyes with dark circles and left her body fatigued. "I had a really weird dream, and I can't get it out of my head," she confessed.

"I've never seen you so rattled before. Are you going to tell me what it was about, or do I need to guess?"

"It was about the day of my own Joining, about a million years ago." Marina chuckled. "You weren't even born yet. It was an exquisite autumn day. The trees had begun to change color, and the forest looked so alive and vibrant. I can still smell the air in the Outdoor Chapel if I close my eyes."

"I wish I'd been there. A Joining is the most beautiful ceremony we have in all of Aether. Ever since I was old enough to understand, I always pictured Hawk up there with me."

The memory tugged at Marina's heart. "Landon was standing next to my grandmother, waiting for me on the dais. The boy next door, literally and figuratively."

Landon and Coal's families resided under one roof right down the lane from Marina's house. They'd grown up like the three musketeers, but on the day of her Joining she'd pledged her love and devotion to only one of her best friends.

Ashlyn waggled her brows. "I bet Abercrombie looked good that day. Were all the girls jealous?"

"He always thought your nickname for him was hysterical. Landon never appreciated how incredibly handsome he was. That day, he took my breath away, and I'll never forget the expression on his face when he saw me walking toward him."

"It sounds like a wonderful dream. What's the problem?" The Fire Guardian asked.

"Hold your horses. I'm getting to it." Marina rolled her eyes. "As I was saying, Bey was officiating, and she looked so proud. Landon leaned in to kiss me, and my grandmother let out a peculiar sounding laugh. I turned away from him and caught her eye twinkling with her usual brand of mischief. But I remember thinking her timing was sort of strange. And when I twisted back around to face Landon, he started to morph before my eyes. His brown hair grew darker, his shoulders widened, and his eyes changed from warm chocolate to midnight blue."

Her friend gasped. "Coal. Dear Goddess, Landon turned into Coal right there on the dais?"

Marina nodded swallowing the lump in her throat. Her words croaked out, "Crazy, right? What do you think it means?"

"Are you seriously asking me that question? You're smart. What do you think it means?"

"I'm crazy, and I'm obsessed with my Kanti's cousin?"

Ashlyn laughed. "Obsessed, probably. Crazy, most likely not."

"Ugh! What am I going to do? I feel like I'm losing my mind. He's all I think about night and day, but I definitely think I may have pushed him too far this time. Running away after our night together didn't go over very well. The funny thing is I think I could be happy if I didn't feel so guilty about Landon." Marina's gaze dropped to the floor.

"Honey, do you really think Landon would want you to be alone for the rest of your life? Coal was more than his cousin. They were like brothers. Who better to love and adore you than Coal?"

"I'm not so sure Landon would agree with you. He was insanely jealous—especially of Coal."

Ashlyn covered Marina's hand with her own. "Why do you think that was? Come on, Marina, Landon knew you had a thing for Coal. He wasn't stupid. From what I hear, you and Coal had as much chemistry back then as you do now. Maybe your dream is telling you where your destiny truly lies."

"I think you've been talking to Lily too much. Besides, it doesn't matter because I totally blew it. I'm sure Coal hates me by now. He must think I'm a pendulum, the way I've swayed back and forth. If I were him, I wouldn't trust me one bit." Ash stared her down with a curious look in her eyes. "Dear Goddess, you're scaring me with that look. It reminds of Lily when she gets a crazy idea in her head."

"I was thinking—"

"Stop right there! That's how she always starts the conversation when she's planning some wacky scheme."

"Well, Lily is a very clever woman. And if you're right about Coal, then I think a grand gesture of some kind is in order. You need to prove to him you're serious this time, and you're not going to change your mind. You're not, are you?"

"No, I'm not. This dream is the final straw. Even my subconscious thinks I should be with Coal. Fighting my feelings has been exhausting. I'm done. I know I've said it before, but I really mean it this time. Since the universe keeps hitting me over the head with the idea, I guess Coal and I truly are destined to be together." Marina let out a huge sigh. "All right, you win. What's your plan?"

****

Coal

Walking into PH a little before noon, Coal found Hawk waiting for him at the reception desk. His lead Protector drummed his fingers on the counter, a scowl plastered on his face. Since the capture of Charles Barrington and his mercenary, every Protector pulsed with tension. They'd each assumed additional duties following their lead Protector's new protocol. Hawk and Quill's vendetta against the arrogant doctor ran deep, and Coal understood his friends' violent impulses toward the asshole. Charles Barrington manipulated everyone he came in contact with, exuding pure evil from every pore. His robotic sidekick, Heller, if that was even his real name, confounded them all, and was the reason Coal had been summoned to Protector Headquarters.

Coal nodded to his lead Protector. "Hey, how's it going?"

"I've been waiting for you, that's how it's going."

"It's barely noon. I was on guard duty, and I couldn't get anyone to take my shift. I told you this was the earliest I could be here. What's so important it couldn't wait?"

Hawk extended his arms and cracked his knuckles. "Sorry. I want everything to be in order before the Joining ceremony. I need to figure out the deal with this Heller character. For some crazy reason, his eyes followed you around the room last time you were guarding him. He's never done that before. He sits in his chair staring straight ahead. He hardly sleeps, and he hasn't eaten. Tell me what you said or did."

Coal raised his hands in surrender. "I didn't do or say anything. I have no idea what's going on with the guy. The lights are on, but nobody's home. All I did was bring him some soup. When I put it down, he looked right at me like he'd just woken up or something. It only lasted for a couple of seconds, and then he was back to staring at the wall again."

"Damn it!" Hawk slammed his fist down on the counter. "We have to figure out what's going on. Kai and Brooke have been running tons of blood tests, but he's pumped so full of different chemicals they can't make heads or tails out of any of it. Kai is convinced Barrington has been controlling this guy pharmaceutically. He also said Heller's medical profile fits an Aetherian to a T."

"Wait a second. Are you saying he's one of us?"

"Yes and no. Brooke and Kai both think Barrington altered his DNA somehow. Heller may not have been enhanced from birth, but it seems he's been reborn an Aetherian. Now we need to jumpstart this guy's engine, or we're never going to know what happened to him."

Pointing to himself, Coal's eyes popped wide. "And you think I can help?"

"Well, you're the only person Heller has shown even a remote interest in. I kind of feel bad for the guy, but he's still a wildcard. Who the hell knows what the doctor did to him." The massive sized Protector leaned back on the desk, his long legs stretched out.

Coal crossed his arms over his chest. "Barrington needs to be put down like a dog. Do you think the Elders are going to allow it?"

"I'm not sure what they're going to do, but I can tell you my grandfather hates Charles Barrington with a passion. And Bear can find a redeeming quality in a parasite. I only hope I get to be the one to end him after the way he tortured Ash, but I guess I'd have to get in line for that job."

"I certainly wouldn't mind taking the son of a bitch out. Poor Brooke, growing up with Barrington for a father must've been hell. How's she doing with all this?"

"She's pretty tough. Definitely a Guardian. You

can take the girl out of Aether, but you can't take Aether out of the girl. You heard what happened when she went to see Barrington, right?"

"Yeah, who hasn't?" Coal laughed.

"Well, Quill went nuts, and rumor has it my grandfather was the one who ended up explaining to good old Charles the way things are done in our world." Hawk smirked. "I can't tell you how much I wish I'd been a fly on the wall. I hope Bear brought the guy down a few pegs."

"Damn, I would've loved to have seen Bear in action."

"Believe me, we all would. It would be fun to go fuck with Barrington, but not today. Today is all about Heller. I want you to go in alone. I'll stay in the doorway and keep you covered. I need to see for myself how he reacts. You good to go?"

"What the hell"—Coal shrugged—"we've got nothing to lose by trying." He gestured toward the room. "After you, my fearless leader."

Hawk flipped him the bird. "I still haven't trained you hoodlums to simply shut up and obey orders. Let's go, Idris. We need to see if a wiseass like you can reach this guy. Who knows maybe it wasn't a one-time thing? Maybe he likes assholes?"

Coal gave him a light jab with his elbow to the ribs. "Very funny."

He followed Hawk down to the power neutralizing room they used for Protector training. Their experts had created this place more than twenty years ago. Coal had no idea how it worked, but it resulted in a level playing field where all Elemental enhancements became null and void.

They reached a red steel door with a bold sign posted on it: *Authorized Personnel Only.* River had required every Protector, young and old, to step behind the door to experience the unnerving sensation of being powerless. Coal's Fire surged through his veins, and his stomach tightened in knots. Endowed with his gift since the age of thirteen, his vulnerable reaction to the room's power drain had been like having his hands tied behind his back.

Hawk punched in the code on the keypad, and the locking mechanism clicked. The door swung open revealing Heller. The mercenary sat unmoving, feet planted in front of him, eyes glued to the wall. Hawk gave Coal an encouraging shove forward, and he stumbled into the room. Straightening, he glared back at his lead Protector, shooting him a dirty look. Even with the noisy intrusion, the mercenary remained in a trance-like state.

The comforting presence of Coal's powers vanished the moment his feet crossed the threshold. He squirmed, an emptiness spreading through him. Coal approached the stationary man and squatted down. Dark, puffy circles marred the soldier's eyes, and a ghostlike pallor covered his skin.

He whispered over his shoulder to Hawk, "Dear God, he looks terrible. The guy looks like he hasn't slept for a year."

Hawk pointed at Heller. "Get back to it."

Coal kept his tone soft. "Hey, buddy? Anybody home in there?" Heller's gaze shifted to him, and Coal jumped back a bit. "Holy crap, you surprised me. Can you hear me?" Coal waited, but Heller remained silent, his eyes focused on Coal's face. "Can't talk, huh? Blink if you can hear me." The mercenary's eyes opened and closed.

Hawk holstered his weapon, striding into the room. He inched closer to Coal, and to Heller he said, "I put my gun away. Now, don't do anything stupid." Hawk leaned in, speaking directly in Heller's ear this time. "I haven't figured you out yet, but if I find out you are with Barrington at any time, you're a dead man. Blink if you get *my* message."

Keeping his eyes locked on Coal, the soldier gave the most imperceptible of nods. His head fell to his shoulder, and his eyelids dropped down.

Coal wrapped his hands around Hawk's massive biceps tugging him away from Heller. "Hey, come on, we don't know that he was a willing party in any of this. It may not be his fault at all. Remember, you said you felt sorry for the guy, and now you're threatening him?"

"Just because I feel sorry for him doesn't mean I trust him. Besides, we can't be sure he's not still being controlled by Barrington."

"I understand, and I'm with you, but if we don't get him out of here, he is going to die. We can't let that happen with all of Barrington's secrets locked inside his head. Look at him; he's passed out cold. Come on, Hawk, the guy looks like shit. Let's get him to the Medical Center."

The Doors song, "Light My Fire," blasted from Hawk's pocket. The giant man flushed. "Um, I'm going to step into the hall for a sec and take this call."

Coal laughed out loud as Hawk left the room. Turning his attention back to the motionless soldier slumped in the chair, he said, "Too bad you have no clue about anything, because that was really funny. Don't worry, buddy; we're going to help you. No one should be controlled. I'm sure you're a good guy who doesn't deserve any of this."

His lead Protector walked in, his eyes focused on his boots. "I guess you figured out Ash has been tampering with my phone. You're going to pretend you didn't hear my new ringtone, and I promise not to kill you. Okay?"

Coal nodded, unable to hold back a smirk. "What ringtone?"

Hawk ignored him. "I'm going to see my grandfather about having sleeping beauty here transferred to the Medical Center. You're not coming with me because Ashlyn said you need to get to the West Tower immediately. I should warn you, she had a tone to her voice that scares the hell out of me a little, so good luck with that."

Slinging an arm around Coal's shoulder, Hawk led him out of the room. The heavy door closed behind them with a loud click. His lead Protector sent him one more devious look before waltzing off down the empty hallway, leaving Coal both confused and curious.

Chapter Sixteen
Brooke

She worked in the lab with Kai, moving in sync, and navigating their way through every task. Shaking her head, Brooke mumbled under her breath, "This is where I've belonged my whole life. With my dad, my real dad, not that monster I thought was my father. I've got to figure all of this out and make everything right here."

Kai's voice lured her from her thoughts. "You okay over there? Did you say something to me?"

"Thanks. I'm fine. I'm going over everything in my head."

His brows lifted. "That can't be good. Information overload. Not to mention an emotional one. I can't help thinking this is at least partially my fault for taking you to see Charles."

"Don't be ridiculous." Brooke waved off his comment. "It was my idea to go in the first place. You only offered to come with me. Believe me it's not only the stuff with him. So much has changed in my life in the past few weeks, and sometimes it's hard to process it all. But there's something that's been on my mind since we found out I'm your daughter. Do you mind if I ask you something that has nothing to do with Barrington, or the lab, or anything like that?"

"Of course not, you can ask me anything."

"Promise me you'll be one hundred percent honest."

"Always." Kai placed his hand over his heart. "I give you my word."

She hesitated before she asked, "Why does Laurel hate me?"

Kai's face fell. "Dear Goddess! She doesn't hate you. Why would you think that?"

Brooke gave him a pointed look. "You're kidding, right? Laurel has avoided me like the plague ever since I let the cat out of the bag at the Medical Center. When I asked Ash about it, she was totally cryptic. Tell me the truth. What's up with her?"

Kai eased the rack of test tubes in front of him aside and turned around in his chair. "First of all, it's not you. Every bad thing that's happened to you is my fault." He lowered his head. "I feel like all I do lately is apologize to you—I'm sorry." Kai brought his gaze up to meet hers, his blue eyes so much like her own. "Has anyone explained to you about reproduction in Aetherians?"

Heat rose to her cheeks. "Um, Kai, my mom had that talk with me when I was ten. Besides, you know I've been shacking up with your best friend for a while now, right? Not to embarrass either one of us, but it appears things work the same way in Aether as in the rest of the world."

"Was it necessary to leave me with that image?" He shook his head, his lip curling up. "Talk about oversharing."

She chuckled. "Sorry, but you left yourself open for that one."

"Quill is a terrible influence on those around him.

You were so sweet and polite when you first came to us. Now look at you." Kai laughed, but underneath he beamed at her. "You're so smart and beautiful, and I'm very proud to call you my daughter. And I know Laurel thinks very highly of you, too. It's really me she's upset with, not you."

"Ash told me you and Laurel weren't together when you knew my mom. Why would she be mad at you?"

"It's true. Laurel and I weren't together at the time you were, um, conceived, but we have been each other's true loves since we were young. You know Aetherians live for hundreds of years."

Brooke nodded. "Yeah, I'm still working on that one."

Kai tucked the hair that escaped her ponytail behind her ear. "It must seem crazy, all of this, Aether I mean. The Elements, magic, a family you've never known, but I'm going to help you work through it. I've always been conflicted as an Aetherian, and I can tell it's the same for you. You come from a world of science. Logic and facts. Trial and error. Magic is based more on belief and instinct, but it's also part science. You'll have to learn, as I did, that these two worlds can mesh together if your mind is open to the possibilities."

She blew out an audible breath. "Believe me, I've been trying for weeks, but I still don't understand. What aren't you telling me about procreation in Aether?"

He cleared his throat. "Well, according to the Elders, the God and Goddess created a plan for the Aetherians and the rest of humankind in order to keep balance on the planet. The population of the village has always remained constant, a system of checks and balances, so to speak. If Aetherian numbers grow too large, then the equity of power would be thrown off."

"I'm a little confused. You're saying the God and Goddess don't want there to be too many Aetherians?"

"Exactly. Elemental enhancements in excess tip the scales too much. Many Aetherians never conceive children, and if they do, it's very rare to have subsequent offspring. So, maybe you can—"

"Oh my God! No wonder why she can't look at me. Laurel thinks you blew your only chance of having kids on my mom. She's a teacher. She's all about kids. I feel like the devil incarnate. *Ahch!* Great. Someone else who hates me." She plopped down on the seat next to him and rested her head on the counter.

"No one hates you, Brooke, especially not Laurel. She's simply trying to come to terms with the possibility of being childless. It happens to a lot of Aetherian couples. The God and Goddess don't want to punish anyone. Couples aren't endowed because they're more powerful, or special. It's simply a matter of random luck. Laurel and I can still be lucky."

"Do you think I should talk to her? You know, tell her I'm sorry or something?"

Kai placed his hand on her shoulder. "You have nothing to apologize for. I'll always feel sad if Laurel and I aren't blessed with a baby, but I'll never be sorry for having you. I'm so glad you're here, in Aether, and part of my life. I love you, Brooke."

She wrapped her arms around Kai's neck, tears filling her eyes. "I love you too, Dad. Thanks for telling me the truth."

He whispered back, "Always."

She glanced over his shoulder, and a glint of blue

sparkled in one of the test tubes, catching her eye. She pulled back from Kai and exclaimed, "Look! This is exactly what we've been waiting for. I think you've figured it out. You're a genius."

"I don't know about that. It was your work on breaking down the compounds which solidified our hypothesis. The combination of drugs Heller was given, in addition to the properties in Ashlyn's blood, were somehow synthesized, altering his DNA. I wish we knew what Barrington did to achieve this result. We need to report this to the Elders." Kai picked up the tube containing the fluorescent colored liquid, swirling it around. Squinting his eyes, he raised the glass tube to the light, examining it.

Brooke pouted. "Can't you see the Elders without me? They still kind of scare me. I feel completely weird when I'm around them."

Kai stroked her cheek. "It's your power sensing the greatness of the Elders' combined strength. You'll learn to channel it."

"Okay, we'll go talk to the old folks." She smirked. "But I really—"

Quill and Hawk rushed into the lab, the lead Protector's deep voice ringing out. "Sorry to disturb you guys at work, but get this, Barrington is insisting on seeing both of you immediately."

Quill's words snarled out. "I said no way you would be willing to see The Nameless Asshole again. Am I right?"

Brooke moved toward Quill. "That depends. Why does he want to see us?"

Hawk took a seat on one of the stools by their workstation. "I'm not exactly sure, but he's definitely worried about Heller. He said if the guy doesn't get medical attention soon, he'll die. Considering the soldier's current state of health, Barrington isn't lying. We need Heller alive. What's in this guy's head could be the answer to stopping the crazy-ass doctor once and for all. I understand if you don't want to face Barrington again, but I'd consider it a personal favor if you would. It's not like Barrington is going to share his plan with us. Heller may be our only chance."

The lead Protector's appeal hit home, and Brooke wrapped her arms around Quill's waist gazing up at him. "We have to trick Charles into telling us if there are any others like Heller out there in the human world. You've been telling me since the first time you saw my mark that I'm a Guardian." Brooke quirked her brow at Quill. "Well then, isn't it my duty to protect the people any way I can? Besides, if we play our cards right, Charles might inadvertently help us." She squeezed Quill tight. "What do you say?"

"All right, but I'm coming with you this time." Quill kissed the top of her head and turned to Kai. "What about you? Are you up for another round with your old friend?"

"It looks like I have no choice. Heller hasn't uttered a single word since he's been captured, but it appears he is no longer catatonic. His eyes have been tracking both objects and people for the past few hours, but the only nutrition he's received is through an IV. We're running out of time, and Charles holds the answers to all of our questions. Brooke and I are relatively certain we've discovered the reason for Mr. Heller's newly acquired powers. We believe the alteration to his DNA is permanent. I'll explain on the way to PH."

Brooke piped in. "Well, let's get the ball rolling. If I know Charles Barrington, we have no time to waste."

****

Quill

Shifting into lead Protector mode, Hawk's voice deepened, "You all know what to do. We each have a role to play, so don't anybody lose your cool and blow it. Remember what the Buddhists say; the key to life is not to know all the answers but to understand the questions."

Brooke laughed. "Wow, you sounded exactly like Bear."

Quill nodded to Kai and Brooke. "Kind of scary, don't you think?"

Hawk sneered with a shake of his head. "No one is listening to you, Quill. And I'm serious. No matter what Barrington says or does, don't deviate from our plan."

"Yeah, yeah, yeah. Don't kill The Nameless Asshole until you say so. I got it," Quill grumbled.

Kai chimed in, "It's no joke. We need him alive, so we can obtain and analyze the rest of his research. Without the information in his records, and the drugs he's created, we don't stand a chance of keeping this situation under control."

Brooke's hands flew to her hips. "Honestly, this situation is already way out of control. Can we please stop talking and get this over with?"

Quill leaned over, whispering in her ear, "Don't be nervous, baby. He can't hurt you." Brooke shoved him hard, and he pretended to lose his balance, catching himself and giving her a playful wink.

Her cute nose wrinkled at the bridge. "You don't

always know what I'm thinking. I'm not nervous—
I'm—"

Hawk's baritone rang out. "You'll be fine, Brooke.
We have faith in you." Hawk threw his best lead
Protector's glare Quill's way. "Let's have less talk and
more action, shall we? Now follow me."

The group walked down the hall in silence. Taking
a deep breath, Quill focused on their plan mumbling a
quiet mantra, "Don't kill the prick. Don't kill the
prick."

Brooke grabbed his hand giving it a gentle squeeze.
"Please, behave. I'm okay. I don't care what he says
even if I act otherwise."

Quill bent down, placing a kiss on her cheek. "I
know. I trust you and our plan."

Their group rounded the corner, and the Protector
on duty resting casually against the wall jumped to
attention. "Hello, sir. Good to see you, sir."

Quill rolled his eyes muttering under his breath,
"Newbies."

Hawk ignored Quill's comment and greeted the
young soldier, "Yeah, uh, good to see you, too." He
handed the kid a slip of paper. "I need you to go get
something for me, and when you come back, we'll be
inside talking to Barrington. You are to wait outside
this door unless I specifically instruct you to do
otherwise. Do not enter this room no matter what you
hear. Am I making myself clear?"

The young Protector's voice squeaked out "Crystal,
sir." He stared at Hawk fidgeting where he stood.

Hawk blew out a forceful breath. "Well? What are
you waiting for? Go."

"Sorry, sir, right away, sir." The kid took off at a

jog down the hall.

Hawk punched the code into the keypad. Quill's powers kicked into action, and he closed his eyes for a moment seizing control of his gift, calling his Air back inside.

The lead Protector pushed the heavy door open, and a memory of River entering Barrington Labs before he'd been shot sent a cold chill down Quill's spine. No gunfire waited for them this time, only Charles Barrington. The disheveled doctor paced the confines of his tiny room. Quill's mouth gaped, and he quickly snapped it shut. Barrington's hair, which had been neatly combed the other day, stood on end.

Charles froze in place. His right hand settled on his hip, and his scuffed shoe tapped in a staccato rhythm on the tiled floor. "Finally, I summoned you quite some time ago. You know I don't like to be kept waiting." The doctor's aggressive tone drew Hawk to him. Their lead Protector unfolded his arms gripping the gun strapped to his side. Charles' posture tensed. He fell silent swallowing a half dozen times in a row, his Adam's apple bobbing up and down.

Brooke pulled her shoulders back. "I'm here now. What is it you wanted to discuss?"

Barrington's voice lost a bit of its malice, "I heard one of the guards saying they were taking Mr. Heller to a medical facility. I insist you bring me to him at once. He needs my intervention, or he will most assuredly perish." The doctor's veneer peeled away a layer at a time exposing his weakening resolve.

"Let's sit down, and we can talk about it." Kai gestured toward a small table and four chairs set up in the corner of the room. A lonely looking partially-eaten sandwich sat on a tray in the center of the table next to a half-filled bottle of water. "Actually, there are a few things we'd like to talk to you about as well."

Charles' eyes narrowed, but he followed Kai to the table anyway. The chairs scraped across the floor in the awkward silence. Brooke, Kai, and Barrington all took seats, but Quill and Hawk stood looming over them.

The doctor studied Kai. "You are not Kai Sanders. I believe you are his son sent here in an attempt to unhinge me. I was understandably stunned by the resemblance between you and your father initially. Therefore, I failed to analyze the facts." Barrington leaned back in his chair. "It won't work. You can't make a fool out of me. Tell your father to come and see me himself if he dares."

A wide smile stretched across Kai's face. "Well, Charlie Boy, I can assure you, I am most definitely Kai Sanders. Perhaps your research isn't quite as thorough as you thought. The life expectancy in Aether is approximately six hundred years. Though some individuals have pushed the boundaries of that number. I believe you met Bear, one of our Elders, the other day. I'm sure you remember him. Extremely large and powerful. The man recently celebrated his four hundred and fiftieth birthday."

A dark red flush rose up from Barrington's neck to his face. "I refuse to allow you to incite me. This farce is nearly over. I will be released from here shortly." He tugged on the collar of his bloodstained shirt and ran his hands down the wrinkled material.

Poised in her calm approach, Brooke addressed Barrington in a matter-of-fact monotone, "In that case, let's move on. Why the urgent need to see Mr. Heller?

Is there something you believe we should know in regard to his condition?"

"I'm the only one who can get through to him. He won't eat or drink anything unless I give him the order. Surely, even you *people* comprehend what happens to a man without any food or water. You must allow me access to him," Barrington's voice held a subtle note of desperation.

Brooke sat erect, her hands folded neatly on the table in front of her. Kai fiddled inside his pocket producing three capped test tubes. Two of the glass vials contained a transparent, colorless fluid, and the third held a blue, fluorescent liquid. Kai rotated the glass tubes again and again clinking them together in a quiet rhythm. The newly formed father and daughter team worked Barrington like a pair of champion interrogators from the FBI.

Charles' eyes followed the movement of Kai's hand and widened with recognition. "What do you have there, Mr. Sanders?"

"It's Dr. Sanders, as you well know. These are a few of our own experiment results." Kai continued toying with the vials and said nothing else.

Barrington ran his fingers through his hair, the salt-and-pepper pieces standing on end. Quill reveled in the pretentious doctor's breakdown, but Brooke had barely moved a muscle since taking a seat, and worry about her niggled at his gut.

Charles' gaze zeroed in on the self-composed Guardian in front of him, and his voice wavered, "Brooke, you must realize these so called, *people*, have brainwashed you. I forgive you. Now take me to Mr. Heller at once, and when I am set free, I will take you with me."

Brooke dug into her pocket yanking out Olivia's hidden flash drive. She slid Barrington's discarded lunch tray aside and placed the memory stick directly in front of him. He pursed his lips, eyeing the tiny piece of technology. Brooke resumed her position clasping her hands in front of her on the table.

She broke the silence after several minutes. "I'm not interested in going anywhere with you. Aether is my home." Brooke raised her hand and pointed to her mark on her palm. "This symbol means I'm The Guardian of The House of Water. This is where I belong. The flash drive in front of you was left to me by my mother. It contains every scrap of information you have on Aether and all of your secret research. Obviously, Ashlyn's blood was the key to your plan coming to fruition. You must know we can't allow you to continue." She refolded her hands placing them back on the table.

A quiet sigh slipped from the doctor's mouth. Small cracks were forming in the haughty man's hard outer shell, and the time to take advantage of the situation neared. Kai adjusted the vials in his grasp noisily, drawing Barrington's focus.

Charles' cheeks flushed a bit. "Are you going to tell me what you're fidgeting with, Sanders?"

"Why don't you tell me what you think they are?" Kai opened his hand displaying the test tubes.

"Colored water? Olivia didn't know anything and neither do you." Charles folded his arms over his chest.

"I'm afraid you've grossly underestimated Aether and our resources, Charles. Our lab is much more sophisticated than you think. Our science far surpasses even the most advanced technology in your world. We've been able to break down the drug composition you created to enhance Mr. Heller, but I'm afraid your research is faulty." Kai plucked the blue tube from the group and held it up to Charles. "According to our experiments, you have permanently altered his DNA, and his body is rejecting the change. I believe Mr. Heller's days are numbered."

Charles rushed to his feet tipping his chair in the process. "Barrington Laboratories is the number one pharmaceutical company in the world, and my labs are cutting-edge. There is absolutely nothing erroneous in my research. You have no idea what you're playing with here."

Hawk pulled his gun from its holster drawing on the doctor. "I think you'd better calm down if you value your life."

"You do not intimidate me in the slightest," Barrington responded in an arrogant tone. "Take me to Heller at once."

Brooke slammed her palms on the table. "That is never going to happen."

"Why on earth not?" The doctor gripped the edge of the table.

Kai's countered, "Let me ask you a question. What would you do in our position?"

Ignoring Kai, Barrington held Brooke's gaze. "We are running out of time. As your father, I'm asking you to take me to my subject."

She leaned in close and spoke softly, "I thought we already discussed my paternity. You are not my father. You're a psychopath. I'm not taking you to see Mr. Heller, who is a person by the way, or at least he was until you turned him into a robot. The line of engineered humans ends with him. We've located all of your labs and are going to destroy your research and samples. Mr. Heller will be the first and last of his kind."

A crimson blush flooded Barrington's cheeks. "You are sorely mistaken. I have a very special subject ready to go as soon as my team comes to retrieve me. My research facility is so well hidden you can search the entire Northeast, and you'll never find it." Charles' volume escalated.

Wrapping his hand around his weapon, Quill inched closer to the doctor, his palms itching to dispatch the smug prick once and for all. Hawk lifted his chin subtly shaking his head, signaling Quill to back down.

Kai responded, "What you're saying is in direct contrast with our findings. Perhaps you can explain it to us?" His sarcasm wasn't part of the plan. "Try using simple vocabulary so we can understand." Hawk put his hand on Kai's shoulder, and his friend's posture relaxed a bit.

Charles stammered, "I-I-don't have to explain anything to you."

Brooke leaned on her elbows. "If you don't want to tell us about your research maybe you can tell us how you managed to get through Aether's protective shields? Or you can explain why you came back here. Do your buyers need more powerful super soldiers?" She waved her hand dismissively in Barrington's direction and addressed Kai, "We should go, Dad, he's bluffing. He's got nothing left, and Heller will be dead by the end of the week."

Charles pounded his clenched fists on the table. "Your information on Mr. Heller's condition is inaccurate. He has been thoroughly tested. Our protocols were set up very specifically to prepare for our true subject. This person's qualifications far surpass those of Mr. Heller. He's not some soldier we yanked off the battlefield in the Middle East. His constitution is beyond the ordinary, and his mind is even more impressive."

Brooke rose to her feet confronting her former father. "You're delusional. How do you think you're going to accomplish anything when you're a prisoner in Aether?"

Barrington shouted; spit flying from his mouth, "My men will come for me! Breaching your pitiful barrier was mere child's play. Since you think you're so smart, why don't you figure out how we got into Aether. And as for Mr. Heller, it's a shame you've destroyed him. He's been a very useful tool, and if he's in any jeopardy right now, it's due to your maltreatment." The doctor's eyes narrowed into slits, and his complexion turned the color of a beetroot. He faced Brooke, venom oozing from his lips. "I can see you're a hopeless case. There's no saving you. Perhaps you *are* one of these mutant aberrations. I should be the only one controlling this power. Everyone in Aether needs to die."

Brooke lost control shouting across the table at the unhinged doctor. "You're the one who needs to die!"

Barrington snapped, diving across the table, his arms flailing in every direction. Unflinching, Brooke stood her ground, but it didn't matter because Quill grabbed the man by the shoulders throwing him into the wall with a loud thud.

The Protector slipped one arm around Barrington's neck, his gun coming up under the man's chin. "One more move and you're dead."

Brooke tucked a few blonde wisps behind her ears. "Don't waste your energy on him, Quill. I think he needs to cool off a bit."

She eyed Barrington's discarded water bottle, and Quill could tell from the look on her face, she was up to something. Placing her marked palm over the opening of the container, Brooke rotated her hand in a continuous circular motion. The water funneled up, churning along with the ascent of her hand. The doctor's eyes followed the path of the clear liquid now floating midair. She flicked her wrist, and the stream of water gathered like a rain cloud above Charles. She squinted her eyes tight, and the water poured down on his head in a mini deluge. Quill broke out laughing. Droplets of water dripped from Barrington's hair. Kai wrapped his arm around Brooke's shoulder and escorted her out of the room without another word.

Quill manhandled the now soaked Barrington into a chair. "Hey, genius, is it starting to sink in yet? You can't beat us." He looked to Hawk. "Can we get away from this asshole now?"

"Wait one second, buddy." Hawk whistled between his teeth to the young Protector waiting in the hall. "Hey, kid, bring that in now."

He entered, handing Hawk a small plastic bag. "Here you go, sir. I'll wait outside the door, sir." The newbie backed out of the room, keeping his eye on them the entire time.

Their lead Protector bent low, speaking in

Barrington's ear, "My young friend over there is going to take you for a shower because your stench is becoming offensive." Reaching inside the bag, Hawk produced a folded article of clothing, shook it out, and placed it in front of Charles. A thin, blue, floral hospital gown rested on the table. "Ashlyn wanted to make sure you had something clean to change into. I hear these are all the rage for guests to don." He picked up the gown tossing it at Barrington. "I know Ashlyn always appreciated your hospitality. We wanted to be sure to return the favor." To Quill, he said, "Let him go. He's a weak, pathetic man. He told us what we wanted to know. We have no use for him anymore."

The door slammed behind them, and Barrington's ranting and raving became a strangled cry in the quiet background of Protector Headquarters.

Chapter Seventeen
Marina

"Hurry up, Ash. He's going to be here any second." Perched on a stool in front of her vanity for the past thirty minutes, Marina nudged Ashlyn with her bare foot. "It looks like a department store makeup counter exploded in here."

"Relax. I'm almost finished. I've been dying to get my hands on you since Brooke's party. Lily did a great job, but I wanted a crack at you, too. You look gorgeous by the way." Ash spun her around to face the mirror. "Look at that face, another perfect canvas." The Fire Guardian dabbed a couple of dots of sparkle in the corner of each of Marina's eyes and pulled back admiring her. "My work here is done. You'd put any supermodel to shame."

Marina dismissed the compliment. "Oh please. Have you looked around Aether? I'm nothing special. Now can you guys finish up and get out of here already? That is part of your plan, right? You know, to leave before he gets here."

Lily poked her head into the bathroom. "Wow! You look stunning. Ash, you're truly an artist. You put my skills to shame. He's going to need to be resuscitated the minute he sees you, Marina."

"Thanks, girls, but I'm not sure anything is going to be enough after what I've put him through."

Lily walked up behind Marina, bent low, and hugged her around the neck. "You'd be surprised what a man in love is capable of. And Coal loves you. And you love him. So, can you please get over yourself already?" To Ash, she said, "Come on, back me up here."

"Honestly, I couldn't agree more. Look what Hawk did to get me back from Barrington's lab. Lily is right. You have to try. You deserve this." Ash enveloped them both in her long arms piling onto their hug.

Marina pushed them off playfully. "Dear Goddess, you're both way too much. I said I'd do it, didn't I? Hello, look at me. You know what I have on under this robe." She nodded toward Ash. "And let's not talk about what The Covergirl Queen here did to me. I'm worried it was all for nothing, and it won't work. What if after all this he rejects me?"

Lily brushed her hands over her expanding belly. "He won't. Trust me."

"If he does, he's crazy. Besides, it's too late. He's going to be here soon." The beautiful Fire Guardian smirked.

"I think I'm going to be sick. How did I let you talk me into this, Ash?" Marina shot Lily a dirty look. "I see you smiling over there. You're not off the hook. I bet the two of you planned this all along." She scrunched up her eyes, scrutinizing her friends.

Muffling giggles behind her hand, Lily's baby bump shimmied with every chuckle. "Sorry. We're only looking out for your best interests. You and Coal make a perfect couple." Her laughing ceased, and she gave Marina a tight squeeze. "You belong together."

"Speak from your heart. Once Coal sees you and

the lengths you've gone to today, he'll know you aren't going to change your mind." Ashlyn fanned her face with her hand. "When he comes in and finds you—"

Lily turned serious. "It's going to be perfect. You'll see. Now let's get you into position, so we can get out of here. You ready?"

Nerves crept through Marina's body. "As I'll ever be." Gazing up toward the sky, she let out a breathy sigh. "Dear Goddess, please don't let me make a total fool of myself."

****

Coal

Opening the door to the West Tower, Coal shouted into the quiet space, "Marina? Everything okay? Hawk said you needed to see me right away."

Her faint voice drifted from the master suite. "In here."

Coal grumbled under his breath, "Things are getting stranger by the minute around here. First, she wants nothing to do with me, then she seduces me. After, she avoids me like the damn plague. What now?" He placed both hands on the door and barged directly into the room. "Look, I'm done with all this bullshit be—"

Coal's body went rigid. He struggled to make sense of the image set before him. Marina was sprawled out on the bed spread eagle, her wrists and ankles bound to the four corners of the frame. Long blonde hair draped across her pillow in a halo. A skin-tight corset, laced up the front, fit the Guardian like a glove, a naughty angel dressed in lingerie, wrapped up like a present just for him. Her magnificent breasts spilled in lush swells from the confines of her sexy garment. He licked his lips.

Marina's words slipped out, sexy and breathy. "Hi, I've been waiting for you."

He found his voice. "What the hell is going on here?"

"We need to talk."

"You're kidding, right?" He flung his hand toward her restrained form. "This is not talking. This is—crazy. I don't understand."

"I wanted to tell you how sorry I am for the way I've been acting."

He cleared his throat. "And this is your way of apologizing?"

"Yes, sort of. I know this seems a little nuts, but I didn't know what else to do. I panicked the last time we were together, but it's not going to happen again. I'm yours, and"—her gaze shifted to her restrained limbs—"I want to tie myself to you in every way." A girlish giggle bubbled out, and a blush crept across her entire body. "I need to prove to you that I'm all in this time."

Coal shook his head never taking his eyes off her. "I shouldn't have pushed you so hard. I can't believe you did this. Who the hell tied you to your bed?" His hand shot up cutting off her answer. "Wait, let me guess, Lily and Ash? I'm not sure what you were thinking, if in fact, you were thinking at all. This is absurd. I'm untying you." Taking a seat on the end of the bed, Coal reached for the silk cord wrapped in an intricate pattern around her ankle.

"Please, don't. Listen to me. I'm trying to show you how vulnerable I am when it comes to you. I always have been. We can't go back and rewrite history, and I'm not sure I would want to, but I'm ready to move forward with you, for good this time."

Coal dropped her stocking-covered foot, meeting her beautiful blue eyes. "I've heard it before, Marina. Why should I believe it's any different this time?"

"Um, maybe you should go check out the closet and the bathroom."

He blew out an exasperated breath. "I'm really starting to worry about you. You're acting crazy."

"Please, go look."

He rose moving toward the large walk-in closet. Flipping on the light switch, Coal's eyes adjusted zeroing in on Landon's side of the closet. Conspicuously empty for some time, the space now held a man's wardrobe. A familiar garment caught his eye. Coal's favorite NYU sweatshirt sat neatly folded on a shelf. His jeans hung on matching wooden hangers, arranged from dark to light. Receiving the same care, his T-shirts lay in precise color coordinated piles. His sneakers and boots were spread out across special angled shelves, their laces tied in careful bows. This little project had Lily written all over it.

Coal stepped out of the closet shaking his head. "I don't get it. Where is this coming from? I've tried to talk to you a thousand times since we got together, but you keep avoiding me. Now, all of the sudden, you moved me into the tower?" He took a seat next to her. "What's really going on with you?"

Marina's soft voice filled the air. "I want you here with me all the time. I want your face to be the first one I see when I wake up in the morning and the last one I see when I close my eyes at night. There's something else, remember I told you about my nightmares?"

"Of course."

Marina continued, "A few days after we, um, were

together, Cassy found me down by the Grand Lake. We sat for a long time talking. I hadn't realized she'd trained as a therapist. Anyway, I've been seeing her every day and working through some of my baggage. Cassy says I have a form of PTSD. She's been a lifesaver. We do relaxation techniques, and she gave me some herbal supplements to help me sleep. I know I have a long way to go, and Cassy says this will probably be something I always struggle with, but I'm doing better. I haven't had a nightmare in quite a few days."

"I'm glad to hear that. I truly am, but what does this have to do with us?"

"For the first time in a very long time, I had a different dream. This time, it took place on the day of my Joining to Landon—"

Coal jumped to his feet. "I'm going. I'll send one of your friends to cut you loose."

He took two steps from the bed, and she cried out, "Stop! Hear me out. That's all I'm asking."

"Why on Earth would I want to hear about your special romantic day? I'll never forget watching the woman I love and my best friend Join. You must know my heart broke that day." He lowered his gaze.

"I'm sorry, Coal, I never meant to hurt you, but I'm starting to think this is the way things were destined to be. Fate is drawing us together and showing me our time is now. The dream I had was about us, not Landon."

He dropped back down onto the end of the bed. "I don't understand."

"In my dream, I was standing on the dais about to kiss Landon, and he turned into you. I know it sounds crazy, but I think it was the God and Goddess' way of proving to me we belong together. Listen, we both loved Landon, but he lied to us. He kept us apart because he wanted me for himself. He wasn't a malicious person, but he put his needs first, and you and I both know love is about sacrifice, about giving up everything for the other person." A single tear leaked out of the corner of her eye and ran in a silvery path down her cheek. "Cassy helped me to see things more clearly. I finally believe, with my whole heart, our love has been written in the stars. Our friends came together to help move all of your stuff here because they agree we with me. I know I didn't say it before because I was too scared, but I'm saying it now. I love you, Coal. I always have, and I always will."

He brushed the tear from her cheek. "I love you, too. But what you're saying doesn't make sense. You had a dream about us kissing, and now you want me to live with you? How is that logical?"

"It's not. Because love isn't logical. It's never made sense to me. Until now. I loved Landon, but something was always missing between us. Never in all the years I spent with him, did I feel the way I feel when I'm with you."

"All those years ago when we were teenagers, I let Landon take you from me because I truly believed I wasn't worthy of your love. I should've trusted myself and my feelings for you. If only I'd kept kissing you and never stopped, maybe things would be different today." He closed his eyes for a brief moment opening them to Marina's incredible blue eyes brimming with tears. "You know, you could've talked to me. None of this was necessary. I would've listened."

"I wanted to show you, so you could see how serious I am. I've done too much talking, too much thinking, too much of everything but feeling. You're the one I've always wanted, and it's not a secret I care to hide anymore. You're my person, Coal, the one I want to share the rest of my life with. Please, I have to know, do you want that, too?"

****

Marina

Coal's soft lips followed the trail of tears flowing down her dampened cheek. "Every minute of every day, I've loved you. Even before I understood what the word meant, I loved you. There's nothing on this Earth I want more than to spend the rest of our lives showing you how much."

The heat of his breath tickled her neck. Goosebumps blossomed, racing up and down her skin. Marina's nipples tightened abrading against the delicate fabric of her lingerie. Her lips parted, hungry for his kiss.

Breathy and desperate, Marina's words rushed out, "You can untie me now."

"You're right. I certainly can, but I think I like you this way." He ran a finger down the laces of her corset. "You look gorgeous. Your friends may be over the top, but they do fine work."

"It was supposed to be a symbolic gesture, not an invitation."

He shook his head. "Yeah, um, sorry, that's not the vibe you're projecting here. It's more of a, here I am, come and get me kind of thing. Honestly, what did you think was going to happen when you had your crazy friends tie you to a bed?" Coal tugged on one of the dangling laces of her corset, and the snug fitting garment loosened, giving way. Her breasts popped free from their confinement. He smiled lasciviously, and her body melted into a puddle.

Marina glided her tongue across her lips. "I guess I didn't really think about the consequences. I needed to prove myself to you."

"Oh, you've definitely proven yourself to me. And now I'm going to prove to you—" He licked a path between her breasts. "—that it was brilliant planning on your part. Those little troublemakers you call your friends are much more devious than I give them credit for. You're impossible to resist like this."

"Come on, Coal, really, untie me."

"Really, baby, not a chance." He grabbed the corset from both sides ripping it open, leaving her exposed to his molten gaze.

Her nipples hardened further under his intense scrutiny, and air rushed from her lungs. "Ooohh—"

"What was that? Did you say something?" He ran his warm hands all the way from her breasts down to her legs. "I love these stockings by the way. You look so sexy."

The unabating electricity between them burned hotter than ever. His fingers danced along her flesh sending shivers down her spine. Coal slid his hands beneath the elastic band holding up her thigh highs. At a maddeningly glacial pace, he rolled her stockings from thigh to ankle, one leg at a time, lighting up every inch of her skin along the way. He dragged the nylons down to the cords tied right above her feet and slipped the thin, silky material through the restraints with ease.

Coal's hands roamed her body in a sensual

exploration. Marina squirmed, an ache forming at her core. She struggled against the silken restraints, bucking up into his sizzling touch. A flood of desire spread through her body.

"You're like liquid fire, Coal. Please, I need more."

"Don't worry, baby, I know exactly what you need—" He skimmed the inside of her thighs with a light scratch of his nails. "—but you're going to have to wait. I'm not done playing yet."

"Now you're being mean." Marina pouted.

He placed his hand over his heart. "I'm offended. I would never be mean to you, my love. Your pleasure is my pleasure." Coal's hands drifted upward finding her heaving breasts.

With her corset splayed open beneath her, Marina wore nothing but a tiny pair of panties. They tied at her hips and consisted of a couple of strings and a narrow strip of lace. Ashlyn insisted the panties were a necessary part of the ensemble, and the laws of fashion required Marina to keep the set intact.

"Untie me, and I'll show you pleasure."

Coal shook his head giving her a sexy wink. "Patience is a virtue." Zeroing in on her breasts, he kneaded the sensitive peaks. He lowered his mouth feasting on her heated flesh.

Marina cried out, "Dear Goddess, you're going to kill me."

"Oh, I'm not going to kill you, baby. I'm just going to torture you the way you've been torturing me." He reached for the strings of her panties, gathered the thin ties in his large grip, and gave them a hard tug. "Mmm, look what I did."

"Coal—" His name drifted from her lips on a soft

whisper.

"You're the most beautiful woman I have ever seen. Say you're mine."

"I'm yours, forever and always. Now please, untie me because if I don't touch you this minute, I'm going to scream. And you know, Lily and Ash will come running if I do, and we don't want that, do we?"

He leaned over kissing her tenderly. "I'll tell you what. I'll untie your legs because I want you to be able to wrap them around me when I'm inside of you. We'll see about your hands, if you're a good girl." Coal kneeled beside the bed releasing the ties at her feet.

She brought her knees up, stretching her legs. "Ahh. Feels good to move again. Now how about another kiss?"

"From where I'm sitting, you are in no position to make demands." Fire danced in his eyes.

"I think you may be enjoying this whole bondage thing a little too much. Stop looking at me like that." Heat rose to her cheeks.

"If you're going to be mine forever, you'd better get used to it."

Her voice shook. "Wait a minute. Get used to what? Bondage? Or you looking at me like that?"

"Both." Coal's lips crashed down on hers, their tongues tangling in a passionate duel.

Her gift opened sensing his love, Fire, and desire. The Protector's emotions flooded her system mingling with her own. He'd worked his way into her soul, joining with her in a way she didn't know existed. Marina gave in to the deluge allowing it to flow through her.

He jumped up untying the remaining restraints. His

shirt flew over his head revealing his beautiful, sculpted chest. Ripping open his button fly, Coal yanked his jeans, underwear, and sneakers off in one swift motion. Climbing his way up the bed, he pulled her close.

Marina brought her fingertip to his lips running it over the sensual bows. He captured her pointer in his teeth with a gentle bite. "Hey!" She protested, but her nipples tightened from the playful nip.

Laughing, he surrendered her helpless digit. "I couldn't resist. You're very biteable." Propped up on his elbows, Coal gazed down at her. "It always feels so natural when I'm with you." He stroked his hand down the length of her hair.

Marina leaned in to his touch. Coal might never understand how much his one little statement meant to her. Being an empath wasn't always easy. Feeling the weight of others' emotions could be pretty draining. Most of the time, she kept her shields locked firmly in place, but with Coal, things somehow felt different. She could peel back her armor and allow their emotions to fuse together. When he touched her, the rest of the world melted away, and everyone and everything ceased to exist.

"I love you so much, Coal." She stretched up kissing his neck. "Mmm, you taste and smell amazing." She licked her way down his muscled chest to his defined abs, appreciating his ultra-fit body. The man was beautiful, and he was all hers. Marina took hold of his erection stroking his length over and over again. She brought her mouth down to his pulsating arousal. Her tongue caressed his torrid flesh, and his fingers tunneled into her hair urging her on.

Coal's ragged words panted out. "Baby, I love your

mouth on me, but you have to stop or I'm not going to last." He gently flipped her onto her back. "Now, that's more what I had in mind before you tried to top me from the bottom."

A warm blush heated her already fiery skin. "It's not my fault. You untied me."

"I'll keep that in mind for next time." Flashing her a sexy smile, he put a hand on each of her knees slowly prying them apart. "It's my turn."

Marina squirmed, and he ignored her, placing lazy, wet kisses on the inside of her thighs. Reaching her core, his talented tongue licked and teased her until she writhed, mad with desire. "Please, Coal, I need you."

Slowly, he kissed his way up her pliant body. Reaching her mouth, he pulled her close fusing their lips together. He entered her with one strong thrust of his hips. Fire surged through her all the way to her toes, every nerve ending alight. He paused, giving her a moment to adjust to his impressive size.

"You feel so good, baby. I've missed being inside you. It's where I belong…" Coal's words fell off.

In a sensual dance, they found their rhythm together, ebbing and flowing as one. Her voice rasped out, "I'm so close, I—"

"It's okay, baby, come for me."

Coal's instruction worked as a direct line to her pulsing core. Marina ground against him driving him deeper. Plunging her fingers into his hair, her breath rushed out in ragged pants. Coal increased his pace setting a massive climax into motion. Little by little the sensations built, and she gripped his shoulders, her fingers digging into his flesh. He pounded into her, and his name broke free from her lips in a scream. Coal brought his mouth to hers thrusting his hips one last time, emptying his seed deep inside her. Marina wrapped her legs around his back, never wanting to separate from this incredible man.

Running her fingers through his short, spiky hair, she gazed into his midnight eyes. "I want my dream to come true. I want to kiss you on the dais in the Outdoor Chapel in front of all of Aether and Join as one."

"Marina Dover Hill, are you asking me to Join with you?"

She kissed his neck. "I suppose, I am. So, what do you say? Will you Join with me?"

Coal tapped the side of his temple. "Hmm. I'm going to have to think about it. You seem kind of high maintenance." He winked and brought his lips to hers with a loud smooch. "You know, what the hell. Sure, why not."

Elbowing him in the ribs, Marina laughed with unbound freedom. "I love you, Coal."

"I love you, too, my sweet, little Guardian. Now come closer and give your betrothed something to celebrate."

Chapter Eighteen
Brooke

Charles Barrington had been quiet since their last meeting. The week passed without incident, and Brooke knew it was never a good sign when her former father fell silent. What devious plan did the doctor have brewing in his warped mind? A sigh fell from Brooke's lips.

At least Heller's condition had stabilized. The vacant look in the soldier's eyes dissipated a bit more each day, but he still hadn't uttered a single word. According to Kai, since Heller had been separated from Barrington, the soldier had shown no signs of violence or aggression of any kind. Brooke and her friends took turns visiting with Heller, but Coal elicited the strongest response from the automated man. One of Kai's latest working theories included suspicions of Heller connecting to Coal's Fire power. Brooke's own theory differed, in that, she hypothesized Coal might have reminded Heller of someone from his pre-Barrington life. Brooke and Kai could debate their theories at a later date, because right now their focus centered on the recovering soldier and the information locked inside his head.

Today, she would set aside her concerns about both Charles Barrington, and the elusive Mr. Heller, and celebrate the Joining of her closest friend in Aether.

Everyone believed Brooke had helped save Ash from captivity in the lab, but in truth, it had been the Fire Guardian who had ultimately saved Brooke. Ashlyn's insistence brought Brooke to Aether where she'd found this beautiful, magical life.

Quill's sexy voice preceded him into the room. "Hey, beautiful, you almost ready?"

"Almost, but don't you think we should check on Charles before we go?"

"Baby, I told you, The Nameless Asshole is secured like always. We have a guard on his door. There's nothing to worry about. Even if he throws one of his epic meltdowns, the Protectors on duty will handle him. Please don't let him ruin your day." He took hold of her hand giving it a gentle squeeze.

"You're right. I know you're right, but I want everything to be perfect for Ash and Hawk. She's the best friend anyone could ask for."

"Wait a minute, I resent that remark. I thought I was the best friend anyone could ever ask for." He tugged her hand, and she careened into his muscled chest. Raising her chin with a delicate touch, he gazed into her eyes. "You're my best friend." He lowered his mouth to hers kissing her deeply.

No matter how many times Quill's lips touched her own, Brooke's knees went weak. The man didn't know how to do anything in a small way, especially kiss. Their tongues tangled in a sensual dance, a wave of heat rushing through her entire body. The rest of the world faded into a blurry background.

Quill pulled back and looked down at her. "See, told you, I'm the best friend ever. Ash only kisses Hawk. Yuck." His hands toyed with the zipper of her hoodie, and he yanked it down in one swift movement. "I like this whole zipper thing you have going here. It's so—convenient." Slipping his fingers under the lace cups of her bra, he tweaked her nipples. "Now let me show you more of the perks of being my best friend."

Brooke's voice rushed out between heavy breaths, "Quill, we can't. We'll be late."

"We have more than enough time. Besides, we haven't had sex in ages."

Her eyebrows shot straight up. "Ages? We had sex last night."

"Exactly. Ages. I need you, baby, and I know you want me, too."

"Duh, I always want you. It's my curse. I'm in love with a man who has the libido of a sex-crazed teenager."

"Let me remind you, I'm far from a teenager. I'm eighty-three years old, and I happen to be very mature for my age by Aetherian standards." Quill crossed his muscular arms over his chest.

She laughed. "Give me a break, will you? By Aetherian standards, you're an infant, but if we were in the outside world, you'd be considered a senior citizen."

"Good thing we're in Aether then." Quill waggled his brows. "Now have some pity on an old man and make love with me. Come on, baby, it will relax us both." He wrapped her in his arms and brought his lips down on hers.

Brooke anchored her hands on his shoulders and pushed back. "Okay, but we better make it a quickie. We can't be late."

Her man didn't need to be told twice. Quill yanked

her running shorts and panties down in one fell swoop, and her sweatshirt and bra followed, joining the pile on the kitchen floor. Ripping his clothes off, he swept her into his arms, and guided them on a current of Air. He deposited her onto the kitchen island with the gentle slap of her butt cheeks on the granite countertop.

Quill's skillful fingers explored her heated core. Brooke squirmed pressing into his hand, and a satisfied look crept across her handsome Protector's face. A powerful jolt of electricity sparked between them, and Quill grabbed her, scooting her toward his waiting erection. He took her in one fast, hard thrust. Brooke held on tight riding the wave of ecstasy with the man she loved. The two rose and fell in unison climaxing with a loud, passionate cry.

Keeping her arms locked around him, she whispered in his ear, "You know, you were right. I do feel much more relaxed now."

His body shook with laughter. "I love you, Brooke Sanders. Now stop distracting me, and let's go get our friends Joined before I really am an old man."

She rolled her eyes and gathered everything she needed for Aether's version of a bridal suite. "Explain to me again what the deal is with these tents and why we need to spend the entire day there? In my world, we do our hair and makeup while sipping champagne right before the ceremony and that's that."

"I have no idea what the women do in their tent, but for us it's a giant pregame. It's an Aetherian tradition. I'm sure you're learning we have a lot of those."

"Yeah, like Ash and Hawk not being allowed to see each for two whole days before their Joining. She's been pretty cranky about it. Human culture has a similar custom but it's usually only the day before."

"If you think Ashlyn has been cranky, you should see Hawk. Between everything going on with Barrington and Heller, and then not being allowed to see Ash, all I can say is, damn. I can't wait for the Joining ceremony to be here already. Hawk hasn't stop complaining about staying at Bear's and how loud the old man snores."

Brooke chuckled. "Well, Ash and Hawk will be back together tonight."

"In that case, Hawk certainly won't be getting any sleep again tonight, but at least he'll have a smile on his face."

"Behave." With a laugh, Brooke smacked him on the arm. "Seriously, I'm so excited about the Joining. When I saw the Fire Guardian ceremony, I really couldn't appreciate the beauty of it. I was still freaking out about being in Aether, but today I'm ready to enjoy myself and celebrate our friends' love. Learning about Aether's ceremonies has been great, but being a part of things is the best feeling in the world."

"Really, I thought we talked about bests earlier? Remember, I'm your best everything, baby."

She elbowed him in the ribs. "You're so full of yourself."

"Another one of the many reasons you love me. Now, can we please get going?"

"Ready when you are, old man."

"Watch it, baby. You don't want me to have to prove my prowess again. I still have those handcuffs you loved so much."

"I'm never going to tame you, am I?" Her eyes

shot skyward, and she gave a subtle shake of her head. "Let's go, wiseass."

Quill collected her bag and sauntered out the door calling over his shoulder, "Glad you know me so well and still love me." He winked and kept walking.

They spotted Laurel approaching from the other direction, and Brooke whispered to Quill, "Great, here comes the president of my fan club. She can start throwing daggers at me nice and early. Did I say I was excited about today? Silly me." Brooke plastered a fake smile on her face and waved to Laurel. "Hey, how's it going?"

The dark-haired beauty waved back. "Good. I'm very excited for our friends."

Stepping up, Quill relieved Laurel of the load she carried. "Let me take that for you."

"You're sweet, thanks. Would you mind bringing our stuff inside? I'd like to talk to Brooke alone for a minute." Laurel placed a hand on Brooke's arm. "That is, if you don't mind?"

Brooke swallowed the lump forming in her throat. "Of course, I don't mind." She turned to face Quill throwing a look of pure desperation his way.

"You two have a nice chat, and I'll drop this off inside for you. I'll see you later, baby." He planted a kiss on Brooke's lips and then leaned in close whispering in her ear, "It'll be fine." Quill sauntered off in the direction of the tent, leaving her to fend for herself.

Laurel paced in a small circle wringing her hands. "Thanks for giving me a chance to speak to you alone. I've wanted to talk to you for a while, but I'm so embarrassed about the way I've been acting. I didn't know what to say to you. You don't need to pretend you don't know what I'm talking about."

Her breath hitched. "It's okay, Laurel. Really, you don't—"

"Yes, yes I do. I'm so sorry, Brooke. I've been a total bitch. I hope you know it has nothing to do with you. Becoming a mother means the world to me, and I've been so afraid that the God and Goddess won't bless Kai twice. I couldn't think straight. Please, forgive me." Tears filled Laurel's eyes, and her head dropped.

Brooke put her arm around Laurel's shoulder. "There is nothing to forgive. You were shocked and upset. It's perfectly understandable."

"You're being too nice. Kai told me you thought I hated you. I need you to know, I think you're wonderful. You saved my best friend. You made the man I love a father." Laurel leaned her head on Brooke's shoulder. "I'm sorry if I made things any harder on you than they needed to be. You belong here, Brooke. I should've welcomed you into our family with open arms, not made you feel uncomfortable. I hope going forward we can become friends, like we were when you first got here, before we knew about any of this."

Brooke nodded. "I'd really like that."

Laurel blew out an audible breath. "Whew. So glad I got that out. I've been a nervous wreck about talking to you. Thank you so much for understanding. Now, how about we go inside and help our friend get ready?"

Brooke hooked her arm through Laurel's. "Sounds like a great idea." Throwing the flaps of the tent open, they entered to the popping of a champagne cork. She dragged Laurel toward the action. "Looks like we got here in the nick of time."

Laurel laughed. "I'll say."

Ashlyn burst from her chair running straight at them. "Dear Goddess, where have you two been? Quill dropped your stuff off eons ago."

"Relax. Brooke and I needed to talk for a few minutes. We're here now. What do you need?"

"For you to drink champagne with me, duh. I got you both robes like mine. Let's get you changed so we can have some fun." The stunning redhead, dressed in a scarlet, satin robe, shoved a glass into each of their hands flashing an infectious grin their way.

"All righty, then. Champagne it is." Raising her glass, Brooke and her friends clinked their flutes together.

"Come and see what my parents did." Ash tugged them along toward the back of the enormous tent. "It looks like one of those fancy spas in here."

"This tent is huge. It looks like the kind they have weddings in where I come from. It's incredible." Brooke spun around in circles taking in every detail.

Muted earth toned furnishings, rugs, and fabrics filled the vast space warming the atmosphere. Ashlyn's mom, Rowan, fussed over Sol, Lily, and Marina who lounged on cushy-looking couches. All four wore robes matching Ashlyn's. They huddled around an enormous coffee table nibbling on fancy puffed pastries and a variety of snacks worthy of a gourmet chef.

Clothing racks housed all of their dresses, and several lighted makeup tables lined the edge alongside the hanging wardrobes. A flash of red out of the corner of Brooke's eye caught her attention. A magnificent gown hung on an antique dress form.

Brooke approached the exquisite garment, running her hands over the delicate fabric. "Wow, all I can say is wow. It's amazing on the mannequin. I can't even imagine how gorgeous you're going to look, Ash."

"You like it even though it's not white like the wedding dresses you're used to?" Ash teased.

"Hey, I'm an Aetherian now." Brooke nudged Ashlyn with her shoulder. "I know the traditions and that you'll be wearing the color of your house. You, my beautiful friend, Guardian of Fire, will look stunning in red. But I still don't get the whole sash thing Quill was trying to explain to me. Someone help me out."

****

Quill

Bear loomed over Hawk, the Elder's enormous chest expanding with each syllable he uttered, "What do you mean you are not wearing the traditional sashes of your houses? I do not understand."

The impact of his grandfather's words drove Hawk backward. The Protector rebounded straightening his shoulders. "Grandfather, we've discussed this a million times. Ash and I want a modern ceremony. She's not wearing her great grandmother's dress, and I'm not wearing those dusty old sashes. It doesn't mean we don't respect our ancestors, we simply want to do things our own way. Please try to understand."

The Elder's volume escalated, and his face reddened, "What in the name of the God and Goddess do you intend to wear?"

Hawk motioned to Quill. "Did you bring it?"

"Yeah, I have it right here." Quill unzipped the garment bag in his hand and withdrew the suit Brooke helped them order online. "That Armani guy charges a pretty penny, but my girl says he's the best, and my friend here definitely deserves the best." He patted Hawk on the back and handed him the suit.

The Elder stomped over and commandeered the suit from Hawk's grasp. "Let me inspect this suit." Bear rubbed the fabric between his chunky fingers. "What is the material and its origin?"

"It's made of the finest Italian wool. I had it handcrafted for the occasion. My tie blends purple and green symbolizing the power of both of my houses. Ash's dress is red." Bear took a breath before his words could break free, but Hawk's hand came up halting his grandfather's speech. "Before you say anything, I haven't seen Ash or the dress. When we first planned our Joining, we talked about the traditions that were important to both of us and wearing the colors of our respective houses was one of them."

Bear's breathing evened out. "What is decided, when decided, is the decision made."

Quill whispered under his breath to Hawk, "I think that's Bear's way of saying, whatever, man."

Hawk dropped a hand on the Elder's shoulder. "I appreciate your understanding. Change isn't always easy." He relieved his grandfather of the suit handing it off to Quill.

"Alrighty then, it looks like we're all on the same page here." Quill hung the garment bag on a nearby rack and scanned the tent for drinks. Tossing his head over his shoulder, he called to his friend, "Hey, Hawk, where's the booze?"

Hawk gestured toward a large seating area in the back corner of the tent. "Kai, Coal, and Mica are hanging out back on the loungers. Go check it out. The bar is set up right next to it."

Quill sauntered over, grabbed a beer from the cooler, and pounced into an empty chair. "Sweet setup. The tent looks nice, but I have to tell you it's not as nice as Ash's. It's still pretty great though." He raised his beer. "Let the games begin." A pillow flew into his face snapping his head back. "Hey, what was that for?"

"Because you were dissing my tent. This is the perfect man cave. You don't know what you're talking about," Hawk protested.

"That's only because you didn't see Ash's tent. It's like a five-star spa in there."

Hawk shoved a giant submarine sandwich into Quill's hand. "Why don't you stick this in your mouth, so we don't have to listen to you anymore? Besides, Ash says we need to eat if we're going to be drinking a lot. And I'm fairly certain we will be drinking a lot."

Quill ripped off a huge chunk, sinking his teeth into the meaty, cheesy goodness. The taste exploded in his mouth, and he spoke around the giant bite. "Mmm, foe goo."

Mica cracked up. "Glad to see your lady isn't changing you, Quill."

Kai chimed in, "Can you please chew with your mouth closed? I feel like I'm with a toddler."

"Funny, that's what Brooke always says." Quill smirked at his friend.

Kai harrumphed. "I honestly don't understand what my daughter sees in you. You'd think she'd have better taste in men."

"Well, her mother sure didn't," Quill retorted, with a playful sneer. "And neither does Laurel for that matter."

Mica held up his hand stopping their banter in its tracks. "Knock it off, boys. I want to make a toast." He cleared his throat. "Hawk, Rowan and I are very excited to have you join our family. You're going to make my Ashlyn a fine Kanti. I only wish your parents were with us to share in this incredible joy. They were our best friends, and we shall simply have to celebrate for them." He raised his glass. "To Hawk and Ashlyn, may you have the beautiful life you both so richly deserve."

Quill could've sworn he saw Bear wipe a tear from his eye. *Time to break free of the heavy moment, my specialty.* "And she's smokin' hot. Let's not forget that little factoid."

Coal smacked him on the back of the head with a flick of his wrist. "Dude, respect please. Ashlyn is much more than a beautiful woman."

"Brooke was right about you, Coal. You've got it bad. I hope you and Marina enjoyed your little sexcapades of late." Quill shot him a knowing look.

Hawk and Kai both shouted in unison, "Shut up, Quill."

"Ahh, hearing you guys say that is truly music to my ears."

"If you young men are quite finished with your tomfoolery, I would also like to say something as well. Hawk, my son and his beautiful Adara would be so very proud of the man you have become, as am I." Bear turned to Mica. "Nothing would have pleased them more than to see their son Join with your brilliant and lovely Ashlyn." Bear placed his hands on Hawk's shoulders. "I am certain they watch over you and know of this great celebration you share with the woman of your destiny. I would like to make this toast to Wolf and Lark Crane. May they feel the joy and love of this occasion wherever they may be."

Everyone stood raising their glasses. "To Wolf and Lark!" They shouted together. The rest of the day passed in a haze of alcohol and celebration.

Bear's booming voice rang out, "Gentlemen, it is time to get ready. Hawk, my boy, let us get you Joined to my beautiful new granddaughter."

****

Marina

Cassy poked her head into the tent. "Hi, ladies, sorry to interrupt, but I have a message from your absentee Guardian. Brynn asked me to tell you that she's running late. She'll be here as soon as she can." She turned to walk out.

"Don't go!" Ashlyn shouted. A smile spread across her pretty face, and her tone gentled. "I'd really like it if you would join us. There's plenty of room, and Lily and my mom went nuts with the food. Please stay."

The dimple in Cassy's left cheek winked. "That's so sweet of you, Ashlyn, but don't feel obligated—"

Ashlyn put her marked palm up. "Pooh, enough, you're staying and that's final. Now please get in here. I'm told I can be temperamental." She turned to Brooke. "What did you say they call it in the outside world?"

Brooke laughed. "Bridezilla."

Marina chuckled, having learned about the culture from reality television. Raised eyebrows and confused looks spread across the faces of the rest of the group. "Guess you don't watch *Say Yes to the Dress*. Brooke turned me on to it. These brides are crazy. You have to check it out. It's hysterical."

Ash piped up, "You know the type, ladies." She raised her pointer, poking her own chest, punctuating each word. "It's all about me, me, me." The whole group erupted in fits of laughter.

Brooke's face lit up with each wave, and joy filled the tent. The scientist's natural connection to the Aetherians had never been more evident. This beautiful and resilient woman belonged here in Aether. She progressed every day learning more about her new role as the Guardian of the House of Water, and Marina's pride swelled.

The afternoon flew by in a haze of excitement, and soon everyone started prepping for the ceremony. Lily stood in front of Ashlyn, placing the finishing touches on her hair and makeup. Her best friend's hands moved to her hips, and her adorable, pregnant belly popped even more.

Stepping back, Lily admired her model and waved her hands in a grand gesture. "*Voilà.*"

Rowan yanked back the towel she'd draped around her daughter's shoulders to protect her dress. "Dear Goddess, Ashlyn, you are so beautiful, not to mention, an exact replica of your great grandmother. I brought her dress in case you change your mind. There's plenty of time for you to put it on."

"Mom, please, we already talked about this. I'm wearing the new gown I picked out. You said you loved it." Ashlyn's lip jutted out like a little girl.

Her mother stroked her arm. "I'm sorry, sweetie, you're right. You look perfect."

The exquisite redhead stood executing a small yet dramatic spin. Her Joining gown, a sublime representation of The House of Fire, had been crafted from a delicate chiffon fabric in a rich shade of deep crimson. The sleeveless style crisscrossed her body accentuating her curvy, sexy figure. Sheer panels discreetly covered parts of her exposed belly and chest. The A-line hem flowed down into a chapel train which only added to the magnificence of the picture.

Marina fanned herself. "Wow, Ash, you look as hot as one of those Hollywood stars on the red carpet. You have to tell me what fantastic designer made your dress. It's so chic."

Ash tossed her a wink. "Don't you worry, my friend. I will totally hook you up." Her gaze drifted up and down scanning each woman from head to toe. "You all look absolutely gorgeous." Clapping her hands together, the Guardian beamed with excitement. "Now let's get this show on the road."

Parting the flaps of the tent, the women stepped out into the warm light of the setting sun. The Outdoor Chapel, bathed in an ethereal glow, shimmered in the fading rays. The splendor of the sanctuary sprang forth from its rich history within Aether, and magic floated in the air all around the incredible space. Nature had provided the people with an amphitheater in the middle of the forest. Gradually steeped inclines were carved into the earth, and the Aetherians created a smooth set of stairs in the midst of the rough terrain. Giant downed timbers were crafted into elaborate benches and row upon row filled the space, wrapping their way around the entire perimeter, with the exception of four wide aisles separating the sections. The slopes all flowed down to a central clearing where the Aetherians had built a raised platform. The incredible meeting place provided more than enough seating for the entire community.

The chapel served many purposes but none as lovely as the Joining ceremonies performed here. Guests filed in looking festive, and the hum of many voices buzzed in Marina's ears. She longed for the day she would Join with Coal in this glorious chapel.

Cassy took hold of Ash's arm, giving it a gentle squeeze. "You are gorgeous, sweetie. I'm going to look for Rayne before he thinks I vanished. I'll be watching."

"Wait, I had seats marked with your names in the front row so you can see better. Make sure you find them. And, Cassy, thanks for sharing this time with me." The Guardian wrapped Brooke's grandmother in a tight hug and sent her on her way.

Rowan leaned over, adjusting Ashlyn's train. "It's almost time. You ready?"

"I've been ready to Join with Hawk forever."

Her mother kissed her forehead and looked toward the group. "Okay, ladies, let's get started. I go first and you girls will follow in the order we discussed."

"Go ahead, Mom, we're right behind you." Ash blew Rowan a kiss, and her mother dabbed her eyes heading down the aisle. The Guardian faced her friends. "Before you guys go, I wanted to say thanks for standing up with me today." Ashlyn wiped a stray tear. "I love you all."

Laurel barreled into Ash's arms, tears streaming down her face. The Guardian gripped her best friend in a tight embrace, the two clinging to each other.

Lily put her hands between the women prying them apart. "Oh no you don't. You're going to mess up my makeup job. I'm officially declaring this a no crying zone until after the ceremony. The wrinkling of garments is also prohibited. Hugging and kissing will be kept to the air variety only."

Marina took hold of Lily's arm. "All right there, tiger, take it easy. This is a celebration, remember? Kissing and hugging are encouraged. Now, let's do as Rowan asked and line up." She came up alongside Ash, placing a kiss on her cheek. "See you down there."

The women entered from one side of the chapel, and the men from the opposite side. Marina spotted Coal across the way straightening his tie. He looked up meeting her gaze, and a huge smile stretched across his handsome face.

Taking her place at the top of the stairs, Marina looked out across the Outdoor Chapel. The Elders waited below, assembled in a row of elegant chairs with the exception of Bear who stood, front and center, ready to preside. Gliding down the lengthy aisle, Marina's gown trailed behind her. The handsome men descended down their aisle from across the chapel, looking like a Hollywood casting call. Meeting at the bottom of the dais, everyone took their places to wait for Ashlyn and Hawk to make their grand entrance.

A strong tug on the back of Marina's dress knocked her off balance. Looking over her shoulder to investigate, Marina's eyes lit up the minute she realized who had done the tugging. Coro, Elder of The House of Air, stood before Marina, hands on her hips. The woman craned her neck staring up from her tiny four-foot ten-inch frame. Her unusual violet-colored eyes sparkled beneath her closely cropped, dark brown fringe of hair. She'd been wearing it in the same pixie cut as Audrey Hepburn in *Roman Holiday* since the film debuted in 1953. The style suited the spunky Elder and matched her powerful personality.

Coro's extrasensory Guardian gift connected her to the spirit realm. It was rumored, the Elder encountered unsolicited visits by spirits who resided in Arcadia. The woman possessed a sharp wit and an even sharper tongue, and she never held back on information sent from the other side.

"Marina, I wish to speak with you," The Elder's tone, authoritative and calm, unnerved her.

"Yes, of course, but wouldn't you like to wait until after the ceremony?" Knots tightened in her stomach.

"No. Now. I will be brief. I have a message from the handsome one, Landon. Kept me awake all night long talking up a blue streak. I shall give you an abridged version of his sentiment. Landon wanted you to know he loves you and Coal very much. He is very sorry for what he did to both you and to his cousin. It is his true wish for you to be happy together."

Marina's mouth dropped open. "Dear Goddess—"

****

Coal

"What the hell is that Elder saying to Marina. She looks like she's seen a ghost," Coal mumbled under his breath.

Quill elbowed him in the ribs. "Did you say something to me, or are you talking to yourself? Don't worry, Joinings aren't contagious you know."

Coal shook his head. Half of him found Quill amusing, but the other half of him wanted to punch his friend in the nose. "In the immortal words of my brothers, Hawk and Kai, shut up, Quill."

The boisterous Protector laughed. "It's a catchy little phrase, isn't it?"

He bumped Quill with his shoulder. "Here they come." He nodded toward the aisle.

"Check out our lead Protector. The guy looks like a badass even in a four thousand-dollar Armani suit," Quill whispered.

"Why are you looking at him? Look at Ash. She's stunning."

"No one deserves a happily ever after more than our friends." Quill's tone turned serious. "After what Charles Barrington did to Ash, these guys getting together is kind of a miracle or something. Don't you think?"

"I couldn't agree more." Coal's gaze shifted to Marina, and her beauty stole his breath. "You know—" He nudged Quill with his shoulder. "—Marina asked me to Join with her. I can't wait until it's our turn to walk down the aisle."

"It sure as hell took you two long enough." Quill smirked. "I'm really happy for both of you. Marina is an incredible woman."

The flash of red from Ashlyn's dress brought them back to the ceremony under way. The long flowing fabric trailed behind her in an elegant sweep. Hawk's ear-to-ear grin lit up his normally stern-looking face. The couple glided down their respective paths, meeting at the bottom of the amphitheater in front of the assembled.

Hawk and Ashlyn joined hands, and a hush fell over the crowd. They gazed at one another with so much love in their eyes it made Coal impatient for his own special day to arrive. A look passed between Hawk and Ashlyn, and he grabbed her around the waist pulling her in for a passionate kiss, inciting loud whoops from the crowd. He settled Ash back on her feet, and a bright red blush stained her cheeks.

The Elder Protector's eyes narrowed, but humor twinkled in the depths of his dark brown orbs. "If you can hold on a little while longer, we will proceed to the kissing portion of the ceremony in short order," Bear said.

The crowd erupted into gales of laughter. Barrington's recent interference in their quiet world had rocked this powerful, magical community. The love between Ashlyn and Hawk had become a beacon of hope for Aether, a representation of its strength and unity.

Hawk gave Bear a sheepish look. "Sorry, Grandfather, I couldn't help myself. Look at my Ashlyn. Can you blame me?"

Bear stroked Ashlyn's cheek. "You are indeed a great beauty and a strong woman to be sure. My grandson is a lucky man." He turned to Hawk. "May we continue?"

"Please, by all means." Their lead Protector gestured with a flick of his wrist.

"Very well, we shall begin. I would like to ask the selected people up on the dais to please form a circle around our couple," Bear instructed.

When the Elder Protector spoke, people listened, and they scurried to their assigned spots. Marina came up alongside Coal, her warm skin brushing against his own. Reaching out, he grabbed her hand, encasing it in his firm grip. She intertwined her fingers with his and flashed him a smile, dazzling enough to stop traffic on a busy city street. Dipping low, in both the front and back, her long, icy blue dress exposed miles of her silky skin.

Bear proceeded. "Ahem. We have invoked the energies of the four Elements by creating this sacred circle in which this couple will be Joined as Kanti and Adara. Within its perimeter, Hawk and Ashlyn will declare their intent before all of Aether." He raised his massive arms and pointed using slow precise movements in each direction. "South, West, East, and North: we align ourselves with these four cardinal directions. Each of our Guardians will come forth with the binding representing her house. Ashlyn, since you are our current Guardian of The House of Fire, Sol will step in for you. Please come forward, Guardians. You may collect the bindings of your houses from the Elders seated behind you." Marina, Zephyr, Brynn, and Sol carried out Bear's instructions with haste.

Marina made her way toward Bear with a braid of royal blue coiled in her delicate grip. She appeared every bit the confident Guardian, and the others fell in line beside her holding the cords of their houses.

The Elder faced the community gathered to witness the special Joining of their lead Protector and The Guardian of The House of Fire. "May the God and Goddess bless this union with energy, passion, and creativity generated from the South and the Element of Fire. Blessed be this union of absolute trust with gifts of the West and the Element of Water. May you look to the East and the Element of Air to find joy in the commitment from your hearts. From the North, may you find fertility and security from The House of Earth."

The Guardians glided forward lining up two-by-two on each side of Bear, presenting their cords. The Elder's voice carried across the amphitheater. "Please clasp your hands together." Ashlyn and Hawk brought their hands together crossing them over creating an *X* and electricity sparked in the air.

Sol lifted the red tie and held it high. "The first binding is thus made with red, symbolic of Fire, that your love may be bright and passionate." She stepped back to her assigned space.

Bear draped the cord over the couples' joined hands. "I ask you now in front of all those present here, will you both help each other grow in spirit and wisdom?"

Ash flipped her hair over her shoulder and gazed up at Hawk. "I will."

Hawk gave her a quick peck on the lips before answering, "I will."

The Elder nodded to Marina and she approached him holding her cord up for all to view. "The second binding is thus made with blue, symbolic of Water, that your love may flow and fill you to your depths." She slid back into place.

Bear wrapped the cord around their hands. "Will you each seek to ease the other's pain and suffering, sharing laughter and joy?"

In unison, they replied, "We will."

"The third binding is made with purple—" Zephyr raised her tie. "—symbolic of Air, that your love may be as limitless as the sky and filled with spirit." Zephyr kissed Ashlyn's cheek and scooted back to her spot.

Bear joined the purple binding with the other two and twisted it over the couple's hands in a figure eight.

"Will you strive to keep romance alive through daily actions and words of encouragement?"

Quill piped in, "Come on, Bear, they don't need any encouragement in that department." The crowd roared with laughter.

Coal watched a silent communication pass between Hawk and Ashlyn. A grin crossed their lead Protector's face, and the Guardian's cheeks reddened.

"See!" Pointing a finger in the couple's direction, Quill continued, "They're doing it right now."

Bear's eyes narrowed, and he shook his head ignoring Quill. "As I was saying."

Hawk smirked, and Ashlyn giggled. "We will."

Brynn approached the couple, stifling her laughter behind her hand. "The fourth and final binding is thus made with green, symbolic of Earth, that your love may be wise and nurturing, and your happiness abundant." She drifted back toward the other Guardians.

The Elder took hold of the four loose ends, fastened the cords together, and addressed the audience. "All will please rise." Bear turned to Ash and Hawk. "You are now bound together, your two lives Joined by love and trust into one life. Above you are the stars and below you is the Earth. Like the stars, your love should be a constant source of light, and like the Earth, a firm foundation from which to grow. You may now kiss your Adara."

Hawk didn't wait for his grandfather to finish his words. Leaning in, he fused his lips to Ashlyn's in a passionate kiss. All of Aether cheered and howled for the couple finally getting their happy ending.

A series of intensely loud bangs and blinding flashes of light pierced Coal's eardrums and scorched his retinas. Strong tremors rocked the Outdoor Chapel, and the world around them erupted into sheer chaos. Clouds of colored smoke filled the air obscuring his vision.

"Shit. Grenades. What the hell?" Sparks ignited and flames burst from the tips of his fingers. Clouds of colored smoke filled the air obscuring his vision, and his Fire sputtered out. A million thoughts ran through Coal's brain, but only one mattered. "Marina," he yelled.

Chapter Nineteen
Brooke and Quill

The ground beneath Brooke's feet shook in violent bursts knocking her off balance. She bumped into someone, but a series of sequentially timed flashes of light made it impossible to see whom. The array of brilliant white strobes burned her eyes, narrowing her vision to nothing but blue spots and a whole lot of pain. She called out, but her lungs seized, filling with smoke. A caustic odor burned her nose, and bile rose to her throat.

Hacking nonstop, Brooke choked out the name foremost on her mind, "Quill?" Her coughing fit persisted, and she bent at the waist easing the spasms slightly. Brooke's words emerged strangled. "What is going on?" Freezing in place, panic climbed the length of her body settling in her belly. "Oh my God, Charles Barrington! I have to stop him." She searched the smoky air trying to get her bearings. A muscular arm emerged through a blue cloud of smoke snagging her around the waist. "Ahh!" Brooke's shrill scream blasted in her own ears.

Quill's coughing broke through the percussive chaos erupting all around, his voice constricted. "Baby, calm down, it's me. Get low." He tugged her to the ground. "Got to stay away from the smoke."

"Can't you clear it with your Air power?" Brooke

rubbed her eyes, the burning unceasing.

"I've got nothing. Believe me, I tried. I think there's something in the gas. I can barely create a small breeze."

Loud shrieks filled the Outdoor Chapel sending chills down Brooke's spine. "We have to do something. People are starting to panic. Do you hear that? It sounds like thunder or maybe more grenades."

Quill took her hand. "I haven't heard any more explosions for a few minutes. The sound you hear is everyone running to get out of the amphitheater. Remember what I taught you about emergencies in Aether?"

She nodded. "Run straight to PH, and don't stop."

"That's what anyone who can is doing right now. I need you to stay calm. Everything is going to be okay."

A booming voice ripped through the pandemonium, "Kai? Quill? Where the fuck are you? Follow my voice and come get us untied. Something hit my grandfather. He's unconscious. Kai? Quill? Anybody? Fuck!"

Brooke grabbed hold of Quill's jacket sleeve cinching it in her fisted grip. "We have to help Ash and Hawk, but I'm completely blind." A series of rapid-fire questions flew from her mouth. "Can you see anything? Do you think Bear is okay? What about everyone else?"

Quill's strong arms encircled her. "Hey, I've got you. I'm going to take care of this. Here's what we're going to do first. Um, don't move."

"What does that mean, don't move? What are you up to?"

"Shh. Trust me." His hands came up under her dress.

Jumping back, she kicked out catching him in the stomach. "Are you insane? Now?"

He didn't flinch from her gut shot but turned, pinning her down. Quill enunciated each word he spoke directly into her ear, his warm breath blowing her hair with every syllable he uttered. "Be still, and listen to me. You can't move around in that dress. I'm going to cut it shorter, and we're taking the heels off your shoes, too."

The cool metal edge of a knife skimmed her thighs, and Brooke held her breath. "You better be careful, buddy. If you cut me, you'll be sorry."

"Believe me, the last thing I want to do is damage your luscious body."

Fabric shredding made a surprisingly loud noise even amid the bedlam breaking out all around the Outdoor Chapel. Her beautiful dress hung in a tattered mess around her legs, but Brooke didn't have time to mourn its loss. Quill yanked her right foot into his lap whispering more orders in her ear, "Hang on one sec. I got this." He squeezed her ankle in a tight grip chopping the heel off her shoe with his blade in one swift motion. Grabbing her left foot, he secured it giving her other shoe the same treatment. "Try standing." Pulling her to her feet, he wrapped his arm around her waist steadying her. "You okay? We've got to find those guys."

"I'm good, but can I ask you a question? Why on Earth did you bring a knife to a wedding?"

"Hello, it's called a Joining. And you should know Protectors are armed at all times. We'd kick your Boy Scouts' asses any day of the week, cause I'm always prepared, baby."

"Maybe you could beat a Boy Scout because on average, they're around twelve." Brooke rolled her eyes and leaned on Quill's shoulder climbing out of the ring of frayed fabric which had once been her beautiful dress. "You're impossible, you know that, right?"

He chuckled. "So, you've mentioned a time or two."

She shook her head. "I'm ready. Let's go."

Planting a quick kiss on her cheek, Quill captured her hand, and led her through the haze of smoke calling out to their friends, "Hawk? Where the hell are you?"

"Over here. Hurry," Hawk roared. "I'm worried about my grandfather. He hasn't moved at all. Where the hell is Kai?"

Quill's hold remained solid as he dragged her along. "I think they're over this way. Hawk, call out again."

Their lead Protector's voice penetrated the pandemonium. "Over here."

Her mangled heels didn't exactly make Brooke any more graceful than normal. Struggling to keep her footing, she latched onto Quill. He dropped his arm around her shoulder securing her close to his side. Their vision obscured by the heavy veil of smoke, Brooke and Quill groped their way along smacking directly into Ashlyn and Hawk.

The force of their collision knocked the couple off balance, and Quill steadied them. "Sorry, guys, but at least we found you."

Waving her hands through the fumes, Brooke couldn't see six inches in front of her face. "Oh my God, Ashlyn, I'm so sorry. Are you all right?"

"I'm fine. None of this is your fault. Charles

Barrington is completely insane. Someone untie us quick. I'm going to fry him." Anger laced her friend's voice.

"Stay still." Quill brought his blade up. "I've got my knife. I'm going to cut you loose."

"No!" Ashlyn shouted in protest. "These bindings are thousands of years old. You can't cut them. Untie us."

Hawk's tone exuded remorse, "I'm sorry, honey, but our people can't wait. We need to take control back from these assholes right now." He nodded toward the bindings. "Do it, Quill."

The thick clouds of smoke cleared a bit, and Brooke could finally see her friends through the haze. Quill sliced through the ancient ropes, and Brooke's stomach dropped. She mumbled under her breath, "Great, yet another thing my former father has taken from Aether." She clutched her hands into tight fists. "He needs to pay this time." The Joining bindings fell into a pile, the heavy cording landing with a loud thud on the hard wooden floor. Brooke shook her head. "Another casualty of Charles Barrington."

Ashlyn choked back tears, but her voice still held a note of fury. "Where are the other Guardians? We need to make sure they're all right and put a stop to this craziness."

Hawk held Ashlyn in his arms. "I want you safe." He pulled back, taking her by the shoulders and gazed into her eyes. "You and Brooke need to get out of here right now."

Ash stood tall. "My safety isn't important. Aether is in trouble, Hawk. I'm the Guardian of Fire."

Hawk shook his head. "There's nothing I can do to

stop you, is there?" He placed a gentle kiss on his new Adara's lips. "Let's get my grandfather squared away and then we'll decide whether you should stay or go. Now where the hell is Kai?" Hawk shouted through the murky fumes, frustration radiating off the powerful Protector, "Damn it, Kai. Bear needs you."

Kai's calm tone cut through the soupy air, "We're here." He came up alongside Ashlyn with Laurel in tow. "We got to you as fast as we could. Are you guys all right?"

Brooke held back tears. "We're all okay, but Bear's not."

Her father stroked her hair. "He's going to be fine, sweetheart. All of the Elders were hit by tranquilizer darts. I'm going to take care of them. You should go with Ash and Laurel. Hide back at PH with the rest of the people until we come for you."

Brooke filled her voice with as much authority as she could muster, "Guardians don't hide." She smiled at her friend. "Right, Ash?" The Guardian of Fire rewarded her with a wink, and Brooke continued without missing a beat, "We're supposed to protect Aether and the Earth. Ash and I will keep Laurel safe and find the rest of the Guardians." She took her friends' hands. "We need to stay together. We're stronger when we work as one. Trust us. Go do your job, and we'll do ours."

Quill came up behind Brooke wrapping his arms around her. "You don't understand what we're dealing with here. These guys mean business. Please, let us get you back to PH where it's safe."

"I think I know better than anyone what and who we're dealing with here. Besides, nowhere in Aether is safe right now, not even PH. Please, don't let them tear us apart. We're going to need to join forces to stop Charles, and we're wasting time." Brooke turned around in his arms and kissed Quill hard on the lips. "Go."

He nodded to Brooke giving her a tight squeeze. "You're right." Quill pivoted to face Hawk. "We're Protectors of Aether, and we need to take these assholes out right now. Our ladies are tough as nails. They can handle this."

****

Hawk held his new Adara close, his voice soft and gentle. "I can't lose you again."

She gazed up at him stroking her hand down his cheek. "You won't. I'm Ashlyn Woods Crane, Guardian of The House of Fire, and Charles Barrington doesn't stand a chance this time. I love you, my Kanti. Please, trust me, and we can save Aether together."

Hawk planted a hot kiss on Ashlyn's lips and released her breathless. The lead Protector's eyes zoned in on Quill. "Promise me you're going to help me kill that bastard Barrington?"

"It would be my genuine pleasure." Quill bowed at the waist. "Lead the way." He could relate to Hawk's hesitation in leaving the women unprotected, but the safety of everyone in Aether hung in the balance. Besides, he wasn't lying when he told his friend Brooke and Ash could more than take care of themselves.

Thick clouds of colored smoke lingered in the air, but a few patchy areas, where it had dissipated a bit, popped up sporadically. Hawk motioned with his head and they crept along, low to the ground, advancing toward the nearest clearing. Quill's hand itched for his

Beretta, and he clenched his fists staving off the impulse to reach for his trusted sidekick.

Hawk's gravelly voice whispered out, "Come on." He tugged Quill's sleeve, leading him toward one of the wide aisles. "This way. I can make out the opening, and it looks like most of the people have cleared this area. It will be way easier going than over the benches, even with all the smoke. Stay low. Let's go. We need to get above this mess and locate these assholes." His best friend began muttering, never a good sign, "How the fuck did they get in here anyway? We have five teams out on patrol, not to mention, all of our protective shields."

"Barrington is a cagey prick. I wouldn't put anything past him." Quill trudged behind his commander. He climbed up to grab the next step, not quite reaching Hawk, and a large hand seized hold of his ankle keeping him in place. Quill's instincts took over, and he kicked back smashing his attacker in the face.

A familiar voice yelled out, "Ow! What the hell, man?" Blood ran down under Coal's nose, and he wiped it with his sleeve. "I've been quietly trying to get your attention for the last five minutes, and you kick me. If you busted my nose, Marina is going to kill you." His eyes watered, and he spit a wad of red-stained salvia on the ground. "Kai sent me to help you."

Contrite, Quill responded, "Sorry, dude, I didn't know it was you. It's still pretty smoky even up here, and let's just say I'm a bit paranoid. You okay?"

"I'll live." Coal moved closer. "Hawk, what do you need me to do?"

The lead Protector bent low, authority lacing his

voice. "Head to PH. Help anyone you find along the way who isn't equipped to fight and get them there safely. Once you do that, grab as many weapons as you can carry, and haul ass back here with every Protector you meet. We're going to stop Charles Barrington and his band of psychos permanently. Hopefully our powers will be active again once the grenade gas clears, otherwise we'll fight hand to hand."

"I may have no Fire power, but I can still kick some ass," Coal assured him.

"I'm counting on you, brother." Hawk gripped Coal's shoulder. "Don't let me down."

Coal dropped his hand on Hawk's opposite shoulder. "Never. I'll be back soon." He slipped away, a determined look in his eyes.

"Okay, what now? Do I get to kill someone?" Quill questioned.

Hawk let out a low chuckle before turning serious. "Soon. Meanwhile, we keep heading to the top. It'll give us a much better vantage point. Let's go, but make sure no one is on your tail this time. We're almost there."

Choking back a snarky retort, Quill reminded himself Hawk was, in fact, his lead Protector not only his childhood best friend. Besides, the guy had a point about staying vigilant, so he swallowed his pride and followed his commander. The two Protectors made their way to the upper ledge of the amphitheater.

Peering down, Quill mumbled to Hawk, "From up here the smoke looks like colorful batches of cotton candy floating in the air, but that is one tricky-ass treat. Maybe getting out of the candy clouds will restore our powers?"

They reached the apex, and Hawk nudged him with his elbow. "My powers are coming back a little. What about you?"

Quill sensed the drain in his powers the moment the gas had hit, but now a twinge of energy flowed to his fingertips. "Yeah, I definitely feel it, too." He stood rubbing his hands together, creating friction on the surface of his skin. He focused on his power. "Come on, damn it. I've got to get my Air back."

"Give me your hand"—Hawk yanked Quill's hand into his oversized one—"and let's see if we can clear some of this smoke together."

"I have to say, this really feels wrong to me."

Hawk's lip curled up. "Shut up, Quill."

"You know it doesn't quite have the same finesse without Kai joining in." He smirked at his friend. "How do you propose we do this? Team up I mean? We're not exactly Marvel super heroes, and this is definitely no comic book."

"Close your eyes and concentrate on the Air."

He obeyed, beseeching his impaired gift to merge with Hawk's. Their palms heated like two sticks being rubbed together, and slowly a small breeze built. He opened his eyes to gusts of Air swirling all around their bodies. The clouds of colorful smoke faded, but only in a twenty-foot radius of where they stood.

Letting out a frustrated breath, Quill ripped his hand from Hawk's grip. "This is bullshit, man. Our powers are spent. I need my goddamn gun. I'm going to destroy these guys."

Hawk jabbed his fist into Quill's bicep cutting off his rant. "Hey, look down there."

The amphitheater lay under a heavy blanket of the

strange colored gas, but at the base smoke billowed away from its center. The five Guardians of Aether stood together, hands joined, in an awesome display of power and beauty.

"Look at them go. We couldn't do shit. Our Air power was like a fart compared to theirs." Quill looked down at Brooke. Her hands were linked with the women of each of the houses' of Aether. She gathered together in strength with her new sisters, taking her rightful place among the Guardians fighting for their home. Pride gushed through him.

A flash in the distance caught Quill's eye. He couldn't see much with the area still cloaked in a heavy layer of smoke, but two shadowy figures broke through the clouds inching closer to their location. Quill said in a hushed tone, "Someone is heading this way. They're right below us." He pointed about ten rows down.

Hawk's gaze searched the area Quill indicated. "It's about time. I'm definitely ready for a fight. What about you, brother?"

"I'm on your six. Let's get these assholes."

"We'll go down a few rows past them and come up from behind. You take the one on the right, and I've got the one on the left." He grabbed Quill by the arm halting his movement. "No fucking around, got me? Dispatch him, and be done with it."

Pulling out of Hawk's grip, he nodded. "I hear you. Kill 'em, and kill 'em quick." Quill took off down the slope giving the mercenaries a wide berth.

The Protectors climbed up and over the empty benches instead of using one of the aisles. If Quill hadn't been staring down at Brooke, he might not have noticed the glint of metal from the guns the mercenaries carried. He whispered under his breath, "These shitheads think they're so smart. We'll show them." Adrenaline flowed through his body, and he sensed the man above him more than he saw him. The thick smoke created a cover Barrington's men had intended to use to their advantage, but the Protectors planned on turning the tables on the unsuspecting assholes.

A black boot tread hovered inches above his face, and Quill could make out every detail including the guy's size twelve etched into the rubber. The clueless soldier continued his climb blithely unaware of the Protector's presence. Quill looked over at Hawk. His lead Protector inclined his head signaling his immediate call to action, and Quill's instincts kicked into high gear.

He jumped up tackling the mercenary. A dark mask, with a plastic shield, covered the soldier's face. "A gasmask? You prick." Quill reached up, snapped the contraption right off the shocked man's face, and clocked him in the jaw. The mercenary's weapon flew from his grip landing on a nearby bench with a loud clunk. "You look like Tom Hardy's character in Batman. No way you get to wear this while I asphyxiate over here." Quill choked from the noxious fumes filling his lungs, and any return of power he'd experienced faded the moment he re-entered the clouds of gas.

The Protector dove for the gun, abandoning the startled soldier. The mercenary was better trained than Quill expected. He popped up, countering with a hard shot to Quill's temple. His neck jerked back, and Quill rebounded, grabbing his head. *Snap out of it. Get the damn gun.* Patting the ground where he'd last seen it, his hand met cold metal. One by one, he wrapped his fingers around the barrel clamping down on it. A hard tug from the weapon's grip nearly separated it from his tight hold. The Protector used his free hand to retaliate with an uppercut to the chin, but the large man didn't back down. Rolling from bench to bench, the two men grappled for the gun. Quill's left shoulder buckled on the last impact, but he blocked out the pain.

With the business end of the shifting gun secured in Quill's fist, a deadly tug of war over the weapon raged on between the two men. Clouds of dirt blended with the smoke hanging in the air. Neither man relented as they choked on the caustic vapors. He had to give props to the mercenary because the guy fought like a highly trained soldier. Quill let out a loud grunt, fighting to keep the other man from making contact with the trigger. He snapped his wrist dislodging the gun from his enemy's possession. The bad news was, he'd also lost his hold, and the gun whizzed by, unclaimed.

They both flew toward the elusive weapon crashing into one another with tremendous force. Quill couldn't see a thing in the haze, but he sensed the moment they both grabbed for the gun. Sweat coated his palms, but he latched onto the pistol battling the mercenary for possession. The loud crack of a gunshot rang in his ears, and the muzzle flashed a bright white light.

****

"It worked! The gas is clearing." Brooke dropped hands with her fellow Guardians. She glanced down and mentally declared her appearance an official disaster area. Tiny colored particles from the gas stained her dress which hung in shreds above her knees. Hacked to bits, her designer shoes wobbled beneath her feet. "I may be a mess, girls, but at least we did it." Brooke turned to Ashlyn giving her the once over. The Fire Guardian's dress barely showed a wrinkle and not a single hair fell out of place. Brooke rolled her eyes. "Are you kidding me? Why do I look like I was dragged down the street by an angry mob, and you still look like you're ready for the runway? It's not fair."

"Oh, Brooke, stop it." Ashlyn laughed, brushing off her comment. "You're a genius. Combining our powers was an amazing idea. We've never tried anything like this before, and it was incredible." Ashlyn looked to the others. "Right?" All of the women mumbled their agreement.

"It's understandable. Aether is all about peace, love, and harmony. None of you has ever had to fight before. Well, except for you, Ash." Brooke squeezed her friend's arm. "I've been afraid of Charles Barrington my entire life. He made my childhood one of fear and self-loathing, but he's taken from me for the very last time. I'm ready to fight for myself and for all of Aether." Brooke's hands clenched into tight fists.

Marina smirked. "Come on, ladies. Is my girl a Guardian or what? My job here is done." She brushed imaginary dust from her shoulder.

Zephyr stepped up. "It was truly a brilliant idea, but I'm afraid we've made ourselves sitting ducks here. We need to find some cover." Zephyr, the Guardian of Air, sounded like the Protector she longed to be.

"I agree. Come on, over here." The Fire Guardian nodded toward the edge of the smoke line leading her friends away from the clearing.

Laurel followed and addressed the others, "Good, because I have to find Kai. I'm sure he needs my help. I appreciate the fact you guys included me in your circle, but I know you were only trying to keep me safe. I don't exactly bring anything to the table. It's time for me to go where I can be useful."

Brooke took Laurel's hand. "Everyone brings something to the table. You're important, Laurel, to all of us."

A sudden onslaught of dizziness overtook Brooke, and she fought to keep her knees from buckling. Swaying, she tightened her grip on Laurel's hand. Another person's arm looped around Brooke's waist steadying her. The faint sound of her name being called registered, but everything except for the vision breaking through the recesses of her mind faded away. Flashes raced across her brain in a rapid-fire staccato picture show. Her vision fine-tuned itself, and an image emerged from the haze into the clarity of her mind. Her powers displayed a picture of three young teens coming straight toward them out of the colored smoke.

Another wave of dizziness hit and more images flooded Brooke's mind. Helpless, she watched on as a grenade sailed through the air, landing smack in the middle of the three kids. The concussive blast sent them each flying in a different direction. Head spinning, stomach in knots, Brooke's vision cut off abruptly, and she would've collapsed to the ground had she not been supported by her friends.

Marina leaned into her space brushing her hair from her face. "Brooke? Are you back with us?"

Regaining her equilibrium, Brooke grew frantic. "The kids. We have to stop them. Please hurry. It's going to happen soon." Pulling away from her friends, she headed off in the other direction.

Zephyr yanked her back. "Wait. Where are you going? Take a breath, and tell me what happened."

"My gift. My visions." She pointed at Laurel. "Your kids. From school. They're coming this way." Breathless, Brooke's heart pounded. "Please, a grenade." She grabbed Zephyr by the dress. "Over that way. Hurry."

This time Zephyr didn't hesitate. "Laurel, come with me. They'll listen to you." She took the teacher's hand and bolted in the direction Brooke had indicated. The Guardian ran full speed, heels, and all, tugging Laurel behind her. The kids appeared at the top of the amphitheater shouting down to their teacher.

Laurel waved her arms back and forth in a frantic motion, her panic palpable. "No! Wren, Briar, Aidan! Stop! Go back. It's not safe. No!"

The trio hesitated for a brief moment squinting down at them. They shrugged to one another and took off jogging down the stairs. A grenade whizzed overhead flying through the air landing directly in the path of the unsuspecting kids. Shockwaves hit the ground kicking up clouds of dirt and smoke, obscuring everyone and everything from view.

****

The mercenary's dead weight pressed down on Quill's chest constricting his breathing. Wedging his hands under the beefy guy's rib cage, Quill lifted him up a few inches, but his injured shoulder protested, and the lifeless corpse dropped back down on top of him. He struggled to extricate himself from beneath the considerable-sized man, when the soldier's body disappeared in a rush landing next to him with a resounding thud. Air filled Quill's lungs, and he inhaled

313

deeply catching his breath.

Hawk's face appeared inches from his own. "Quill, buddy, did he get you?" His friend patted him down with a bit too much force.

"I'm fine, but your giant paws are pounding me into the ground. Do you mind getting the fuck off me?"

"Oh shit—" Hawk backed off. "—sorry, I thought you got shot again." He gestured toward another dead soldier lying face down on the ground. "My guy is toast, too. If you're all right, get that asshole's gun, and let's get moving."

Quill ripped his hanging shirtsleeve from the seam and tossed it aside. Grabbing the mercenary's semi-automatic handgun off the ground, he nodded to Hawk. "Ready."

Hawk tossed Quill an extra clip for the Glock he'd picked up. "No, now you're ready. Let's make tracks." Hawk ran off without a backward glance.

Dusting off his suit pants, Quill straightened before his scuffed dress shoes hit the dirt once more. Grumbling, he raced up the steps two at a time. "No rest for the weary."

He reached the apex of the amphitheater, and found Hawk flanked by Coal, Skye, Brack, and two other Protectors. Skye still wore her fancy dress, but she had donned a pair of black combat boots instead of heels. If she didn't have a giant gash on her forehead, it might've made for an amusing picture. The other Protectors looked equally roughed up with cuts and bruises marring their faces. At their feet, four men kneeled, hands zip-tied behind their backs, in much worse shape than his fellow Protectors.

"Glad you could make it to the party, Quill." Coal

smiled through a split lip.

Skye reached into a black duffle next to her and produced a 45mm pistol. "Gun?"

Quill held up the Glock he'd confiscated from the dead soldier. "You can never have too many guns I always say. I'll definitely take that one."

She tossed him the pistol. "Sorry, I couldn't find any Berettas. We were in a hurry."

"I appreciate the thought, but the .45 is great." Quill tucked the extra gun into his waistband.

Frantic shouting and a scurry of activity down at the base of the amphitheater redirected everyone's focus. Laurel's voice penetrated the chaos and the heavy layers of smoke hovering in the air. Waving her arms above her head, she screamed at the top of her lungs at three teenagers Quill recognized from her class.

Across from him, on the other side of the amphitheater, the kids hurried toward a stretch of open air. The whistle of a grenade flying overhead buzzed in Quill's ears. His eyes followed its trajectory, helpless to change the outcome of its pending destruction. The ground beneath his feet rocked, and a cloud of smoke rose in the air obscuring everything below.

"Holy shit, the kids. Did they take the hit?" Brack leaned over peering into the abyss.

Hawk grabbed Coal's arm. "I thought you said everyone was accounted for."

Coal's shoulders slumped. "I'm sorry. I saw the kids back at PH, and they asked me if they could help. I told them to stay put. They must've snuck out."

Hawk's posture stiffened. "It's not your fault, but we need to get down there and assess the situation.

Skye, Brack, go around to the other side, and see if you can find whoever tossed that grenade." He pointed to the other two Protectors. "You guys stay here, and keep an eye on this group. Stay frosty. I'm sure there are plenty more where they came from. Quill and Coal, follow me. We're going down this way." He gestured with a nod of his head.

He and Coal obeyed their lead Protector's command, racing down the steep walkway toward the site of the blast. Glancing at Coal, Quill mumbled to his friend, "Everyone better be all right down there."

"Damn straight, brother. Let's keep moving," Coal replied.

****

A concussive shock hit the ground, and they took off at a dead run toward the source of the explosion. Brooke raced along with the others skidding to a halt in front of Zephyr as the Guardian was helping Laurel to her feet. Masked behind the thick soot filling the air, the soft muffled cries of the kids carried through the haze.

Ashlyn grabbed Brooke's hand. "We need to clear this smoke." Zephyr, Brynn, and Marina stepped up forming a circle, and the Guardians made quick work of the offensive clouds.

The fog lifted revealing the kids scattered in three different directions. Laurel gasped and bolted through the lingering clouds heading for her students. Kai and Rayne caught up to her racing toward the wounded children, who looked to be more dazed than seriously injured.

Cassy rushed up to her. "Brooke, sweetheart, are you all right?"

"I'm fine, Gran." Shortly after they'd learned the

truth of her paternity, Cassy had insisted Brooke start calling her by the nickname. The two had been spending so much time together it flowed from Brooke's lips with a natural ease.

"I saw what you and the other Guardians did, and I'm so proud of you." Cassy took Brooke's hand. "But don't you think it's time you get to PH?"

"Maybe I should be saying that to you? Why aren't you back at PH with everyone else?"

Her grandmother thrust her chin out. "For the same reason you won't go. It's my job to be here. A lot of people have been injured and drugged. Don't forget, I'm of The House of Water, too."

"Okay, I get it." Brooke nodded. "We both have jobs to do." She pointed to the kids. "They seem okay. At least they're all sitting up."

"Kids are resilient. They'll be fine." Cassy's brows lifted. "How did Laurel know about the grenade?"

"She didn't. It was me. I had a vision." Brooke's head dropped. "It was so scary. Those poor kids."

Cassy wrapped her arm around Brooke's shoulder. "You did a wonderful thing. You slowed them down. If you hadn't, they would've been directly in the path of the grenade. You saved their lives. You should embrace your gifts." Cassy took hold of the tattered remnants of Brooke's designer gown. "Dear Goddess, what happened to your dress, and your shoes?"

Brooke laughed. "Quill. Need I say more?"

"No. I think I understand. Well, as much as anyone can understand Quill." Cassy chuckled. Voices from across the aisle pulled their attention back to the injured kids being helped to their feet. "Look, the children are all walking out on their own steam. They may be a little worse for wear, but you definitely saved them. You really are a Guardian of Aether now."

"Isn't this sweet. Brooke Barrington saves the day." Out of a dark patch of smoke lingering in the air, a chilling voice penetrated straight to her bones.

All of the oxygen in Brooke's lungs rushed out in a single breath. Flanked on each side by a soldier, Charles Barrington strode up, coming to a halt a few feet in front of Brooke and Cassy. The click of a gun being cocked sent a cold chill down Brooke's spine, but she refused to stand down.

Her hands settled on her hips in a defiant stance. "You mean, Brooke Sanders. I don't know anyone named Brooke Barrington."

"Aren't you the brave one?" Venom oozed from every word Charles Barrington uttered. "You and your friends thought you were so smart, but I engineered this entire scenario all along, and you fools fell right into my trap. The only downfall was the ruination of my experiment, Mr. Heller. No matter, repeated attempts to drum the morality out of that man were becoming a terribly bothersome issue."

Cassy remained silent beside her, but her chest rose and fell in a rapid rhythm. Brooke angled her body protecting her grandmother from the ranting man. Facing off against the doctor, Brooke demanded, "What do you want from us now? Can't you leave us alone?"

"I will do no such thing. This place, this power, should not belong to these people. Control over the Elements is my destiny not yours." The maniacal doctor's face turned crimson. "I have the perfect subject to help me see my plan to fruition. Unstoppable. Brilliant. Strong. *Loyal.*" He emphasized the last word

318

shooting daggers at Brooke.

The other Guardians slowly crept toward them. Brooke distracted Barrington with a question challenging his over-inflated ego. "Where is it you have this perfect individual tucked away?"

Ignoring her question, Charles' gaze shifted to the approaching Guardians. "Stop right there, Ashlyn. I see you and your friends." His chest puffed out. "Did you like my little present? I made the power stripping gas with you in mind." Fire sparked from the tips of Ashlyn's fingers, and she continued inching closer. "If you take one more step, my men will kill you." The soldiers on either side of him raised their guns.

Ashlyn's Fire retreated, and she halted in her tracks. "We don't want any more trouble from you, Dr. Barrington. We'd like you to take your people and leave."

"I have no intention of leaving until I get what I came for." He pointed the gun at Brooke, his hand shaking. "You see, Brooke is under the impression this is her birthright, but she is sorely mistaken." The doctor squinted his eyes in anger, a huge vein bulging in his neck. "No one is smarter than I am. Not that fraud, Kai Sanders, and certainly not you."

The gun teetered from side to side in Barrington's unsteady grip, and Brooke's stomach tightened in knots. Desperate to diffuse the situation, she switched gears appealing to any remnants of Charles' paternal bond. "Please, Dad. Stop this before anyone else gets hurt."

"Oh, so now I'm Dad, am I? You're a bigger a phony than that idiot you're calling your father. I'm not leaving without samples of blood from them"—he gestured with his head toward the other Guardians—"and you're going to get them for me, or I'll shoot you and take them myself."

"I don't care what you do to me; I'm never going to help you." Brooke stood firm, her heart pounding.

"Well, not everything is about you. Your mother may have thought so, but she was wrong. If Olivia had spent less time worrying about you and more time worrying about what I was doing, perhaps she would've figured out I was injecting her with cancer cells instead of vitamin B."

Brooke's face fell, and her legs wobbled. "What did you say?" Her voice hitched, fury filling her veins.

"You heard me. I gave that meddlesome bitch cancer and killed her. Now you're going to join her." His dark eyes glazed over flooding with rage.

Any hope she had that a sliver of humanity remained inside of Charles Barrington faded away with the revelation of her mother's murder. "You're insane." Brooke's fists clenched at her sides, her voice shaking. "That's not possible."

"Let me assure you, it most certainly is possible."

"You son of a bitch!" All rational thought left her, and she flew at Barrington. The loud click of the slide dropping into place, on the pistol Barrington held, barely registered.

"No!" Cassy screamed jumping in front of Brooke.

Everything happened in slow motion from the moment the bullet left the gun. Shouting erupted all around Brooke, the sound distorted in her ears, like an old record player set on the wrong speed. People moved at a glacial pace, and her vision clouded.

The dark figure of Heller emerged from the smoke

swooping in, a gun in each hand. Brooke's world spun on its axis, and time accelerated once again. Rapid fire shots rained down on Charles Barrington and his soldiers. The men didn't have time to blink slamming one by one into the hard wood floor.

Cassy crumpled to the ground at Brooke's feet. Following her grandmother down to the floor, Brooke pulled her into her lap. Cassy clutched her chest, blood pouring out between her fingers. Brooke covered her grandmother's hands with her own applying pressure to the gushing wound. "What did you do, Gran?" Tears trailed down Brooke's face.

Blood bubbled from the corner of Cassy's mouth and gasping for breath, she whispered, "Saved you." Her grandmother's eyelids shuttered down, and her hands slipped away from her chest falling to her sides.

Chapter Twenty
Quill

By the time they'd arrived at the base of the amphitheater, all hell had broken loose. Quill swept in taking a sobbing Brooke into his arms. Kai and Rayne worked on Cassy at a frantic pace. Hawk barked orders at the Protectors emerging from every direction. Everyone huddled together, hugging, and speaking in hushed tones. Quill stroked Brooke's back in slow circles, her body shaking non-stop. The hardened Protector's heart broke. If Barrington hadn't already been dead, Quill would have dispatched the evil prick with pleasure.

Emerging from one of the lingering clouds of smoke, an ATV pulled up skidding to a halt. Two Protectors hopped off and assisted Rayne in lifting Cassy onto the rack. Kai moved along with them straddling the seat backward, his hands pressed firmly to his mother's wound.

Kai shouted over the roar of the engine, "Dad, are you okay to drive? I can't stop applying pressure, or she's going to bleed out."

"I'm fine. You just save my Adara. Let's go." Rayne squeezed onto the ATV taking off in a cloud of dust.

They pulled away, and no one moved or said a word. A scuffle erupted a few feet from where Quill stood breaking the heavy silence. A couple of Protectors wrestled Heller to the ground. The mercenary, as docile as a newborn kitten, laced his hands behind his head, emotionless. A gunshot rang out echoing in the acoustics of the amphitheater, freezing everyone in their tracks.

Fury filling her eyes, Zephyr held a smoking pistol in her steady grip pointing it in the air. "You let him go this minute. He saved us all." She brought the weapon's sites in line with the Protectors holding Heller down.

Hawk came up beside her placing his hands over hers and lowered the weapon before he removed it from her tight fist. "What the hell, Zeph?"

"These guys are acting like he's the enemy. Heller is the one who shot Barrington. You can't do this to him, Hawk. He didn't ask for any of this. Look at him. He's not even fighting."

Brooke left the safety of Quill's arms addressing the lead Protector, "I agree with Zephyr. I'd be dead right now if it wasn't for Mr. Heller. We all would."

Hawk nodded to his men. "Ease up there, guys. Let's show some respect to our guest." He faced off with the two women. "I'll tell you what's going to happen. We're going to get out of here and head to the Medical Center to get checked out by Kai's staff, including Mr. Heller. You have my word; he will be treated kindly. And, Zeph, no more guns, okay?"

"Next time, I'll make sure I have my crossbow." Zephyr snarled.

The lead Protector stepped into her space, an imposing figure. "Watch it. I'm pretty sure we've discussed this issue ad nauseam. You can't be a Protector unless the Elders give the go ahead." Hawk studied the young Guardian. "Listen, you know if it was up to me, it would be a done deal already, but it's out of my hands. So, can you please give me a break here?"

Zephyr kicked the dirt beneath her feet. "Fine, but I'm going with those guys to make sure they don't hurt him."

Quill studied the young Guardian. *Holy shit, she's into the freaky robot guy. This will go over well with the Elders, not. Do not respond, not a single sound. You can do it. This is not the time for a joke.* Hawk snapped out orders sending everyone scurrying, and Quill swallowed audibly, restraining his wise-cracking impulses.

"It's going to be one hell of a long night." Quill let out an exhausted breath, grabbed hold of Brooke's hand, and headed toward the Medical Center. They settled in, waiting for Cassy to come out of surgery and for news about the three kids hit by the grenade.

Laurel entered the room, looking to Brooke. "Sorry, no word on Cassy yet—" She sat beside Brooke, picking up her hand. "—but I have some good news about the kids you saved. Wren has a broken wrist, Briar, a sprained ankle, and Aidan took seven stitches to the head, but my feisty Three Musketeers are going to be as good as new thanks to you."

Brooke offered the teacher a small smile. "I'm so happy to hear that, but nothing short of a miracle with Cassy is going to make me feel any better."

Quill wrapped Brooke in his arms. "It's a dark day for all of us, baby. Aether lost four kickass Protectors today, but have faith, Cassy's a fighter. And remember, Barrington is gone, and he can't ever hurt you again."

His beautiful Guardian's eyes filled with tears. "I

know but even with his last breath, Charles managed to turn the most beautiful day into one of sheer horror." He had no words of comfort to offer Brooke, only the warmth of his embrace.

People came and went throughout the interminable wait, but Brooke refused to leave, or do anything except sit and stare into space. Around hour two of her silent meditation, Quill's concern grew. Hour three came and went, and finally, a weary looking Kai appeared.

Brooke jumped to her feet racing into her father's open arms. Agony filled her voice, "How is she?"

"She's going to make it. I'm not going to lie to you. It's bad. She's in for a rough recovery. The bullet entered under her right breast straight through her lung shattering several ribs in its path. It lodged in her chest nicking her aorta, but my surgical repair seems to be holding. Her healing powers are kicking in now that the gas is out of her system." He took Brooke by the shoulders examining her. "Let me look at you. Are you okay?"

"Seriously? You're asking her a dad question?" Quill grabbed Brooke's hand pulling her to him. "She's fine."

She planted a kiss on Quill's lips. "I love you, but he is my dad, and he's allowed to ask me dad questions."

"And I'd like to ask a lead Protector question if you guys don't mind," Hawk interjected shaking his head at his friends. "Kai, I know you're dealing with a lot, but do you have an update on the wounded?"

The doctor nodded. "Yes. I received a preliminary report during surgery. Most of the people who were near the flash grenade suffered from disorientation. The explosion produces a flare of light seven million candelas strong which activates photoreceptor cells blinding the subject for several seconds, but not to worry, the effects are only temporarily. The loud blast produces an additional set of issues. Victims are left with a short-lived deafness, and the sound waves disturb the fluid in their ears causing a loss of balance."

Quill snorted. "So, to translate from Kai speak into English, the effects are not going to last, and everyone's going to be fine, right?"

"Well, yes. Those who were impacted by the grenades will recover quickly." Throwing a scowl Quill's way, Kai continued, "The rest of the injuries were minor. A couple of stitches here and there, some broken bones, but mostly everyone was sent home."

Hawk ran his fingers through his hair. "That's good news, but what about my grandfather and the other Elders?"

Kai smirked. "Actually, I wanted to talk to you about Bear—"

Before Kai could get the words out, the double doors leading to the treatment area swung open. Bear burst through wearing nothing but a hospital gown and an irritated grimace on his face. "There you are, Hawk." He all but snarled at his grandson.

A young nurse trailed after him. "Please, sir, you need to get back in bed."

Bear turned around to face her, and the back of his gown split open giving anyone in visual range an up-close look at the Elder's bare ass. Horrified gasps escaped from both Brooke and Ashlyn.

Hawk shook his head. "Grandfather, please, you're frightening the ladies. Go to your room, and get back into bed."

The lightweight fabric strained against the Elder's massive shoulders. The big man spun around, moving his hands to his hips, and raising the gown in the process. The women paled in the wake of the full frontal view of Bear's package.

"I feel perfectly well and wish to return home at once. Thank you for your kind hospitality, Dr. Sanders." Bear headed for the door, exposing his backside once again.

The room filled with laughter, and Quill sensed things were going to be all right. It would take time, but Aether and its people would recover.

****

Brooke

Cracking the door to the house open, she shoved Quill inside and jumped into his arms. Cassy was going to live, and Brooke wanted to do the same starting with having crazy sex with the man she loved. Wrapping her legs around his waist, Brooke brought him closer. Quill responded to her sexual aggressiveness with fervor. The delicious bite of his hands digging into her ass sent her reeling.

Quill's breath rushed out in heavy pants, hot against her ear. "Not that I'm complaining mind you, but who are you, and what have you done with my girlfriend?"

Brooke leaned back in his arms and laughed. "I'm so happy Cassy is going to be okay." She peppered his face with kisses. "I love you so much, Quill. This is the best feeling ever. The Nameless Asshole is gone forever. I'm ready to let loose and be free for the first time in my life—with you."

He spun them around pushing her against the door, closing it with the force of their bodies. Quill's mouth found hers, hungry, and wanting. He angled his hips hitting the perfect spot every time he ground against her. Excitement coursed through her body, and her legs tightened around his waist.

"Sorry, baby, this first time is going to be a quick one. I need you so much. Tell me you're ready for me." He kissed along the slim column of her neck and lowered her feet to the ground.

"Oh, I'm more than ready." Brooke pulled her tattered dress up and over her head. Reaching down, she tore away her lacy thong tossing it aside.

"That's my girl," Quill said, dropping his pants and boxer briefs in one quick motion. He scooped her back up entering her with a hard thrust.

More than ready for him, Brooke gripped his shoulders driving him deeper. "Please, Quill, I can't wait. I need it fast and hard."

He didn't need to be told twice. Shifting her in his arms, he picked up the pace pounding into her tight channel so fast her body hit the door like an overzealous visitor knocking. His mouth latched onto her nipple triggering an intense climax. Quill's head fell back, and the hardened bud popped free of his lips. His husky voice shouted out his release filling the quiet room.

Breathless, he rested his forehead against hers. Quill lowered Brooke to her feet placing a gentle kiss on her lips. "You okay, baby?"

"Of course, I'm great." Her shredded dress and mangled shoes lay in a heap at her feet, and she pointed at them laughing. "Well, I guess I could use some clothes, and I definitely need a shower."

"I'm going to have to say no to the clothes but—" He scooped Brooke into his arms. "—a shower sounds great." He kissed her the entire way to the bathroom.

Brooke looped her arms around Quill's neck, her lips fused with his. He pulled back, kicking the door open, and set her down on the tile floor. His heavily lidded eyes brimmed with lust, locking onto her naked body. Brooke felt her skin flush under the burn of his seductive gaze. The sexy Protector flashed a grin and reached into the shower cranking on the water. Quill tore off the remnants of his tattered shirt, tossed it on the floor, and took her by the hand pulling her under the heated spray.

He pushed Brooke's hair back from her face. "You are so beautiful."

She gave him a playful shove. "How can you say that? I'm a total mess."

"No, you're not. You're my beautiful Guardian. The Water really suits you." He waggled his brows. "I love you all wet." Quill dropped to his knees, his mouth meeting her tender flesh.

Brooke's fingers tunneled into his wet hair. Lifting her leg, he tossed it over his shoulder bringing his tongue closer to her sensitive bud. Quill added a finger sliding it in and out of her wet heat. A moan broke free echoing in the tiled space. The stroke of his tongue combined with the glide of his finger inched her toward a massive orgasm. She shouted out her pleasure, his name a harsh cry on her lips.

Quill rose to his feet, a satisfied smirk on his face. She leaned in, her tongue catching the droplets of water cascading down his muscled chest. Brooke's hands teased every inch of his skin working her way down his body. He backed her up to the bench in the corner, and her butt hit the cool marble seat. She wrapped her fingers around his thick erection, her tongue caressing the tip with slow, tormenting strokes. Quill's head fell back. Brooke increased her efforts, her hand and mouth moving in tandem. His fingers tangled in her wet hair urging her on. Steam filled the stall, and heat rose in waves off their bodies. Brooke gripped his ass squeezing his firm cheeks.

He pulled back. "Baby, wait. I'm going—"

"I know. I want you to. I need to taste you."

Quill reached down lifting her chin. "Next time, okay, baby? If I don't come inside you, I may die." Taking her hands, he tugged her to her feet. "I want you in our bed." He wrapped them in an oversized towel, drying them off, and rushed her, hair still dripping, into the bedroom.

Laying her gently on the bed, he trailed his fingers up and down her arms. Brooke stared up at him, love filling her heart. Bending his head, Quill brushed his mouth against hers, and her lips parted inviting him in. Their tongues tangled in a passionate duel fueling the fire of Brooke's need. She slid her arms around Quill's back, straining against him, but he would not be rushed. He explored her body murmuring words of love. Every nerve ending buzzed with the intoxicating pleasure. Quill took hold of her legs spreading them wide and plunged deep into her heated core. Brooke countered his movements, rising and falling in time with his rhythm, taking them both over the edge in a mind-bending climax.

Brooke began to doze off, but Quill leapt from the

bed startling her. "Quick, I need my pants."

"Um, is there somewhere you need to be?"

He clicked his tongue and shook his head. "No, silly. I need to get something from my pocket. Where are my pants?"

"Probably by the front door. What is wrong with you? You're acting really weird even for you." Ignoring her, his beautiful, naked butt turned in her direction, and jogged straight out the bedroom door. She admired the fantastic view.

Two minutes later Quill returned wearing the said pants. "I found them."

"I can see that. Now take them off, and come back to bed."

He shook his head. "Not yet." Quill huffed out a breath. "This isn't how I wanted to do this. I wanted everything to be perfect, but then I realized the only perfect thing in this world is you."

Sitting up on her elbows, Brooke rolled her eyes. "Hardly. Now what brought on all this sweet talk?"

Quill fell to his knees beside the bed taking her hand. "If you'd give me a second, you'd realize I'm trying to ask you to marry me." He reached into his tattered pants pocket producing a bright blue box.

Brooke's marked palm flew to her mouth covering a loud gasp. "Oh…my…God."

"I wanted it to be like the show the Bachelor. I've been watching with Ashlyn and Lily to learn how the outsiders do it. I was planning to propose tonight in the Outdoor Chapel after the Joining, but obviously that didn't work out." Quill cracked open the lid revealing a stunning solitaire diamond nestled in a classic Tiffany box. "So, Brooke Sanders, will you marry me?" He plucked the ring from the box sliding it onto her finger.

Brooke gazed down at the sparkling stone adorning her hand and threw her arms around Quill's neck. "Of course, I will. There is nothing I want more than to be your Adara. I love you more than anything. I don't need a wedding. Being together forever is all that matters to me."

"I love you, too, and I want to honor both of our traditions, so how about a wedding and a Joining?"

"It sounds perfect." She leaned down and kissed him. "And by the way, you were right you know?"

"Really? I like the sound of that. What was this thing I was allegedly correct about, Dr. Sanders?"

"I am The Guardian of The House of Water. You know what else you were right about?" She smiled brightly gazing into his eyes with all the love in her heart. "I'm yours, Quill Robbins, forever and always."

Epilogue
Zephyr

The gray sky fit Zephyr's dark mood. She tugged on her Hunter boots, tucking her pants inside. Rain had poured down for the past three days leaving Aether a soggy mess. Quietly, she cracked open the East Tower's old wooden door slipping outside and closing it behind her.

"Going somewhere?"

Zephyr jumped back, her hand flying to her chest. Her heart pounded like thunder under her marked palm. "Dear Goddess, Skye, you scared me half to death. Why are you hiding out here?"

"Because I know you've been sneaking out, and I think you're setting yourself up for disaster."

"I have no idea what you're talking about," Zeph shot back. "I was up early, and thought I'd take a walk. You know, to clear my head."

Skye's lips stretched into an enigmatic smile. "Give me a small break here, will you? You may be five minutes older than me but that doesn't mean you're smarter." Her smile fell away. "I know where you're going."

"You think you know everything."

Skye's hands moved to her hips. "I may not know everything, but I know you. Why are you staring at me like that? You know exactly what I'm talking about."

Dropping her hands to her thighs with a loud smack, she retorted, "I'm worried about you. The guy was catatonic, then suddenly wakes up, shoots someone, and you've gone to see him, what five or six times already. Are you out of your mind?"

Zephyr crossed her arms over her chest. "You're acting like a total bitch. You're not even giving Heller the slightest chance, and that's not like you. I don't understand." She leaned back against the tower's rough stone wall. "Do I need to remind you, he didn't kill a person; he killed the bad guy. Charles Barrington wanted to steal our powers and wipe us all out of existence."

"Believe me, I remember. No one in Aether can forget what happened. We lost four Protectors that day, and dozens of people were injured." Skye took her sister's hand, her tone softening, "But I can't stand the thought of you getting hurt. We know nothing about this man except he's a killer, and he was with Barrington."

Zephyr yanked her hand back. "Not because he wanted to be, and you're only upset because he got to the crazy doctor first. The point is Heller killed Charles Barrington, which makes him a good guy."

"Oh please, sometimes you sound so naive for twenty-five. How do we even know Heller is his real name?"

"I don't care what his name is. I only care what I see in his eyes," Zephyr countered.

"I think I'm going to be sick. You're attracted to him. How did I not see it immediately?" Skye looked up to the heavens shaking her head before meeting her sister's eyes. "Just because Coma Guy looks like an action hero does not make him one. You can't fall for the science experiment. You're a Guardian. If you think the Elders have a problem with you also wanting to be a Protector, wait until they find out you have a thing for this freak."

"He's not a freak, and I'm not attracted to him. I—I feel sorry for him. He didn't ask Barrington to turn him into a mind-controlled fighting machine. He's a soldier. You can tell the minute you look at him. That psycho doctor made him this way. No one in their right mind would choose to be experimented on."

"Exactly! How do you know Heller didn't sign on the dotted line to participate? Maybe Doctor Looney Tunes didn't force him. We don't know where this guy comes from, or where his allegiance lies." Skye put her hand on Zephyr's shoulder. "Not everything in the outside world can be based on instincts and a blind belief in destiny. Some people just suck, and that's all there is to it. Wake up, Zeph. You're way too smart to be acting so foolish."

"And you're way too young to be acting like an Elder." Zephyr wrinkled her nose scoffing at her sister. "I'm ignoring you. See you later." She waved to Skye skulking off toward the Medical Center.

Dawn inched its way closer. Trudging along the mud-covered path, the only sound was that of Zephyr's boots sloshing as she made her way through the silent village. A faint mist hung in the air coating every surface of the Square with an iridescent shine. Light streamed through the windows of the Medical Center giving the dusky sky surrounding it a warm, rosy glow.

Zephyr approached the building keeping to the shadows. Taking a deep breath, she wrapped her fingers around the cool metal door handle and pushed her way inside. She'd rehearsed an excuse for whoever might be on duty for the early morning shift. Scanning the area, she wiped her boots on the entryway welcome mat. Zephyr's eyes zeroed in on the empty front desk, and she took advantage of the moment, slipping through the double doors which led to the patient rooms.

Creeping down the quiet hallway, her rubber soles squeaked across the tile floor, and she cringed at her lack of stealth. She came to a halt in front of an ordinary door and traced the number 5, raised in gold on the panel with the tip of her finger. Dropping her hand, her fingers hovered over the knob.

Zephyr mumbled, "Skye's right. I should go home." She turned on her heels and bumped straight into Coal.

The handsome Protector stared down at her. "Morning, Zephyr. Is there something I can do for you? It's kind of early for a visit don't you think?"

Busted. "Oh, hey, Coal. How's it going?" She batted her lashes.

"Sorry, kiddo, that's not going to work on me. I told you yesterday, I think you should stay away. I know Heller seems docile, but he's still a wildcard."

"Please, I know you don't think that. He's all alone in there. Come on; let me in. What harm could it do?"

Coal's brows lifted. "Seriously?" He rolled his eyes and let out an audible breath. "Fine, but only for a little while, and the door stays open."

"Wow, you sounded exactly like my dad did when I was a teenager. I'm a little worried about you." She shook her head, clapped him on the shoulder, and pushed past him.

The door creaked open revealing the most beautiful man she had ever set eyes on. Zephyr's breath hitched. Heller slept, his long, muscular frame stretched out on the tiny hospital mattress. She froze taking in the peaceful expression blanketing his handsome face. With tentative steps, she forced one foot in front of the other approaching the bed. His blond military-style haircut had grown out a bit since he'd been in Aether.

Unable to resist the urge, Zephyr reached out brushing away a few stray hairs hanging down on his forehead. Heller bolted upright grabbing her hand and clamping down on it. She pulled back but his strength far surpassed hers. The soldier's eyes widened, and he loosened his grip but still kept hold of her hand. Heller's other hand came up and stroked her cheek. She remained motionless staring into his sparkling, blue eyes.

Heller's raspy voice broke the silence uttering only a single word, "Zephyr."

A word about the authors...

Born and bred on the shores of Long Island, the dynamic duo of romance writing, M. Goldsmith and A. Malin (aka Melissa and Anita) have been close friends for many years. They met when their daughters were in the same first grade class, and discovered a shared love of reading, retrievers, and all things romance, especially paranormal adventures.

Join them on a magical journey into the world of Aether where the Elements rule.

Visit at:

www.mgoldsmithandamalin.com

Follow at:

Facebook.com/MGoldsmithAMalin
Instagram.com/m.goldsmith_a.malin
Twitter.com/Goldsmith_Malin